Advance praise for *Sister Dear*

"A stunning achievement! Just when I thought I knew what was going to happen, Hannah Mary McKinnon proved me wrong. Beautifully plotted story with characters that left a mark."
—Samantha Downing, author of #1 international bestseller *My Lovely Wife*

"Loss, love, revenge, buried secrets and greed add up to make *Sister Dear* an electrifying read."
—Mary Kubica, *New York Times* bestselling author of *The Good Girl* and *The Other Mrs.*

"A brilliant, breathless thriller that crackles with suspense and heart-thumping twists. I finished this absorbing, creepy and downright sinister novel in the wee hours of the night."
—Heather Gudenkauf, *New York Times* bestselling author of *The Weight of Silence* and *Before She Was Found*

"Creeps up the back of your neck then explodes into an ending that I guarantee you won't soon forget... Smart, addictive, and genuinely surprising."
—Kimberly Belle, internationally bestselling author of *Dear Wife*

"Dark, twisty, compelling and also heartbreaking.... Unputdownable and I truly enjoyed reading it to see how the intertwined lives would unfold. Highly recommended!"
—Karen Hamilton, internationally bestselling author of *The Perfect Girlfriend*

"Fabulous, with a bombshell twist you won't see coming. I devoured it."
—Kaira Rouda, internationally bestselling author of *The Favorite Daughter*

SISTER
DEAR

HANNAH MARY
McKINNON

mira

Recycling programs
for this product may
not exist in your area.

ISBN-13: 978-0-7783-0955-0

Sister Dear

Copyright © 2020 by Hannah McKinnon

Use of quote kindly permitted by The Society of Authors, on behalf of the
Bernard Shaw Estate.

This edition published by arrangement with Harlequin Books S.A.

For questions and comments about the quality of this book, please contact us at
CustomerService@Harlequin.com.

Mira
22 Adelaide St. West, 40th Floor
Toronto, Ontario M5H 4E3, Canada
BookClubbish.com

Printed in U.S.A.

To my sister Joely, who always put on funny voices when reading me bedtime stories, and who, thankfully, didn't inspire this novel.

Also by Hannah Mary McKinnon

Her Secret Son
The Neighbors

SISTER DEAR

If you cannot get rid of the family skeleton, you may as well make it dance.

—George Bernard Shaw

CHAPTER ONE

THE POLICE DIDN'T BELIEVE ME.

A jury wouldn't have, either, if I'd gone on trial, and most definitely not the judge. My attorney had more than a few reservations about my story. Ms. Allerton hadn't said as much. She didn't need to. I saw it in her eyes, could tell by the way she shuffled and reshuffled her papers, as if doing so might shake my lies clean off the pages, leaving only the truth behind in her inky, royal blue swirls.

After our first meeting I'd concluded she must've known early on—before she shook my hand with her icy fingers—that I was a liar. Before she'd walked into the room in shiny four-inch heels, she'd no doubt decided she'd heard my excuses, or a variation thereof, from countless clients already. I was yet another person claiming to be innocent. Another criminal who'd remained adamant they'd done nothing wrong, it wasn't their fault, *honest*, despite the overwhelming amount of evidence to the contrary, a wall of impending doom surrounding me.

And still, at the time I'd believed the only reason Ms. Allerton had taken on my case pro bono was because of the amount of publicity it gave her firm. Reducing my sentence—for there would be one—would amplify her legacy as a hotshot lawyer. I'd accepted her help. There was no other option. I needed her knowledge, her expertise, saw her as my final hope. I now know her motivations were something else I'd miscalculated. All hope extinguished. Game over.

If I'm being fair, the judgments Ms. Allerton and other people had made about me weren't completely wrong. I *had* told lies, some, anyway. While that stripped away part of my claim to innocence, it didn't mean I was entirely guilty. Not of the things everybody said I'd done. Things I'd had no choice but to confess to, despite that being my biggest lie of all.

But I'll tell you the truth. The whole truth and nothing but. I'll start at the beginning and share everything that happened. Every last detail leading up to one fateful night. The night someone died because of me. The night I lost you, too.

I won't expect your forgiveness. Our relationship—or lack thereof—will have gone way beyond that point. No. All I can hope for, is that my side of the story will one day help you understand why I did the things I did.

And why I have to do the things I've not yet done.

CHAPTER TWO

Fifteen months earlier

MY HEELS DRAGGED AS my legs took shorter steps than usual, an unmistakable sign my feet weren't heading in a direction I wanted to go. The hems of my old frayed jeans dragged on the sidewalk, soaking up the gray slush—the final vestige of the snow dusting most of Maine had received earlier that Friday afternoon, dumping the majority of it right on top of Portland.

The freezing, soggy fabric of my pants had turned into frozen fingers snatching at my ankles, and I cursed myself twice. Once for not believing the weatherman when he said snow would hit mid-October, and again because I'd donned comfy sneakers as a pathetic sign of protest. At almost thirty and an East Coast native, I really should've known better.

While my heart protested, my brain made me quicken my pace toward Monroe Hospice. I tried hard not to imagine what Dad might look like today. If I did, I feared I'd turn around, scuttle home to my little apartment, which had become more of a refuge since his diagnosis. Never mind my pathetic and humble abode's dire need for odorless carpets, proper windows to keep out the draft and paint that didn't come off the walls in banana-peel strips. Despite its state, I longed to be at home, close the curtains, pull on two sweaters and hide for the weekend, trying to pretend Dad wasn't sick. Wasn't dying. That this wouldn't be his last Thanksgiving, and he *would* make it to Christmas.

Forty-eight hours had passed since I'd visited. Even in such a short amount of time I wasn't sure what condition I'd find him in—the pallor of his face, how much more sallow his skin had become as it stretched over his jutting cheekbones, translucent as raw phyllo pastry.

Pancreatic cancer—the inoperable, terminal kind, the doctor had said eight weeks ago, although it felt as if multiple lifetimes had passed since our world had been turned upside down. I'd refused to believe it when Dad told me. Insisted they'd made a mistake, handed him somebody else's test results by accident. The thought of losing my father, the one person I cared for the most in the entire world, filled me with horror. At the rate of his decline, we'd be lucky if he made it another month.

I'd barely slept since the diagnosis, the only advantage being I'd stayed ahead of schedule with the website designs for my clients, even though I caught myself staring into space far too often. Working so much couldn't prevent my mind from traveling the path marked Life after Dad. It was bleak down there. Empty and cold. Lonely. A place filled with despair, anger and hate. Somewhere nobody should be forced to go, yet a destination almost everyone ended up at some point, and in my case, before I'd done something—anything—to make him proud.

I hoisted my bag over my shoulder, wishing for the umpteenth time I'd emptied it before setting off, and had left my notepad-cum-sketchbook and camera at home. The latter was an older, large digital Nikon. It had belonged to my neighbor's deceased husband and had therefore been free—a big part of the appeal—but it now made the straps of my bag dig into my skin.

"You're an idiot," I said and shifted the weight. Even if Dad let me take his picture, I'd be incapable of focusing the lens on him without bursting into tears.

I took another few steps, caught sight of my reflection in the store window and quickly looked away, stuffed my hands deeper into the pockets of my jacket, which already bunched more snuggly around my middle than it had when I'd bought it at the thrift store a few weeks ago. We'd never been on good terms, mirrors and I—it was why I preferred holding the pencil or being on the other side of the camera—and I had more reasons to avoid them now. Unhappiness did peculiar things to people. For me, it translated into lank, greasy hair, a total lack of makeup, and a pattern of shoveling as much comfort food—translation: any food—down my throat as fast as I possibly could.

I'd never lost anyone before, nobody close anyway, no one I'd sobbed into my pillow for, or bargained over with a higher power. It petrified me. Seeing my dad—a strong and burly truck driver with a marshmallow heart—be reduced to no more than a shell within a matter of weeks was already frightening enough, but I suspected the worst was yet to come.

I shuddered, pulled the hood of my jacket over my head to stop the bitter winds from assaulting my ears and remembered our conversation about the "technical arrangements" for his funeral, more specifically, what he *didn't* want.

"Get them to play 'Another One Bites the Dust' by Queen," he'd said.

"Dad, there's no way I—"

"Kidding. 'Knocking on Heaven's Door' will do fine. But not

Bob Dylan's version, it's too soft. I want Guns N' Roses, and make sure it's the one with Slash's awesome guitar riff."

"Are you serious?"

"Deadly serious."

"You're not funny."

"'Course I am. Anyway, we'll make the whole thing cheap and cheerful—"

"Cheerful? You expect your funeral to be cheerful?"

"Yes, Eleanor," he said, his smile disappearing. "It's to be a celebration. I don't want you to be sad. Promise me you won't be sad."

Keeping my word was about as probable as healing his cancer with my bare hands, but I'd given it to him anyway, understood it was something he needed to feel better, to at least try to rid himself of the guilt of leaving the people who loved him behind.

I shook my head and looked up at the swirling skies, so lost in thought I'd already arrived at Monroe Hospice, a stone-clad, two-story building tucked away on a dead-end road. Despite my stalling tactics, the walk from my apartment on Sherman Street hadn't taken much more than an hour, and not for the first time I wondered why they'd built Monroe in an area called Pleasantdale. When I'd shared this with Dad during my last visit, he'd laughed.

"At least it's close to the cemetery. Transport will be cheap," he'd said and I'd burst into tears, which had led to him apologizing for his crass attempt at gallows humor, blaming the dark, English sense of wit he'd inherited from his mother.

Taking a deep breath to prepare myself, I pushed open the doors. Although they'd tried hard to make the place homey and comfortable—cheery, abstract, multicolored artwork adorning the walls, a sitting area filled with high-backed sofas so soft you could lose yourself within—the distinct odor of a hospital environment had mixed with the invisible but constant death and sorrow, all of which now clung to the place, tearing my heart in two.

I gave Brenda, the petite receptionist, a small wave, pretending I didn't hear when she asked how I was doing because I wouldn't have known how to respond. The elevator took me to my dad's floor, where I gave Nurse Jelani a nod as she greeted me with a well-honed, compassionate expression. How she, or anyone else, worked in this place day in, day out—surrounded by illness and grief, knowing patients would rather go home so they could die in the relative comfort of their own surroundings—was an awesome mystery to me, filled with superheroes in scrubs. In comparison, my website job was a walk in a beautifully serene park. The annoyance I felt when I gave even my most demanding customer the sun and the moon, only to have them ask for the entire solar system, seemed petty and meaningless in contrast.

When I got closer to Dad's room and heard voices, specifically my mother's, I paused. Her unmistakable tone—considerably more nasal and irritating than usual—still had the power to send jolts down my spine, never mind my moving out as soon as I'd finished high school, determined never to depend on her again.

I hadn't expected her to be at the hospice. The fact she'd visited Dad a few days earlier had already been a surprise, considering she'd ordered him to pack his stuff and leave almost twenty years ago, and had hardly spoken to him since. He'd only mentioned she'd visited because I'd told him I'd spotted her coming out of Monroe, and had ducked behind a fir tree to avoid her. It had been at least six months since I'd had any contact with her, almost a year since we'd been in the same room for my sister Amy's lavish twenty-seventh birthday party. Even that amount of time and distance hadn't been enough to treat the festering wounds, or get rid of her voice, which constantly berated me in my head.

I'd always questioned, but never understood, why she despised me. I'd asked Dad, too, but he hadn't given me a proper answer, only said she was a complicated woman. As much as I pretended

I didn't care, part of me still wanted to know. She was caring and loving toward Amy, but had only constant resentment for Dad and me—yet here she was, at his bedside. Maybe there was still hope she'd give treating him like an actual human being another go. After all, she must've loved him once.

I leaned against the door, tried to hear their conversation and hoped she was on the verge of leaving, in which case I'd slip into the bathroom or find a supply cupboard to sneak into.

"I still don't understand, Bruce," she said to Dad without a hint of warmth. Her glacial tone would freeze hell over when she left this world. No way would she go anywhere but south when she did.

"I've already told you, it's done," my father said. "I'm not changing my mind." Although determined, his voice sounded throaty, no doubt in equal parts from his illness and the effort of standing up to my mother. I wondered how long she'd been there, if she'd helped him drink some water, bent the straw at the proper angle so he could make the least amount of effort.

"Why are you doing this?" she asked, her voice veering into banshee territory. *"Why?"*

If she wasn't careful, Nurse Jelani would ask her to leave. I crossed my fingers, but my mother regained some of her composure and brought the volume down a notch. "What, exactly, are you trying to accomplish?"

"I'm not *trying* to accomplish anything, Sylvia," Dad replied. "I'm doing what's fair. Everything's split fifty-fifty between the girls. Why are you so upset? It won't be much, so—"

"Exactly my point," my mother said. "You never were much of a provider, were you? You barely have anything now, and Nellie—"

"Eleanor," Dad said. "She hates being called Nellie."

"Well, there's Nellie for you." My mother sniffed, and I imagined her steely eyes drilling into Dad as he dared defy her. "She always was overly sensitive."

"Because Amy sang 'Nellie the Elephant' on a loop for three years, remember?" Dad said, and I wanted to rush in and hug him. "The pair of you have poked fun at her for years. You know it's why she's convinced she's ugly. She thinks her legs look like highway bridge supports."

"If she's that bothered about her looks, why doesn't she do something about them? I did, and well before her age. I've kept my weight in check ever since, and—"

"There's nothing wrong with her, Sylvia," Dad said, sounding exhausted.

My mother sighed deeply. I wondered how much self-control she'd burned through trying not to argue with a dying man. Not all of it, apparently, because she clicked her tongue before quietly saying, "*Eleanor* doesn't need money—"

"How would you know? You never speak to her."

"The phone works both ways. Besides, you said she's perfectly content with her freelance job, her little apartment—"

"With the old windows—"

"—and don't forget she's never had the same ambitions my Amy has."

My Amy. How often had I heard those words? My sister, the golden child, the girl wonder, the rising star actor living in LA who'd been blessed multiple times over by the Good Gene Fairy and had fallen into the Unlimited Pool of Talent. Me, the dispensable forethought, the unnecessary prologue to my mother's childbearing life. I'd always known I was the tubby one. The dowdy one. The disappointment. Now, as the toxic green-eyed monster inside me snarled, I pulled its leash tight. Bitterness, jealousy and resentment had to be some of the most unattractive traits bestowed on mankind, and—in my case at least—the hardest ones to change.

"I don't know why you're insisting on giving Eleanor anything at all." My mother's voice had filled with her special blend of acrid determination that brought the fiercest of opponents to their knees, accepting their fate with bowed heads as she read-ied her proverbial sword.

Not this time, I decided, not with a sick man, *my dad*, as her victim, but before I could take a step forward, she spoke again, her next words changing my life forever.

"You're forgetting one thing, Bruce," she said. "Eleanor isn't your daughter."

CHAPTER THREE

ELEANOR ISN'T YOUR DAUGHTER.
       I felt my face contort itself into a bizarre grimace as my breath caught in my throat. I put a hand against the doorframe to steady myself, tried to stop the hallway from closing in on me. For a few seconds I worked hard to dislodge my mother's words from my brain. Shook my head to rattle them around my skull long enough for her sentence to make sense. Any sense. The attempt didn't work and I remained in the hallway with my mouth open, brow furrowed.

"Of course she's my girl." My father's voice broke the deafening silence, sounding stronger than he had in days. A rush of relief flooded my body. I'd misheard. Misinterpreted what she'd meant. But Dad coughed and continued, his voice strained once more. "I've always treated Eleanor as if she were mine. How many times have you said I love her enough for the both of us?"

My hand flew to my mouth as I tried to stop the cry from escaping between my fingers. It couldn't be true. Dad was exactly that. My *dad*. There had to be some mistake, they had to be talking about someone else.

"You're missing the point," my mother snapped. "You can't—"

"We should tell her."

"I beg your pardon?"

"You heard me, Sylvia. She should—"

I'll never know what he was about to say next because as I leaned in to hear more clearly, my heavy bag swung off my shoulder. It banged against the door with a loud thud, forcing it open with a croaky creak.

Dad's head turned. "Eleanor. You're here."

My mother spun around, following Dad's cancer-patient-in-the-headlights gaze until her eyes landed squarely on mine. She didn't waver, but lifted her chin, signaling her acute annoyance at my presence as she observed me in the way a spider might watch a fly trapped in its sticky web.

"How are you, Freckles?" Dad's use of the nickname my nose and cheeks earned me one blistering summer two decades ago was an obvious but unsuccessful attempt at masking the tremble in his voice. "I was hoping you'd come. Did you—"

"Is it true?" I took a step and put a hand on the soft, sky blue armchair—the one I'd spent three nights in during the past week alone—to make sure I didn't stumble. My bag felt as if the weight of the sketchbook and camera had multiplied tenfold, and it slipped farther down my arm. I let it drop to the floor with a dull clunk, put one foot in front of the other despite my brain screaming at me to turn and run. "You're not my dad?"

My mother spoke first. "Look, Nellie—"

"Eleanor," I said, teeth clenched. "Didn't you hear what Dad said about your stupid nickname? Why don't you ever listen to him?"

"That's quite enough, *Eleanor*," she said. "There's no need to make a scene."

"A *scene*?"

Her shiny red lips pursed as she exhaled through her nose, nostrils flaring. I prepared for another of her pointed rebukes, wrapped myself up in the imaginary armor I'd developed as a child, held up an invisible shield to deflect her attack, vowing I wouldn't let it hurt me this time. One thing I'd mastered while living with a dragon for years was the ability to recognize when it was about to open wide and incinerate me.

"There's no need for you to be so dramatic," she said evenly, eyes ablaze.

My hands went to my hips, ordering me to stand my ground, make myself larger to scare off the enemy I knew so well, yet had never come close to understanding.

"But there's always drama with you, isn't there?" she continued. "You thrive on it—"

I snorted. "How rich. You're the one who always—"

"Stop it, both of you. *Please*."

The pain in Dad's voice tore my gaze from my mother's face and made me look at his instead. He must have pushed himself up before realizing it was too much effort, and slumped down again. His pillow had slipped, too, so he now lay lopsided, resembling a skinny rag doll, left on the bed in an abandoned heap.

I lunged, slipped my hands under his arms, tried to ignore how the only thing I could feel was skin and bone, not the bulky biceps he used to bear-hug me with. Once he was upright again, the pillow set firmly behind him, I offered him a drink of water but he waved his skeletal hands.

"No," he said. "Thanks, but not now."

I lowered my voice to a whisper, pretended my mother wasn't there. "Dad...you have to tell me the truth. Are you... Are you my dad?"

He stared at me. One second. Two. Three. I wanted him to smile and say, *Yes, of course I am, silly.* Needed him to tell me this was all a terrible mistake. The silence grew, stretching out between us. After another long moment, he slowly shook his head and I swallowed hard, felt my legs tremble.

"But...but...then, who is?"

"He—"

"Bruce." The word was a sharp warning from my mother. "We agreed. It's in the past."

"But it's *my* past," I said, doing my best to ignore her death stares, a thousand tiny needles piercing my skin. "And it's my present. Can't you see? Why didn't anyone tell me? Why didn't either of you think I should know?"

"I'm sorry, Eleanor," Dad said gently before turning to my mother. "Sylvia, isn't it time we told her the truth? She—"

"No." My mother looked me up and down. "You know what you're implying, don't you, Eleanor? You're saying your father hasn't been enough for you."

"No, I never—"

"Hasn't he always treated you well?"

"Yes, but—"

"Hasn't he always done *everything* for you?"

"Of course he has." I raised my voice again as I stared back at her. "I never said—"

"Then why does it matter, *Nellie*?" my mother snapped. "This is exactly why I insisted we never tell you. I knew you wouldn't be mature about it. I said you'd overreact and—"

"No." I shook my head, held up my hands, palms facing her. *"No.* I won't let you turn this around and blame me. Not today." I looked at Dad, who lay in his bed with a pained expression on his face. He seemed so small, so sick and defeated, and yet all I could think of was I needed to leave, that I had to get out of there. Now. "I'll come back tomorrow, Dad, okay? We can talk then, and—"

"You don't have to go," he said.

I looked at him, and then at my mother, trying to come to grips with the fact they'd lied for my entire life, both of them complicit. That my mother had withheld the truth didn't surprise me, but my father's betrayal, that he had—yet again—been unable to stand up to her, made me want to scream. My heart thumped, blood whooshing in my ears as I understood he was never going to tell me unless she agreed. If I hadn't overheard their conversation, he'd have taken this secret to his early grave. I couldn't believe what he'd almost done. Couldn't accept he was going to die. It was unfair. All of it was so unfair. The cancer. The fact it was taking him instead of her. The lies. *Everything.*

Decades of hatred and suppressed anger I felt for my mother—coupled with the last two months of grief, despair and sleepless nights—all billowed and surged inside me. The feelings strained against the shackles I'd tried to tame them with, snapping their chains one by one with their pointed teeth. When the last one broke, red-hot fury shot from my belly and raced up to my mouth, where it transformed itself into twisted words of disgust, spewing forth like lava.

"How could you do this?" I said to Dad. "That *she*—" I pointed at my mother but kept my eyes firmly on him "—would treat me like utter shit is nothing new. But *you*? I trusted you. You were supposed to be on my side. You lied to me."

"I'm sorry, Eleanor, I—"

"I don't care you're sorry," I shouted, hating—detesting—myself all the more, but unable to make myself stop, to regain control.

"Freckles, please." He held out his hand but I stepped back, shook my head.

"Who's my real father?" I said, and watched Dad wince at the word *real*. Still, both he and my mother stayed silent, making me back away toward the door, because, I realized, I was terrified they might answer. My next words came out a trembling whisper. "I can't deal with this. I need to get my head straight. I'll come back tomorrow."

Dad pushed himself up with his elbows and opened his mouth to reply, but the only thing coming from his lips was a string of deep, chesty coughs, like sounds of gunfire bouncing off the walls. His chest rose and fell at an alarming pace as his face turned more ashen. Before I got to him, a machine went off, beeping loudly, adding to the noise and confusion. Dad opened his eyes wider, transforming them into sunken black holes.

"Dad!" I shouted as two people rushed into the room. *"Dad!"*

"You need to step outside," Nurse Jelani said, shooing me and my mother in no uncertain terms into the corridor while continuing to talk to her colleague in medical terms I didn't recognize, let alone understand.

"But I have to—"

"Let us take care of him, Eleanor. I'll come and find you when he's settled, okay? It'll be all right." She gave me a final push and pulled the door shut.

If we'd been anything resembling a normal family, my mother and I would've hugged each other, offered support, whispered words of reassurance and comfort. Instead we stood ten feet apart, eyes locked on each other, waiting for the other to attack. We were about as far away from normal as you could get.

She adjusted the perfect creases in the sleeves of her deep red silk blouse and looked at me, her eyes lethal daggers. "This is your fault. Yours and yours alone."

"I didn't—"

"Your father, because that's exactly who he is and don't you forget it, is *sick*."

"I know, I—"

"You pushed him. You *upset* him."

"I didn't mean to." Tears pricked the backs of my eyes and I swiped at them with my hand. How many times had this woman, my *mother*, made me cry? A thousand? Ten thousand?

"Go home," she said. "Leave."

"I want to see Dad and—"

"Why?" she snapped. "So you can upset him again? No, *Nellie*, you've done quite enough for one evening, don't you think?"

I wanted to answer back. Willed myself to put her in her place once and for all. As I looked at her fury-filled face, my determination dissolved like honey in hot tea. My mother had always come out on top as far as the two of us were concerned. She'd always won. I was weak, pathetic, unworthy of the love and attention she bestowed on Amy, unworthy of being loved by anybody else, too. I wasn't deserving. Wasn't good enough. Had never been good enough.

And so, clutching to Nurse Jelani's reassuring words about Dad going to be all right, I fled. Down the corridor, where I flung the stairwell door open, making the handle bounce off the wall before I flew down the steps as fast as my feet would allow. When I stumbled past Brenda at reception and out of the hospice's main entrance, I grabbed hold of the steel trash can with shaking arms and bent over, trying not to throw up.

As I gulped in the cool, misty air, and with it the faint smell of garbage and stale cigarette butts, I vowed I'd call Dad when I got home. Surely he'd be settled by then, and, with any luck, my mother would have left, too. The trip back would give me a bit of time to figure out how to apologize to the man who'd always taken care of me, who'd been the best father a girl could wish for. I owed him that, and so much more.

If I hurried, I decided, taking quicker steps, I'd soon be making amends.

CHAPTER FOUR

I DIDN'T GET MUCH FARTHER before remembering I'd left my bag in Dad's room. For a few seconds I debated whether to go back and get it, but decided to make my way home without. The keys to my apartment were in my jacket pocket, and as it was six thirty on a Friday, I could get by without my phone and wallet for the night. It was the weekend. Most of my clients wouldn't expect answers before Monday, and my social life had been on hiatus for years. Besides, I could check email and social media on my laptop when I got home. I had some emergency cash in a coffee jar at the apartment, something Dad always insisted I do.

Still, I hesitated, right up until a rare taxi drove past. I flagged it down and hopped in, grateful for the shelter and warmth it provided, my cheeks already numb from the wind.

"Good evening, miss," the driver said as he smiled at me in

the rearview mirror, the gap between his front teeth half a finger wide. "Where to?"

"Sherman Street, please," I said, and, deciding to be up-front and honest about my situation, added, "I don't have any money—"

"I'm sorry, miss." His smile faded as he put the car back in Park. "No money, no ride. I'm afraid you have to get out of—"

"But I have some at home. I'll run up and get it—"

"No." He shook his head. "I really can't. I've been taken for *those* rides more than once."

"But—"

"Look, you seem nice, and so did they. Since then I don't make any exceptions."

Despite pleading with him again, it became clear he wouldn't give in. I fumbled for the handle before stepping out of the car and watching him drive away, my heart sinking straight to my sneakers. These were my two options: walk home or go back to the hospice to get my bag, but I couldn't face Dad, not after I'd upset him so badly, and I certainly couldn't face my mother.

I'd call Nurse Jelani from my neighbor's apartment as soon as I got back to make sure Dad had settled. He needed his rest and I'd return first thing in the morning. Decision made, I set off, heading for Casco Bay Bridge.

The light had long faded, spindly shadow-fingers elongating as they'd inched their way across the streets. I slowed my pace, winded from the effort of walking so fast. No point wondering when I'd become so out of shape. I'd never particularly been *in* shape, unless pear-shaped counted. Photographic evidence readily demonstrated the soft, pudgy kid I'd been during my elementary years. The ugly duckling fairy tale I'd desperately wished for had never come, and I'd morphed into an equally pasty-looking adolescent in high school. Every year I'd remained the odd one out, unpopular, a misfit, a nerd with teeth too big for my face and puppy fat I'd never got rid of. The other girls had thick, shiny locks, about as diametrically opposed to my curly blond mop as you could get, and their gravity-defying breasts and backsides could've given a freshly picked peach an inferiority complex.

I pushed away the memories of being made fun of, called names or ignored, tried to leave them behind, although they still followed me down the road, snapping at my heels. As much as I insisted it was years ago, that I should get over myself and none of it mattered anymore, the scars were still there, ready to be picked—or quashed with yet another bagel or muffin my mother would have tut-tutted over and told me not to eat.

I focused on the walk home, longing for my crappy little apartment. I'd lived there for a few years now and wouldn't be upgrading anytime soon, not since I'd started the website business six months prior. Going out on my own had never been a burning desire—my mother was right about my lack of ambition, if little else—but when a former boss's hands had wandered once too many, I'd semipolitely told him to stop, or I'd report him to HR. The next day I was laid off, told my IT support role had been cut because of "efficiencies," ironically by the woman who turned out to be my boss's girlfriend.

In a way it was a relief. I'd been unhappy there for a while but too scared to do anything about it. I'd never been the type to make decisions unless I got some kind of shove.

My business had increased, and I'd acquired a couple of regular maintenance contracts. Quite the contrast from the third month in, when I'd had none and couldn't make rent. Seeing no alternative, I'd asked Dad for help, which he'd been happy to provide, my promises of paying him back falling on deaf ears.

"Consider it a gift, Freckles, okay?" he'd said. "End of story."

The thought of my father took my breath away. Although I wanted to cling to it forever, I attempted to rid my mind of the image before it sliced my heart straight through. Instead, I allowed myself to think about Dad not being my real father—

no, not real, *biological*—and debated whether it mattered. Did it make me less upset he was dying? Stop me from caring?

I shook my head. He was my dad, the one person I'd always looked up to, who'd always tried to be there for me. He'd read to me every single night he'd been home, taught me how to fish, how to ride a bike when I'd been terrified I'd fall. He was the one who'd encouraged me to take computer sciences, applauded when I told him about my new business venture. And amid all that, he'd taken the brunt of my mother's fury whenever he possibly could so I didn't have to.

No way could I let him think I hated him for hiding the truth. His intentions had no doubt been to protect me, as he always had, but what about him? When had he found out he wasn't my father? Had he always known, or discovered it later? Had it had something to do with their divorce?

Walking faster still, I hoped Dad would be awake when I got home. I wanted to talk to him now so I could tell him I loved him no matter what, and when he was ready and strong enough, maybe he'd give me some answers.

About fifty yards from my building's front door, the winds picked up, carrying with them the smell of sea salt, and stripping leaves that still desperately clung to the trees. I buried my chin in my scarf and dug my hands deeper into my pockets. The sky was completely black now, hardly anyone left on the streets save for someone a short distance behind me, the clunk-clunk sound of their boots on the sidewalk echoing in my ears. Had they been there long? I hadn't noticed because of the deafening noise of my thoughts.

I glanced over my shoulder, saw a tall man dressed in black walking behind me, and who, judging by the length of his strides, seemed in as much of a hurry as I was.

I slowed to let him pass, but instead of him walking by me, a heavy hand gripped my shoulder. At first I hoped he had an inappropriate way of asking for the time or directions, but when

I spun around, his hoodie covered the top half of his head, and the shadows obscured the rest of his face. Other than the tip of a badly shaven chin, and the ghostly white skin beneath, I couldn't make out any of his features. Something shiny in his right hand caught my eye. I looked down and gasped at the knife glinting in the moonlight.

"Your money." He sounded raspy, and his breath smelled of stale booze. "Now."

"I—I don't have any. Please. I forgot my bag—"

"Pretty but stupid, eh?" He grabbed my shoulder again, his thumb digging underneath my collarbone. His knife was so close it grazed my stomach, catching on my jacket. "Give me your fucking money. *Now*, bitch."

"I—I'm sorry," I stammered, feeling small, pathetic. "Honestly, I left it—"

I didn't see the punch coming. Only knew it had happened when his fist connected with my cheek. A crunch—from his hand, my face or both—vibrated in my ears as searing pain shot across my jaw. I stumbled sideways. He came at me again, pushed me to the ground where I lay on my back as he pressed the cold blade against my neck.

"Move and I'll cut you."

I didn't budge, but he grabbed my hair anyway and slammed the back of my head against the concrete. Bright white stars exploded in front of my eyes and I heard myself let out an incoherent groan. I felt him patting down my chest, my pockets, cursing and swearing. His breath, coupled with the pain in my head, made me want to retch. When his fingers went inside my pants pockets, I attempted to swipe at his hand, but he swatted me away and punched my head again as he fired off another string of expletives about not finding my money.

My eyes rolled into the back of my head. As I gave in to the pain, wondering if I would die right there, in the middle of the street, I heard a yell in the distance.

"Hey!"

Because of the pounding in my ears I couldn't tell how far away the voice was, or if the shout had been directed at us. Noise sounded strange, muffled, as if I'd been dropped into a swimming pool and was sinking to the bottom, left to drown.

"Hey!"

Definitely male. Deep and gruff. Closer this time, wasn't it? The sound of what I thought were footsteps approached, fast and heavy, followed by another yell.

"Get away from her!"

When the man with the knife took off in the opposite direction, I rolled onto my side, chest heaving, mouth gulping for air as I curled up into a shivering ball.

Moments later someone crouched beside me. Someone smelling of sandalwood and laundry detergent. It was a familiar, comforting scent, but one I couldn't place. I tried to push words from between my lips but nothing came out, and when my vision blurred again, making the human shape above me fuzzy, I closed my eyes, searching for relief.

"Eleanor? Eleanor! It's you. *Jesus!* Talk to me."

I wanted to answer, but couldn't speak or open my eyes.

"Shit...*shit*... Hello? Yes, I need an ambulance."

Through the brain fog, I grasped he'd called 911, and my woolly mind made quantum leaps to connect the dots. The voice belonged to Lewis Farrier, my upstairs neighbor. He was here to help. It meant I was safe. Tears snaked down the side of my face, pooling in my ear.

"It's going to be okay," he said as the weight of something soft and warm—his jacket?—spread over my chest and I felt him stroking my hair. "You're going to be all right, I promise. I promise, Eleanor, it's going to be okay."

I wanted to look at him, to thank him, but the more I tried to focus, the darker everything around me became. The last of the light and all the remaining sounds merged into one, before fading to nothing, taking my words, my thoughts and every other part of me with it.

CHAPTER FIVE

THE FAINT BEEPING SOUND became louder, cutting through the murkiness that had taken hold of my brain, making fragments of memories fit together like jigsaw puzzle pieces. I'd been attacked. A man had hurt me. The smell of his rancid breath lingered in my nostrils and I felt the sharp tip of a blade pressing against my skin. Was I safe? Was he still here?

My heart pounded as I forced my eyes open, squinting and wincing at the pain when the light hit my face full on. I pushed myself up, tried to take in the unfamiliar surroundings. I wasn't dead, at least I didn't think so, but this wasn't my bedroom with its teal-painted walls and the blossom branch decal I'd painstakingly stuck above my bed one rainy afternoon. The windows in this room had blinds, not the turquoise satin curtains with the blackout backing I'd found at Target and silently thanked the gods of retail for because they'd been seventy-five percent off in the sale.

No, this wasn't home, but when I tried to move my head again to figure out where I was, another sharp pain shot from the middle of my head right down my spine.

I lifted my hand to identify the source of the pressure on my finger. It took a while to focus, recognize the object as one of those things to measure—what was it again?—yes, that was it, oxygen levels in the blood. Why was it such an effort to think?

My gaze followed the cable to a machine standing on wheels to the left of the bed, its display jam-packed with colorful numbers I couldn't decipher, but which gave me a clue. A hospital. I was in a *hospital*. But who had brought me in, and how long had I been there?

As I tried to remember, my next thoughts went to Dad. He was sick. He needed me. I had to make sure he was okay. As I searched for a phone, trying not to move my head or my eyes too much, a nurse walked in. She was thin as six o'clock, with chicken-feathered, eggplant-colored hair, and when she saw I was awake she tilted her head to one side, her face breaking into a comforting smile.

"Welcome back, Eleanor," she said. "I'm Miranda, and I'll be your nurse today. Do you know where you are?"

"Hospital." My voice croaked and broke over the single word.

"Yes, very good. You're in ICU for close monitoring, okay? You had a bit of a rough time, didn't you? How are you feeling, dear?"

I tried clearing my throat but winced again. "I...I hurt... My head feels really bad."

"You took quite the blow to the back—"

"There was a man. He grabbed me and—" I stopped as tears filled my eyes, increasing the pressure in my skull, making me bite my lip as anger and frustration built within me. I'd never been attacked before. Had always thought I'd scream and kick, scratch and bite. When it came down to it, my fear and the element of surprise had been on his side because every single one of my muscles had frozen, and I'd done nothing to defend myself. Nothing at all. I gulped in some air, said, "Uh, I think my neighbor...Lewis. He helped me."

"Lewis Farrier?" Nurse Miranda smiled again. "He should be here soon."

"What time is it?" I said, trying to lift the covers. "I have to call my dad."

"Nine thirty."

Nurse Miranda rearranged the sheets and blankets on top of me, tucking me in as if I were a child. I sank back onto the pillow as she handed me a glass of water. Dad would be asleep now, which meant I could call him in the morning, except when I looked at the light coming in from the window, it didn't add up.

"But it's bright outside."

Nurse Miranda nodded, taking the glass from me. "It's Saturday morning, dear."

My heart sped up again as I struggled against the blankets, kicking them away, scrambling to get them off me. "No, it can't be. I have to leave. I've got to see my—"

"You can't go anywhere." She crossed her arms, looking down at me with the sternest of expressions, sending a clear message she wouldn't put up with any of my nonsense. "You took a severe blow to the head and you were unconscious for a while, drifted in and out all night. We'll wait for the doctor—"

"I'm fine. I'll be fine," I said, trying to ignore the fact my head pounded so hard, I thought I'd pass out. Nurse Miranda's face, the walls—the entire room—began to spin, making my stomach churn. Not quite defeated, I slumped onto my side, refusing to give up. I needed to get out of there. "You don't understand. My dad's sick. I have to see him. Please let me—"

"Eleanor?" Lewis's deep, gravelly voice made me stop fighting and turn around. He stood in the doorway, his blond hair looked damp, as if he'd not long ago stepped out of the shower. As he moved closer, he brought the unmistakable scent of sandalwood with him, the one I'd smelled last night as he'd held me, whispered everything would be okay. The familiarity of his aftershave, the instant security it provided, made me choke on my tears.

"Mr. Farrier." Nurse Miranda's face lit up, looking like a kid who'd been presented with an ice-cream sundae for breakfast. "Good to see you again. Maybe you can help me talk some sense into this young lady. She's trying to leave."

"Oh, no, no. You can't." Lewis only needed two strides to get to the bed, where he reached out and patted my hand, making my skin tingle. "You have to stay here so they can make sure you're okay. There's no way you can leave."

Nurse Miranda looked down at me with a told-you-so expression, and as Lewis removed his hand from mine, a scarlet blush shot straight up my arm, all the way to my face, where it set my cheeks on fire.

As neighbors went, Lewis and I didn't know each other well, had crossed paths in the apartment building a few times since he'd moved in last August. The first instance was when I'd gone to the mailboxes, hoping to find a check from one of my clients, the funeral home called Worthy & Moore. They hadn't paid the final installment for their website for over two weeks, despite three calls from me and multiple assurances from them they were satisfied with my work.

"Ours is but the most important of businesses," Mr. Moore, an impossibly tall man with a glass eye, had said in a grave voice as we signed the contract a few weeks prior. "After all, it's the last purchase you'll ever make."

Obviously, paying their suppliers on time wasn't important to Mr. Moore, because when I got to my creaky old mailbox, it was still empty. "Crap," I said. "Crap, crap, *crap*."

"Anything I can help with?"

The voice made me jump. I hadn't noticed anyone come down the stairs behind me, or the man who now stood three mailboxes away. He looked about my age, and I tried hard not to stare at his smooth olive skin, big green eyes and blond hair reaching his wide shoulders. Not nearly as hard as I fought against letting my gaze linger on how his T-shirt grazed his flat middle and strained against his toned arms.

A familiar voice crept into my head, whispering I should've changed out of my panda-print pajamas before lunchtime. At least *attempted* to put on makeup. Done more with my hair than shove it on top of my head, where I'd secured it with an old, faded, blue velour scrunchie that probably had its heyday in the '80s. Chasing the words in my head away and chastising myself for caring one iota what he—or any man—might think, I'd muttered, "No, thanks, I'm fine," and scurried back upstairs.

The next time we'd met hadn't been less embarrassing; in fact, it had been worse. I'd decided to do laundry in the basement, a place I ventured only in desperate times. It was creepy, dark and dingy, and the hallway should've been nominated as "most probable place for a Portland murder." That hadn't happened so far—the nomination or the murder—not as far as I knew anyway, but I tried to spend as little time down there as possible. As I rushed around the corner to the laundry room, I collided with the person coming in the opposite direction, sending his bottle of detergent, my basket and all the clothes in it crashing to the floor.

"I'm so sorry," I said, realizing who I'd rammed into. The mystery mailbox man.

"Totally my fault." He took a step back and looked at me. "Hey, it's you."

I frowned, unsure what he'd meant with his comment. To avoid further humiliation, I kept my face down while bending over to pick up my clothes.

"I wondered where you'd got to," he said. When I looked at

him with a puzzled stare, he quickly added, "I mean because I haven't seen you around. I'm Lewis, by the way. Lewis Farrier. We met at the mailboxes. I think I live in the apartment above you."

I nodded, my lips glued shut by an invisible force.

He leaned in, stage-whispered, "This is the bit where you tell me your name."

"Oh, uh, Eleanor Hardwicke," I said, grateful for the landlord's penny-pinching approach to lighting the communal areas, and hoping the low-wattage bulb above us would do a good enough job at hiding yet another ridiculous expression that had no doubt taken over my face.

"Pleased to officially meet you." Lewis held out a hand, and as I extended mine, I looked down at the pair of polka-dot underwear still clenched between my fingers. *Unwashed* polka-dot underwear. I wished for a meteor to fall on my head or a sinkhole to open up beneath my feet, but no such luck. Instead I pulled my hand and the offending object away as I mumbled something about being late for an appointment and made another run for it.

Mrs. Winchester—my oldest neighbor, who'd lived in the building forever and knew everybody's business—was only too happy to inform me the next morning that the "rugged man living upstairs" was a personal trainer. She'd secretly named him Luscious Lewis and insisted he should be on the cover of *Men's Health*.

"You read *Men's Health*?" I said.

"Got a copy in the mail by mistake once. Read it cover to cover. Five times." She winked and chuckled, then waggled her eyebrows. "Would it surprise you to know he's single?"

"How do you know?"

"I asked him, silly girl. Invited him in for a cup of coffee and a chat. He's excellent company, you know. Very polite. Anyway, my point is you're still single, too, aren't you? And I can't understand why. You're clever, independent and attractive—"

"I'm not—"

"Maybe I'll get him to ask you out. Who knows what might happen?"

I'd coughed and spluttered, told her going out with a neighbor was a terrible idea. Of course the real reason was because I'd identified Lewis as at least a million levels out of my league from the first time I'd set eyes on him. Not that it mattered. I wasn't looking for any kind of a relationship. I'd been perfectly happy on my own for years.

I'd avoided Lewis from then on, which wasn't too difficult. I saw him leave for work early, generally before six when I stood at my window with my first cup of coffee, and didn't hear him moving about upstairs again until well after ten at night. He kept busy, which made it easy for me to keep out of his way. Except now, as he stood over my hospital bed with a face full of concern, avoiding him had become impossible.

Nurse Miranda didn't appear to be in much of a hurry to leave, either. She took my vitals and checked the machines for the third time in five minutes. Her diligence, I presumed, was perhaps a little less about the state of my health and more about getting a longer look at Lewis. Who could blame her? He was one of those people who could've been sculpted from a block of granite before stepping off the pedestal, destined to walk among us lesser mortals.

"I'll call Dr. Chang." Nurse Miranda directed the words at me while beaming at Lewis. "She'll be with you shortly. I'll leave you two to catch up in the meantime."

I wanted to ask her to stay, tell her that, other than watching Lewis come and go on his fluorescent-green mountain bike from my living room window, I didn't know anything about him. As he stood in front of me, I couldn't find the courage to ask.

"I'm sorry," he whispered after she'd left, his voice urgent. "I'm really, really sorry."

Of all the things I'd expected to hear, this wasn't one of them. "Why?"

"For not getting to you sooner." He shook his head, stuffed his hands into the pockets of his jeans as he rocked on his heels like a boulder. "I've been cursing myself since last night. If I hadn't left my bike key at the gym, or if I'd left thirty seconds earlier, I'd have been able to stop the guy. Hell, if I'd left a *minute* earlier, he might not have touched you at all."

"It's not your fault. Don't forget, if you'd left a minute later, the back of my skull might be stuck to the sidewalk."

Lewis smiled, his shoulders dropping. "Are you always this pragmatic?"

"I'm glad you arrived when you did," I whispered, forcing the lump in my throat back down. "Thank you for helping me."

"Of course. Anyone would have done the same." He sighed, shook his head. "I wish I'd caught the guy, though. I wanted to go after him, but I couldn't leave you, you know? It's probably better for him. I'd have beaten him to a pulp." He exhaled deeply, looking at me with his big green eyes and I dropped my gaze. "The police asked me for his description, but I didn't see him properly. Do you remember anything?"

"Not much. He wore a black hoodie… I think he had white skin, stubble and definitely needed a toothbrush. Not exactly a lot for them to go on, is it?"

"But you'll file a report? Which reminds me—" he dug around in his pocket and pulled out a business card "—these are the detective's contact details, although he said he'd be in touch. Hopefully with what you tell them they'll be able to catch the guy."

"I doubt it. I mean, I'm another statistic, right?" My laugh sounded false, and the pressure in the back of my head made me stop. Without warning, a sob escaped my lips, followed by a steady trickle of tears, which refused to slow even as I squeezed my eyes shut to keep them in.

"Hey," I heard Lewis say as he placed his hand over mine again, his touch warm and reassuring. "You're safe now, Eleanor, I promise." He waited until I opened my eyes again, and then reached for a chair, pulled it over and sat down. "Have you spoken to your folks?"

"My parents? No, I—"

"They didn't call? The super gave me your emergency contacts. Your dad didn't answer but I left a message on his voice mail, and on your mom's, too. I told them where you were. I can check with the nurse if—"

"No, you don't need to," I whispered.

"I hope I didn't get the wrong number. Your mom's name is Sylvia, right?"

"Yes," I mumbled. I'd forgotten I'd added her as another contact because there wasn't anyone else, and I never thought she'd be called. Luckily I'd only been bumped on the head—I'd have to be missing all four limbs before she'd make an appearance. I sat up. "I need to call my dad. I don't have my phone or my wallet, and he's—"

"Here, use mine." He dug around the back pocket of his jeans, and when he held his cell out to me, it could've been a toy nestled in the palm of a giant's hand. "You didn't have a bag with you, either. Was it stolen? Can you remember?" When I shook my head, he said, "We should cancel your credit cards and have your locks changed, too, if your keys—"

"No, there's no need," I said as a pleasant warmth spread throughout my chest. He'd said *we*, as if we were in this together somehow. "I forgot my bag at the hospice."

"Hospice?" Lewis's brow furrowed. "Are you all right?"

I swallowed hard and exhaled quietly, trying to ensure that when I spoke, my words would be steady enough for Lewis to understand. "It's my dad. He has pancreatic cancer—"

"God, I'm so sorry."

"—and, uh, he wasn't doing well when I left last night. I need to find out what's going on. I have to call. To make sure he's okay."

"Which hospice?"

"Monroe. It's in Pleasantdale."

He looked it up and passed the phone to me. "Take your time," he said, standing up. He gave me a quick glance and an encouraging nod as he moved to the door. "I'll be right outside."

I clutched the phone, preparing myself for what I'd say to Dad. First, I'd tell him I loved him, I didn't care about him not being my biological father, it didn't matter one bit. Then I'd apologize, say I was so, so sorry I'd left. I'd been selfish, stupid. He'd say, *Freckles, it's fine, nothing to forgive.* The thought made my chest expand as I hit Dial.

"Good morning, Monroe Hospice, how may I direct your call?" Brenda the receptionist's voice was a true balm for the soul. She'd given me a hug the first day I'd visited Dad. Held me after I'd walked out of the elevator where I'd let go of the emotions I'd kept inside since I'd arrived an hour earlier. Not once did she complain or try to pull away as I clung to her, not even when a damp patch of my tears soaked into her soft yellow cashmere sweater.

"Hi, Brenda. It's Eleanor Hardwicke." I pressed Lewis's phone against my ear, hoping the whooshing in my head would stop soon.

"Eleanor…" Brenda's voice became gentler still. "How are you?"

"Not great, to be honest. Can I please speak to Dad? Is he awake?"

Her silence lasted forever. With every passing nanosecond, it squeezed my gut a little bit more before going for my lungs, wrapping itself around them. "Brenda? Can you put me through to his room?"

"I'm so sorry, Eleanor," she whispered, and instead of my blood running cold, it froze solid in my veins. "I'm afraid your father passed away last night."

CHAPTER SIX

LEWIS'S PHONE SLIPPED FROM my fingers and clattered to the floor. My little remaining strength evaporated, turning my voice into a tiny, inconsequential noise when I tried to speak. I put my head back and let out a scream that sounded closer to the noise a wounded animal might make.

Within a heartbeat, Lewis appeared in the doorway. "Eleanor?" He saw the expression on my face, took three steps in my direction, his eyes widening. "What's wrong? What happened?"

"My dad. He…he's…" The word *dead* wouldn't come out, I couldn't push it past my lips. Brenda had got it wrong, mistaken me for someone else because Dad wasn't gone. Not now. Not like this. Not after the way I'd spoken to him and walked away.

"Jesus. I'm so, so sorry," Lewis whispered. "When did it happen? Last night?"

As I nodded, he sat on the side of the bed and held out his

arms. I collapsed against his chest, let him pull me against him as I sobbed.

"He can't be," I said, crying louder still, and when the reality of the situation slammed into me, the fact I'd never see Dad again, I let out another wail. "He was supposed to have four months. It's what they told him. Four months. We're not even halfway there." I pushed Lewis away. "Why did he wait so long before going to the doctor? Why? It's not fair, it's not *fair*."

Nurse Miranda must've heard the commotion because she rushed into the room. "My goodness, what's going on in here? Is everything all right?"

"Her father passed away," Lewis said in a low voice. He hadn't moved, and I sank against him again, bunching his shirt beneath my fingers, hoping he could stop me from feeling as if I was suffocating in that godforsaken hospital bed.

"Oh, you poor thing." Nurse Miranda's face filled with pity as she pressed one hand to her chest. "I'll give you some time and come back in a while, okay? Can I get you anything?"

When I didn't answer, Lewis shook his head, and the door closed behind her. It took a long while for my tears to stop, but when no more came, Lewis helped me lie back down and handed me a tissue.

"What can I do?" he said. "How can I help?"

The compassion in his eyes, the fact this quasi stranger would offer any kind of assistance threatened to set me off into a blubbering mess again. It had been such a long time since anyone but Dad had showed me affection, I'd all but forgotten what it felt like.

"Is there someone I can call?" he said, retrieving his phone from the floor. "Shall I try your mom again? Maybe this is why she hasn't contacted you? God, she must be devastated."

Despite everything, I almost laughed. "Devastation isn't in my mother's range of emotions," I said, and Lewis raised his eyebrows.

"They've been divorced for almost twenty years and… Let's just say it's always been complicated between her and me."

"Yeah," he said. "Families can be tough. What about a brother? A sister?"

"Amy lives in LA. We rarely speak."

"Right. Look, are you sure you don't want to call your mom?"

Lewis had no idea what I'd meant by things being complicated. I knew my mother hadn't gone to see Dad out of concern for his health last night, that much had been evident from the conversation I'd overheard. She'd tried to make him change his will, leave the little he had to Amy. Now I'd taken the possibility away from my sister, and even through the fresh fog of grief, I could clearly see another reason for them to despise me. I remembered my mother's words about how I'd brought on Dad's collapse. She was right, it had been my fault. He'd died last night because of *me*. She'd never let me forget it. She didn't need to. I'd never forgive myself.

"I don't want to talk to her," I whispered.

"What about your boyfriend?" Lewis said. "Or a girlfriend, maybe? There must be someone who can be with you. You shouldn't be alone, not after what's happened."

I looked away, didn't want to say there was no one to call. I'd only had a handful of relationships—all of which ended in disaster—and never had many friends. Telling him would have meant admitting how isolated I'd become, how alone I felt, despite trying to convince myself otherwise. It was of my own doing, I knew. I'd been hurt too many times, put down and let down far too often. Being alone was easier. *Usually* easier, but only because I'd had Dad.

Before I could speak, the door opened and a woman in a white overcoat walked in. A red stethoscope hung around her neck and she carried a chart of some sort under her arm. She came over to the bed and shook my hand, her long fingers cold as Popsicles, and in direct contradiction with the warm smile on her face.

"Good morning, Ms. Hardwicke," she said with a hint of an accent. "I'm Dr. Chang. Miranda told me about your father. My deepest sympathies." She paused, folded her arms across her chest and looked down at me. I fought the urge to cry again as I wished I could disappear, fade away to nothing—it would be penance for hurting Dad. I didn't deserve Dr. Chang's condolences, didn't deserve anyone's sympathies.

"I've got good news," she said, oblivious to the turmoil going on inside me. "The blow to your head was quite severe and it had us worried, but your CT scan is clear. No signs of internal bleeding or cranial fractures. Miranda told me you woke up a few times during the night."

"I don't remember," I said. "Not until this morning."

"But it's still great news, isn't it?" Lewis said, squeezing my hand.

"Great news indeed," Dr. Chang replied.

"When can I leave?" I whispered. "I want to go home."

"Ah, not quite yet." Dr. Chang shook her head. "I want to keep you in for observation for at least twenty-four hours, preferably until tomorrow morning. Get plenty of rest until then. Let us take care of you, okay?"

"Okay," I mumbled, held still as she went through her notes, examined my head, my eyes, asked me questions about headaches and vision and nausea. I lied, told her there was no pain, no blurriness, no queasiness. I'd had a concussion at school once, I knew what she was looking for. As soon as she and Nurse Miranda left, I pushed away the covers, but yanked them swiftly back up. My clothes had been removed at some point, and I was now dressed in nothing but a hospital gown with a gaping hole at the back.

"What are you doing?" Lewis put his hand on mine as I reached for the IV needle in my arm. "Stop. You heard what she said. You have to rest."

"I can't." I tried to push him away but he held firm. "I want to see my dad. I have to get to the hospice. I need to—"

"I get it, I do," Lewis said, letting go.

"Do you?" I snapped, carefully pulling the IV out of my arm and pushing down hard to stop the blood. "Because I can't afford what they'll charge me for being here, either. I don't have insurance. I have to get out of here."

"But you were hurt. I saw it and it scared the living daylights out of me. I thought he'd… I thought you'd…" He took a deep breath. "You can't leave."

"Yes, I can." Anger rose inside me. Who the hell did he think he was? I'd known him all of five minutes, really, and he had some kind of savior complex going on? I didn't *need* saving. "What are you going to do? Stop me?"

He must have seen the flash of fury in my eyes because he raised his hands, palms turned outward, got up and took a step back. "No, of course not," he said gently. "But if you insist on leaving, at least tell me how you'll get to the hospice."

"I'll figure it out."

"Didn't you say your bag's there? With your wallet and phone?" When I didn't answer, he said, "It's settled then. I'll take you."

"You don't need to," I spat, my voice harsh, ungrateful, too reminiscent of my mother's, which was no surprise really, considering she constantly lived in my head.

"Please, Eleanor. It's your decision, but listen to the doctor. She said you're supposed to be under observation. It's not smart to leave the hospital in the first place, but going all the way to Pleasantdale on your own…?" He brushed his hair off his face, shook his head. "Let me make sure you get there safely, please? And then I'll leave you alone, I promise."

I wanted to argue but knew Lewis was right. Walking to the hospice with the pounding in my head would be akin to riding his green bicycle through a pool of molasses with my feet tied together. "Fine," I said with a curt nod. "Fine."

"I'd better track down the doctor right away." Lewis headed for the door. "They'll probably want you to sign something. You know, for liability reasons, or whatever."

After he disappeared from the room, I swung my legs over and put my feet on the cold floor, reached for the back of the chair to stop the room from spinning. When I was sure I wouldn't pass out or empty my guts, I searched for my clothes, found them folded up and stored away in a plastic bag in the closet, my shoes and jacket underneath. I gathered up my things, tried to ignore the shaking of my hands as I took slow steps to the bathroom.

I winced when the fluorescent lights came on, and, once I'd pulled on my clothes, dared to take a quick peek in the mirror. A wicked bruise—already a frightening shade of deep blue and purple—stretched across the left side of my temple and almost to the bottom of my cheek. The dark circles under my eyes blended with the hue of the bruise, making the rest of my skin appear paler than flour. Meanwhile, my hair had tangled itself into a cross between a bird's nest and a tumbleweed and had piled itself on top of my head.

Lowering my gaze, I splashed water onto my face before running a hand over the back of my head, gently touching the tender golf ball–size lump protruding from my skull. As I glanced at myself in the mirror again, the voice inside me began to whisper.

Dad's dead. He's dead. *It's your fault.* Your *fault, you pathetic loser.*

I exhaled, pushing the air from my lungs to drown out the words, but all it did was make more room for the guilt that had already taken hold, let it burrow deeper inside me, feelings I knew would be silenced for even a moment if only I had something to eat. I returned to the room, where Lewis stood by the bed, his arms crossed.

"Can I talk you out of this?" he said.

"No." I slipped on my sneakers.

"At least let me try?"

I didn't answer and headed for the door. Nurse Miranda wasn't impressed with my decision to leave, either, sighing as I completed and signed the necessary Against Medical Advice forms without bothering to read them through.

"You bring her back if she passes out, has blurred vision or complains of headaches, all right?" she told Lewis. "Same if she throws up, has slurred speech, numbness of any kind or anything that looks even remotely like a seizure. Get her to a doctor immediately."

After Lewis promised he would, he walked me to the entrance, asking half a dozen times if I was okay, if we should slow down, if I needed a rest. I almost told him to stop fussing, I was a grown woman, and he should let me be, but kept quiet. Dad always told me I shouldn't look a gift horse in the mouth, let alone take it behind the barn and shoot it, and most of the time his advice had been sound. I forced myself to stop thinking about Dad, and focused on putting one foot in front of the other without letting Lewis see how unsteady I was.

"You're sure I can't take you home?" he said, zipping up his jacket when we got outside. "I can collect your stuff from the hospice later."

I shook my head. "I have to do this."

He nodded, a grim look on his face. "I understand. I'll find us a cab."

My heart made its way into my throat and stayed there, a giant, uncomfortable lump I couldn't swallow or dislodge. The spiteful voice in my head started whispering again, and this time I couldn't make it stop.

You have nobody left. You're alone now. All alone. And it's what you deserve.

CHAPTER SEVEN

WE SAT IN SILENCE for most of the drive. Lewis glanced at me on a regular basis and I was grateful for the dark and gloomy weather. Brighter skies would've caused me to shut my eyes, and that might have been enough for Lewis to tell the driver to take us back to hospital.

As I stared out of the window, I caught sight of a couple with matching blue-and-white-striped bobble hats perched atop their heads kissing in a doorway, arms wrapped around each other as if it were the end of the world. I wished I had my camera as I imagined them planning Thanksgiving and Christmas, debating whose family to visit first, what gifts to buy and for whom, and which explosive subjects were best avoided over dinner. I looked at my hands folded in my lap, picked at a hangnail. The holidays weren't important anymore. With Dad gone, there was nothing left to celebrate.

From nowhere, my next thoughts went to my biological father, and that he was out there somewhere.

I pushed the idea away. I would not think about him. I would *not*. But all that did was send my mind racing back to Dad and the fact he was dead. Snatched away even earlier than we'd thought. It was enough to make me want to scream, pound my fists against the doors of the taxi, smash the windows with my bare hands. My chest rose and fell more quickly as my breath became shallow, and when I sensed Lewis's eyes on me again, I seized the opportunity to start a conversation, to talk about anything—preferably a topic as bland as three-week-old vanilla pudding—in the hope it would distract and calm me somehow.

"You usually work weekends, don't you?" I said, forcing my voice into neutral, hoping Lewis wouldn't detect my thinly veiled hysteria or mistake my banal question for not giving a shit about Dad. "I see you leave early every morning." When he looked at me, I felt a blush creep across my cheeks. Dear God, now he'd think I was the building's stalker in residence instead. "I mean, I hope you won't be in trouble with your boss on my account."

"I asked one of my team to open up this morning," he said. "Gym owner's privilege."

"I didn't know you own a gym. Mrs. Winchester never... Uh, I mean, that's impressive."

Lewis waved a hand. "It's nothing, really, only a small place on Forest Avenue."

"What's it called?" I had to keep him talking; it was the only way to drown out all the other terrible thoughts whispering inside my head, telling me over and over again what a despicable person I was.

"Audaz."

"Is that Portuguese?"

"Spanish. It means bold and fearless. I chose it because of my maternal grandmother. She was a total badass."

"Was she a bullfighter or something?"

Lewis chuckled. "No, but her parents died when she was young, and her uncle who was supposed to take care of her was a complete ass. When she was sixteen, she woke up one morning, packed her things and walked out of the house without looking back."

"I can relate."

He nodded. "She said it was the best decision she ever made."

My heart had slowed, but now my interest felt real. "What happened? Where did she go?"

"Well, after hitchhiking to the coast, she found a ship bound for America and talked her way into working her fare as a cook."

"What a great story."

"There's more. She arrived in Boston with twenty bucks in her pocket and four years later opened her own restaurant. Now, that's what I call impressive."

"Didn't you want to follow in her restauranteur footsteps?"

He shook his head. "No, they sold the place when I was a kid. But I'm kind of in the industry if you think about it. I get people to work off all the paella they eat." He laughed and despite myself I joined in. I had a feeling Lewis was doing everything he could to keep me distracted, help me forget about what was going on if only for an instant, and I was grateful.

"We do personal training and boot camps," Lewis continued, "prepare people for obstacle runs and stuff. You should come once your head's better."

"Uh, no, thanks. Working out is about as appealing as using knitting needles to clean my ears. Thanks for the offer, though, Drill Sergeant Farrier." I gave him a salute.

"Captain Farrier, if you please." He laughed again, a warm sound that made my heart skip a couple of beats, and I told it to knock it off. "Figured I'd put my army experience to good use, and bossing people around a gym seemed a natural fit."

"I didn't know you were in the army."

He smiled again. "Ten years, and I want to say we barely know each other, but you've seen what laundry detergent I use, so it wouldn't be an accurate statement, would it?"

I'd hoped our basement polka-dot-underwear encounter had somehow been erased from his mind, or, better still, I'd dreamed it. The heat rose to my face again, and I could barely stop myself from pressing my forehead against the cool window.

We arrived at the hospice not long afterward, helping to avoid more humiliation but regenerating the havoc inside me. As the cab came to a halt, the mood shifted, as if we'd driven under an invisible yet oppressive cloud.

"Want me to come with you?" Lewis said after he'd paid the fare.

"I'll be okay, thanks. You can go now if—"

"I'll stay right here, and I'm not in any hurry, so take as long as you need."

As soon as I stepped inside the building, Brenda rushed out from behind the reception desk and hugged me hard, squeezing more tears out of me as she asked about the bruise on my face, patting my hands when I told her. She led me to a sofa where we sat as she put her arms around me, waiting for my crying to subside. How many times had she been in this situation? How many spouses, partners, fathers, mothers and children had she comforted? I clung to her, inhaled her perfume, not wanting to let go.

"I—I shouldn't have left last night." I took a gulp of air to suppress another sob.

"You didn't know it was his time, sweetheart," Brenda whispered.

"But he was struggling and I shouldn't have gone," I said, and she hugged me again, gave me a tissue from a bright orange box on the table and waited for me to speak. "We argued last night. I said some awful things… He died thinking I meant them. I should've stayed. I should've told him I loved him. Why didn't I stay?"

She rubbed my shoulder. "He knew you did, honey. He knew. And he loved you, too. Only the other day he told me how proud he was, what a fantastic daughter you are."

"Did he? Did he really say that?"

"Yes. He said you were the best girl a dad could ever hope for."

I closed my eyes and bit down on my lip, the memories of my father so strong, so real, it felt as if he was sitting there with us, leaning back into a comfy chair, his cheeks full again, his skin pink. How could someone who was gone still feel so present? And what would happen to me when those feelings and the memories began to fade?

"Do you know what happened?" I said.

"I shouldn't—"

"Please, Brenda. What difference does it make if you tell me? I want to know now."

She looked at me, seemingly debating whether I'd cause trouble if she gave me the details, and deciding I wouldn't. "They think his heart gave out, and with the DNR, well..."

I nodded, remembering how Dad and I had fiercely debated the do-not-resuscitate order when he told me he was going to sign it. I insisted it was selfish; if they could help him live longer, he should let them. His eyes had filled with sadness, and he'd shaken his head.

"I'm dying, Freckles. And while I know it's hard, you have to accept it. If I go, I'm going, okay? I don't want to be kept alive by machines or be a vegetable. You have to let me go. It'll be easier for you in the long run."

In the end I'd agreed, but sitting here now with Brenda, I wished I hadn't. Why had I come here? What had I expected to find? That Dad wasn't dead? It had all been some kind of mix-up or a distasteful joke? I needed to leave, get outside, clear my throbbing head, but my legs had become heavier than sandbags, pushing my feet into the floor.

"I left my bag here yesterday," I mumbled. "Do you have it?"

"It's behind the desk," Brenda said, getting up.

"Where's Dad now? Did Worthy & Moore already come to, uh, *get* him?"

"Yes, last night. You can go there now if—"

"I will," I said, the fear of seeing my father's body threatening to overwhelm me.

"Have you spoken to your mother yet? She—"

"No. I can't face her. She blames me for Dad…for him…"

"You can't listen to things like that," Brenda said. "People lash out when a loved one passes, trust me, it happens more than you think." There was no point explaining the deeply rooted animosity between my mother and me, so I stayed silent, and she continued, lowering her voice. "Nurse Jelani mentioned something your father said last night."

"What was it?" I said, my head spinning. "What did he say?"

"It might not mean anything, but we thought you should know in case it does." As Brenda paused, I held my breath. "He had a lucid moment, right before he passed. Nurse Jelani said he was a hundred percent focused, his voice clear as day. He grabbed her hand like this—" she pressed her fingers over mine and squeezed, hard "—then opened his eyes and said, 'Tell Eleanor about Stan Gallinger.' He repeated it three times. Does it mean anything to you?"

Tell Eleanor about Stan Gallinger. I rolled the words around my head, my brow furrowing. I didn't know of a Stan Gallinger and couldn't remember any of Dad's friends or acquaintances of that name, either. Could it be…? Could Dad have left me one final gift, knowing he was slipping away, and we'd never see each other again? Was it his way of making amends somehow, of making things right between us?

Stan Gallinger. *Stan Gallinger.*

He was my biological father, I was sure of it. My heart rate quickened. Now that I had the information, I was no longer sure I wanted it.

CHAPTER EIGHT

SEEING DAD AT THE funeral home a short while later was the hardest thing I'd ever done. I broke down in front of his body, whispering a thousand times "I'm sorry" and a million "I love yous" as my tears choked me. Somehow I managed to keep my voice steady after Mr. Moore guided me to his office, where we went over the paperwork and Dad's wishes. I dug my fingernails into the armrest when he told me Dad left the final approval, and the right to change anything, exclusively to me. I wanted to shout I had no right to do anything.

"It's all been arranged for Thursday," I told Lewis in a shaky voice when we were back in a taxi and on our way home. He'd kindly insisted on coming with me to the funeral home after Brenda had given me my things and we'd left the hospice, even though I'd lied and told him I'd be fine alone. "Dad preplanned everything, right down to the last detail. He said he wanted to make it as easy as possible for me. Can you believe that?"

"I'm so sorry," Lewis said. "You were very close, weren't you?"

"Not as close as I thought." The words slipped out before I could stop them.

He frowned, waited a few beats for me to elaborate and I found myself hesitating, suppressing a sudden urge, an unexpected but undeniable need to talk. But I barely knew Lewis, never let people in, certainly not a relative stranger. I pressed my lips together and stared out the window, and Lewis didn't push me for more information.

Back at the apartment I insisted on paying the fare and tried to shove money into Lewis's hands but he wouldn't hear of it. I continued arguing with him until he walked me up the stairs of our apartment building, and all the way to my front door.

"Enough," he said. "Now, are you absolutely sure you'll be all right? You really don't want someone to come and stay with you?"

"I'll be fine," I said, hoping I could ignore the throbbing in my skull for another minute, at least long enough to get inside my apartment and collapse on the sofa.

Lewis let out a sigh and I could tell he saw through my charade but didn't know what to do about it. "Okay, listen, if you need anything, I'll be upstairs for a while. Text me your number?"

"My phone's dead."

"Then I'll send you mine if you give me your details."

I didn't want to argue so I reeled off the digits and he typed them into his phone.

"There," he said. "I've sent you a text so you have my number now, too. Promise you'll call if you need help? Anytime, day or night."

"Thank you." I tried to tamp down another little flutter going on in my stomach by focusing on retrieving my keys and unlocking the front door. "I'm sorry I caused so much trouble."

"No trouble at all," he said quietly. "Take care of yourself, Eleanor. I'll see you soon."

With the door closed behind me, I breathed in deep, grateful for the utter silence and the familiar, delicate scent of the lemongrass potpourri I'd treated myself to a couple of weeks before. I dropped my bag on the floor, plugged in my phone to charge and looked at my laptop on the coffee table. I took a step toward it, then backed away as if it were a venomous, toothy creature ready to bite. My mind sped up, repeating two words on loop, louder and louder until they were impossible to ignore.

Stan Gallinger. Stan Gallinger. *Stan Gallinger.*

Another few seconds, and my fantasies about my possible biological father ballooned to Hollywood-esque proportions. The excitement—was it excitement?—felt as delicate and fragile as butterfly wings. Part of me wanted to grab my laptop and start researching him, but another part refused for fear my illusions would shatter into millions of pieces, shards of jagged glass crashing down around me.

Still, I couldn't stop thinking of another word. *Family.* I had more family, possibly in Portland. A biological father, perhaps a stepmother and maybe siblings. People I might be able to hang out with, who wouldn't judge me, but instead accept me for who I was and see me as one of their own.

My brain sped into overdrive. What did Stan know about me? Had he waited all these years, hoping I'd make the first move, wishing for a letter, an email or a phone call from his estranged daughter? What would I say if I contacted him? What would *he* say?

"Stop it!" I said out loud, making my head ache. How could I allow myself to think these things? Dad hadn't yet been gone a day and I was fantasizing about a reunion with my biological father? I heard my mother's voice in my mind, telling me I was a disgusting, despicable, ungrateful traitor.

Hanging my head, I quickly walked to the kitchen and grabbed half a dozen cookies, berating myself as I stuffed them down, two at a time, before reaching for more. My stomach rumbled, reminding me I hadn't eaten since last night, and that I should have something more substantial, but my throat closed up as my mind went back to Stan, that he was out there somewhere, maybe just a phone call away.

I almost picked up my cell, wanted to dial my mother's number and demand the truth, but knew she'd refuse. She'd made her position crystal clear at the hospice. No, this was something I'd have to do alone—just...not yet.

As I continued resisting the temptation to search for anything about Stan Gallinger, I headed to the bathroom. Stripping down, I avoided looking at any part of me in the mirror and stepped under the warm water. I stood there for a long time, letting it run over my body, making sure I avoided my tender head, willing it to wash away my grief, take the feelings of revulsion I felt for myself with it. Neither happened, but body clean, hair shampooed and conditioned as carefully as I could, I pulled on a fresh pair of pajamas, got myself a glass of water from the kitchen and picked up my revived phone, noticing the number of new emails and missed calls.

They'd started the night before, shortly after I'd fled the hospice, and had resumed early this morning. A few calls were from the hospice, the rest from Kyle Draper, my biggest client. Judging by the sound of his voice in the messages he'd left, he'd become increasingly frustrated as he reminded me I'd committed to fixing the outstanding issues on the website for his newest nightclub, The Hub.

"We're opening tonight," he'd said in his last message, and despite the loud techno music in the background, I could tell he was almost in major meltdown mode. I imagined him standing in The Hub with its eclectic mix of purple velvet chairs, steel bar and expensive art-deco lighting. No doubt he was dressed in his standard outfit of black shirt and pants, his goatee shaved with exacting precision—precisely how he ran his nightclub and corporate event businesses, and why he'd become a self-made millionaire by the age of thirty-five. "Where are you, Eleanor? Where's your team? Why isn't anyone answering the phone? Call me back."

I wished I'd never fibbed to Kyle about having employees. I'd lied for good reason. I knew what I was capable of, but he'd never have believed I could manage to build the new site he wanted, plus maintain his five others, without assistance, even if he knew I didn't have a life outside of work. I'd never let him down until today. Not only was Kyle my best and most regular client, but he'd referred me to three others. I couldn't afford to lose his business. I should've taken care of everything before leaving for the hospice yesterday evening, instead of planning on finalizing the corrections when I got home.

I'd told Lewis things could've been worse if he'd showed up thirty seconds later, which was true, but things could've been so very, very different if I'd got to the hospice a little later. Not only would Kyle be happy, but I'd have missed my parents' secret conversation altogether. My world wouldn't have been turned upside down. I wouldn't have been attacked and—most important—Dad would still be alive.

As much as I wanted to dissolve into a puddle on the floor or rewrite the past, I couldn't. I had to focus, do what needed to be done, and so, after another handful of cookies, I took deep breaths and dialed Kyle's number, deciding it was best to get it over with.

CHAPTER NINE

A **SUCCESSION OF LOUD KNOCKS** woke me up with a start. Save for the faint streetlight glow sneaking in through the windows, darkness had engulfed the living room. I fumbled around for my phone, trying to figure out the time—and the day. When the doorbell rang three times in a row, I realized whoever had their finger on the buzzer must have been the source of the banging noises, too.

"Gimme a minute," I yelled, stumbling into the hallway, stubbing my big toe on the table in my haste. I swore, hobbled another few steps as the knocking resumed, and reached for the handle. "God, enough already. Where's the fi—"

The rest of my sentence withered and died as I saw Lewis standing in front of me, a paper takeout bag in one hand, the other poised midair.

"Is everything okay?" he said. "I thought you'd passed out or something."

"I'm fine." I wrapped my cardigan around my middle. "I must've fallen asleep on the sofa. What time is it?"

"Six forty-five." When he caught my confused look, he added, "Saturday night. God, for a moment there I wondered if I should break down the door."

"For a moment there I thought you had."

He grinned and held out the bag. "Hungry? The fish-and-chip shop around the corner always serves monster portions. There's enough for two."

I looked at him, tilted my head to one side. "Fish and chips? You mean every personal trainer's nemesis? Don't you think carbs and fat are the work of the devil or something?"

He grinned again, faint lines appearing around his eyes. They complemented the dimples in his cheeks I'd almost convinced myself I hadn't noticed. When he leaned toward me, I could feel my pulse tap-tapping in my neck.

"After training for two hours today, I think I'll be all right," he said, then whispered, "but promise you won't tell the work-out police?"

"Two hours? That's more than I've done in a year. Come in before you pass out."

He followed me to my tiny galley kitchen. I pulled out two polka-dot-covered plates, knives, forks and some napkins from the cupboard and drawers, retrieved ketchup and mayo from the fridge and set everything on the table along with glasses of water. Meanwhile, Lewis opened the various containers, releasing the glorious smell of deep-fried food, making my stomach growl. I wouldn't eat much, I promised myself, not after all the cookies I'd had, and I hated dining with others anyway because I always felt judged, that people were thinking, *I wouldn't eat that if I were you.*

"Was that taken in Portland?" Lewis gestured to the framed

picture hanging on the wall. The photograph was of couple standing outside a café on a cobbled street, lost in an embrace while huddled under a red umbrella. You couldn't see their faces, but it added to the charm.

"Yeah," I said. "I took it on Wharf Street."

"It's yours? You're a photographer?"

"Amateur. I dabble."

"I'd say it's more than dabbling. It's captivating," he said. "Do you know who they are?"

"Haven't the faintest idea."

"Really?"

"Yeah. I enjoy taking pictures of people when they don't know I'm there..." I rolled my eyes. "God, that sounded weird."

Lewis grinned. "Only a bit."

"I meant I enjoy capturing something that isn't rehearsed or staged. It makes it more...intimate, I guess, more interesting. I've always wondered if they'd been together long."

"Now you've got me wondering if they still are. It's a great photo really," Lewis said as we sat down at the table. After taking his first mouthful, he added, "How's the head?"

"Much better," I lied, popping a greasy chip into my mouth, trying not to shovel in another, reminding myself I wasn't supposed to have anything until morning as a punishment for my earlier indulgence. I looked at Lewis, whose fingers still hovered over his plate. "Honestly, I'm fine," I said, but could tell he wasn't quite buying it. "I worked for a bit—"

"You *worked*?"

"I didn't have a choice. One of my clients wasn't exactly happy with me." I tried not to shudder as I thought about how stern Kyle had sounded when I'd called him back, how frustrated and annoyed.

"You work from home, don't you? What do you do?" Lewis picked up a napkin and wiped his mouth before taking a sip of his water, waiting for my reply.

"Website designs. I set up my own business a few months ago."

"Congratulations." Lewis smiled. "I wish we'd met before I'd opened Audaz. I'd have asked you to do my site."

We both fell silent again. Self-consciousness coupled with the renewed realization Dad was gone and the conflicting thoughts about him and Stan—which I kept trying to push away—made my stomach turn itself into uncomfortable knots. I'd never been great at conversation, and felt so out of practice, we might as well have been speaking different languages.

"Did you get ahold of your mom?" Lewis put his fork down when I shook my head. "How come? Is everything okay?"

I wanted to nod and brush him off again, but without warning my face crumpled. Putting a hand over my mouth, I shut my lips and eyes tight, trapping the sobs and tears inside.

"Hey." Lewis reached over the table and put his hand over mine. "Eleanor, I'm here. You can talk to me. You don't have to do this alone."

I opened my eyes, taking in his kind face full of worry, and once again an urge to talk rose from deep within me. This time I didn't ignore it, but instead I took a few seconds to get my thoughts in order, hoping it would help me articulate them properly.

"Last night..." I paused, forced all the air from my lungs in one big push and started again. "Last night I found out that Dad isn't...*wasn't* my biological father." Each word resounded in my ears like thunder, hurt harder than a punch to my gut, making me wince.

Lewis's eyes went wide. "Fuck... Sorry, I mean, hell, that's a lot to take in."

"Yeah...that's precisely how I feel," I said with a shake of my head.

"He told you all this before he died? Was it a confession or something?"

"No, and that's exactly it. I wasn't supposed to find out. I overheard him and my mother talking and I confronted them, got angry and...and then he collapsed." My lips wobbled, stretching across my bottom teeth and I struggled to keep control. "My mother told me to leave and, coward that I am, I did. Then I got mugged, and Dad died and I feel like such a shit because I have all these unanswered questions I don't know what to do with, and—"

Lewis squeezed my hand. "I'm sure he didn't mean to hurt you."

"I know," I whispered. "But I hurt *him*. How can I ever forgive myself for that? And he died with all these secrets and I don't know how to deal with them. It's such a mess."

I paused again, wondered how much more I should say. I noticed the way Lewis leaned forward, giving me his undivided attention. He was there out of some kind of savior's guilt, perhaps, yet I felt I could trust him, and he'd listen. With everything that had happened in such a short amount of time, the protective bubble of self-preservation I'd wrapped myself in wasn't enough tonight. I needed a friend.

"One of the last things my dad did was give the nurse a name," I said. "I—I think it's my biological father's."

Lewis raised his eyebrows. "Do you know him?"

"No."

"Could you ask your mother?"

"Definitely not. Like I said, things between her and me are—"

"Complicated. I remember. Has it always been that way? Difficult, I mean?"

I almost laughed. "That question will take eons to answer."

"I'm not in a hurry," he said gently. "You said your parents divorced?"

"Yeah. Dad was the nicest, most hardworking man you'd ever meet," I said, wanting to smile at what would only ever be the memory of him, and unable to get my mouth to cooperate because of it. "It wasn't enough for her. I guess he didn't meet her expectations. She threw him out when my sister, Amy, and I were at school one day. The day before my eleventh birthday."

Lewis whistled. "What a crappy gift, to say the least."

"It was horrible, and I'll never forget him showing up at the bus stop that afternoon. He gave me this massive hug, smelling of Old Spice, and his beard prickled my forehead. I was so happy until he gave me a kiss and said he couldn't live with us anymore."

"And you couldn't go with him?"

I shook my head, remembering how I'd longed to do so. After he'd dropped us off at what became "Mom's house," I'd rushed inside, packed a bag and patiently sat on my bed, waiting for my mother's curt instructions to join him. The order never came. "Dad traveled a lot for work, and Mom wouldn't let me. I don't know, I think it was her warped way of punishing us both because we got along so well. She got custody of Amy and me, and that was that."

"Christ, no wonder things with your mom turned sour," Lewis said.

"Oh, no, they were bad way before. Our relationship had already been strained for years." I pushed my plate away, stretched out my legs. "I know this sounds petty and juvenile, but she's always favored Amy. I guess I always felt—no, *knew*—my mother didn't want me around despite insisting I live with her. Like I said, it's complicated, and the put-downs, the lack of interest, the punishments—"

"She beat you?"

"Oh, no, it was never physical. She was a little more subtle, but locking me in the basement whenever I'd done something she considered wrong was fairly typical." I shuddered at the memory of the first time it had happened. I'd been seven, had swiped a cookie from a plate intended for Amy's tea party with her dolls and been caught chocolate-handed with fresh crumbs around my mouth.

"This is for your own good," my mother had insisted as she forced me downstairs. "Stealing is bad. And you don't need cookies, not with your physique." Her footsteps had faded away while I'd sat on the creaky wooden floor, knees close to my chin, crying—begging—for her to let me out or put the light on for a while, and that I was sorry, I was so, so sorry.

I didn't share any of that with Lewis, but simply said, "She's not a nice person."

"What about your sister, or your dad? Didn't they stick up for you?"

"Dad did when he was around." I looked away, not wanting to say I'd been angry with Dad at times, not only for him being away so often, but also because he wouldn't stand up to my mother as much as I thought he should. "She only did it when he was away, and when I told him, she ordered him to mind his own business, said disciplining me was up to her because he wasn't there. And Amy? Well, she was always the good girl, on Mom's side."

"I've never understood how a parent can have a favorite kid," Lewis said. "Then again, I don't have any and I'm an only child, so I'm hardly an expert."

"What about your parents? Do you get along with them?"

Lewis folded his napkin in half and dropped it onto his plate. "Mine divorced, too. I was about fifteen and lived with my mom after my dad left. God, we fought like crazy, her and me."

"Because of the divorce?"

"No, because I was a dick. My dad had a lot of issues. He drank and gambled. I kept telling her to leave him but she wouldn't. She couldn't see she deserved better. Then he met someone else and she was devastated, and I despised her for that, too." He shook his head. "Frankly, I was a stupid kid who didn't know how complicated life can be, how difficult it is to get away from an abusive relationship. The only thing I knew was that I wanted to leave and told her so on a regular basis."

"Is that why you joined the army?" I said.

"Partly, I guess. I mean, I wanted to serve my country, but the added bonus was being on the other side of the world, away from all the crap at home." He smiled, let out a small, wry laugh. "Get this, the day before I left for my first tour in Afghanistan I yelled at her, told her I knew she was glad to see the back of me. I said I bet she was hoping I wouldn't come home."

"Ouch. That's vicious."

"It was bullshit. A self-preservation thing, you know? I was scared out of my mind to go but wouldn't admit it. Anyway, when I got back, she hugged me so hard I thought she'd break me in half, and that's saying something. She's barely five feet tall." He smiled again, the dimples in his cheeks deepening. "Distance has a funny way of putting things into perspective. She lives with my stepdad in Colorado now. They're great together, but I wish I could go back in time and be more supportive, help her when she needed it most."

"What about your dad? Do you still see him?"

Lewis shook his head. "He died last year."

"Oh, gosh, I'm really sorry."

"Me, too." He paused. "He was all alone, barely any friends or family, no money. Mom flew back to help sort out all of his things. When I asked why she'd do that after the way he'd treated her, she said it was her way of making peace with him, of forgiving him."

"She sounds like a strong woman."

"She's awesome." He paused again, let a few moments pass. "Look, you're right when you say I don't know your mom, but maybe it's not too late to salvage the relationship."

I let out a laugh and waved a hand. "Trust me, that bridge has been blown up, not burned."

"Maybe not forever," Lewis said. "And she might have more

answers about your biological father, when you're ready to ask her."

"Unless I decide the questions don't matter."

"Can you?"

I looked at him, shrugged. "I'm not sure."

"Lots to think about." Lewis reached for my plate as he stood up, and when I was about to protest, he added, "You sit. I'll take care of this."

I watched him walk across my kitchen, his frame so big he took up the majority of the space. There being another person in my apartment felt almost alien, but Lewis moved with such confidence, putting leftovers in the fridge, washing and drying the plates and cutlery before stacking them in the cupboards, it was as if he'd been there a thousand times. Like he belonged. I reprimanded myself for imagining anything other than a distant friendship developing between us, that he could be more than the guy upstairs who said a friendly hello in the hall.

"I'll let you rest," he said, snapping me out of my daydream. "Will you be okay?"

"Yes. I'm sure I'll be fine."

"I hope you sleep well, Eleanor," he said as he walked to the door where he paused, his fingers on the handle. "Thanks for the chat. Call me if you need me. Anytime. Okay?"

I had a sudden impulse to rush over, stand on my tiptoes and kiss his cheek, take in the scent of his aftershave, feel the warmth of his skin, the stubble on his chin. I didn't want to be alone. For a fraction of a heartbeat I wondered what he'd say if I asked him to stay, and what his reasons might be if he said yes, but it was too late because he slipped into the hallway and pulled the door closed behind him.

CHAPTER TEN

AFTER LEWIS LEFT, I sank onto the sofa, staring at my laptop on the coffee table. All I needed to do was open it and run a search. *Stan Gallinger.* It would take a second. I shook my head, squished my hands under my thighs to prevent myself from touching the computer, and still my mind raced. It was a bit of research. Something to satisfy my curiosity. That was all. No harm done.

My fingers reached for the laptop, hovered over the keyboard as I opened it. This could be the start of a new chapter in my life, and yet the mere thought felt like the ultimate betrayal toward Dad, as if I would leave him behind somehow. I'd never replace, let alone forget, him. He was my dad, my true father, but I couldn't stop myself from thinking about Stan Gallinger, and that he was family, too. If I had another chance to belong somewhere, I had to look into it. At the very least I needed to know where I came from. Surely Dad would understand why, maybe he even wanted me to, especially since he'd given Nurse Jelani Stan's name.

With trembling fingers I typed Stan Gallinger Portland in the search bar, trying to talk myself into—and subsequently out of—hitting Enter. When I couldn't bear it any longer, I held my breath and pressed the key.

Within an instant pages and pages of hits flooded my screen. News articles. Interviews. Blog entries. All of the same person. And right at the top was a picture of him. Stanley Gallinger from Portland. My biological father. *Alleged* biological father, I reminded myself as I peered more closely, zooming in on the photo.

Dad had always made jokes about being vertically challenged, barely reaching five foot seven in his shoes, and I'd always assumed I'd inherited my distinct lack of stature from him. He'd had a round, friendly face, which complemented his soft, squidgy belly, and he'd proudly sported his bald head, saying oncoming drivers could spot him more easily because their headlights bounced off his skull. The only suit I'd seen him in was when he'd dressed up as Santa, making Amy and me squeal with delight when we were kids.

Stan Gallinger was about as diametrically opposed to Dad as could be. He looked immaculate in every photograph I examined, including the ones from thirty years prior. The definition of his features was so sharp, you could cut yourself on it, and his ice-blue eyes, salt-and-pepper hair and the custom-tailored suits all screamed money and success.

If this man was my father, then determining what my mother had seen in him—at least on a superficial level—was hardly a challenge. He could have been a sophisticated, suave model, and, two clicks later, there he was again, gracing the front of the local newspaper with his charming bright white smile. They'd written an entire feature about him and his company, Gallinger

Properties, detailing his journey from past to present, including how he'd inspired hordes of up-and-coming entrepreneurs, in Portland and beyond, to follow in his footsteps.

I opened another tab, brought up my mother's LinkedIn profile, which she meticulously kept up-to-date, and remembered how she'd proudly boasted there wasn't a single gap in her career save for two *"exceedingly"* short periods of maternity leave. I scrolled down, my breath catching as I spotted the company name. She'd worked at Gallinger Properties as an accountant the year before I was born.

"Jesus," I whispered as the certainty that Stan was my biological father cemented itself onto my bones.

I reminded myself to breathe and flicked back to the article. A quick calculation and I figured he was sixty-four, which made him thirty-four when I was born. He'd grown up locally, came from a modest background. His father was a steelworker, his mother a hairstylist. After winning a college football scholarship, he'd studied business, but during his third year he'd been involved in an accident when the rear wheel on his girlfriend's car came off, sending them straight into a tree. His girlfriend was killed on impact, whereas Stan sustained injuries so serious, he was almost taken off life support. He'd been forced to drop out of university and, after his yearlong recovery, worked three jobs until he'd saved enough money for a down payment on a decrepit factory nobody wanted. Everyone called him crazy until he converted the building into trendy office spaces and sold them for a hefty profit. Gallinger Properties was born, and the privately held company was now valued at millions.

I tried to digest the fact my biological father was a real estate mogul, a self-made multimillionaire. When I couldn't get my head around all the information, I read on.

"After the accident I went to a dark place," Stan told the interviewer. "Ultimately it was my wife, Madeleine, who got me through it. I owe her everything."

Madeleine was French-Canadian, two years Stan's junior and his late girlfriend's roommate. Her father was an automobile magnate who specialized in classic cars; her mother had died during childbirth. After the accident that almost killed Stan, he and Madeleine found solace in each other. She'd visited him in the hospital every day, and he'd proposed nine months later.

"I knew she was the one," Stan said. "Never a doubt in our minds." They'd married when he was twenty-seven, she twenty-five. Almost forty years. My eyebrows shot up, and I didn't need to do the math. I wasn't yet thirty. I was the product of an affair.

My mother had married Dad two months before I was born— I'd seen the pictures of them standing on the steps of City Hall, Dad beaming in a brown suit, white shirt and tie, my mother in a black shift dress stretched over her swollen belly, her face even. I wasn't clear on the details about how long they'd dated, and it was something else I'd never get to ask Dad about. But once again I wondered if he'd always known he wasn't my father, or if she'd cheated but pretended I was his.

I went back to reading the article, scrolled down to a photograph, my fingers freezing midair when I recognized Stan sitting between two women. My eyes darted to the caption.

Stanley Gallinger with his wife, Madeleine, and their daughter, Victoria.

Their *daughter.*

While Madeleine was the embodiment of chic—her neck long and swanlike, her blond hair tousled just so—it was Victoria who made my mouth fall open. She'd inherited her parents' best features and made them her own.

Long, thick mahogany hair, almond eyes and a bone structure that would make the most famous of supermodels whimper, all of which exuded elegance and confidence. At the time of the article she'd been twenty-five, which made her twenty-nine now, the

77

same as me. I sped through the last paragraph and modified my search to Victoria Gallinger. The security settings on her social media accounts were shockingly lax, and I quickly determined she lived in Portland, too, and she'd been born two months after me.

I stared at one of her profile photographs. Her hair had been swept to the side, her lips were slightly parted, as if she'd asked a question and was waiting for the answer. Again I noticed her eyes—as striking as her father's—but a shade of warm emerald green, not his frosty blue.

The more I stared at her, the more elation built and mushroomed inside me. No longer able to contain the excitement, it exploded from within in a fit of childish giggles. I had another *sister*—half sister—and we were the same age. I imagined us as young girls with ponytails—hers brown, mine a dirty blond—sharing secrets and midnight feasts. As teens we'd have swapped clothes and complained about our boyfriends, all the things I'd never done with Amy. Victoria and I weren't kids anymore, but was it too late to have the kind of relationship I'd always dreamed of?

I told myself to stop being ridiculous and went back to my snooping. Judging by the photographs taken on various beaches, at art gallery openings, horse races and après-ski functions in Whistler, Victoria's days were glamorous and fun filled. Comparing our lives felt as if I was watching the original *Wizard of Oz* movie—mine was the black-and-white part, whereas hers burst forth in rich, opulent Technicolor. Despite the obvious differences in our upbringing, I wondered if we might still be friends.

The longer I studied Victoria's pictures, the more I wanted this to be a gift, another chance at having a family, a way to no longer feel abandoned and alone, something I'd pretended so hard I didn't care about, I'd almost had myself convinced. I fought the impulse to send her a Facebook message, introducing myself as her half sister. No. When—*if*—I contacted any of the Gallingers, it would have to be slow and steady. This wasn't a situation to be rushed; I needed to be sure, and I needed to be careful.

As an army man, Lewis would've told me the first thing to do in unfamiliar territory was recon. Lots and lots of recon, which included being certain they really were my family, and who knew what about me.

Whispering a thank-you to the creators of social media for allowing me the ability to spy on others from the comfort of my living room, I continued piecing Victoria's life together. She'd married a guy called Hugh Watters two years ago; they had no pets or kids. If the looks of affection and the way they wrapped their arms around each other were anything to go by, they were very much in love, and they had a set of equally attractive, wealthy-looking friends.

I opened another tab and typed in Gallinger Properties, headed to their Contact Us page and didn't blink until my eyeballs had gone dry. Their offices were on Exchange Street. My biological father worked a mere fifteen-minute walk from my apartment. We'd probably passed one another in the street, maybe grabbed some lunch or a coffee from the same place at the same time. I hadn't known of his existence. Had he known of mine? If he'd seen me coming, had he put his head down and crossed the street, pretended to be interested in a window display until I'd passed?

Head spinning, I went through my options, ranging from doing nothing to showing up at Gallinger Properties unannounced. I imagined Stan stepping out of an important meeting, demanding to know who had interrupted his busy schedule. As soon as he saw me, he'd rush forward with open arms and a tear in his eye, telling me he'd always hoped I'd find him.

Then again he might have zero clue who I was.

After mulling things over some more, I decided *if* I was going to contact him, by phone would be best, providing my throat didn't close up before I got out a single word. Maybe sending a note was more sensible—not an email, but a handwritten one, perhaps a fancy greeting card I'd put in a padded envelope. Except...what if I sent it and he didn't respond? What then?

The scenarios spun around my head, gathering speed, merging into an indecipherable blur.

Enough. I slammed down the cover of my laptop. While I'd thought I could choose to ignore things, a different path ahead was already coming more and more into focus, crystalizing in my mind. I couldn't spend the rest of my life *guessing* if Stan Gallinger was or wasn't my biological father, what he did or didn't know about me, might or might not say.

No. Guessing wouldn't do at all.

I needed to *know.*

CHAPTER ELEVEN

I **SPENT MOST OF SUNDAY** in a contradictory combination of trying to rest my head, pretending to ignore what I'd discovered, overanalyzing everything I'd seen, spending more time researching the Gallingers and trying not to reach for the cookies as my stress levels rose. That pattern was interrupted midafternoon when an overworked-sounding detective called about Friday's "incident," asking for details and a description of my assailant. When I told him I couldn't help, he almost sounded relieved. No doubt within a few days, my case would be buried underneath a pile of more solvable ones, already forgotten and gathering dust—which suited me fine.

My mother didn't contact me, as was to be expected, but neither did Amy, and by now she had to know about Dad. This was an all-time high in the pathetic levels of our family's dysfunctionality, but by late afternoon I decided I had to discuss Dad's funeral arrangements with my sister. He might have left the final decisions to me, but she was his daughter, too. *His real daughter.* I swatted the voice away and picked up my phone.

"Hey, Eleanor, how are you?" Amy said in her overly enthusiastic stage voice. "What's going on? Are you out of the hospital?"

Her comment threw me. "You knew?"

"Mom said she got a message from your neighbor? I'd have called, only—"

"You were busy?" I said, trying—failing—to keep the sarcasm at bay.

"Yes, I was, actually," she said, her tone sharp as a glass cutter. "I was at auditions all weekend, if you must know. I got home all of two minutes ago."

I counted to ten. "How are you coping with the news about Dad...?"

"Oh, it's awful, isn't it?" she said, her voice cracking. "I've been crying on and off. We knew it was coming, but that doesn't make it any easier."

"No, it doesn't," I whispered, wondering if we might finally bond a little, if the death of a parent was the thing we'd needed to bring us closer. "Listen, I, uh, I've made all the arrangements for the funeral. The service will be on—"

"Thursday, I know. Mom had the info. I'm sending flowers."

"Okay, thanks. I guess you'll stay with her? When do you fly in?"

"I can't come, Eleanor."

"What do you mean, you can't come?"

She sighed. "You know how my work can be."

"No, I don't. Why don't you fill me in?"

"I told you, I had auditions all day." Amy's voice shot up. "One of them is a huge part in a soap opera which my agent says would really put me on the map—"

"But you can't—"

"—and the callbacks are scheduled over the next week, plus

I have a commercial to shoot the day after the funeral. I'm already booked."

"It's not—"

"Mom's fine with it," she snapped. "Why can't you be?"

So much for sisterly bonding. "Because he's your dad, Amy. Your *dad*."

"I'll be there in spirit. I'm sure he'd understand. Besides, you'll be there, and *you* were his favorite, weren't you? Always two peas in a pod."

The sickly sweet tone with a sour undernote told me Amy had already known about the family secret I'd only just discovered. Of course she had. Our mother shared *everything* with her. I loosened the grip on my phone so I didn't shatter the screen between my fingers.

"When did she tell you?" I said.

"Tell me what?"

"That Dad isn't my father."

She let out a long sigh, making it sound as if we were talking about something as trivial and bothersome as bad weather. "About a week after he was diagnosed. When I came back for a quick visit, remember?"

"Yes." Although, as I recalled it, I didn't know she was in town until Dad brought it up, by which time she was on a flight heading back to LA. "Why didn't you tell me about Stan?"

Amy clicked her tongue but didn't question who Stan was, which meant I was right. He *was* my biological father. My pulse raced as she started talking again.

"First of all, it was her secret to tell, not mine. And do you think it's any better now that you know? I mean, you can't do anything about it, can you, Nellie?" She laced her words with defiance and I could see her in my mind's eye, standing in her perfect apartment, dressed in one of her perfect outfits, judging me with her perfect face, her expression tight, exactly like our mother's except with fewer wrinkles and higher cheekbones.

I wanted to scream, but she spoke first. "Mom did what she thought was best. It's not her fault you were eavesdropping."

"Oh, look, you're taking her side. What a fucking surprise."

"Dad hid it from you, too. Why aren't you mad at him?" She paused for what I knew was dramatic effect before letting out another Oscar-worthy sigh. "I'm not looking for a fight—"

"Then show Dad the respect he deserves and come to the funeral. Because until then, we've got nothing more to say."

I disconnected the call, silencing Amy's protests. Despite knowing I'd more than likely not hear from her—or my mother—again, my chest heaved as the anger inside me mounted in a rolling crescendo. Although it wasn't a huge surprise our mother had confided in Amy about Stan, the fact she'd done so while continuing to lie to me and talking about me behind my back made me want to slam my fists into the wall until my knuckles bled.

I headed for the fridge and wolfed down the leftover fish and chips without bothering to heat them up, opened an abandoned can of pears from the back of the cupboard and finished them all, including the sugar-laden juice, which I gulped straight from the can. During the few minutes it took to stuff myself, I kept thinking about Victoria and Madeleine, couldn't imagine them behaving the way Amy and my mother had. They'd be respectful, compassionate and understanding, not petty, self-involved, lying little *bitches*.

The conversation with Amy and her total disregard for Dad rattled me so much, I tossed and turned when I went to bed, falling into fits of broken sleep around three. When I woke up again Monday morning, it was almost nine, but despite the several hours of rest, my head felt as if it had been stuffed with bags of fluffy cotton wool.

Both Nurse Miranda and Dr. Chang had warned that my body would need time to recover, but at least that pain had become a dull ache I could pretend to ignore. Staring at the screen far too long the day before hadn't helped, especially when I'd found the home addresses for Stan and Madeleine, and Victoria. I hadn't got any closer to the answers I wanted or reached a conclusion on what to do and felt like the vilest of traitors, especially when I switched on the radio to drown out the voice in my head, only to hear The Beach Boys singing "God Only Knows," one of Dad's favorites.

I buried my face in my hands as a fresh wave of grief and loneliness hit me, not wanting to listen to the lyrics but incapable of switching them off, wishing he were there.

After pulling myself together, brushing my teeth and fixing a quick cup of coffee, I opened my email, homed in on a note from Kyle, in which he asked for last-minute updates. Reluctantly, I got to work, replacing the carousel photos as he requested and doctoring the home-page layout according to his specs. Forty minutes and a brisk shower later, my intentions of going through the rest of my inbox evaporated. Instead I found myself rereading the entire article about Stan, examining the photos of Victoria and pulling up the Contact Us page on the Gallinger Properties website.

I looked at my watch. Almost lunchtime. Before I changed my mind, I grabbed my phone and dialed.

"Gallinger Properties, Steven Marshall speaking. How may I direct your call?"

"Uh, hello… I…uh…"

What the hell was I doing? I ordered my fingers to hang up, but the phone remained at my ear, as if hot-glued there, my heart thumping so loud, I was sure Steven Marshall and everyone else at Gallinger Properties would hear its galloping tune.

"Hello, miss," Steven said in a smooth baritone. "How may I be of assistance?"

I need to speak to my father. I gave my head a shake, making my headache come back with determined vengeance. "Uh, I, uh…" My brain kicked in, making my mouth move. "Is Mr. Gallinger in today?"

"He certainly is. I'll put you through—"

"No." Think. *Think.* "I mean, no, thank you… Uh, I have a delivery for him."

"Oh, I see, well, you can leave it with me at reception. I'll make sure he gets it."

"But it says I have to deliver it personally," I blurted.

"Okay, let me check his schedule," Steven said, giving me a few seconds to try to regain some of my composure. "He's stepping out for lunch soon but he'll be back around one thirty. Then he has meetings for most of the afternoon, but if you don't mind waiting, I'll let him know you're here and we'll squeeze you in."

"Oh, uh, great."

"Can I help you with anything else today? Directions to the office?"

"No, thank you," I said in more of a squeak than actual words, before hanging up and lobbing the phone onto the sofa as if it had scorched my fingers.

He's stepping out for lunch soon.

Steven's words ran around my head over and over. There was no harm in me going to the Gallinger offices and waiting outside, was there? Not if my only intention was to catch a glimpse. The man was my father. I wouldn't actually *do* anything, *say* anything. Not now and maybe not ever, but I had an insatiable desire to see him, if only from afar.

As I hurried to the bedroom to get changed, I stopped in front of the photograph of Dad and me, the one I'd taken last Christmas, well before his diagnosis. After showing him my latest drawings and draft company logos, I'd put my Nikon on a timer and taken an old-fashioned selfie in which we wore lopsided paper crowns, the ones you get in Christmas crackers along with plastic toys and lame jokes.

Pulling crackers was a tradition Dad had kept from his early childhood in England, and something we'd done every year without fail. We'd spent the day together, exchanging presents and eating roasted chicken—neither of us liked turkey—along with buttered mashed potatoes and honey-glazed carrots. After gorging ourselves silly, we'd collapsed on the sofa with a bottle of red wine, munching our way through a box of Belgian chocolates while one-upping each other with the Christmas cracker jokes.

"Where does Santa keep his money?" Dad popped a hazelnut swirl into his mouth and waited for my answer, his grin growing and spreading as I wrinkled my nose. He almost loved this ridiculous tradition more than I did. "Giving up already? It's the snowbank."

I groaned, peering at my joke. "You'll never get this one. What do elves learn in school?"

"Wait, wait, I remember that from last year. It's…it's…the *elfa*-bet."

"Yes." I giggled. "God, these are dumb."

"Yup." Dad let out a contented sigh, passed the box of chocolates to me and stretched out on the sofa. "Merry Christmas, Freckles."

"Merry Christmas, Dad," I said, before noticing him looking at me with a frown as he rubbed his stubble with a hand. I shoved my third cherry truffle in my mouth and, when I couldn't ignore him any longer, said, *"What?"*

"Nothing."

"Why are you looking at me like that?"

"Like what?"

"You know…all weird."

"I'm not—"

"Dad."

"Okay, okay. I'm wondering if you're going to spend all day here."

"What do you mean? Of course I am, it's Christmas."

Dad tutted. "Yes, I know. I meant, are you going to visit your mother?"

I examined the chocolate in my hand and bit it in half with fervor. "Nope."

He knew better than to challenge me. "Hanging out with a boyfriend later? Got any cute-couple Christmassy things planned?"

I stuffed the rest of the chocolate in my mouth and looked at him as I chewed, raising an eyebrow. "Really, Dad? Cute-couple Christmassy things? Don't you know me at all?"

He waved a hand, took a sip of wine and smacked his lips. "You know what I mean."

"And *you* know I don't have a boyfriend."

"Yeah. Exactly my point. You've been single forever."

"Are you trying to get rid of me or something?"

"Absolutely not. You know how much I enjoy your company, Freckles. I'm sure a man your age would, too. Cute and clever as you are, you—"

"I don't need a man," I fired off with a snort. "And I don't see you dating anyone. Any sexy trucker women you like?"

"No. Frankly, I'm too tired these days, anyway. All I want to do is sleep."

"How come?" I looked at him, scanned his face, for the first time taking in the dark circles under his eyes. How long had they been there? Had he lost weight, too? Come to think of it, he hadn't polished off his mammoth helping of food, despite his plate rivaling the height of the Portland Head Lighthouse. When I'd mentioned it, he'd said he was watching his diet—Dad never watched his diet, and he'd been the same weight forever.

I sat up. "Are you okay?"

With a dismissive wave, he drank more wine and reached for another joke. "I'm fine. What do you call Santa when he takes a break? Santa Pause."

I'd laughed, topped up our glasses, feeling a little smug about steering the conversation away from my love life without him noticing. Now, standing in my hallway, looking at one of the last pictures I'd taken of us together, I felt like a heartless monster.

"I'm sorry, Dad," I whispered. "I should've paid attention. Told you to see a doctor, I should've dragged you there. I'm *sorry*."

He smiled back with his purple paper crown and rosy cheeks.

"I have to see what this Stan guy's about," I said, still talking out loud, my voice cracking. "You understand, don't you? Please don't be mad."

I put the photograph facedown and went to my closet, squeezing myself into jeans and choosing a loose sweater. Hair and teeth brushed, I grabbed my camera, bag and jacket, put on my boots and headed outside.

The crisp wind carried the promise of snow, so I pulled my hood over my head and retrieved my blue-and-white polka-dot mittens from my pocket before remembering they'd been a gift from Dad on my last birthday. I gulped. I didn't believe in signs or messages from beyond the grave, but I shoved the mittens back in my pocket regardless, doing my best to ignore them and my freezing fingers.

When I finally got to Exchange Street, I took a few deep gulps of air, stood on the opposite side of the road, slightly to the left of Gallinger Properties's front door. I panicked—maybe I was too late, or Stan never used the front door but a side entrance, perhaps one at the back—and wondered if I'd blown it. As it turned out, I'd picked the right time and the right place, too, because five minutes later the front door swung open, and a woman stepped outside.

Madeleine Gallinger.

From across the street, I couldn't get a good enough look at her, so I raised my Nikon and zoomed in. Before I knew what my fingers were doing, I snapped a picture, then another, taking photo after photo, the click-click-click of the shutter ringing in my ears. She looked more elegant in real life—an almost impossible feat. Her honey-colored hair was in a perfect bob, accentuating her long, slim neck. The deep burgundy dress complemented her pale skin tone, and her cream-colored woolen coat, which reached halfway down her high-heeled, black leather boots, must have cost three times my rent. She moved with ease, class and grace—gliding rather than walking—as if she were some kind of celestial being. Another person accompanied Madeleine, and my gaze landed on him.

Stan.

He wore a dark suit underneath his long black coat, and his shoes had been shined to perfection. Although his hair had become more salt than pepper since the most recent photos I'd seen online, his frame was still lean and fit, easily making him appear ten years younger.

I snapped another dozen pictures, watched as he took Madeleine's hand, said something to make her laugh, and she rested her head on his shoulder. Anyone observing them could tell they were in love, but the way they carried themselves—the confidence they exuded—sent another message, too. They were a force to be reckoned with, the kind of power couple sparking awe and envy in equal measure.

I wondered what it would have been like to grow up as their child. Privileged in terms of money, that much was a certainty, but were they warm and caring, or cold and distant? Too preoccupied by career, status and how they appeared to the outside world? All these thoughts—and then some—ran through my mind until a shiny black Mercedes with tinted windows pulled up in front of the building. Stan held the back passenger door open for Madeleine, and within a heartbeat they'd disappeared inside.

I wished I could follow them, listen to their conversation without them realizing I was spying. Not an option, so I hurried to a nearby café, where I grabbed a coffee and a chicken wrap, and settled down in a window seat, giving me a direct sight line over the street and the entrance of Stan's company. My fluttering stomach didn't appreciate the food despite having skipped breakfast, something that hadn't happened in years, and I ended up sipping my coffee too fast, scalding the roof of my mouth and leaving half of the drink untouched.

An hour later I needed the bathroom, and more than one person had given me the evil eye for sitting in a prime spot with half a cup of cold coffee, but I refused to move. At exactly one twenty-five, the Mercedes pulled up again. Stan got out alone and headed inside.

I told myself I'd got what I'd came for, a glimpse. Not only had I seen Stan, but Madeleine, too, and I'd taken reams of pictures. Time to go home, mull all of this over and decide what—if anything—I'd do next. While I knew it was the sensible thing to do, the *only* thing to do, my brain and my feet were still at odds, and the latter won.

As if on autopilot and without allowing myself to think it through, I got up, walked out of the café, crossed the street and headed straight through the front door of Gallinger Properties.

CHAPTER TWELVE

"GOOD AFTERNOON."

The man at the reception desk greeted me with a smile as I walked in, and I recognized his deep voice as Steven Marshall's, the person who'd answered my earlier call. He looked a few years younger than me, wore a pin-striped suit with a lilac tie and a pair of vintage glasses.

"Welcome to Gallinger Properties," he continued, and I could tell he was trying very hard not to stare at my bruised face. "How may I help you?"

As I took in the white reception desk with curves rivaling a cello's, and the large silver letters spelling out the company name on the stone-tiled wall behind him, I shifted from one foot to the other, a trickle of sweat running down my back. "Uh, I'm here for Mr. Gallinger."

"Do you have a meeting scheduled?"

"No," I said quietly. "But I need to see him. It's important."

"All right," Steven said. "May I take your name and can you tell me what it's regarding?"

I shouldn't have come, told myself to turn and run—but knew if I did, I'd never have the courage to come back. "I'm Eleanor, and it's...personal." When Steven raised his eyebrows I blurted, "I really need to see Mr. Gallinger. *Please*."

He looked at me as if trying to decide whether I was a crazy person who'd cost him his job if he let me in, or if he'd get fired if he didn't. A few more beats passed in our bizarre standoff until he said, "Let me see what I can do. Why don't you have a seat?"

"Thank you." I took a step back, eyed the leather sofa next to the low coffee table with a pile of business magazines on top, which had been arranged in an artistic spiral. No way would I sit. I wanted to be ready to make a dash for it in case I lost my nerve.

Steven pressed a button on his computer and mumbled something into his headset. Not long after, he gestured to me. "Mr. Gallinger will see you in the small meeting room," he said, sounding almost as surprised as I felt. This had to be a sign. A good one.

We walked past a few closed doors and into a meeting room the size of my apartment. It had an oval-shaped wooden table with eight high-backed black leather chairs on either side. The far wall was covered in matching oak paneling and housed the biggest TV I'd ever seen. The artwork on the opposite wall featured abstract trees in various shades of green, gold and brown, lending the room a calming effect rather than making it ostentatious and overbearing.

"Mr. Gallinger will be right with you," Steven said. "Can I offer you anything to drink in the meantime? A coffee, some water, perhaps, or tea?"

"No, thank you." I was incapable of keeping anything down considering I was about to serve up a huge helping of family drama right there in the conference room.

"He won't be long," Steven said and disappeared, closing the door behind him.

My palms felt as if they'd transformed themselves into sweaty sponges, and I wiped them on my pants as yet another bead rolled down my spine. What the hell was I doing? This wasn't recon—it was a suicide mission. I'd found out about Stan Gallinger two days ago. Now I was in his office, no clue how I'd introduce myself, what I'd say or what I wanted from the man. *Get out of here*, my mind yelled, but the door swung open.

Stan stood before me, tall and assertive. Imposing. A flicker of something passed over his face, but he stayed silent as he looked at me.

I took a step back and bowed my head. "This is a mistake. I'm sorry, I'll go and—"

"Have a seat." His voice was firm as he pulled out a chair, blocking my escape.

I didn't realize how badly my legs had been shaking until I sank down on the soft leather without saying a word. I opened my mouth but nothing came out so I shut it again.

"What happened to you?" he said. "You look hurt."

"I—I was mugged. But I'm okay. That's not why I'm here."

He observed me for a little while before talking again. "Why *are* you here, Eleanor?" Although the words were spoken softly, the way his blue eyes observed my every move, I couldn't tell if he was friend, foe or somewhere in between.

I exhaled, trying to buy myself time. I could make my excuses and go, leave the building and never, ever come back, do what I usually did with confrontation. What my mother would expect from me. Hide.

No. Not this time. I gave my head a small shake and forced myself to speak. "I found out some information about you and, well, my mother, and I…I wondered…"

Stan waited for me to continue, but when I didn't, he said, "Who's your mother?"

I hesitated, whispered, "Sylvia Hardwicke."

He sat back in his chair, put his fingers in a steeple under his chin. I couldn't tell what he was thinking. I couldn't read him, so I let him continue observing me, trying not to squirm.

"You look a lot like her," he said. "It's the eyes."

A hand flew to my mouth as the room slipped out of focus, becoming like the blurry trees on the wall. I pressed my palms onto the smooth table, pushed my heels into the floor. "Does that mean it's true? You're my father?"

"Why are you here, Eleanor?" he repeated. While his voice remained gentle, his tone demanded the truth, and I found myself unable to do anything but comply.

"I wasn't going to come." My words spilled forth like water from a burst pipe. "I only found out a few days ago my dad— well, the man I thought was my dad—wasn't actually my dad. He told me your name and…and I looked you up online and read articles about you and found out where you work. I stood outside and when I saw you and your wife—"

"You saw my wife?" he said, eyebrows raised.

"Yes, earlier, when you went for lunch. But I wasn't stalking you or anything, I promise." I hoped he wouldn't ask me to turn out the contents of my bag because all the photos on my camera told a different story. "I…I needed to see you because—" I looked away, his gaze too intense "—because my dad… He died."

"I'm sorry. This must be hard and confusing for you."

My shoulders dropped. "Yes, yes, it really is. My mother… We, uh, don't get along, you know?" I made myself stop. I was coming on too strong, sharing too much, too quickly. I wasn't allowing him—or myself—time to digest any of it. "And, well, here I am."

"With all that in mind," he said, "would I be wrong to presume you came because you're looking for…family? For us to have some kind of a connection or relationship?"

"*Yes.*" This was incredible. We'd met all of three minutes

ago and were so much in tune already, he'd picked up on what I wanted to say. "Yes, please, maybe—"

He held up a hand, shook his head. "I'm afraid that's not going to happen, Eleanor."

All the air left my lungs as if I'd taken a hit to the chest. "I'm sorry? Why—"

"Sylvia and I had an agreement—"

"An *agreement*?"

"Yes, a financial one."

"But...but that means you knew about me? And you *paid* her? For *me*?"

"Enough for you, for your education—"

"But I paid for college. I mean, I was given a scholarship, but I still took out a loan and...she never told me anything—"

"Whether she did or didn't isn't my concern, I'm afraid. I paid what we agreed on years ago." Stan clasped his hands in front of him, speaking as if we were in a business meeting, discussing the details of a property transaction. How could he be so detached and unemotional, so cold? I was his daughter, his own flesh and blood, not a building to tear down and redevelop.

"I don't care about money," I said. "I want to get to know you, I—"

"I've told you it's not possible." Stan's face remained unchanged, his voice even.

"But...but *why*?"

"In the simplest of terms, there's no room for you in my life."

"No *room*?"

"What I mean is I already have a family. Your presence would be...upsetting."

My mouth fell open as I struggled to process his words, grasp their meaning. My absolute worst nightmare about our meeting was happening right in front of my face, and I felt powerless to stop it. "I'm your *daughter*."

"Yes. However, at this point I'm afraid it's irrelevant."

"How can you—"

"I wish you the best, Eleanor, I really do, and I'm sorry about your father—"

"Wait, I—"

"—but I can't have any kind of connection with you. Not now and not in the future."

I looked at him, my mouth still half-open, my brain filled with nothing but static buzz. "I don't understand," I said when I found my voice. "What about your wife? What about Victoria?"

He narrowed his eyes. "What about them?"

"Do they know about me?"

"What are you implying?" Stan said, his voice sharp.

"Nothing, I—"

"Good. Because whatever you're thinking of doing, I strongly advise you against it. There will be no more money."

"No, I'd never—"

"I have another meeting I'm already late for." Stan got up and headed for the door, where he paused and turned around. "I really am sorry about your father, Eleanor, and I do wish you the best of luck, but I don't expect to hear from you again."

He opened the door and waited, so I grabbed my bag, jumped up and pushed past him, fled down the hallway, sped by reception—from where Steven wished me a good day— and straight out the door. The tears I'd held in because of the shock rather than determination now rolled down my cheeks, blurring my vision. I didn't see the person coming in my direction until I'd collided straight into them, almost sending us both crashing to the sidewalk.

"Gosh, are you all right?" the woman said, gripping my forearms with perfectly manicured fingers, stopping me from falling. As I breathed in the scent of her subtle floral perfume, I looked up into her emerald eyes, took in her mahogany hair.

Victoria Gallinger. Her smooth, flawless face mere inches from mine.

"Are you all right?" she repeated, a frown crossing her face as she let go.

I turned and darted across the street. Ignored the squealing tires. Didn't care about the drivers who had to slam on their brakes to avoid hitting me. I almost wished they hadn't bothered as my world imploded around me for the second time. Dad was gone. Stan had rejected me. No doubt he'd already decided I was a loser, a waste of space, and he was right. *Everything* my mother had always thought and said about me was right. I *was* nothing. Nobody. Pathetic. Useless. Fat. Ugly. Stupid.

I ran down the street, trying to rid myself of the words, knowing they were right behind me and I'd never be free. As I picked up the pace, my lungs burning, I willed the shards of my shattered life to not only be figurative daggers to my broken heart but literal ones, too.

CHAPTER THIRTEEN

WHEN I GOT HOME, I slammed the door shut, threw my bag on the floor and balled my fists as I let out a piercing scream. I clamped both hands over my mouth, forcing another yell to stay inside, trying to calm my nerves in case Mrs. Winchester rushed over to see what was wrong.

Waves of rage, sadness and desperation pounded my skull, threatening to crack it in half as I dug my fingernails deeper into my skin in an attempt to stop more cries from escaping. I wanted to pick up a chair and throw it at the wall or through the window, got as far as lifting it a few inches off the floor before letting it drop with a defeated clunk.

Breathing hard, I walked to the kitchen, opened the fridge and pulled out a carton of apple juice. Drinking directly from the box, I ignored the steady trickle dribbling down my chin. The cold liquid soothed the inside of my throat, raw from running through the cold air, and I almost finished the whole thing without stopping.

I moved on to food. First the leftovers from an Indian takeout I'd bought a few days ago, followed by thick wedges of cheddar cheese, handfuls of walnuts and slices of stale bread, which I slathered with peanut butter. My heart pounded as I ate, my fingers opening cupboards as my brain raced ahead, deciding what I'd gorge on next and after that, too.

The following six, seven minutes were spent in a trance as I randomly crammed as much as I could into my mouth without choking, forcing everything down with huge gulps of juice. The food had barely settled, expanding and bloating my gut, but making my nerves subside. By the time I finished off another slice of bread and some more nuts, my hands had stopped shaking. This was a temporary reprieve, the tiniest of windows during which all seemed under control. Before long, a familiar sense of hate and self-loathing would rear its ugly head.

Emotional binge eating, a shrink labeled it a few years ago, after I'd filled in a random survey about eating habits in a magazine, answering each question with an emphatic *yes*. I didn't need to read the results section to know I had a problem, and a few weeks later decided to talk to someone. I contacted a psychologist called Dr. Hope, which I'd taken as some sort of sign.

She'd been older, small and wiry, with elfin features, spiky gray hair and huge rainbow-colored glasses, magnifying her eyes like an owl's as she stared at me over her leather-bound notepad. Her lips had formed into a bored smile as she'd waited for me to speak, reveal my deepest flaws—things I'd never told anyone and hardly admitted to myself—her pen poised to make a permanent record of it all.

I'd let out a nervous laugh. Thought about telling her, with my history, she should invest in a thicker notepad. Later, when she asked if I'd ever considered I might be attempting to fill the void inside me with food, I knew there was no point going again. That chasm was so old and ran so deep, it would never be satisfied.

Standing in the kitchen, my face and hands covered in food debris, I knew the hole had become even bigger, and with Dad… *gone*, more impossible to fill. I braced myself, ready for the familiar, chastising voice to begin, surrendering to it, accepting its victory.

No wonder nobody wants you. You're pathetic. Look at you. Just look at you.

I ran to the bathroom, as I did every time, with the intention of making myself throw up, but stopped as soon as my crumb-covered, peanut butter–smelling fingers touched my lips. Tears rolled down my cheeks and I swiped at them with the back of my hand as the voice continued.

You can't even do that, can you? You waste of space. You. Are. Pathetic.

I turned the shower to cold and set it full blast to drown out the words, but they still came.

Being overweight is a choice, Nellie. Your *choice. You're so weak. So hopeless.*

I stripped down, averting my eyes from the mirror. I must have lost at least three hundred pounds over my lifetime. Shame it was a hundred and fifty times the same two I kept putting back on again. I clenched my teeth as I stood under the freezing water, forced myself to stay until my fingertips had shriveled and turned blue.

"Stop," I said through chattering teeth. "Enough now. You have to stop."

Once dressed in my clean, blue-and-red-plaid pajamas and the softest cotton T-shirt I could find, I crawled under the duvet and curled up into a ball, shivering until I fell asleep.

By evening I was hungry again, but I wouldn't allow myself to eat. I knew the routine—I wouldn't touch anything for a while. It was the way we worked, food and me, this impossible love-hate relationship, the endless struggle for control. To avoid thinking about eating or at least distract myself from it, I decided to get outside and try to clear my head.

The temperature had dropped and the misty air swirled around my face as I walked down the street, undecided on the direction in which to head. I passed the local bakery without as much as a sideways glance, stepped aside for groups of friends heading out for the night, laughing and joking. More anger bubbled beneath the surface, and I felt the urge to push it down with something—a candy bar, chips, donuts—anything to stop it from erupting.

"No," I told myself, putting one foot in front of the other, faster and faster, away from the jovial banter.

"Excuse *you*," a woman said as I bumped into her, almost sending her and her two full-to-the-brim shopping bags flying into the street. "Why don't you watch where you're going?"

"Fuck you," I snarled, giving her the finger. I'm not sure who was more surprised, her or me. This wasn't how I reacted. On a typical day I'd have apologized and rushed off.

I knew where I was headed now and sped up, turning left on Deering Avenue and onto Bramhall Street, sticking close to other people so I was never completely alone and vulnerable, finally reaching the corner of Western Promenade. I recognized the house from a hundred yards away and had examined it so closely on Street View, I could've drawn it from memory.

Redbrick, three stories, green shutters, a balcony-covered porch complete with Roman columns. All that glamour set atop a manicured lawn and encircled by a three-foot-high decorative black iron fence. An impressive house, by anyone's standards, one worth close to two million dollars if the comps I'd found were to be believed.

When I reached the house, I stopped and stood still, pressing my back against a tree, glancing left and right every few seconds to make sure I could run if I saw someone threatening coming, my breath escaping my mouth and nostrils in steamy clouds. Even from across the street I could see in through what I determined to be the living room window. The curtains weren't yet drawn, and I easily spotted the people inside. I grabbed my Nikon and zoomed in, taking picture after picture of *them*. Stan and Madeleine.

They sat on the sofa, each of them engrossed in a book, looking like they didn't have a care in the world. I wanted to know if he'd told her about my visit. Confessed he'd had an affair resulting in a secret daughter. Had Madeleine vowed to stand by him? Told him it was so long ago, it didn't matter? *I* didn't matter? Or had he said nothing at all? Gone home to a posh dinner of foie gras and chateaubriand, washed down with an exclusive bottle of Bordeaux, my visit already transforming into a distant and insignificant memory.

I loosened my grip on the camera and flexed my fingers as I stood, transfixed, watching them. Madeleine lifted her head and gazed at her husband before reaching for his hand. They seemed the perfect couple, married for decades, still in love, this moment no doubt one of many examples of their mutual devotion.

Something deep, more primal and despicable than poisonous jealousy pummeled my insides. I couldn't imagine them fighting the way my mother and Dad had, couldn't picture myself perched on the stairs of this house with my hands pressed over my ears, wishing my mother's words of hatred would stop, hoping Dad would finally leave her and take me with him.

Dad had loved me, there was no question, but my childhood, even while he'd still lived with us, had been riddled with palpable tension, which had seeped through the walls and into the bones of the house. Because of it, I'd hardly brought friends over—there weren't many to begin with—and, according to teachers, became more withdrawn. It was easier to keep people at a distance, and ensure nobody figured out the truth. It was one of the only ways Amy and I were similar, except she'd escaped to other people's houses and had always taken my mother's side, blaming my father for their problems. Had Victoria ever felt that way about her parents? Had she experienced anything similar?

I shook my head. I'd been so lost in thought I hadn't noticed Stan leaving the living room, not until the front door opened and he stepped outside with a large brown dog by his side. At first I wanted to turn in the other direction, but once again my feet did the opposite, only allowing me to take steps forward. This man was my father. I couldn't let him swat me away as if I were an annoying fly.

My heart threatened to leap out of my chest as I stowed the camera in my bag and crossed the road, running after Stan. He must have heard me approach because he turned, stopping dead as soon as he caught sight of my face.

"What are you doing here?" he said before ordering the massive dog—a drooling Great Dane—to sit. It did so without hesitation and looked up at me, panting, its tongue hanging out, and a lopsided grin on its face, mocking me.

"I have questions," I said, forcing myself to stand tall. "And… and I feel I deserve answers. It's the least you can do."

His jaw made tiny, sinewy movements. "What did your mother tell you about me?"

"*Nothing.* I overheard them talking the night Dad… When he died. It's how I found out—" I looked at him, willing myself to stay strong, to not cut and run "—that you're my father."

Stan sighed, shook his head. "Without being delicate about it, your mother and I had an affair. It meant a lot more to her than it did to me—"

"But I'm the result. Doesn't that mean anything to you?"

"It doesn't," he whispered. "It never did. Not back then and not now. I'm sorry. I paid your mother a hundred thousand—"

"*How much?*"

"—and I've already told you there won't be more."

"I don't *want* your money!"

He looked at me. "And I can't give you what you're looking for. Goodbye, Eleanor. Please don't contact me again."

I'm not sure how long I stayed there. Long enough to watch him and the dog disappear around the corner and for my whole body to go numb. The darkness wrapped itself around me, reminding me I was alone, I had nobody, there wasn't anyone left who cared.

As I stood there, I wondered how long it would take for me to be reported missing if I walked to the water and catapulted myself off the Veterans Memorial Bridge. Who would be the first person to notice I was gone? Not my mother. Not Amy. None of the friends I'd distanced myself from. None of my few ex-boyfriends who'd broken my heart, making me more defensive and bitter. It would either be my landlord because I'd missed rent, or Kyle Draper looking for his website updates.

I *was* all alone because it was what I deserved.

I imagined falling, my body hitting the water, pulled under by my sodden clothes and heavy boots, arms flailing, lungs filling...and then blackness, stillness. Peace.

With a shudder I lowered my head, turned and hurried in the direction of my apartment. Away from the water, away from the bridge.

You're a coward, the darkness whispered inside my head. *I don't want you, either.*

CHAPTER FOURTEEN

THURSDAY. DAD'S FUNERAL. The rain had been relentless since early morning, coming down in thick, translucent
strands stretching from the skies all the way to the ground. Big
fat drops thudded off my red-and-white polka-dot umbrella, the
only one I had, but which now seemed disrespectfully cheery
as I stood by Dad's grave.

The crowd had dispersed in a relative hurry, mourners making their way to the warmth and comfort of the Fiddler's Head,
the traditional English pub across the street in which my ever-
organized father had planned what he'd called a goodbye party,
with good food and unlimited pints on tap. I wasn't ready to
join them, partly because I didn't want to leave Dad, but also
because my mother had gone inside the pub.

She'd arrived with a few of her friends who'd come to the
funeral to offer moral support as she played the part of the ex-

wife in mourning. When I'd first spotted her at the church, I'd been surprised to see her and wondered why she'd come, decided it was for appearances' sake—and to make sure Dad was truly gone so she could somehow get his money into Amy's hands. As soon as our eyes had met across the crowded church, she'd waltzed over, grabbed my elbow and pulled me to one side, her fingers digging into my skin.

"We need to talk." Her tone had been more bitter than usual, the fact we were in a church for a funeral having zero effect on her kindness and empathy levels. "You look terrible. Couldn't you at least have used some concealer to hide that bruise?"

I had, but obviously not to her satisfaction. I shook her off, hoping God—if indeed there was one—would make her burst into flames, providing it was possible to burn a bona fide ice queen. "I've got nothing to say to you," I said, taking a step back as she tried to grab me again.

"You went to see Stan." She nodded slowly as she registered my look of surprise. "Oh, yes, I know all about your little visits. I haven't spoken to the man in decades, then he calls me, demanding to know what's going on. What the hell do you think you're doing?"

"None of your business." I took another step back but she inched closer, her face in mine, eyes turning to narrow slits, her red snake mouth hissing her next words.

"How was your reunion?" she said. "Did you hold hands and sing 'Kumbaya'?"

I looked away, my shoulders falling. Her gaze, her very presence, making me feel like half a person. I hated myself for it. For being so weak, for—after all these years—still questioning why she'd never loved me or accepted me and, goddamn it, for part of me still *wanting* her to despite the way she'd treated me.

The day I'd moved out with four bags and a drooping houseplant under my arm, I'd relinquished the key to her place, too. She'd stood in the hallway of the three-bedroom house in Oakdale she'd bought after Dad had left, and which she'd long filled with new furniture and memories that excluded him. An oversize baby blue sweater hung casually from one of her tan shoulders, and her black leggings showed off legs she always reminded me she'd worked hard to achieve and she thought looked better than most of those belonging to women half her age.

In lieu of a hug and good-luck wishes, she'd given me her customary disapproving head-to-toe scan, raised her eyebrows and held out her palm toward me. "You won't need your key anymore," she'd said, before instructing me to phone ahead if I wanted to visit—which I'd done fewer than half a dozen times in as many years—and to ring the doorbell when I arrived.

All my life I'd envied women who had close relationships with their mothers. I'd see them going to the movies, shopping for clothes or having lunch together. The likelihood of the two of us even going for a watered-down coffee and dry toast felt as probable as an all-expenses-paid trip to Bora-Bora—but I'd still wished for it. Her behavior had brought me closer to Dad, but instead of being relieved I wasn't around her, I'd made her hate me more, furious he'd always taken my side when he'd still lived at home, and after that, too.

"I'm not having this conversation with you," I said, catching the eye of the pastor, who gave me a wave and walked in our direction, his hands clasped over the Bible, a deep look of sympathy on his face.

My mother leaned in. "Listen to me. You will keep quiet about this. All of it. You will *not* ruin my reputation or my business, do you hear me?"

"I don't care about either," I snapped, knowing full well her tax advisory company was the one thing that rivaled Amy when it came to my mother's attention. She was proud of the business, and with good reason. She'd gone back to night school for accounting classes once my sister and I had been old enough to take care of ourselves. Within three years she'd started her own firm, which she'd grown to over a dozen staff. She was a determined, brainy woman, I owed her that much acknowledgment, although I'd only ever do so silently.

"I swear, Eleanor, if you tell people that man's your father... if you *embarrass* me with this, then you're no longer welcome at my house, or in my life, do you understand?"

"Wait, you mean up until now I *was* welcome?" My laughter oozed with sarcasm. Two could joust when they had equally long, sharp lances aimed at each other's jugulars.

She stared at me—her eyes narrower slits—no doubt wishing I'd turn to stone, but as the pastor approached her transformation back into grieving ex-wife was instant, and she greeted him with a perfectly practiced small, sad smile, readily accepting his condolences.

I'd avoided her during and after the service, made sure there were other people between her and me as Dad's casket was lowered into the ground, ensuring she couldn't trap me graveside, too.

No doubt she was already charming the guests at the Fiddler's Head, her aim to leave them thinking Dad had been a fool to let her slip through his fingers. I knew better, knew her for what she was: a manipulator, a cold, calculating, spiteful witch. Dad wouldn't mind if I didn't go to the pub, and I couldn't face the throngs of people anyway, what with their solemn faces, which would brighten with every sip of beer, the memories of Dad already fading from their minds. I whispered a lengthy goodbye to him and went home, stood by my window until the sun had long disappeared behind the buildings.

A few hours later I heard familiar footsteps in the hallway. Lewis, whom I hadn't seen since he'd stopped by with the fish and chips. Maybe if I accidentally-on-purpose bumped into him, he'd ask how I was. Perhaps he'd offer to come in for a chat, allowing me the illusion of normalcy for a few minutes. God, I needed that.

As I opened the door and saw Lewis, a smile made its way across my face, but it vanished all too quickly because he wasn't alone. He held the hand of a girl with long dark hair in a high-set ponytail, a button nose and big brown doe eyes adorned with fake eyelashes so long and heavy she blinked in slow motion. Her yoga pants showed off her toned legs, and her cropped top—not the most practical of shirts on a cold day even when worn under a hot-pink jacket with a downy collar—accentuated a tiny waist. She wrapped her arms around Lewis's middle, pulling him closer.

"Hey, how are you?" Lewis said as he tried to extricate himself from her octopus grip.

"I'm okay, thanks," I said, wishing I could hit a magic "rewind time" button. "You?"

"Good, yeah, great. Uh, this is Janique. Janique, this is Eleanor."

"Nice to meet you." Her expression was in direct contradiction to her words as her eyes moved from the top of my head to my feet. She looked at Lewis. "*This* is your neighbor?"

Heat shot to my cheeks. What had he told her? How I'd embarrassed myself by almost shaking his hand with a pair of dirty underwear the size of a tent? That he'd had to defend me from some jerk because I couldn't do it myself? She'd probably loved the last one, fluttered those ridiculous eyelashes at him before jumping his knight-in-shining-armor bones.

"I forgot something on the stove," I said, trying to rid my mind of the X-rated images of Lewis and Janique together and slamming the door shut. As I rested my forehead against it, I heard them moving to the stairs and a peal of Janique's laughter rang out. It made me bite down on my lip so hard, I tasted blood. I headed for the kitchen and opened the fridge.

Sunlight streamed in through the windows the next morning, not only an indication of a welcome change in weather, but also of how late it was. Usually I was up hours before, ready to dive into my latest project. I decided today had to be about new beginnings—not family, but business—which meant making cold calls and chasing new clients, something I enjoyed, much to Dad's amusement.

"It's surprising, is all, Freckles, considering you don't really like people," he'd joked.

"But I know what I'm talking about," I'd said. "It's easy. And I like people."

"No, you don't," he huffed.

"I like *you*, don't I? You're people."

"Touché, but still, you're a bit of a hermit, like me, and yet you enjoy cold-calling. That makes you an anomaly. And it's a good thing." He'd ruffled my hair, making me feel like a five-year-old. "I certainly wouldn't give it a go, and your mother hated sales so much, she hired someone else to do it. She couldn't sell anything to save her life."

"Except her soul," I said, and Dad turned away, but not before I'd caught his smirk.

The memory of him pinched my heart so hard, I thought it might stop beating. Jagged waves of realization kept slamming into me, over and over. I'd never see him again. Hear him again. Be able to call or laugh with him again. I had no idea how to cope with that, so I did the only thing I could think of; open a little box in my mind into which I forced the memory of our conversation and shut the lid tight.

I switched on the kettle and fished a jar of instant coffee from the cupboard. Despite trying not to, I couldn't help but wonder if my penchant for prospecting had anything to do with Stan. After all, he hadn't become a real estate highflier without picking up the phone. It got me thinking if I'd inherited any of his other traits. When I was younger, people had often remarked how much I looked like my mother, which had made her scowl deepen. I knew I reminded her of what she called her "worst physical attributes"—big hips, large thighs, crappy metabolism—things she'd been determined to rectify all her life and told me I should focus on, too, chastising and ridiculing me when I didn't, because if she'd managed to do so, I should, too.

I pushed the thoughts of my mother and her obsessions aside. What were the similarities between me and Stan? I'd studied his photographs, tried to determine if I had some of his facial features—our lips were similar, which was nothing to go by— but I was more curious about personalities than looks. Did we share opinions? Think the same way? Have the same reactions?

I almost laughed. The way I'd cut my mother and Amy out of my life was reminiscent of what he'd done to me, although the reasons were different. And mine were valid.

After I'd made my coffee, I sat down with my laptop and a buttered bagel. The memory of my recent binges made the food taste stale, the coffee bland, and I pushed both away, un- finished, and focused on work. My emails didn't take long to go through. Most of my clients' projects were over, and the two who'd signed up for regular monthly maintenance—with ridiculously low fees—had already been handled. Kyle had sent a quick thank-you note, telling me everything was in order. It wasn't until I was about to make my first call that I noticed an unread email sitting in my spam folder.

Dear Eleanor,

I'm looking to redesign the website for my bakery chain, Bread'n'Batter, which you may have heard of. As well as our six corporate stores in Maine, we have franchisees in another twenty- five locations (soon to be twenty-eight) across the country. Kyle Draper highly recommended you and I'd love for us to meet. Could you please contact me on my cell (below) at your earliest convenience to discuss?

Excited to hear from you,

Aliyah James

CEO

It had arrived a week ago, the evening Dad died, and for whatever reason, gone straight to spam. It was a folder I checked regularly, but with everything that happened, I'd missed it.

Crap. Shit. *Fuck.*

Bread'n'Batter was a Portland success story, everybody knew it. Aliyah James, a single mother of four, had started the company with a hundred bucks of supplies, waking up at 3:00 a.m. to make bread and cookies while her kids slept. At first she'd sold her goods to friends and neighbors. They'd told all their friends and neighbors, who, in turn, had told all of theirs, too. Within a year, she'd hired staff and moved her production to a commercial kitchen. Within two, she'd won a local Entrepreneur of the Year award and had appeared on television. When a major coffee shop chain added her cookies to their stores, her already impressive sales exploded.

Redesigning her websites was a killer opportunity, a huge contract, and one I couldn't afford to miss. I snatched up my phone, dialed Aliyah's number, willing her to pick up while I tried to think of a good enough reason for not responding to her request any earlier.

"Aliyah James."

"Ms. James, hi. It's Eleanor Hardwicke." I pressed the phone to my ear, hoping my words hadn't come out garbled. "You emailed me about your website project."

"Oh, yes, I remember," Aliyah said, her voice smooth. "Thanks for getting back to me."

"No trouble. I'm sorry about the delay." I decided honesty was the best way to go and let out a small laugh. "User error, I'm afraid, or at least an overly protective spam filter. When can we meet? I love your bakeries and your story. I think I could—"

"Apologies for cutting you off," Aliyah said, "but before I contacted you, I reached out to other developers, then I saw Kyle and he gave me your details. When I didn't hear from you, I assumed you weren't interested—"

"Oh, gosh, no. I definitely am. It's been a bit of a rough week."

"I'm sorry to hear it," Aliyah said. "But I'm afraid I signed a contract with a company yesterday. I really wish I'd heard from you. Kyle sang your praises loud and proud."

"But what if I sent you some designs? Is there any chance—"

"I'm afraid not," Aliyah said. "Going back on my word isn't my style. I'll keep your details for the future, though. Hopefully we'll still get the opportunity to work together. Thanks again for calling. All the best to you. Bye."

I sank back onto the sofa. I was never late, never this disorganized and I couldn't believe I'd blown an opportunity that could've given me the financial wiggle room I needed.

Although I knew what I'd see, I opened my banking app. Numbers didn't lie, whether it was the dusty scale I'd shoved into the depths of my bathroom closet or my bank balance.

I ran a finger down the screen, double-checking the withdrawals and the occasional deposit. I had a few thousand dollars, enough to cover a little while, but if I didn't get another contract, I'd be in trouble. At some point there'd be the inheritance money from Dad—we'd agreed him appointing an executor would be more sensible than me trying to settle on anything with Amy—but it wouldn't be much. My mother had nearly wiped Dad out financially during the divorce, and he'd never recovered, especially not when he'd gotten sick and had ludicrous medical costs to pay. My belly tightened again. I'd have a bill for my stint at the hospital, too, something I couldn't afford.

Not for the first time I wondered if Dad had known about Stan's payment to my mother. A hundred grand. I shook my head. He couldn't have, or he'd have ensured at least some of it was set aside for me—or maybe he knew and my mother told him it was none of his business, and it had zero to do with him because I wasn't his. Anything was possible, and for a brief moment it made me angry at Dad, which immediately made me feel guilty. I missed him so much, wanted him to come in through the door, plop down on the sofa and say, *Okay, Freckles, let's figure out what you're going to do.*

My thoughts went back to Stan and our last conversation. Rage pushed away the grief as I remembered how he'd brushed me off, discarded me as if I were something he'd trodden on in the street. He already had a daughter—a beautiful, smart, successful one—he didn't need another. But I was Victoria's sister, goddamn it. I was family, too.

Fingers trembling, I opened her Facebook profile again. How easy would it be to blackmail him, after all? Demand cash or I'd tell Madeleine and Victoria who I was? I could threaten him with sending one of them a message, maybe.

Hi, Victoria,
This will no doubt come as a shock but I recently found out I'm your half sister, and I'm not sure what to do. Can we please meet or speak on the phone? I'd love for us to get to know each other. Hope to hear from you soon.

Or something entirely different.

Hi, Victoria,
Guess what? Your dad's a fucking cheater and I'm the result.
Don't believe me? Ask him who I am.

He might pay up, but I'd meant what I'd told him. I didn't want his money, wasn't capable of extortion, and at this point I wasn't sure I wanted a father-daughter connection with him, either. He'd had his chance, and he'd thrown it away. Twice. This was a game to him, one he'd already decided he'd won. It made me sick, *he* made me sick, and I wanted him to hurt, too. Suffer way more than taking a few thousand bucks from his inflated bank account ever could.

I sat back in my chair, thinking about what Victoria might do if she found out about me. Discard me like Stan had? Despise him like I did? Whatever the case, no matter what her reaction, the fact remained I knew about my half sister's existence.

Wasn't it fair she knew about mine, too?

CHAPTER FIFTEEN

I LOOKED AT MY HANDS, now balled into fists, my nails transformed into tiny knives, digging deep into my palms. I winced and straightened my fingers, considered calling Stan or drafting him a message when there was a knock on the door.

"Hi," Lewis said as I opened up.

He was alone, dressed in workout gear, his chest and arms glistening with sweat. I tried hard not to imagine what he and Janique had been doing to each other since last night.

"Can I come in?"

"Uh, sure."

He walked through to the living room, where he stood facing the window, hands on his hips, before abruptly turning and looking at me, making me shiver. His eyes were so intense, and his golden hair, backlit by the light coming in from the windows, transformed him into a mythical creature who'd stepped out of the pages of a fantasy book.

"I wanted to apologize," he said, crossing his arms, his biceps bulging, and I forced myself to look at his face instead of the solid contours of his muscles.

"Apologize? What for?"

He sighed, dropped his hands. "First off, for not offering to come to your dad's funeral."

"Oh..."

"Yeah. I really should have."

"But you didn't know him."

"Maybe, but that's not really the point." He paused. "Look, a couple of days ago, I told Janique about your dad and about you being mugged. I hope that's okay? It was on my mind and I wanted a woman's opinion, so I asked if she thought I should offer to come to the funeral..."

"What did she say?" I said, and should've made a hefty bet on his answer.

"That it would be weird because we don't know each other well. Was she right?"

"To be honest, I could've done with the company."

Lewis rolled his eyes. "Yep, I'm an idiot. I should've asked *you*, not her. And then she made that comment, the '*this* is your neighbor' one? Let me put it into context—"

"I don't think I need a translation. The message was pretty clear."

"That's exactly what I told her." He suppressed a grin. "She left shortly afterward."

"Did she?" I tried my best to sound more surprised than victorious.

"Yeah. I mean, talking about another woman on the first date and having an argument about her on the second is rarely a good sign, right? Anyway, enough about Janique. Tell me how the funeral went. And how are you? How are you coping with everything?"

"It comes and goes in waves," I said, surprised again at how easy it was to be honest with him. "One minute I'm fine and the next I'm either about to turn into a blubbering mess or I want to punch someone." He nodded, and I continued, "The funeral was—" I shrugged "—well, whoever put the word *fun* into *funeral* is an asshole."

Lewis smiled, properly this time. "You haven't lost your sense of humor. Good. I'm glad, given the circumstances and everything. I've been worried about you."

I looked at him, this man I hardly knew but who kept coming to check on me. Dad had always taught me to look after myself, and my mother, in her own way, had instilled that, too, but once again, with Lewis standing in my living room, I didn't want to be so independent. I felt vulnerable and alone.

Lewis must have sensed something, because he frowned. "What's wrong?" he said.

I hesitated. For all I knew, he was the biggest gossip in Portland. Then again, there wasn't anybody else to talk to. Maybe his opinion would help put things into perspective. He seemed genuinely interested, and having someone help make sense of it all was something I couldn't pass over.

I told him everything. About my terse discussion with my mother, my research about the Gallingers and my two encounters with Stan, even bumping into Victoria outside the office. By the time I'd finished, he'd flopped on the sofa, eyes wider than my windows.

"This happened in the past few days? Jesus, it's enough to make your brain explode."

"Tell me about it," I said. "Exactly what I needed on top of my sore head."

"About that. Your bruises have faded a lot, but the memory of the attack—"

"I'm fine," I said, and when he stared at me, I added, "Really. I can handle all that way more than the fact I have two families who don't give a crap I exist."

"But you don't know for sure," Lewis said. "I mean, what about your half sister? Victoria, is it? Who's to say you two wouldn't get along?"

I let out a laugh. "I don't think we're cut from the same cloth, so to speak. Different side of the tracks, worlds apart and all those other clichés."

"Not necessarily. You share fifty percent of your DNA. You might be surprised at all the other things you have in common."

"The wildly wealthy pedigree? Boarding schools and country clubs? Flights to the Bahamas on a private jet?" I didn't know how Victoria had grown up, but I couldn't imagine it being anything other than excessive and exclusive.

Lewis wasn't buying it, and waved a hand. "Details."

"Ha. Really? Not from where I'm standing. I live in a crummy one-bedroom apartment with a temperamental and regularly striking heater, and do my laundry in a basement, where I hope I won't get murdered or eaten by rats. Meanwhile Victoria lives in a townhouse on Newbury."

"You know where she lives?"

"Uh, well. I looked up her address. It's an end unit in a new building."

"Not the one on the corner they renovated a couple of months ago? With the floor-to-ceiling windows?" Lewis let out a whistle. "Sweet."

"As I said. Wildly wealthy. And privileged. Guess who developed the place?"

"I'll take Gallinger Properties for fifty points."

"You got it. He probably gave it to them for their wedding anniversary, as a birthday present or a 'congrats it's a Monday' gift or whatever. See? Worlds apart." I leaned back, let my head sink onto the cushion. I couldn't help imagining the look of disgust on Victoria's face when she learned about me and found out we were related. Mildly unfair, perhaps, but the rich daughter likely didn't fall far from the money tree. If I knew for sure it would cause conflict between her and Stan—or Stan and Madeleine—it would almost be worth going through with contacting her, except, sitting there next to Lewis, I didn't think I could be that kind of person. Besides, once the initial shock dissipated, all the hatred would be redirected at me.

Having exposed all this information about my family secrets now made me feel self-conscious and raw. I wished I hadn't opened up, needed to be alone so I could try to stuff it all into another box inside my head and label it Do Not Open.

"I should get back to work," I said, gesturing to my laptop.

"Yes, sure. Okay," Lewis said. "I suppose I should get going, too. Will you be all right?"

"I'll be fine."

"You keep saying that," Lewis said as he got up. "You know, I can't help thinking life's really short. You said you don't get along with Amy... Maybe you could approach Victoria when the time feels right? I mean, her father is a dick, but doesn't she deserve to know about you so she can make up her own mind instead of you doing it for her? Besides—" delicate lines formed next to his eyes as he smiled "—you're an awesome person. How can she not like you?" When I let out a small laugh, he looked at me. "You are. Really. Think about it, okay?"

I spent an hour calling potential new clients, circling back with existing ones and going through job postings offered on four contractor-for-hire sites. The amounts people were willing to pay were paltry, less than minimum wage, but I couldn't be picky or my business would fail, and I'd promised Dad I wouldn't let that happen. If I did, I knew it would only be more evidence about the kind of person my mother said I was.

A while later, curiosity whispered in my ear, making Lewis's comment about Victoria rattle around my head, and my day-dreams about us becoming close friends drained the rest of my focus.

As far as I could tell, Victoria was an only child. No postings about siblings or mention of a brother or sister in any of the articles I'd read. There were numerous Instagram photos of her and someone called Charlotte, who I'd gathered was her cousin, and they seemed close. Perhaps Lewis was right; maybe I should approach Victoria, but I couldn't do so the way I'd contacted Stan. If—and it was still a big if—I wanted to meet her, I'd do it slowly, gently, and I didn't want Stan or my mother to know, at least not for now.

I looked through Victoria's social media accounts, saw she'd checked into a spinning class thirty minutes earlier, adding a bicycle and biceps emoji to her post. The studio was a local one I recognized, and a short walk from my apartment, so I gathered my things and hurried outside. While I had no intention of joining the class, I often visited the arts and crafts store directly across the street, which I knew offered the perfect vantage point.

I meandered around the store for a while, checked out the on-sale graphite sticks and sketchbooks, while keeping one eye on the fitness studio's front door. Twenty-five minutes later, Victoria emerged, accompanied by another woman I didn't recognize from any of the photos I'd seen. They were both dressed in similar outfits, multicolored spandex pants showing off their mile-long legs, and colorful hoodies underneath their thick jackets.

I grabbed my Nikon and snapped pictures of Victoria and her friend until the store clerk gave me a funny look and walked toward me. Not wanting to draw more attention to myself than I already had, I shoved the camera back in my bag and headed outside. I crossed the road, trying to get close enough to hear the conversation without my eavesdropping becoming obvious, and made sure I stood in the opposite direction to Victoria's apartment, so when she headed home, we couldn't cross paths.

My plan backfired. Before I was able to make out their words, Victoria hugged the woman, turned and walked directly at me. I panicked, thinking she knew who I was, she'd recognized me from our brief encounter outside Gallinger Properties, or Stan had showed her my picture and told her all about me. She was coming to confront me, ask me why I was following her, taking pictures of her. I wanted to move, but my feet had become heavy as blocks of ice, frozen to the ground, forcing her to sidestep me. I stood, mouth agape, as she walked past, didn't move until a rush of pure relief flooded my veins. She had no idea who I was. Not the tiniest of inklings.

"Sorry," I mumbled but Victoria didn't respond and kept walking, and for a split second I imagined shouting *I'm your sister!* but managed to keep quiet, cursing myself for being so stupid. If this was my idea of a soft approach, then God help me.

CHAPTER SIXTEEN

ENSURING I LEFT A steady thirty-foot gap between us, I walked behind Victoria, watched her silky ponytail swish-swishing against the back of her coat. I relaxed as I kept moving, repeating to myself she had no clue who I was, had no more than glanced at me and there'd been no flicker of recognition. I was safe.

Two blocks later Victoria walked up the steps of a gastropub called Le Médaillon, where she pushed open the ten-foot door and disappeared from sight. I stood outside for a good five minutes, taking a couple of pictures of the building before deciding my behavior was ridiculous at best, and it was time to go home.

I half turned before looking up at the restaurant again. It was new and there'd been a lot of buzz on social media about it. The food was said to be delicious, albeit too expensive for my budget, but the mere thought of a proper meal almost made my stomach turn on itself from hunger and offset the potential discomfort of eating in front of others. There was no reason I couldn't go inside, was there? I wouldn't order much, and it wasn't like I was doing anything wrong.

The more I thought about it, the more I wanted to know who Victoria was meeting. What did my half sister do after spin class? Hang out with friends? Her husband? What if she was cheating on him and meeting a lover? Like father, like daughter, perhaps?

The apple-cheeked hostess smiled when I got inside. If she was fazed by my jeans, scuffed boots and tatty jacket, she didn't show it. "Table for...?" she said.

"One, please," I answered, scanning the restaurant. I didn't spot Victoria and suspected she'd gone to the back, obscured from view. "Somewhere quiet? I've got a bit of work to do."

"Of course, follow me."

We made our way to the rear of the restaurant, past the chunky maple tables and the funky mix of multicolored, upholstered chairs. The place was busy but not packed, the ambient lounge-type music at a volume where you could still hold a conversation without raising your voice. Servers with long black aprons walked past, carrying plates piled high with thick-cut fries and pan-seared fish smelling of tarragon.

My mouth watered and my stomach grumbled again. It was almost nine. I hadn't eaten anything since lunch. Binge punishment was still on the menu, and I hadn't found the time or energy to go grocery shopping. Come to think of it, for the first time in forever, stocking up the fridge hadn't even occurred to me. Maybe it was an illusion, but my jeans didn't seem to pinch my middle quite as much, either.

"How's this?" the hostess said, gesturing to a smaller table tucked away in a corner.

I quickly looked around, stumbling when I spotted Victoria sitting with two other women in a horseshoe-shaped booth across the room. I recognized both of them—blond bob, long neck—unmistakably Madeleine. The other had dimpled cheeks and long red hair—Charlotte, Victoria's cousin I'd seen in the multiple Instagram posts.

I hesitated. I'd bumped into Victoria twice now, what if she realized I was following her? But I needn't have worried because none of them glanced our way; they were too engrossed in conversation.

Funny how fear can be replaced by courage in an instant. I pointed at the empty booth next to them. "Can I sit there? It would give me more room for my stuff." I didn't have "stuff" with me, save for my camera and sketchbook in my bag, but the latter would suffice to help with the charade of keeping myself busy.

The hostess gave me another smile and guided me over, handed me a rolled-up parchment paper menu. "Trinity will be right with you. Enjoy."

I sat with my back to Victoria's table, hoping to home in on their conversation as I scanned the menu, immediately identifying the prices of the entrees as more than two times out of my reach. When Trinity bounded over—her hair a mass of corkscrew curls, her eyes the color of amber—I decided to go for the cheapest thing; a bowl of tomato and red pepper soup and a glass of tap water. When she asked if I wanted garlic bread, I opened my mouth to request a double helping before imagining Victoria sitting behind me. No doubt she'd chosen a tiny salad with the dressing on the side. Her cheekbones sat high and proud—not hidden beneath a puffy layer of skin like mine.

"No, thank you," I said to Trinity, smiling when my stomach growled again, protesting my refusal of the habitual buttery, carb-loaded treat.

After she left, I pulled out my sketchbook and pencils to keep up the pretense of looking like I was doing something other than prying, and leaned back while I doodled, pressing my spine against the seat, wishing the trio behind me would speak a fraction louder.

"You're such a hoot, Charlotte," Madeleine said, her voice husky, her French accent transforming the words into *an oot*. "I can't believe you told Malcolm that."

"Well, you know me," another voice said. Charlotte's, I presumed. "He had it coming, don't you think?" As the laughter erupted, I wanted to join them at their table, find out who Malcolm was and what, exactly, Charlotte had told him. I longed to share their inside jokes instead of skulking around on the sidelines.

"How's Dad?" The third voice had to belong to Victoria. It was low and sultry, sexy, and I straightened my back and sat completely still, waiting for the answer.

"Oh, he's wonderful," Madeleine said. "Busy, busy, busy, as usual."

"I popped in to see him the other day," Victoria said. "He seemed a bit upset."

"Your father was upset you stopped by?" Madeleine said.

"No, I don't think that's what it was," Victoria said.

"Was this on Monday?" Madeleine asked.

"Uh, let's see… Yes, it was. After you'd had lunch with him, I think," Victoria said. "But don't worry. I didn't take it personally. You know what he can be like with work."

Madeleine laughed. "Oh, yes, I certainly do. Actually, I remember him coming home that day. *Mon dieu*, he was a bear with a migraine. He calmed down over dinner, then got worked up after he'd taken Zeus out for a walk. He was gone for almost an hour."

"I thought Zeus collapsed after twenty minutes," Charlotte said.

"Exactly," Madeleine said. "When he came back, he was muttering about people not respecting business deals, so I gave him a whiskey, went to bed and left him to it."

"We all know how serious Dad is about people respecting terms," Victoria said. "Remember the agreement about minimum achievements when I started high school?"

"Yes, I do." Madeleine laughed. "And it worked, didn't it?"

"Yeah, well, speaking of contracts," Victoria said, her voice filling with excitement, "he took me to the Commercial Street location. I loved it. Not too big, not too small, it was—"

"Goldilocks," Charlotte said, and they all chuckled.

"This is the one," Victoria added. "It'll be perfect for my new business."

While Charlotte and Madeleine expressed their approval in varying degrees of appreciative noises, I made a mental note to find out what business they were talking about. As far as my research had revealed, Victoria worked as an interior designer for a company called King, had been there for the past four years and specialized in transforming upscale houses. Her LinkedIn profile was full of recommendations, compliments and praise. Apparently she was as successful in her professional life as in her private one, although I couldn't help thinking it had to be easy when you started off a few rungs up the privilege ladder.

"Hugh must be so proud," Charlotte said, sounding equally so.

"I couldn't do this without him," Victoria said.

"I know, darling," Madeleine said. "Have you settled on a name yet? My favorite is still Victoria by Design. It has such a wonderful ring to it."

"Why don't you call it Gallinger Designs?" Charlotte said. "I mean, everybody knows Gallinger Properties and—"

"Exactly," Victoria said. "Which makes it pretentious, so—"

"You think our name's *pretentious*?" Madeleine said.

"Of course not, Mom," Victoria said. "And don't take this the wrong way, either, but I don't want something as recognizable. I really, *really* want to make my own mark. Be successful in my own right."

"You already are, *ma chérie*," Madeleine said. "Remember,

there's nothing wrong with taking advantage of who you are. But you're the boss. Besides, you know your father's rules. If you bid on any of his projects, you won't get any special treatment."

"Of course he says that," Charlotte said with a click of her tongue, "and it may be true, but you'll have the edge, Victoria. You know exactly what he's looking for, how he works, what his expectations are. You'll win those bids in a heartbeat."

Victoria laughed. "How about I get this company off the ground without too much nepotism, okay? Anyway, I need more than the name. There's the logo, the marketing, the—"

"Customers." Charlotte giggled. "Don't forget the customers."

"Yes, those, too," Victoria said. "Let's hope there are lots of them."

"My neighbor could help with the marketing bit," Charlotte said. "He did some stuff for the flower shop, it looks really good."

"Great," Victoria said, and, without seeing her face, I could tell she didn't mean it. "I'll let you know when I'm ready and you can put us in touch."

Trinity brought me my soup and I took a few mouthfuls as I processed every scrap and morsel of information I'd learned. Victoria needed marketing for her new business. Did it include a website? I doodled as I ate and continued listening to them chat about her new venture before moving on to Madeleine and Stan's upcoming trip to the British Virgin Islands. Not a cross word was spoken between them, they offered one another nothing but encouragement and support. They were the same with Trinity, too, complimenting her on her hair, asking where she'd got her silver bracelets from. They were so kind, so thoughtful and sweet, it made me feel as if I was rolling around in a tub of glitter while watching an episode of *Strawberry Shortcake*.

By now I needed the bathroom, and after waiting as long as I could, I tore myself away from the conversation, headed to the restrooms and darted to the back stall. When I was about to flush the toilet, I heard the main bathroom door open. Madeleine's and Victoria's now-familiar voices rang out. I lowered the seat without making a sound and sat down, pulling my feet up and out of sight, deciding to wait until they'd gone.

A minute later, as they were washing their hands, Madeleine said, "Charlotte has no idea, does she? She'd have said something if she did."

"I still can't believe Malcolm's cheating on her," Victoria said, and I spied through the crack in the door, making out a sliver of my half sister. She'd dried her hands and was looking at a selection of creams in the wicker basket on the counter. "Are you sure?"

"I told you, one of my friends saw him having dinner with another woman in Cape Elizabeth." Madeleine shook her head. "What was he thinking? Really, if you're going to cheat, you may want to make more of an effort to hide it."

"But she could've been a work colleague, couldn't she?" Victoria said. "I mean, he—"

"Had his hand halfway up her skirt, which looked more like a belt, according to Geneviève," Madeleine said. "Apparently she was barely legal."

"What are we going to do?" Victoria said. "Should we tell Charlotte?"

"I don't think we can. Imagine what it'll do to her. She's barely over her postnatal depression and that took her years. It'll devastate her. It could send her right back to square one."

"But we can't do nothing, Mom. That bastard—"

"Who said we'd do nothing? I'll speak to Malcolm."

"And say what?"

"I'll put the fear of God in him. Or the fear of the Gallingers, anyway."

Victoria shook her head. "Either way, it's horrible. I can't imagine being in her shoes."

"First of all, she doesn't know she's in them. And second,

you'll never have anything to worry about." Madeleine patted her shoulder. "Hugh worships you. He'd do anything for you. Which is exactly how it should be. Exactly how I taught you, remember, darling? You call the shots, even if he thinks he does."

As they left the bathroom, I stood up, my legs shaking so hard I had to steady myself by holding the wall. I didn't know what to do with the news of the affair, or whether it was of any relevance or importance to me. Regardless, I stored it in the back of my mind, in the virtual file marked Gallinger, which had started taking up an awful lot of space.

I washed my hands, walked over to the lotion basket, picked up the lavender one I'd seen Victoria use and opened the tube. It smelled divine, calm and comforting as a summer breeze, and I rubbed some into my hands and elbows. When I put the tube back, a glint of something caught the corner of my eye. An engagement ring—a platinum-and-diamond one by the look of it—carefully placed on a hand towel.

I stared at the shiny band, mesmerized by the small stones adorning it, marveling at how the large square-cut one set on top caught the light. My mind raced as I reached for the ring, picked it up and held it between my fingers, watching it sparkle.

It had to be Victoria's—there was no way she wouldn't have seen it as she'd chosen the lotion. She must have taken it off when she'd used the cream on her hands, become distracted as she'd talked about Charlotte's husband. How long before she noticed she'd left it behind? How much time before she came rushing back to the bathroom and found me standing there with her engagement ring in my hands?

As much as I didn't want that to happen, I couldn't put it down and leave—what if someone else took it? Equally, I didn't want to walk up to their table and hand it to Victoria. Option three meant giving it to the restaurant's manager, but what if they kept it for themselves? Later I tried to convince myself otherwise, but the real reason for what I did next was the fact I didn't want to part with something belonging to my half sister, something so personal, so intimate.

Before anyone entered the bathroom, I slipped the ring into my pocket and hurried to my table, where I slid a twenty-dollar bill under my plate, not bothering to wait for change. I headed for the front door, expecting a hand to clamp down on my shoulder, or the yell of a gruff voice saying, "Stop, thief!"

But neither happened, and so, with a mixture of terror and triumph churning in my belly, I rushed home. With every step, I ignored the screaming voice in my head ordering me to turn around, questioning who I was becoming and demanding to know what the hell I'd do next.

CHAPTER SEVENTEEN

A SPIKY BALL OF ANXIETY nestled itself into my lungs, where it grew overnight. A shower, coffee and two headache pills for safety's sake later, and it still hadn't moved. I skipped breakfast, pulled on a clean pair of sweatpants—working from home came with its advantages—and settled at my table, trying to make myself research new clients.

Victoria's ring, though, had other plans. Despite it sitting on the counter, out of sight and carefully wrapped in a napkin, it burned a relentless hole in my forehead, demanding attention. After fifteen minutes of failing to ignore the damn thing, I snatched it up, unwrapped it and let it sit in the palm of my hand. Whatever bravado I'd felt the night before had long vanished, leaving me with one question: What the actual *fuck* had I been thinking? I'd swiped Victoria's jewelry. The ring wasn't mine. I was a thief. It was wrong to keep it, plain and simple.

I'd already known that before I'd left the restaurant. No, scratch that—before I'd picked it up.

I had to take it back to Le Médaillon, but what if they'd already called the police? What if stealing it—even for a few hours—meant I'd be charged? The ball in my lungs fell into my belly, digging itself into my gut. Had someone been to the bathroom after me, automatically becoming a suspect, too? Did the restaurant have security cameras? If so, had the footage caught my face? I'd paid cash for my food, they had no way of knowing who I was, but it would be easy enough to take stills and post them online, asking for help to identify me. My mind buzzed, trying to justify my actions, arguing with itself.

You can't keep it. You know it's wrong.

Yes, I can. It's not my fault she forgot her damn ring.

Oh, so you're victim blaming, are you? You'll get caught. You know you will.

They might have me on camera, but they can't prove anything.

The last one happened to be true. Unless there was hard evidence Victoria forgot her ring, it was a classic case of her word against mine, although I suspected a judge would favor her version. Victoria didn't need to commit insurance fraud, whereas anybody could tell a cash injection would do me no harm. My mind continued its interrogation.

What would Dad think? What would he say?

The thought of him watching over me, knowing what I'd done, made my knees buckle. I couldn't keep the ring, had no choice but to give it back somehow. I'd been worried about him dying without me ever making him proud, and now this? Perhaps going to the police was the way to go. Maybe I could drop the ring off anonymously, otherwise they'd ask questions I didn't want to answer. I weighed up the options over and over until another slithered into my brain with a soft whisper.

Take the ring to her apartment.

I could slide it into her mailbox—it was bound to be secure—

or give it to the doorman, if the building had one. It wasn't a perfect idea, but I had to pick from the solutions I'd come up with or think of an alternative. Stealing it had been an impulsive, stupid thing to do, and I needed to make it right before the cops came knocking.

I decided to do whatever offered the least potential interaction with anyone—going to Victoria's apartment building. As I changed, a pang of hunger hit me, reminding me I hadn't eaten since I'd had the bowl of soup at Le Médaillon. I ignored it as I shoved the ring in my pocket, darted down the hallway and burst outside, where I pulled my hood down over my face. I pushed away the thought of walking straight into a pawnshop and taking whatever they offered, despite knowing if I did, it would lessen the financial pressure of finding work for a while.

"I'm not pawning it, no way," I said out loud, the force and tone of my voice startling an elderly woman hobbling ahead of me. She turned around, her bright yellow cane shaking in her hand. I apologized and picked up the pace as I walked past her, the spiky ball of discomfort growing larger still and continuing to dig itself deeper.

I'd never stolen anything in my life—not unless you counted the cookie from Amy's tea party. A few years later, as I'd come home from school one afternoon, I'd spotted a shiny brown wallet lying in the grass on the side of the road. I'd picked it up and peered inside to find ten crisp twenty-dollar notes. Even at that age, I knew the cash was somebody's rent money or food budget. Whatever it was, it wasn't mine, and I wouldn't have slept properly keeping it. Maybe it was my personality, or my mother's unforgettable punishment—whatever the reason, I'd handed it in and never taken anything that wasn't mine, not even a paperclip from work. Yet, here I was with a diamond ring in my pocket, one I'd stolen with hardly any hesitation.

Since last night I'd continued asking myself who I was becoming. Stalking my biological father, now my half sister. Stealing her things. That wasn't me. I shuddered. Dad would be mortified if he knew. Then again if he hadn't died, maybe I wouldn't be in such a mess. If only he was still here, if only we'd had more time, maybe I wouldn't be turning into a crazy person.

I walked east, wrapping my jacket around me as I headed to Newbury Street. The wind picked up, whipping my face as I buried my chin in my scarf, taking faster and longer strides until I arrived at Victoria's building, yet another place I'd examined from every possible angle on Street View, adding to my list of ridiculous behavior.

My nerves got the better of me, made me stumble as I crossed the road. Before I reached the entrance, a woman wearing a long houndstooth coat and carrying a Prada bag you could fit a small child in pushed the door open, stepping out into the cold. As she turned and walked down the street, I reached for the handle before the door swung shut again. Fingers trembling, I pulled it open a fraction more and slipped inside.

The lobby was such a marvel to behold, it was as if I'd stepped into another world. In comparison to my building—where dim lights flickered, beige paint bubbled and peeled from the uninspired walls, and the pattern on the brown hallway carpet was an assortment of indecipherable stains—Victoria's place was a magical fairy-tale palace. Shiny black marble floors you could eat your supper off. White walls, which looked as if they'd been painted the night before. A futuristic silver light fixture as big as a small car, and probably more expensive, hung from the high ceiling, lending the place a welcoming glow.

The air smelled of pumpkin spice, and while there was no doorman, an annoyingly early six-foot Christmas tree stood sentry in the corner instead, decorated with silver and purple ribbons and baubles, with matching gift-wrapped parcels underneath. Even the letterboxes were smart-looking, not dented and scratched like the ones in my building. These golden handles were pristine—not a single scuff—the name tags engraved with a swirly font Santa himself could have penned.

I cursed myself for dashing out of my apartment on impulse, for not coming prepared. Usually I was Little Miss Planner, always thinking ahead, expecting the worst and preparing for it, too. I should've at least put the ring in an envelope. Now the tatty tissue would have to suffice.

As I was about to pull the ring from my pocket, the elevator bell dinged, announcing someone's arrival. There was no time to make a run for it, I wouldn't have reached the door. I considered crouching behind the Christmas tree before deciding to hide in plain sight, pretending to look for a resident's name on the mailboxes.

Turning my head slightly toward the doors, I glanced at the reflection of the elderly couple stepping out of the elevator, both of them smartly dressed in tweed jackets, their hair an identical shade of white. The woman looked at my back through her round glasses, but neither of them said a word. Maybe this was something else money provided—discretion and anonymity—and it couldn't have come at a better time.

Once alone in the lobby again, I touched Victoria's mailbox, which was marked Victoria E. Gallinger & Hugh F. Watters. Her middle name was Elizabeth, his was Francis, and the more I read the names, the more regal and *entitled* they sounded.

Dad had told me the story about how he'd chosen my first name because it meant "bright, shining one." It was something I'd never felt I lived up to, but I liked it all the same until Amy bastardized it to Nellie. Hardwicke, on the other hand, became "hard dick" by taunting peers around fifth grade and stuck until I'd left high school.

I bet Victoria had never been teased, and while it was pure assumption, I couldn't help imagining her in an elite, prestigious and obscenely expensive private school where she was popular, revered by students and teachers alike. Head of student council, possibly. Valedictorian, probably. Definitely not a wallflower who'd been picked on for wearing her younger-but-taller sister's hand-me-downs, which were a size too small around the waist.

As I stood there and imagined Victoria's perfect life, not only with a doting father but also a mother who *wanted* a relationship with her, the green-eyed monster within me woke up again and snarled, snapping its ugly, sharp teeth.

Maybe I could keep the ring for a little longer, I decided. Was there really any harm? Would Victoria even miss it? Okay, that was ridiculous considering it was her engagement ring, but still. By now she'd probably claimed it on insurance, spoken to the jeweler and had a new one on order. Those things were easy for people like the Gallingers. And while I could accept money couldn't buy happiness, it sure as hell had to make life a lot easier.

When I heard the whoosh of the elevator being summoned upstairs, I decided not to risk another chance encounter with anyone else in the building. Within a heartbeat I'd pushed the front door open and gone back outside into the frigid air.

I almost turned around on four separate occasions, wishing I'd shoved the damn ring in Victoria's mailbox instead of letting it sear a hole in my pocket as if it were a blowtorch. I tried to justify my most recent bad decision by insisting it would've been foolish to leave something so valuable where it might be stolen—again—even though those mailboxes looked as impenetrable as Fort Knox.

I slid my hand in my pocket, closed my palm over the ring. *Victoria's* ring. My heart sped up and I didn't bother trying to stop the smile from spreading over my face. I'd taken something from her. She didn't have a clue, had no idea I existed.

How had she felt when she'd realized her ring was missing? Had she cried when she'd rushed back to the bathroom and seen the empty spot where it had been? I imagined her, teary-eyed as she told Hugh. How had he reacted? Did he hug her, tell her it didn't matter? Whisk her out to buy a replacement? Was everything always so easy for her?

It isn't fair she's got a perfect life, is it? Don't you think you deserve all of that, too?

Instead of smacking down the voice in my head, I encouraged it, let it slither and slide around my brain, tell me it wasn't right she had everything when all I'd ever done was struggle. Victoria was younger than me. I'd been born first and yet had been discarded by my biological father, unwanted by my mother, raised by a man I'd loved but who'd lied to me and who'd ultimately left me, too.

I squeezed my fingers shut, pushed the stones into my skin, hoping they'd leave indentations, a perfect, permanent print. The satisfaction of knowing I'd taken something from Victoria, that I'd made her life a little less perfect, spread through my veins like a virus. But instead of it making me sick, it made me stronger. As I walked down the street, back to my sad little life, a tiny part of me—not far beneath the surface—wondered what else I could take from her, too.

CHAPTER EIGHTEEN

UNABLE TO FACE SITTING alone in my dingy apartment with thoughts pinging around my mind as if it were a psychotic pinball machine, I decided to visit the grocery store. My fridge and cupboards had gone from almost bare to destitute, begging to be filled.

At first I stuffed the usual suspects into my basket: pretzels, chocolate, a frozen lasagna, mac and cheese for one. Cooking wasn't a skill I'd cared to develop, and I preferred things I could shove in the microwave or, in a pinch, the oven. Today, all of those choices seemed as appealing as a bowl of hair soup. I put the items back, wandered over to the produce aisle, where, with a suspicious eye, I examined the yellow zucchini, green beans and fuzzy brown kiwis as if they'd arrived from an alien planet.

I'd overheard Victoria order the maple balsamic salmon at Le Médaillon ("no rice, extra vegetables") whereas Madeleine had chosen a plate of perch ("same, and no butter"), and Charlotte the braised ribs with duchess potatoes ("I'll take all the trimmings"). The dishes had sounded mouthwateringly delicious, and I could still smell the delicate fish and rich gravy. They'd been far too expensive for me to try, but now I felt the urge to eat something homemade with more flavor than a piece of cardboard. Well aware I wasn't proficient enough to tackle an elaborate recipe, and after looking at a couple of videos on my phone, I settled on fresh chicken breast, baby carrots, a small head of butter lettuce, half a dozen shiny apples and a box of green tea, something else I'd overheard Victoria order.

I recalled seeing a cookbook somewhere in the depths of my kitchen cupboard, as well as herbs and spices I'd bought on a whim, but rarely used. By the time I left the store, the prospect of making myself a healthy meal filled me with more excitement than I'd felt in weeks.

I'd been home for no more than five minutes, had half unpacked the groceries and put the kettle on, when there was a sharp knock on the door.

I jumped up, hoping it was Lewis. Because I'd slept in late every day, I hadn't heard him upstairs much. Not that I'd ever say it out loud, but I kind of missed him, which was ludicrous considering we barely knew each other. In any case, his gym had to be a raging success and keeping him busy, which was fantastic, but I still hoped he'd come to check on me again. I pondered whether to suggest we grab something to eat or offer to cook dinner, and groaned out loud. The idea was nothing but a recipe for disaster.

I grinned as I opened the door, but my smile slid off my face when I saw my mother. She was dressed in her ankle-length red coat, adorned by a single row of large buttons, a black fedora sitting on top of her head. She removed it and smoothed down her hair, and although she'd colored it the same hue for years,

I noticed it was similar to Madeleine's, although not as expensively done or nearly as flattering.

"Hello, Eleanor," she said. I was about to tell her to go away, but she spoke again, this time in the soft, gentle voice usually reserved for Amy. "Please, may I come in?"

Curious, I opened the door, staying mute as she stepped inside, readying myself for her withering looks and scathing remarks about my apartment, which she'd never seen. Instead of giving the place the once-over before lampooning the color scheme— or lack thereof—and my choice of decor with verbal spears, she said, "How are you?"

"Uh… I'm okay."

"I'm so glad your bruises have almost gone. I've been worried about you."

"Sorry?" She'd seen me but a few days ago, had been furious. Now she was concerned?

"The attack, your father's passing and finding out about… Well, you know." She said the last two words with extra care, as if she'd covered them in Bubble Wrap to make sure they didn't hurt me. "I had to come by to see how you are. Do you need anything? Can I help?"

I wondered if I'd fallen in the shower, smacked my head on the floor and been taken back to the hospital. Maybe I was in a coma, and Nurse Miranda was speaking to me through the fog in my brain, somehow taking on the shape of Sylvia Hardwicke. I gave my head a shake.

She took a step forward and I thought she'd grab my hands or give me a hug, at which point I'd have known for certain I'd stumbled into an alternate reality. "Eleanor, what's wrong?"

"Nothing, I'm fine," I said, debating whether I should offer her a coffee, but deciding it would mean us spending at least enough time together for her drink to cool to a palatable level. The chances of us killing one another before that point were already at DEFCON 1.

My mother walked past me to the living room and let herself drop onto the sofa, where she patted the cushion next to her. "Let's sit down and have a chat."

"A *chat*?"

She looked at me, pressed a hand to her chest. "You must miss your father so very much." When I bit my lip, unable to answer, she sighed, adding, "I've been seeing things from your point of view. I owe you an explanation. More than one, actually."

She laughed at her feeble attempt of a joke, but it came out too shrill, too loud and it wasn't funny to begin with.

As she set her hat on the cushion beside her and undid the buttons of her coat, I lowered myself onto one of the dining chairs, observing her as if she were a deadly viper, waiting to strike.

"I want to tell you about Stan," she said. "About what happened. Would that be all right?"

"Yes," I whispered, working hard not to break the spell by blurting out *who are you?* Or *how come?* Or *why now?*

"I met him at work," she said quietly. "He'd started Gallinger Properties a few years prior, and the company had taken off. I worked in their finance department, a temporary thing, you know? Covering for somebody's sabbatical for a few months." She paused, dropped her gaze as her cheeks reddened. "Stan was—"

"Married?" I offered, unable to help myself.

She met my stare, nodded and looked away again. "I was going to say my boss, but yes, he was married, and yes, I knew it, right from the start. He was intelligent and charming. Handsome. *Exceedingly* handsome."

"Quite the catch, apart from the obvious," I said, wishing I could stuff the words back into my mouth. My mother had come with information about my biological father. This wasn't the time to be snide. "What happened?"

"I liked him right away. Offered to work late and the flirting began," she said, her tone wistful, making her sound my age. "It led to lunch and then dinner and, well…other things. I loved him deeply, and…and he said he loved me."

"And you believed him?"

She let out a sigh. "I was young, stupid and terribly naive."

I almost snorted. My mother was many things: cold, hard, tenacious—naive had never been one of her attributes. I could picture her thirty years earlier, with Amy's looks and a knock-out figure she'd worked hard for, digging her sharp claws into Stan, deciding she wanted him, and married or not, she'd have him. Naive? Give me a break.

"The affair lasted a few months," she continued. "When I found out I was pregnant, I was sure he'd leave her for me. He didn't. Instead he insisted I get rid of the baby. When I refused, my contract was terminated and they escorted me out of the building as if I were a criminal."

"Did you see him again?" I said.

"He wouldn't return my calls so I waited outside the office one day." She looked at me. "It was incredibly humiliating, Eleanor, the way he treated me. You have no idea."

"Oh, I can imagine."

"Yes, well—" she smoothed down her clothes "—now you know why I've always told you to become self-sufficient, and why I've never begged a man for anything."

I raised my eyebrows. "Was that before or after you took his money?"

"It wasn't—"

"Wasn't it?"

"*No.* I know it sounds cold and calculating, but we reached an agreement. He'd pay me and I'd never publicly or privately speak of what happened or that he was your father. Not to anyone. Not even you…" She fiddled with the buttons on her coat. All her feelings—remorse, guilt, shame—seemed genuine. My mother had never worn her emotions on her sleeve, but right now they were wrapping her up like a blanket.

As I looked at her, I tried to put myself in her situation: in love with a married man who'd said he loved her, too, but walked away as soon as he'd found out about the baby. My mother, alone and pregnant and, by the sound of things, without a job, too. Had she tried to trap him, wanted to force him to leave Madeleine? If so, she'd made such a classic mistake it was almost laughable, except I was the result, and there was nothing funny about it.

"Basically Stan gave you money so we'd disappear from his life forever?"

"That's right. He worried about his marriage collapsing, and of course his reputation would've been in tatters if word had got out. Can you imagine? The golden boy of Portland falling from his bejeweled pedestal?" She shook her head, leaned toward me. "But his main reason was family, Eleanor. More to the point, his wife's. His father-in-law gave him a loan to buy his first property—"

"I read he'd worked multiple jobs, saved all his money—"

"True, although not enough to buy the building. But playing the poor kid who became successful through elbow grease and grit is far more appealing to the masses than him getting a leg up from his wealthy Canadian father-in-law." Her eyes narrowed, and I could see even after all these years she still despised Stan Gallinger, possibly more than I did.

"I found out Stan and Madeleine had a prenuptial agreement," my mother said. "If they'd divorced, he would've had to pay back the loan plus interest, and it would've ruined him financially. His business was stretched thin, it could've gone under."

"How do you know that?"

"I worked in their finance department, remember? Besides, when it came down to it, he loved *her* more. You can't force someone to love you, however hard you try."

I blinked, the irony of her statement settling between us with the subtlety of a brick wall. "So when he offered you money, you took it," I said.

"It made financial sense. Nobody wanted to hire a pregnant accountant, so it gave me time to get back on my feet, and I was able to buy a house."

That explained why Dad had left the marriage with next to nothing. Up until then, I'd assumed it was because he was too kind, too soft, and let my mother have whatever she wanted, because it was how their relationship had always been. "Where did Dad fit into all of this?"

My mother didn't answer straight away. She blinked a few times, and finally, she said, "I told you the truth about how I met him in a café, when I spilled my coffee on him and he bought me another."

"He told me you got pregnant a few months after meeting him."

"I did, it wasn't a lie," she said. "But I met him while I was involved with Stan. Bruce and I became friends, and when Stan left me, Bruce asked me out and I agreed."

"But you were pregnant?"

"Yes."

"And Dad knew?"

"From the start. Bruce didn't care I was carrying someone else's child, he said it didn't matter. He told me he loved me on our third date, asked me to marry him a week later."

"Really?"

"Believe it or not, I wasn't always such a hard woman," she said. "I swore Bruce to secrecy about Stan, and we agreed it wouldn't make sense to tell you the truth—" she put a hand up when I opened my mouth in protest "—and I can see now how that was wrong. You had every right to know, and I'm sorry."

Her apology, her whole demeanor, head bent, fingers still fidgeting with her coat, threw me again. I'd never seen her this way before. "Didn't Stan want to see me after I was born?"

"No, and it still makes me so angry, him treating us like that."

Us. I searched her face, saw vulnerability and, for the first time, understood how much effort it took for her to let her guard down. It was a glimpse of what Dad might have seen when they first met, a side to my mother I'd never discovered or knew she had. Like me, she didn't let many people close, had never remarried or had another longtime partner, at least in part because she'd been hurt. I couldn't begrudge her that, could I?

"Why do you hate me so much?" I said, the need to know forcing the words out.

"I don't—"

"But you've always pushed me away."

She tilted her head to one side, her eyes searching my face. "I blamed you for a lot of things," she said quietly. "Marrying a man I didn't love as much as another—"

"But Dad was—"

"A good man, I know that, Eleanor, but I'm ashamed to say I felt trapped. If I hadn't got pregnant with Stan's child, or if he'd wanted to be with me, my life might have been different. More glamorous, more exciting." She looked away but I didn't dare interrupt. This was the most we'd spoken in years. "You remind me of him sometimes. The way you move, your hand gestures. Sometimes it was more than I could bear, and I'm truly sorry, because none of this was ever your fault." She let out another breath. "Stan still riles me. I don't want to have anything to do with him. I don't want my name associated with his. I hope you understand."

"I do."

"Are you sure? Because I don't think you know what kind of person he is," she said. "Do you know what he told me when he called about your visits? He said if you contact him again, he'll go after my business, convince my clients to change accounting firms."

"*What?*"

"He wasn't who I thought he was in the end." She swallowed, her bottom lip quivering. "But that's not your fault, either, and it doesn't mean we can't be friends. Would you... I mean, do you think it's possible? Could we try at least?"

My heart thudded. These were words I'd longed to hear my mother say ever since I was little. At times I'd vowed I'd throw them back in her face with a vehemence reserved for only the most appalling of enemies. Now, with her sitting in front of me, a hopeful, desperate look on her face, I couldn't do it. It meant something, her coming here and confiding in me. No, not something—*everything*. Maybe Lewis had been right, and it wasn't too late for us, after all. Perhaps she and I could somehow find our way to the relationship I'd given up on years ago. Maybe I could still have a parent in my life.

"Yes, Mom. I'd like that, too."

"Oh, thank you, Eleanor, thank you. Would you... No, never mind."

"Would I what?"

"Well...I was going to ask if we could start by going out for coffee."

"You mean now?"

"Yes, if you're free? I saw a place a block down. The Coffee Pot, I think it's called. Have you been? Their chocolate cake looks delicious."

"It is," I said, remembering the huge slice I'd bought for half price on opening day, and decided I'd only have coffee this time. "And yes, I'm free."

"Wonderful. I'll take a minute to freshen up and we can go talk some more."

She smiled at me again as she made her way to the bathroom, closing the door softly behind her. I couldn't shake the surprise from my face, couldn't believe this was happening. My mother, the person who'd shoved me away more times than I could count, wanted to spend time with me. But the best part was hearing her say it hadn't been my fault. She hadn't disliked me for me, per se, but because of Stan. The way she'd treated me, alienated me and pushed me aside wasn't something I could easily forget, but in time and with effort on both sides, maybe there was still enough to salvage.

An image invaded my brain: her, Amy and me sipping margaritas on a sunny afternoon, the three of us laughing at an inside joke the way Victoria, Madeleine and Charlotte had. I was still smiling when I heard the buzz of a cell phone. Not mine, but Mom's, half-wedged between the sofa cushions. I picked it up, a frown hijacking my face when I saw the twinkling words on the screen. A message from Amy.

Seen N yet? What did she say? Will she do it?

My mother's security settings were infantile. Two guesses and I'd figured out her passcode—Amy's birthday—and opened the message app. As I read the exchanges between my younger sister and my mother, the pink and fluffy, happy-family thoughts vanished one by one, replaced by the familiar rage-filled storm clouds swelling inside me.

Mother: I've found a way to pay for your acting classes & coach

Amy: How? So expensive :(

Mother: Nellie will get money from S

Amy: He'll pay her?

Mother: She'll make him

Amy: Wth??? N agreed???

Mother: She'll do as she's told

Amy: How? She won't tlk 2 u

Mother: I'll become her best friend and make her think he threatened my business

Amy: Sneaky! BTW aren't u my BFF? LOL

"Ready to go?" My mother had returned from the bathroom, wearing what I now identified as a masterful but fake expression on her touched-up face. "Sweetie, are you okay?"

Sweetie. She'd never used the name, any pet name, not once. With the single word, she'd not only revealed her hand but thrown it away, and I couldn't believe she'd almost succeeded in deceiving me.

I held up her phone, waggled it midair. "You dropped this."

She took a step. "Oh, thank you. It must've fallen—"

"Amy sent a text."

"Did she? I'll read it later. She can wait."

"I'm not sure she can," I said slowly, deliberately, every word a sharp, piercing blade aimed at her heart, at her soul—except she didn't have one anymore because she'd sold it thirty years ago for a hundred thousand dollars. "She wants an update on how the blackmail plans are going. Probably wondering if I'll *do as I'm told.*"

My mother's eyes flashed. "You read my messages? You're invading my privacy—"

I laughed out loud, could hardly stop long enough to say, "Nice try, *Mom.* You came here for one reason only. Use me to get money from Stan. For *Amy.* Didn't you?"

"Eleanor—"

"What, were you too chicken to try to blackmail him yourself? Worried he really would go after your clients if you did?

You know, you almost had me convinced. I wanted to believe deep, deep down that you're a decent person and could be a real mother, but—"

"I can, Eleanor," she said, but she'd forgotten how well I knew her, for how many years I'd studied her, trying to get her to love me. She had no idea how the tone of her voice betrayed her now. Maybe she should've considered hiring an acting coach for herself rather than Amy.

My blood boiled, spilled over, raced through my veins, throbbed in my temples, threatening to make my head burst. "Get out," I said, teeth and fists clenched. "I never, ever want to see or speak to you again." She wouldn't move, not until I shouted at her once more to leave, grabbed her arm and yanked her to the front door.

"You're making a mistake," she said as I shoved her again. "We could—"

"Get. *Out*."

She stared at me with her foot over the threshold as she adjusted her sleeves. "You know, I was like you once, Eleanor, years ago. Not quite as heavy of course, but with little backbone. The difference is I grew more. Made something of myself. Took pride in my appearance, and worked hard. But you? You'll never be *anything* unless we—"

Ignoring her foot, I slammed the door, pushed my back up against it in case she had the strength to blow it down like the big bad wolf I knew she was. She knocked a few times, demanded I let her in, but I didn't move, not until I heard Mrs. Winchester's voice.

"What's going on out here?" my old neighbor said. "Why are you making such a racket?"

"Mind your own business," my mother snapped, banging on the door again. "Eleanor!"

"I'll call the police if you don't leave," Mrs. Winchester wheezed. "Right now."

My mother didn't speak again, but I heard her footsteps beat a hasty retreat down the corridor. A moment later there was a soft knock on the door.

"Are you okay, Eleanor?" Mrs. Winchester said. "Is everything all right?"

I bit my lip, telling myself not to cry. I would *not* cry. This was a dance my mother and I had practiced for years, our sickening pas de deux taking us closer and closer to the precipice before we'd finally plunged over the edge. Did it matter? Did I care?

"I'm fine," I called out. "Really."

"Mmm-hmm," Mrs. Winchester replied. "Come find me if you need to talk. You hear?"

"Yes, Mrs. W. Thank you."

I slunk to the window, waiting for my mother to leave the building, and stood a few feet back in case she turned around and spotted me, but shouldn't have bothered. Sylvia Hardwicke strode across the street and out of my life, her steps determined, red coat flowing behind her as if she was going straight back to hell. And this time, I vowed, she'd been exorcised for good.

CHAPTER NINETEEN

THE NEXT COUPLE OF days passed in a blur. I spent my time working, doing a few website fixes in between hunting for new business, a search that remained unsuccessful. I hadn't heard from Kyle Draper, either, odd considering he was late emailing me his weekly list of updates. He was the kind of person who regarded being on time as late, but he was also a busy man, and he had a reputation as a terrible delegator. Maybe for the first time since I'd met him he'd become overwhelmed and had dropped a few of the hundred balls he typically juggled with ease. I briefly wondered if I should call him, decided it would be best to wait until he contacted me rather than risk upsetting him by pointing out he was behind his self-imposed schedule.

At least his payment for the last month had arrived. Still, I had too much time on my hands and on Wednesday morning, after I'd spent an hour examining the clown-shaped water stain on the ceiling, thinking about Dad, my mother, Amy and the Gallingers, I decided to get outside before I drove myself insane.

I hadn't been to the cemetery to see Dad since the funeral the week before, and the thought made me feel like an utter piece of garbage, however hard I tried justifying my absence. My headaches from the mugging had all but disappeared, and I'd read enough about PTSD to know so far I wasn't suffering from it, but the cemetery wasn't a busy place, and being there with nobody else around made me feel on edge.

When I got to Dad's grave, despite vowing I'd be chirpy and bright because I'd promised him I wouldn't be sad, the first thing I did was cry.

Tears spilled over my cheeks, seeped into my scarf as I clenched my fists. I missed him more than I'd ever missed anything or anyone. Grief was an absolute bastard, and while I'd known there were different stages—denial, anger, bargaining and so forth—what I hadn't appreciated was that a song on the radio, a commercial on TV, a similar voice, a photograph, the smell of cherry pie or whatever else happened to trigger a memory could slam you right back to the beginning. Yes, grief was an absolute bastard, and a spiteful, malicious one. At home I'd been coping—barely—but here I felt unmoored, without compass, as if I'd float around in this ocean of despair, forevermore trying to find my way home. I sank to my knees, the cold ground making an immediate assault on my legs.

"I miss you," I whispered. "I miss you so much. What am I going to do without you?"

When my phone rang, I jumped, my heart insisting it was a sign from Dad before my brain kicked in, reprimanding me for my wishful thinking. "Hello?" I said, my voice unsteady.

"Hello? Eleanor Hardwicke?" The man's deep voice wasn't one I recognized.

"Yes. Who's this?"

"I'm Scott Burkett, your father's attorney," the man said, and when I didn't respond, he added. "From Herbert, Regnell and Associates. Did I catch you at a bad time?"

"No, it's fine," I replied. "Uh, how can I help you?"

"I'm hoping it's the other way around," Mr. Burkett said carefully. "I'm calling about your father's will. Did he mention I'm the executor?"

"Yes," I said, finally placing the name. "He mentioned it."

"Great. That's great. Well, I was hoping you could come and see me."

I wasn't sure I could face talking about my father in the past tense, hear about how he'd divided up his things. I didn't care about his stuff. All I wanted was to have him back, put my arms around him and give him a hug, swap another set of crappy Christmas jokes.

Mr. Burkett must have sensed my hesitation. "I understand how hard this can be—"

"Do you really?"

He let a beat go, then another. "I lost both my parents last year. It's tough."

"Oh. I'm sorry. I shouldn't have—"

"Don't worry, please. When could you come and see me?"

It didn't take long for me to decide. While talking about Dad might be upsetting, it was an opportunity to spend time with someone who'd known him, who'd had actual conversations with him, even if it had been only to discuss his affairs. "I'm free now."

Mr. Burkett gave me the details and we agreed I'd arrive within the hour. I stayed at the cemetery for another little while, growing colder by the minute, but not quite ready to leave as I promised Dad over and over I'd come see him again soon. By the time my ride-share arrived, my fingers and toes had gone numb, and I clambered into the back of the car, grateful the young female driver wasn't in a chatty mood. I settled into my seat, wrapping my arms around my body in an attempt to get warm.

I arrived at the offices of Herbert, Regnell and Associates twenty minutes later. The name made the firm sound glitzy, upscale and expensive, with heavy oak doors, marble floors and glass-paneled conference rooms. As it turned out, the place consisted of small, dank rooms with a frayed green carpet and desks that could've been relics from the seventies. The lone assistant might have been plucked from the decade, too, her bouffant hair and multicolored eye makeup a tribute to ABBA.

"Take a seat, dear," she croaked in a voice suggesting a long-standing love affair with nicotine, and gestured to the scratched plastic chairs lined up next to a sticky table covered in well-worn copies of *US Weekly*. As I sat down, I felt her gaze land on me, so I picked up a magazine and pretended to be interested in last year's celebrity news.

"Ms. Hardwicke." Scott Burkett came out of the back office five minutes later, hand outstretched. He was a plump man, probably midfifties, with sun-kissed skin, a shiny bald head and huge brown eyes. After the customary introductions and an offer of a glass of water, which I declined, he invited me to follow him to his office, where he pulled out a chair for me.

I sat down, glancing at his rickety desk piled high with precarious stacks of dusty papers, which threatened to topple over and bury us both. From the disheartened look in Mr. Burkett's eyes, and the palm tree poster on the wall, I speculated he'd much prefer sitting on a beach or a sailing boat somewhere warm.

"Your father was a good man, Ms. Hardwicke," he said. "Very kindhearted."

"Yes, he was," I whispered. "Thank you."

"We played darts together for a while. Bruce always won." He tapped the notepad in front of him with his index finger. "I'm not sure if he spoke to you about his financial situation?"

I shifted in my chair. Why did talking about Dad's money make me feel so uncomfortable and wretched, like a bloodsucking leech? I reminded myself Dad had appointed Mr. Burkett and that he'd called me, not the other way around. This was his job.

"A little," I said.

"I'm afraid his illness took most of the money he had left. The life insurance lapsed and he couldn't renew it because of the cancer." He interlaced his fingers in front of him, looking even more desperate to be somewhere else. "Bruce remortgaged his apartment to pay for treatment, so the bank will take most of the money when it sells. Then there's the funeral—"

"Yes, I know. We chose everything together. I know how much it cost."

"You probably knew he prearranged for his things to be taken from his apartment and sold at auction, too?" Mr. Burkett said, and I nodded. "Estate sales don't typically net much, nor did he have anything of notable value. He mentioned you'd already taken what you wanted?"

I nodded again as I pictured the giant snow globe filled with trees and mountains, which Dad had brought back from one of his long-haul trips to Denver, and now sat on a shelf in my bedroom. He'd given me the photo albums he'd put together when I was a kid, too, the ones with pictures of us camping and fishing at the lake during the summer, while Amy and my mother had stayed in Portland or gone to New York for my sister's acting lessons. The only other things I'd taken were his Manchester United soccer shirt and the World's Best Truck Driver mug I'd given him for his birthday when I was nine, and he'd used daily since. My heart couldn't withstand being surrounded by more of his things.

"Yes. Dad gave me everything I need."

"All right, then." Mr. Burkett made a note with his pen and replaced the badly chewed cap. "Well, after all the deductions and fees and so forth, there will be little to share."

"I know." I felt guilty about the tinge of disappointment bubbling inside me. I'd known there was no surprise inheritance waiting for me at a lawyer's office, no hidden treasure beneath the floorboards or dusty Picassos forgotten in a closet. "I wasn't expecting anything."

"Ah, yes, well, there's another reason I asked you here." Mr. Burkett's voice wavered. Glassy beads of sweat appeared on his forehead and he swiped a tissue from a nearby box to mop them away. "Uh, your sister's attorney called."

"My sister?"

"Yes—" he flipped through his notes "—she, uh, informed me Amy's contesting your father's will." He shuffled in his seat. "She's alleging Bruce wasn't well enough to make decisions and that his physical state adversely influenced his mental capacity."

"But there was nothing wrong with his mind—"

"I agree, and I'm confident we can prove it, too." He grimaced and an apologetic look settled over his face. "But until we clear things up, the inheritance will be delayed."

"Or you could give everything to Amy."

"You don't have to—"

"Will it make them go away?" I said, knowing that the fail-safe Dad and I had put in place by appointing an executor hadn't worked. Of course not. We'd been stupid to believe it would.

"Who?" Mr. Burkett shook his head. "Make who go away?"

"My sister and my mother. If I give Amy everything, will they leave me alone?"

"Uh, I...I don't know. But you don't have to—"

"No, but I want to." The small room closed in on me, the stacks of paper becoming bigger and taller and increasingly threatening—ink-filled monsters preparing to flatten me. I needed to get outside, fill my lungs with fresh air before I suffocated. I stood up. "I'll sign whatever you need. Send me the documents and give her the money."

Ignoring Mr. Burkett's calls for me to come back, I hurried past the ancient receptionist, who might have fallen asleep, bounded down the stairs and ran out into the cold. Snow swirled in the gray skies, settling on the ground in a thin, slippery layer.

My mother was lightning fast, I had to give her that. She'd probably called Amy as soon as she left my apartment, told her to contact Mr. Burkett and dig into Dad's money, planning every last detail to maximize the pain and damage on my side in the hope I'd give in to blackmailing Stan, and my little sister had agreed. Except they'd miscalculated. Instead of hurting, I felt free. Conceding the money to Amy would make them think I was weak, and they'd won. *Let them*, I thought, because I knew it made me stronger.

I felt my hate for my mother, Amy and the Gallingers grow, hardening my heart but straightening that elusive backbone. Alongside Dad, I'd always been the quiet one, the one who wouldn't say boo to a fly let alone a goose, the person every-body overlooked and underestimated. Maybe we were the ones people needed to be extra careful of. We lived in the shadow of others, but didn't that also mean we were the ones who snapped when everyone least expected it? And when we did, every single person in our vicinity got hurt.

Including—*especially*—family.

CHAPTER TWENTY

AS SOON AS I got home, I retrieved Victoria's ring from where I'd stuffed it into my bedside table, and unfolded the tissue without touching the metal at first, as if afraid it might brand me somehow. I held the ring in my palm, turned my hand left and right, letting the pretentious little show-off diamonds catch the light. How much was it worth? Enough to solve my financial issues for a while, yet I still didn't want to part with it, not when it could fuel the hatred for both my families. Selling it was a cop-out. Keeping it when I desperately needed the money, another victory.

I gently slid it onto the ring finger of my right hand, surprised when it didn't stop at the knuckle as I thought it would, but continued to the base, as if custom-made. My fingers didn't much resemble Victoria's French-manicured digits, but I held them out all the same, admiring the jewelry, my lips curving into a smile. I wandered to the bathroom, slipped Victoria's ring off my right hand and put it on my left. I gathered my hair behind my head, holding it in the loose ponytail Victoria had worn at Le Médaillon.

As I observed myself in the mirror, I wondered how she'd felt when Hugh had proposed and where he'd asked her to be his wife. In front of family and friends in a public demonstration of his love for her? During an intimate dinner, the ring delivered by a waiter in a crystal flute of overpriced champagne? I shook my head. Too cliché. Victoria was the kind of woman who'd settle for nothing less than extraordinary, something she could brag about to her friends, listen to them oohing and aahing about how *lucky* she was. Once again I found myself asking how it would be to live like her. To *be* her.

"Hi," I said to my reflection. "I'm Victoria Elizabeth Gallinger." When I heard the sound of my voice, I let my hair drop. We looked nothing alike, she and I, save perhaps for our eyebrows or maybe our pinky toes, although I suspected her feet were dainty and faultless, not boat-size and in desperate need of a pedicure. Her nose fit her symmetrical face whereas mine could've been a stuck-on potato. She had straight white teeth, too, not misaligned tombstones. My mother hadn't seen the benefit of fitting me with braces as she had Amy—according to her, great teeth weren't necessary if you didn't have a flawless face to go with them, something I'd overheard her say to a friend on my thirteenth birthday.

Even the color and texture of Victoria's and my hair were different. Hers thick and luscious. Mine thin and strawlike in every sense. The saying "blondes have more fun" held zero truth as far as I was concerned, and I'd always become suspicious whenever someone told me I was pretty or attractive—leaving me wondering what their motives were.

I cocked my head from side to side, for once really examining my reflection rather than turning away from it. Maybe a change of style would help—it certainly couldn't do any harm—but I couldn't afford to go to a salon to have my hair done. One of those home-dye kits could suffice, I decided, although a wig might also be an option.

"Hi, I'm Victoria Elizabeth Gallinger," I repeated, batting my eyelashes.

How difficult would it be to look like her? Walk and talk like her? Was it all genetics, or could I learn some of it, pick up her traits, habits and gestures if I got close enough?

I pulled out my Nikon and flicked through the photographs of Victoria coming out of her spin class, recalled what she'd said at Le Médaillon about needing marketing for her business. I hadn't found any details about her venture online, but it didn't mean I couldn't offer her my services. My gut clenched. Chances were she'd refuse, but what if she didn't?

"Then you'll get to know her," I said out loud, uttering the thoughts I'd been repeating in my head for days. "And you can find out everything about her."

I closed my eyes, didn't want to look at myself. Those thoughts belonged in the head of a crazy person—a weirdo, a psycho. Same as thinking about dyeing my hair or wearing a wig to look like Victoria, or stealing her ring and slipping it on my finger instead of giving it back.

"You're not crazy," I whispered. "You're not."

But I *was* almost broke. Knowing someone who might need a website developed and not acting on it was foolish, careless even. Okay, so it was Victoria, but she didn't know we were related. Disregarding this business opportunity—*that* was crazy. There was no harm in at least considering the option, playing around with it in my mind. I pulled out my phone, looked up her Facebook profile and hovered my finger over the message button. I'd draft a note, I decided, then sleep on it, wait awhile to send it. I began to type.

Hi, Victoria,

No, this was stupid. If I contacted her via social media, it had to be professional. I headed over to LinkedIn, searched for her profile and opened up a new message. My belly fluttered as I thought about her reading my note, going over my profile, checking out my credentials. It was daring, exciting, so far out of my comfort zone, the zone was a distant dot in a galaxy far, far away. If this was how it felt to be adventurous, I'd been missing out.

Dear Ms. Gallinger,

Yes, better. Far better.

I offer professional, fresh and reasonably priced website designs for small to midsize companies. Might this be something of interest for your business? I'm based in Portland and could easily come to your offices to discuss my portfolio and options.

Looking forward to hearing from you.

Yours sincerely,

Eleanor Hardwicke

I reread the words, crinkling my nose as I made changes, agonizing over sentence structure until satisfied everything was perfect. After I'd added the links to my website and Kyle Draper's restaurants and bars as examples of what I could offer, I sat back in my chair and exhaled. I was good at my job, had a knack for layout and design.

Still, the more I thought about it, the more I decided sending Victoria a message was a terrible idea. If she ignored me, I'd feel rejected. If she was interested, it meant speaking with her, potentially meeting face-to-face. And Stan would know. Was I ready for that?

Screw the adventurous crap from five minutes ago. I couldn't handle it. As much as I wanted to think I'd become a badass overnight, the best thing was to ignore it all—my so-called family and the Gallingers—and move on with my life. Sort out new contracts. Keep Kyle happy. Maybe take up a hobby—kickboxing or something else people did to vent their frustrations.

My phone twinkled and buzzed with an incoming message.

Are you busy?

I smiled at Lewis's note, baby bird wings flapping around in my stomach as I answered.

No.

Within a minute there was a knock on the door and I found him standing outside looking rugged, casual and oh-so-sexy in a pair of jeans and a green V-neck sweater. My face broke into another smile. "You just sent me a text," I said, noting how breathless and girlie I sounded, telling myself to stop it, stop it right now. "Do you need something?"

"Laundry detergent?" Lewis grinned.

"Oh, sure." I forced my face back into a neutral expression. "Hold on, I'll get it—"

"I'm kidding. I picked up a bottle yesterday."

"Okay..." I said as he took a step closer, his eyes softening.

"I want to ask you to dinner."

"Dinner?"

Lewis tilted his head to one side. "Yeah, you know. On a date."

"But...why?"

He laughed gently, the sound adding to the warm fuzzies in my belly. "Is that a trick question?" When I didn't answer and continued staring at him because I couldn't think of how to respond, he said, "Because I like you, Eleanor. You're... different."

I let out a snort. "I'm not sure that's a good thing."

"It is, believe me. You're smart and funny. You're—" Lewis shrugged "—real. I hope we can get to know each other better, if that's okay?"

I started to laugh, quietly at first, but when a loud chuckle escaped, I covered my mouth with both hands. "I'm sorry," I said when I could finally talk again. "I'm wondering if I'm having an out-of-body experience."

"Is that a no, then?" He was grinning now, too. "Honestly, I'm a bit confused."

"No, I mean, yes, dinner sounds great."

He took another step toward me, gently tucked a lock of hair behind my ear. The gesture felt surprisingly intimate, his touch making my skin tingle with—what was it—lust? Desire? As sudden images of the two of us, naked, galloped around my mind, I lost the grip on my phone, and it clattered to the floor. Lewis bent over and picked it up, held it out to me. Our fingers touched, lingered, making my heart beat faster and the number of naughty images quadruple.

"Thank you." I pulled my hand away, wrapped it around my phone.

"Dinner then. How about tomorrow night?"

"Sounds perfect."

"Can I pick you up at seven?"

"Yes, please," I whispered. "I'll see you then."

From the way Lewis looked at me, I thought he might kiss me, and I let myself imagine his lips pressed against mine, his hands slipping around my waist, pulling me closer. Instead, he smiled again and left, closing the door behind him without making a sound.

My grin threatened to break my face but vanished when I

looked at my phone. The LinkedIn message to Victoria was no longer a draft. It had been sent, hurtling through cyberspace, straight toward her inbox.

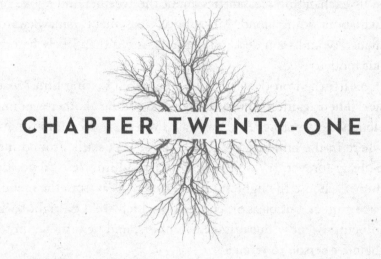

CHAPTER TWENTY-ONE

MOST OF THE NIGHT was spent attempting to calm my frayed nerves, which had shot off in all directions, disappearing down "what if" rabbit holes, robbing me of any potential sleep. By the time morning came, I was still trying to convince myself not to worry. Victoria wouldn't answer. She *wouldn't*. How many times had I emailed or contacted prospects through social media or left voice mails, only to hear nothing but crickets?

Experience taught me there were always a few dozen rejections before I got to the elusive "yes," it was the simple reality of sales. Sure, Victoria wasn't a regular prospect as far as I was concerned, but she didn't know. Like so many others, she'd probably see my message and hit Delete, and on the off chance she replied, I'd ignore her. Simple.

I dragged my exhausted body to the bathroom and looked at

myself in the mirror. The yellow sheen of my bruises had faded at last, and I decided I'd ignore the deep purple bags under my eyes. I had something else to focus on. Dinner with Lewis.

But the more I thought about it, the more I knew it was a bad idea. He'd said I was different, which was kind of lovely, but we didn't have much—anything—in common, which would lead to us exchanging pleasantries about the weather and a joke or two about doing laundry in a spooky basement. An awkward silence would soon descend upon us, more than likely before our food arrived.

As I turned on the shower, I considered texting him I was sick. Then again, the prospect of not spending another evening alone was tempting. And anyway, I'd have to face him somewhere in the building eventually. I couldn't skulk around the hallway forever, trying my best to avoid him. Yes, I'd go for dinner, choose the lightest, easiest thing to eat from the menu, have a quick but pleasant chat, after which we'd go right back to being friendly but distant neighbors, and he'd move on to the next person to rescue.

Except going out with Lewis presented another dilemma. Other than my usual outfit of jeans and a black T-shirt, what would I wear on a date? My dress pants would surely still be too snug around the middle—prompting scary visions of me splitting the seams after my first mouthful—and if I wore any of my work stuff, I'd look like I was on a job interview. No, there was no future with Lewis, that was a given, but it didn't mean I wanted to appear as a total loser on my first date in almost two years. God, had it been that long since I'd kissed a guy?

My last relationship had lasted only four months. I'd met Tony, a colleague who worked in the legal department, in the lunch room when he'd confused my tuna sandwich for his. Deadpan, he'd asked if I knew what happened to the tuna fisherman, and said, "He got canned." Profuse apologies for the terrible pun followed, but he'd made me grin, so when he asked me out, I said yes. Things had gone quite well for a while, the sex transitioning from awkward to mostly enjoyable, but when Tony told me he loved me, I froze.

"What's wrong?" he'd said with sad puppy eyes. "Don't you love me?"

Maybe I should've said yes, but I didn't want to lie. I'd been hurt before when I'd said it to previous boyfriends, heard it parroted back before finding out I'd been cheated on. And so I'd hesitated before telling Tony I wasn't there yet, and I saw the hurt etch itself across his face. A week later we'd broken up. Another six months and HR collected donations for an engagement present for Tony and Laura, a girl from Sales. I'd chucked in twenty bucks because I hadn't missed him once, which said an awful lot about me I didn't want to know.

But, as strange as it felt, I missed Lewis. As I'd lain in bed last night, trying not to think about the message I'd sent Victoria, I'd pictured him instead. The shape of his back. The definition of his arms. The sound of his voice. The way he'd looked at me. How it might feel if he were there, in my bed… While all those thoughts had been a helpful distraction, they'd stopped me from sleeping, too.

My legs wobbled, and I shut off the shower, ordering myself to get a grip. I added up the cash in my bank account, deciding I could spend a few bucks on a new shirt at least, although my old jeans would have to suffice. Mind made up, I got ready and headed to the local thrift store, where I rummaged around long enough to find a "new" three-quarter-sleeved shirt that would cover what a gym teacher had once referred to as my "boilermaker" arms. The top was silky smooth dark gray satin, slightly tapered at the waist and had a plunging neckline embroidered with small white flowers.

"Great find," the store clerk said, looking up from the pile of sweaters she'd rearranged. "I think it would really suit you. You can try it on if you like."

I wrinkled my nose, still unsure, wondering if it was something Victoria might have worn a few fashion seasons ago. No doubt she was the kind of person who discarded her entire wardrobe twice yearly, always going with—and pulling off—the latest trends. Thinking about her riled me again, and I told the jealousy to climb back in its box, but it refused.

"I'll take it," I told the clerk, paying seven bucks and going back outside. When I passed the drugstore, I doubled back, hesitating in front of the entrance. I'd never had a talent for makeup, limiting my efforts to a swipe of mascara, some blush, the occasional touch of a peach-colored lipstick I'd had for years. Victoria's face always looked expertly done in her photos, even after her spin class the other night. In every single picture, she seemed flawless, also when barefaced. Like Amy, Victoria was the kind of person who didn't need artificial help, but knew exactly which tools would enhance her impeccable features some more.

I'd read somewhere that when the economy tanked, lipstick sales went up, something about it being perceived as a small yet affordable luxury. Well, I reasoned as I walked into the drugstore, my job prospects weren't fantastic so that had to mean a new lip gloss was in order. I perused the different brands and colors, took my time trying out darker shades on the palm of my hand, incapable of figuring out what might suit. When a sales assistant with long auburn hair and choppy bangs walked over, she reached for a tube of shiny, pale pink lip gloss.

"This is great if you're going for a neutral look," she said. "Here, see what you think." She dabbed a little onto my hand, her fingers butter-soft as she rubbed the gloss into my skin. "See how it blends but leaves a little shimmer? Beautiful."

"It's lovely."

She beamed. "Anything else I can help you with?"

"Uh…no, thanks," I said, but as she turned I added, "Wait, yes. My eyes. Any suggestions how to get rid of these bags before Samsonite comes looking for them?"

She laughed. "Sure. And for the record, your eyes are a lovely shade of blue. Let's see…"

Thirty minutes later I clutched a little basket filled with foundation, applicator sponges, concealer, eyeliner and eyeshadow, mascara and the shimmery lip gloss. Penelope, my new best friend, had showed me how to use everything, giving me a mini makeover right there in the store.

"See," she said, holding out a mirror when she was done. "You're stunning."

I couldn't see what she did, and knew flattery was part of her job, but I had to agree my reflection was a vast improvement. The dark bags had all but disappeared, my lips looked plumper and somehow Penelope had unearthed my cheekbones with the skill of a veteran archeologist. When she took me to the counter and rung up all the items—over sixty dollars' worth of products—I balked.

"Oops. I almost forgot the ten-percent discount for your birthday," Penelope said.

"But it isn't—"

"Sure it is." She winked. "And I'll include a load of samples, too, okay?"

Treating myself felt unfamiliar, but even so, before I left the store, I ended up two aisles over in front of the boxes of hair dye. My eyes glanced over the hues, finally settled on a rich mahogany, the exact shade of Victoria's hair. I reached out to pick up a box, but pulled my hand back before sticking my arm out again and grabbing it, knocking three others off the shelf in the process. Penelope had disappeared so I couldn't ask her opinion, and the new clerk stood at the counter picking her fingernails, barely glancing at me as I paid for the dye. I didn't care. I was too eager to get home and continue my transformation.

An hour later I stood in front of the bathroom mirror, staring at the reflection of someone I no longer recognized, wishing I'd waited for Penelope after all. As much as I'd detested my yellow mop, I wanted it back.

The promised color on the box had translated into a peculiar shade of mud brown on my head, and instead of subtle highlights, it looked like a kid had taken a Sharpie to sporadic strands. Despite the new makeup, my face appeared ghostly white, appropriate for an audition in a zombie movie, perhaps, but nothing else. Worse, there was little under an hour left before Lewis would pick me up, during which time I'd have to wash and rewash my hair to rid it of the color. After five rounds of good scrubbing, it had barely budged, and, if anything, looked more lackluster. I grabbed the box and read the instructions, desperate for some magical solution but finding only that I'd bought *permanent* dye, not a wash-out one.

Cursing profusely, I blow-dried my hair, retouched my makeup so Lewis wouldn't think I was one of the undead coming for his brains and practically leaped into my jeans and new shirt, which, I saw at the last minute, had a small hole under the right armpit. There was no time to change again, because, right on cue, the doorbell rang.

"Hey," Lewis said with a smile. "You changed your hair."

"Uh, yeah." I ran a hand through it, pulling it back into a ponytail, wishing I could come down with an instant bout of flu. "It didn't go as planned."

"I think you look great. Are you hungry?"

"Starving," I said automatically, realizing I hadn't eaten all day. I was about to ask where he wanted to go, but my cell rang. I fished it from my bag, didn't recognize the local number. "Sorry, Lewis, do you mind if...?"

"Go right ahead," he said, heading for the door. "I'll step out."

After he pulled the door closed behind him, I put the phone to my ear. "Hello?"

"Hi, is that Eleanor Hardwicke?"

My entire body stiffened, my brain desperately trying to connect to my mouth because I knew exactly who was on the other end of the phone. "Yes, this is Eleanor."

"Great. I'm Victoria. Victoria Gallinger. You sent me a message about website designs?" As she waited for my response, I swear she must've heard the panic rising inside me. When I still couldn't speak, she continued, "Is now a good time?"

No. No, it absolutely isn't, was what I should've said. I'd practiced the sentence, or a variation thereof, a hundred times already. Now, faced with the option of having an actual conversation with my half sister, the person I'd speculated and played movies in my head about, convinced myself I hated, was too good to pass up.

"Uh, yes. Now's great," I said, my heart slowing as I told myself I was the one with all the knowledge, I was the one in control.

"Fantastic," Victoria said, her voice as friendly as a hug. "I love your designs, and your website's gorgeous. Your timing's impeccable, too."

"It is?"

"Yes. I'm in desperate need of a web designer." She laughed, a sound that made me smile, despite trying not to. "Yikes, I should've kept quiet. You'll double your prices now."

"I wouldn't do that," I said, flustered. Did she know I was broke? Had she figured out who I was? Seen footage from the restaurant? Worked out I was the thief?

"I'm kidding."

My heart rate slowed again. Of course she didn't know who I was or what I'd done. My photograph was on my website and LinkedIn. There was no way she'd be this friendly if she'd recognized me as the person who'd stolen her ring.

"Uh, so you liked my work?" I said, now the one sounding desperate.

"I really did. It's slick and beautifully laid out. I love how you made sure each site is completely different, too, not a copy-paste job. I find that's what some companies seem to do these days—roll out the same design except with different pictures."

"Each of my clients is unique. It's important their sites reflect that."

"Exactly." Her amplified smile practically beamed through the phone like a ray of sunshine. "Look, uh, this is a little delicate, not to mention confidential, but I'm not calling you about the website for the company I work for."

"Oh…?"

"Yes… I've decided I might want to go it alone."

"Congratulations," I said. "What a huge step."

"Honestly, I'm terrified," she whispered. "You have your own company, right? Please tell me the fear of failure goes away."

"Absolutely," I lied. "Best decision I ever made."

"I'm hoping to be like you in the future," she said with a sigh. "Running a successful business you built yourself must be incredibly rewarding. Maybe you can give me some tips?" She laughed again as I tried to digest the fact she'd said she wanted to be like me. Like *me*. "Anyway," she continued, "I'm not there yet, it's not even off the ground, so before I get ahead of myself, could we meet and talk about website options?"

"You want to *meet*?" I said, trying to contain my gasp.

"If it's okay? Face-to-face is so much better, don't you think? I'd love to have your input on the site. I've researched a few developers, but when I saw your stuff…"

This was it. Time to tell her I'd signed a new contract with another client—ten new clients—and couldn't possibly take on anything else. My brain compressed my throat, wrapping it with an invisible noose, trying to keep my next words in, but my heart won the battle raging inside. "I'd love to. When?"

"How about yesterday," she said with a laugh. "Or next week. Whenever you're free?"

I thought about my date with Lewis. As much as I'd wanted to spend the evening with him, what for? It would never go anywhere. "I'm free now," I said, hardly believing I'd spoken the words out loud.

"Really? I don't want to spoil your plans if—"

"No plans, it's fine. But if you can't—"

"Actually... I could meet now, for a little while, anyway. If you're sure?"

My mind screamed, No, no, *no*, but my mouth said, "Where would work for you?"

"You said you live in Portland?"

"Sherman Street."

"No way! You're really close to me. I'm on Newbury."

"Are you?" I said, my voice dangerously high. "What a co-incidence."

"There's a new coffee shop on Congress and Temple called Jake's Cakes. That's kind of in the middle. We could meet in, say, half an hour. It shouldn't be too busy on a Thursday night."

"Great. I'll see you then."

"Perfect. I'll find you, okay? I'm sure I'll recognize you."

Once we hung up, I opened my front door. Lewis leaned against the wall, hands in his pockets, his face breaking into a smile that almost had the power to change my mind.

"Everything okay?" he said.

"One of my clients is having a meltdown."

He nodded. "I'm guessing you need a rain check?"

"Yes, I'm really sorry."

"Don't be. You do what you need to do. My next couple of days are crazy but I'll text or stop by and we can decide on another date. How does that sound?"

"Great," I said. "That would be nice."

"Good night, Eleanor." He leaned in, his soft lips a gentle whisper brushing against my cheek. "And I meant it," he murmured, "you look beautiful."

A few days ago I would have died on the spot if he'd said those words. Now I couldn't wait for him to leave. Because in thirty minutes, I was officially going to meet my sister.

CHAPTER TWENTY-TWO

NO GOOD CAN COME of this.

I repeated the sentence—my new mantra—over and over after Lewis left. This was a bad idea, a terrible idea. I walked the length of the living room, back and forth, back and forth. Sweat poured down my back, transforming my badly dyed hair into a frizzy mess, and I felt incapable of stringing together a coherent thought, let alone a sentence. I wanted to go to the kitchen and grab a fistful of cookies or chips or cake—preferably all three—but told myself to calm down, it would be okay, everything would be fine.

If I was to go through with this "business" meeting, I had five minutes to change into one of my old office outfits. It wouldn't be difficult to choose between the few pairs of pants and couple of jackets and shirts—they were all dark, drab colors I'd picked because they allowed me to blend in, gave me the ability to hide—but bland or not, all of the clothes fit ten pounds ago. When I'd last tried them, the pants had pinched my thighs and dug into my hips, and the shirts had pulled across my chest, leaving open gaps between the buttons.

I'd stay dressed how I was. It didn't matter; this *wasn't* a business meeting. Once we met and my curiosity about my half sister was satisfied, I'd send her a note, tell her something had come up and I couldn't work with her. I grabbed a beanie and shoved my hair underneath, trying not to think about how much money it would cost to have the color fixed. For the next year while it grew out, I'd have to accept my ombré-gone-wrong look and invest in more hats.

All too quickly I ended up twenty yards from Jake's Cakes, palms sweating as much as the rest of me, the mantra about it all being a terrible idea still trundling around my head. I wanted to go home, but the image of Stan, the memory of how he'd ordered me to disappear into the night, wouldn't let me. Fuck him. What would his precious daughter and dutiful wife think when they learned their tight family unit wasn't so perfect, after all? What might happen if in fifteen minutes Victoria phoned Stan demanding to know the truth, if a woman called Eleanor Hardwicke was his illegitimate offspring? The choice to reveal the truth was mine. I held all the cards, no, the entire deck. Of course, doing so would mean I'd ruin my chances of ever being invited to become part of the Gallinger clan, but my illusions of that happening were long gone. Besides, I couldn't imagine forgiving Stan's betrayal.

I pulled open the door to Jake's Cakes and looked around. The place was trendy yet cozy, with open shelves, black-and-white handwritten chalkboards and a collection of tables and chairs. Two-feet-high bright red letters spelled out the coffee shop's name and hung above the reclaimed-timber counter standing next to a fridge stacked with multicolored frosted cakes.

There were a couple of people in the store. Two older women

sat deep in conversation over their giant mugs, their beverages piled high with whipped cream and sprinkles. A few students huddled together in another corner, by the sound of it discussing a science syllabus.

A table near the front seemed the safest bet to meet Victoria; away from everyone but close enough to the front doors to allow for a quick escape should the need arise. I ordered the cheapest decaf from the hipster-bearded barista, refusing the offer of treats. Once again I'd picked at little food all day, had enjoyed the sense of control it gave me when I had a handle on little else. As I yanked up my jeans that had slipped below my hip bone—a body part hidden underneath soft flesh for years—I wondered if I should've given my uninspired office outfits another chance.

My heart bounced around my rib cage as I took a seat and ran through my options, trying to decide if I should tell Victoria outright we were related, and if I did so, what she might say. I imagined an entire catalog of her expressions, settled on astonished disbelief, a reaction I'd anticipate with an extra helping of relish.

It felt good going into a situation knowing the advantage was mine, except, until then, I'd never thought of myself as a calculating person. I was a people pleaser, a good girl. I mostly kept to myself, followed the rules, never cheated or lied and paid my bills on time. I'd spent many nights at the office in my previous job, taking on more projects than I could reasonably handle, never having the courage to say no. Where had all of my goody-two-shoes behavior got me?

I drummed my fingertips on the table, looked at the time. Victoria had said to meet in thirty minutes. It had already been forty. What if she'd changed her mind? If she'd decided she couldn't be bothered, would I have the nerve to contact her again? Another minute passed. As I was about to discard the half-empty coffee cup and head home with a mix of relief and disappointment settling in my chest, the café door opened, and Victoria stepped inside.

If someone had asked me to describe my half sister in one word, I'd have said *glowing*. In her photos she looked perfect, but still they didn't do her justice. Awestruck, I took in her delicate nose, smooth skin and long hair, which fell around her face in an effortless "this is how I wake up every morning" look. Dressed in fitted black pants, high-heeled leather boots with silver buckles and a pine-green coat pulled in at her tiny waist, she could've come directly from a modeling shoot. As I looked at her, a nasty, vicious feeling bubbled up inside me. One I'd fought hard in my past. Something I still felt every time I set eyes on Amy. Sheer envy.

"Eleanor?" Victoria said, her voice as soft and pleasant as it had been on the phone. "I'm *so* sorry I'm late. Thank you for waiting." She held out her hand and I shook it, the skin of her slim, tan fingers velvety, her grip assertive and strong. My gaze dropped to her left hand, my belly fluttering when I saw the empty spot next to her wedding ring.

Guess where your precious diamonds are, I wanted to whisper.

"It's no trouble." My voice came out too high. I tried again. "And it's nice to meet you."

"Same." Her face broke into a smile as she put a hand on my arm. "I was so excited to get your message yesterday. Give me a few minutes to get a coffee. Can I get you anything? Another drink? A muffin or something?"

"No, thank you," I said, trying to stop myself from pulling away. "I'm good."

"Back in a second."

I watched the barista fall under Victoria's spell as she walked up to him, her hips swaying ever so slightly, her shampoo-commercial hair bouncing behind her. A blush lit up his face as she leaned in and said something that made him laugh. When I'd asked him for a coffee with cream and sugar, I'd received a friendly "Anything else, Miss?" in return. Nothing to complain about, but his entire demeanor changed during their short exchange. Another word to describe her was *enchanting. Bewitching. Fascinating.* No doubt people were unaware she'd ensnared them before it was too late, and she'd got what she wanted from them. *Not this time,* I thought. *Not with me.*

Victoria walked back to our table, the barista's gaze planted firmly on her ass. When he looked up, his eyes met mine, and he blushed harder still, grabbing a cloth to wipe the counter.

"Thanks again for waiting," she said as she sat down. "I was talking about a potential property and got so excited, I completely forgot the time."

"What kind of property?" I said, heart thumping. "Are you moving?"

"Oh, gosh, no, not at all, we only got to our new place a few months ago. This one is for work, for my own company." She leaned in, lowered her voice to a whisper. "I know we've just met, but I hope I can speak to you in confidence?"

"Of course." My chest tightened at the thought of us sharing a secret. "What happens at Jake's Cakes stays at Jake's Cakes."

"Who *is* Jake, anyway? The coffee guy's name tag said Phil." Victoria grinned, and I found myself doing so, too. "Anyway, after the call tonight, I'm a hundred steps closer to quitting my job."

"Wow. That must feel scary." Except it wasn't. Not when you had a wealthy family and a husband doubling up as your safety net so you could play at being entrepreneur. I highly doubted *she'd* been refused a small business loan, or that she'd even applied for one. Daddy darling's pockets were deep enough.

"It's terrifying," Victoria said. "I've never done anything like this before. I'm petrified."

"I completely understand. What line of business are you going into?"

"Same as now, interior design. I'm tired of working for

someone else, them calling all the shots, taking all the credit for my work." Her eyes flashed, telling me she didn't think highly of her boss. "Now that I'm ready to quit, I have to get the website figured out, stat. I need something edgy to make me stand out from the crowd."

She already knew she stood out from any crowd, but I wouldn't give her the satisfaction of saying so. Instead I sat, silent, waiting for her to continue.

"As I said on the phone, I loved the sites you did for those bars," she said. "What was the last one called? The Hub? It's fantastic. I was thinking…" She spent the next few minutes describing her company's vision, how she wanted to start out with upscale apartments and then get into new developments. "My father's in real estate, too," she said with a smile.

"How fortunate." I wanted to congratulate myself for keeping the acidity out of my tone.

"Yes, I know. I'm a fortunate, lucky, spoiled brat." Pulling a face, she added, "But I'm going to work my ass off. Show everyone I can do this."

"What's the name of your company?"

She shook her head, took a sip of her black coffee and dabbed the corners of her mouth with a napkin. "You'd think I'd have figured that out by now, what with the months of planning, but I still can't decide. I was trying to go all fancy, even mulled over using the Latin word for *interior*, but it's—"

"*Penitus,*" I said. "Or *penetralis.*"

Victoria stifled a giggle. "God, what am I, twelve?" She laughed again, and I joined in despite myself.

"Your last name's Gallinger." I made sure to keep my face steady. "You're not related to a Stanley Gallinger, by any chance, are you?"

Her face lit up even more as she put a hand to her chest. "Yes! He's my dad. Don't tell me you know him?"

"Only by reputation," I fake-gushed. "He's the living legend of Portland."

"Ha. I'll have to tell him you said so. He'll get a kick out of it, I'm sure."

"Please do." I leaned back in my chair, let those last words sit, wondering if she'd mention our encounter to him, if she'd refer to me by name, or simply as "a website designer."

As I studied her, it dawned on me if I told her who I was, right here, right now, it would be the end of it. Stan would demand she cut contact, and of course she'd bow to his orders. We'd never see each other again, robbing me of the chance to learn anything new about her. The more I looked at her, the more information I yearned for, the deeper I wanted to delve into her life. Now she was in front of me, my appetite to find out *everything* about my half sister felt insatiable—and maybe I could have a little bit of fun doing it.

"You could call your company Victoria Gallinger Designs," I said.

She shook her head and frowned. "Don't you think it's a little—"

"Pretentious?"

"How funny. That's exactly what I thought. You said so yourself, my father's a legend. Everyone will know who I am."

"Isn't that the point? I mean, why not capitalize on it?" I said, silently thinking—hoping—most people would see it for what it was, a spoiled princess using the family name to get ahead. "There's nothing wrong with that. It's not your fault you were born into such an *amazing* family. Use the leverage. I certainly would."

"Would you?"

"Yes. I have an idea for the logo, too."

She clapped her hands and leaned in. "Can you show me?"

I pulled out my notebook and flipped through the pages.

"Are those yours?" Victoria said, stopping me midflip. She

pointed at the sketch of a woman I'd drawn. She was naked, sitting on the floor with her knees pulled to her chest, her head buried in her hands. "Gosh, that's amazing. Did you go to art school?"

"Computer science."

"Seriously? And you can draw, too? She's so…melancholy. It makes me want to know exactly who she is and what she's thinking. Why is she so sad?"

I'd rather die than tell her it was supposed to have been a self-portrait, so I shrugged and hastily turned the pages until I got to a blank one, where I drew a circle, wrote *VG* in italics inside, adding the word *Designs* underneath, and shaded the letters to make them appear in relief. By the time I was done, it looked great.

"It's a rough idea," I said. "Obviously the finished product would be far better."

Victoria put a hand to her chest, touching the diamond-encrusted heart pendant nestled between her perfect round breasts. "It's what I've been looking for. You're amazing, Eleanor, really. How is it we barely know each other, yet you understand exactly what I want? You—"

The noise of her cell phone interrupted her, and she fished it out of her bag as I basked in the glory of her words. A delicious shiver ran up and down my spine. She *approved* of me.

"Hey, baby, is everything okay?" she said into the phone, her voice even softer, her smile dropping as she listened. "I'm with Eleanor… Yes, for the website…" She looked at me, mouthed, "Sorry," and frowned. "What? Oh, no. Really? Yes. Of course I'll come back… Yes. I'll pick some up right way. Be there in twenty. Okay. Bye."

"Is something wrong?" I said as she slid her phone back into her pocket.

"My husband's got a migraine and we've run out of pain pills.

I have to pick some up." She put on her jacket, her expression changing from excited to flustered in an instant.

"But the website—"

"I know, I know. There's still so much to discuss." She stopped wrapping her scarf around her neck and hesitated, glanced at her watch. "When can we meet again?"

"Well, uh…"

"How about the day after tomorrow, late afternoon if you're free?" She laughed. "Never mind, it'll be the weekend, and way too short notice for you, I'm sure. It's just that I'm overexcited now, but I expect you're too busy, so—"

"No," I said, jumping at the chance, seizing it with my entire being. "It's no problem."

Her face lit up again, the worry replaced by another effervescent smile. "Are you sure? We can put it off until next week. You must have other plans for a Saturday."

I pictured my empty apartment. "Nothing I can't rearrange."

"Really?"

"Yeah. Uh, my friends will understand."

"That's so kind of you," she said, a hand to her chest. "Would around five be okay? Do you want to come to our apartment? I've got tons of books and magazines. I can show you my favorite designs and styles. Maybe it'll help us for the website?"

"Definitely. I'd love to."

"Great. I'll send you the address. You can meet Hugh, too," she continued, almost babbling now. "He wants to meet the people I work with, you know, uh, so he can give me advice. And his ideas are fantastic. He's really smart. What do you think?"

"Yes," I said with a laugh, getting caught up in her enthusiasm. "Sounds great."

This time I wasn't lying or putting on a show, and my plans solidified as I looked at her lit-up face. I couldn't tell Victoria who I was, not now, in a rush over an empty coffee cup at Jake's

Cakes. She'd offered me the opportunity to get a glimpse of what was behind the luxurious curtain of her life.

Only a fool wouldn't take it.

CHAPTER TWENTY-THREE

INSTEAD OF GOING HOME after Victoria rushed off to tend to Hugh, I headed south on Union Street. Thanksgiving was almost upon us, Christmas coming soon after, and the Portland party brigade had already begun working their seasonal magic. Soon the place would be transformed into a winter wonderland with sparkling, multicolored trees, giant red-and-white candy canes and glittering garland. No corner, storefront or lamppost would be spared, no street could escape the festive makeover. Eager shoppers already hurried by, bags laden with gift-wrapped boxes. Even the crisp air had joined the party, filling itself with the scent of gingerbread.

My mind, which had skipped the overdrive stage, zooming straight into warp speed, felt as if it might explode. To escape all the hustle, bustle and razzle-dazzle, I pushed through the crowds, walked past the restaurants and went to the end of the wharf. It was marginally quieter there with fewer people, but still not enough to calm the mile-a-minute thoughts in my brain.

I'd expected my brazenness to have disappeared since I left Jake's Cakes, thought it would melt away like chocolate in the summer sun. Victoria had invited me to her apartment, I reminded myself, waiting for the tsunami of panic to hit. In under forty-eight hours, I'd get what I'd been wondering about all this time—a look into her life, the inside scoop. Not too long ago the prospect would've terrified me, left me tongue-tied and red-faced, ready to run. Now a calmness enveloped me, a thick stone shell keeping any nervousness in check.

I couldn't wait to get to her place. Couldn't wait to meet Hugh, either. I'd examined his face in the photos, already sketched them both in my book, although I'd torn the page out and left it in the kitchen. As for Victoria, well, if tonight was anything to go by, she thought we were on the fast track to becoming firm friends.

An image of Stan flitted through my brain, and I conjured his voice into my mind. I imagined his praise and congratulatory words of encouragement when Victoria told him about her new website designer, how she'd taken another step toward being an entrepreneur. Then I saw his face paling, falling, knew his pulse would quicken when she mentioned my name, when he understood I'd gone against his orders and found my way into their lives after all.

I smiled as I looked across the dark water. Playing a game when you were the only one who knew the rules—and made them up as you went along—felt exhilarating and intoxicating.

The wickedness I never knew I had inside me clambered from the bottom of my heart like a demon. Instead of pushing it away, I greeted it, let it crawl to my ear, tell me this wasn't a fairy-tale life where things worked out in the end. I had to take charge, and it wouldn't happen by letting people walk all over me, as I always had. It was time to come out of the shadows, reclaim all the ground I'd given up and rebuild my confidence that had been eroded like cliffs on a storm-battered beach.

Could it be that simple—deciding I wouldn't take any more crap from anyone? That from now on I'd go after whatever I desired, live life on my terms? I wanted to believe it; then again, this strange assertiveness—if that was indeed what it was—could shrivel up and die by sunrise. For that reason exactly, I decided I'd cling to it, revel and bathe in it, hope some of it would seep into my skin and latch onto my bones. If only for one night, I wanted to believe I was an invincible gladiator who could do anything, be anything. Be *someone*.

As I walked home, I pulled my hands out of my pockets and straightened my back, looked a few people in the eye as I passed them, smiling and saying hello, making them notice me. A few streets up, the crowds thinned out and I walked on alone. Three men stepped out of a bar a dozen yards ahead, laughing and hollering, pushing and shoving each other.

When they turned in my direction, my breathing became patchy, my pulse throbbing. The memories of the mugging were still all too fresh, the bruises and lump on my head barely healed. Walking around after dark on my own made me a target, and while I could've crossed the road, turned or zipped up a side street, I didn't. I *wouldn't*. Instead I pulled my shoulders back, refused to move off the sidewalk or bow my head, and raised my chin.

The men quieted, each of them stepping out of the way with a polite "hello" as I walked past, all of them unaware a river of sweat had seeped into the back of my jeans.

No more hiding, I told myself. No more being a doormat, no more complying with points of view I didn't share to avoid conflict. There would be no more.

Later I lay in bed whispering to myself that I shouldn't forget how powerful tonight had felt, and while my body succumbed to exhaustion, I begged the change deep within me to still be there come dawn.

Friday sped by, and on Saturday morning I was up by six, and bounded out of bed with energy I hadn't felt in weeks. I searched for a change of heart, any indication I might bolt in the opposite direction to the one my life had taken two nights ago. Although my stomach fluttered with the anticipation of seeing Victoria again, my hands held steady, my heart stayed still.

I'd hoped my subconscious would formulate a plan over the last two nights, complete with detailed strategy and a clear endgame. But the only thing I felt sure of was that I'd go to Victoria's, see how her life was up close before deciding my next move. Not having a clear plan made another shiver zip down my spine. Rebellion and impulsiveness was an addictive combination, although when I looked at the photograph of Dad, guilt and shame tried to take its place, and I pushed them away.

I spent the next hour in the bathroom, washing my hair another half a dozen times in an effort to get rid of the dye. The end result was a bleaker shade of brown—dull and lifeless as old leaves stuck to the ground after a late-winter storm. Having searched for online advice, I abandoned the idea of returning to the drugstore for a second kit. With my luck, I'd only make things worse. I pulled my hair into another ponytail. This would be the norm until I'd saved enough cash to get it taken care of. Maybe I'd ask Victoria which salon she went to and, in time, book an appointment there.

Although we'd never become twins—not even if her hairdresser, colorist and stylist all materialized into one ginormous fairy godmother—perhaps, just *maybe*, if I hung out with her a little longer, I'd continue to feel like less of a waste of space. It was undeniable. Being close to her on Thursday at Jake's Cakes felt as if I might have absorbed some of her power, and I wondered if she'd woken up with a little less.

I made myself a coffee, forgoing the cream and sugar—Victoria took hers black. My jeans sat a little farther down my hips and at this rate I'd have to invest in my first belt. When I'd looked in the mirror after I'd washed my hair, I'd noticed my face appeared less puffy, too—my missing-in-action cheekbones Penelope had discovered at the drugstore were making more of a comeback, and I wondered what Dad would say if he saw me.

Regardless of all the distractions, his death weighed heavily both on my mind and in my heart, whenever I let it, which seemed to be less and less often. Years of handling my mother's lack of affection had allowed me to develop a handy knack for compartmentalizing, and so I shoved my grief into a dark corner of my mind. I knew I'd have to take it out and deal with it at some point, but I also knew I wouldn't function if I constantly thought about Dad, or what he'd say about my recent actions, and I couldn't bear thinking about it.

I took another sip of coffee and glanced at my phone. Two missed calls. One from Amy just after two—she'd yet to care about the time difference between Maine and California—the other from my mother, an hour ago. With utmost satisfaction I swiped and deleted, sending their voices to the virtual garbage. I had no desire to listen to their messages, never mind speak to them. They could both go to hell, and take their pathetic plans to blackmail Stan with them.

I now knew for certain taking his cash wouldn't give me any kind of satisfaction—all he'd do was make more, maybe find a way to write the amount off as a tax break, calling it a "charitable contribution." But somehow I needed to counterbalance his act of pushing me away—twice—and the more I thought about it, the more my befriending his daughter would be the perfect slow-burn revenge. Knowing—at least believing—he'd not sleep well at night because he couldn't figure out what I was doing, or why, was a more tantalizing prospect by far.

When I was ready, when I'd ingratiated myself into her life, become friends, I'd tell her who I was and watch him hurt. He'd been so adamant about keeping my existence quiet, like my mother, terrified I'd tarnish his reputation. I smiled at the realization. Stan Gallinger, formidable businessman, Prince of Portland, was *scared*. I covered my mouth to keep the laughter in, before dropping my hand and letting the sound out, not caring who heard.

As much as I wanted to sit there and giggle all weekend, work had to get done, and so I went about checking my email for replies from all the prospects I'd contacted. One of them sounded promising. Stefanie Schneider, owner of a baby apparel store called Kind, wanted her site redone as quickly as possible. It was usually a good sign when someone said they were in a hurry.

"My budget is one thousand dollars maximum," Stefanie said a few minutes into the conversation, after informing me *kind* meant child in German, and describing the work she wanted done, which included updating her entire e-commerce backend and payment system.

I needed cash, and not long ago I would've agreed to her measly terms, worked day and night to get it done on time and to spec—but that no longer fit with my decision to stop people from taking advantage. Doing so would only eat into my time for finding proper paying customers, time I didn't have.

"My rate for the site you're looking for would be three times more," I said, my back stiffening.

"*Three* times?" Stefanie said, sounding as if I'd asked her for her firstborn *kind*. "I'm afraid that's not possible. It's far too much."

"I understand you might think so, but it's what my time and experience are worth."

She fell silent, no doubt hoping I'd change my mind if I talked first. Tough luck, I decided, she'd have a long wait. "Okay," she said at last. "Let me think about it."

"Sounds great. I'll touch base with you soon."

Around three, I decided to stop willing my empty inbox to fill itself with deals, and shut off my laptop. Lewis hadn't called or stopped by to rearrange our dinner but there was no time to dwell. I put on my new makeup, my first attempt making me look like a toddler who'd broken into her mother's bathroom. By the time I'd repaired the damage, it was already four thirty. I'd skipped lunch and my fridge was almost bare again, so I drank a glass of milk to stifle the grumbles, grabbed my things and headed downstairs, impressed by my self-control.

The feeling didn't last. I stopped at my mailbox, which I'd ignored for days, and unlocked it. Inside was a single white envelope with a logo I knew by heart. The hospital. I didn't dare open the letter and find out how much money I owed for my overnight stay, and now wished I hadn't been quite so bold in my negotiations with Stefanie. I plucked the envelope from the box and stuffed it into my bag, deciding to ignore it for the night and focus on where I was going or, more specifically, who I was meeting.

Once again, the anticipation of seeing Victoria, of being invited inside her home, made my hair stand on end. I kept imagining Dad's voice as I walked, asking me what I was doing, and a few times I almost turned around. My gut squeezed itself into a ball, churning the milk so hard, it must have become a lump of butter by the time I reached Victoria's apartment.

I stood outside the building, not yet ready to venture inside, so I pulled out my Nikon and snapped a few photos of the facade, focusing on the large windows, the patterns of the redbrick walls. When I saw Victoria by one of the windows, I stepped back into an alcove and took picture after picture, zooming in on her face, her hands. The sound of the shutter steadied my nerves, and when I felt ready, I smoothed down my jacket, ran my fingers through my hair before crossing the street. I pressed the buzzer to Victoria E. Gallinger and Hugh F. Watters's apartment, holding my breath.

She let me in, and I took the shiny, pumpkin-spice-aroma-filled elevator to the second floor.

Victoria stood in the open doorway, dressed in black leggings and a white button-down blouse that skimmed her miniscule waist and hips. Her long hair cascaded over her shoulders like a chocolate waterfall, and her eyes lit up with an infectious smile.

"Eleanor. Good to see you. Did you have trouble finding us?" As her smile broadened, I shook my head, unable to formulate a coherent response, because it felt as if my tongue had glued itself to the roof of my mouth. "Come in, come in." She gestured with a hand, ushering me inside. "Don't be shy. Make yourself right at home."

Stepping over the threshold was akin to crossing into another dimension. Victoria took me across the white marble floor, away from a long corridor off to the right, which I assumed led to the bedrooms and bathrooms, and into an open-plan living area. I almost gasped at the amount of space, the apartment's high ceilings the first indication of its size. The huge glass windows at the front spanned the entire length of the place, seeming even bigger than from the outside. Yet somehow they'd pulled off making an airy, industrial-looking space both cozy and glamorous. Splashes of color—turquoise sofa, mustard cushions, red carpet—dotted the room, and the timber truss table with a shiny white stone finish gave the apartment an urban yet earthy feel.

Blown-up photographs adorned the walls, including one of Victoria and Hugh's wedding day. I'd spotted the picture on social media, had studied their beaming faces gazing at one another. I'd thought it over-the-top when I'd first seen it, especially when I noticed it had received well over three hundred likes. Looking at it now, hung on their living room wall, it warmed a tiny piece of my heart, their happiness somehow burning away some of my envy.

"Thanks again for coming," Victoria said. "I hope your friends didn't mind?"

"My friends?"

"Yes. You said you'd have to rearrange things with them."

"Oh." The heat from being caught in a lie flooded my cheeks. "It's fine."

"Great, that's great. Can I get you anything? Are you hungry or thirsty?"

I shook my head. "No, I'm fine."

"Are you sure? I was going to have a glass of wine. Do you want one?" When I shook my head again, she leaned in and whispered, "Don't make me drink alone. I'll look like a sad loser."

I laughed and held up my hands. "I doubt that, but...okay, then."

"Excellent." Victoria went to the fridge in the huge designer kitchen, where she pulled out a bottle of white wine with a name I couldn't pronounce before retrieving two large glasses from a pantry bigger than my clothes closet. She set them on the island with a clink and filled them halfway, grabbed a remote, pressed a button, filling the air with the sound of soft jazz.

"Here you go," she said as she walked over and handed me a glass. "Cheers."

Within an hour, the website designs had been discussed, and the bottle of wine had all but disappeared. Victoria seemed completely sober, but my head spun to the point where I'd put off going to the bathroom for fear I'd collapse. Note to self: not eating all day and mixing milk with wine was not an experiment to be repeated.

"You're really going to take my project on?" Victoria said with a sigh, flopping back onto the cushions and folding her long legs beneath her. "You can fit it into your schedule?"

"Of course," I said, the excitement about having a proper contract again, the fact it was for my sister's business and the booze all making me feel giddy. "I can't wait to get started."

"And you're sure about the budget?" she said. "Five thousand doesn't seem much."

I bit my tongue so I didn't laugh. I'd doubled my usual quote for a site this simple. Clearly five grand was nothing to her. She probably spent more on clothes each month.

"I'm happy to give you a break on the price," I said.

"You're amazing," Victoria said. "I mean, I'll have to clear it with Hugh, but I'd imagine he'll be fine with it. He handles all of our personal finances and insurance and stuff. To be honest, I'd rather poke myself in the eye." She let out another long, contented sigh. "Gosh, I'm so happy you got in touch with me. I feel you've got my back, you know? And I'm so pleased to be working with a woman. I spoke with a couple of developer guys and they were so full of themselves."

"Trust me, I know the type."

"Right?" Victoria winked at me. "We sisters have to stick together."

As the front door opened, she missed my sharp intake of breath at her choice of words, and she jumped up as Hugh stepped inside.

He looked even better in person than he did in the photos; tall, slim, short brown hair and clean-shaven skin. He wore black jeans and a red polo shirt, a leather jacket slung casually over his arm. I knew he wasn't only an attractive man, but a smart one, too, had graduated summa cum laude from Harvard. No wonder they'd gravitated toward each other. They were the perfect power couple, the image of her parents.

"Hey, you. How was your day?" Hugh walked over to Victoria, slipped a hand around her waist before softly kissing her. Had I imagined it, or had she flinched ever so slightly when he'd touched her?

"I'm good." Victoria took a step back and bit her lip. "Uh, this is Eleanor."

He turned to me, his head tilted to one side. Closing the gap between us with a single step, he held out a hand, his grip businesslike. "Nice to meet you, Eleanor."

"Pleased to meet you, too, Mr. Watters," I said, enunciating every word.

"Yikes, call me Hugh, please. I'm not my father."

Victoria sat down, and when Hugh did, too, this time I was sure she moved her leg away a fraction of an inch when his knee touched hers. "We've been discussing the website," she said. "Eleanor's ideas are amazing. You should see her designs. I know you'll approve."

"Fantastic," Hugh said, looking at me. Were his eyes always so blue—bottomless, exotic pools, inviting you to jump in? "I take it the project's a go?"

"Yes," I said, unable to contain my excitement. "I'll start as soon as I get home."

"After I show you everything, Hugh," Victoria said quickly. "The budget, too."

"Oh, I'm not worried," he said with a frown as he looked at me. "Victoria's a formidable businesswoman. Never once has she made a bad decision."

"My husband's the sweetest," Victoria said, but her expression had shifted, lost some of its shine and luster. "Well, if there's anything else you need to discuss before we start, Eleanor, you have my cell. Call or text anytime, and I'll make myself available."

"All right." I got up, acknowledging my cue to leave, not wanting to outstay my welcome. Not when my plan was to come back, hopefully more than once. I'd been unable to make it to the bathroom because of the effects of the wine, and that had meant no opportunity to snoop through their cabinets or take a peek at the rest of the apartment. We hadn't talked about her family, either, or her upbringing. There was still so much I wanted to know about my half sister but it wouldn't be today. Either I'd find a way to come back, or we'd meet somewhere else. I'd tell her I needed to discuss the designs face-to-face again and wanted to go over the layout with her. She was paying me so much money, I could afford to drag the development out a little.

"Bye, Hugh," I said, holding out my hand.

"Nice to meet you." His fingers wrapped around mine, his touch warm and manly, and as he took a step closer, the scent of his citrusy aftershave filled the space between us. "I'll see you again soon."

As Victoria accompanied me to the front door, she glanced over her shoulder, absentmindedly tapping her taut thighs with her fingertips. "Thanks again."

"No problem," I said, not quite ready to leave. "I'll get a contract to you and get to work on the designs."

"Great," she said, her voice quiet, subdued, her enthusiasm all but gone. "Don't forget to include your bank details so we can organize the down payment once I've confirmed everything with Hugh."

"Fantastic. Thanks—" the door was already closing "—bye, Victoria."

As I walked home, I kept wondering why Hugh's presence had made her so on edge. She'd been jumpy when he'd phoned her at Jake's Cakes, too. Perhaps I was reading too much into it, but could things between them not be as picture-perfect as they seemed at first glance? While I'd never been one for gossip—I'd despised it when Amy had repeated rumors she'd known to be untruths, turning them into out-of-control wildfires she helped spread—I wanted to know what was going on in my half sister's marriage. If Hugh and Victoria had secrets, especially ones I could use to my advantage, I'd make it my business to find out.

And something told me all I needed to do was dig.

CHAPTER TWENTY-FOUR

BY NOON ON SUNDAY I'd already drafted the development agreement for Victoria and played around with concepts and layouts. The website would take no time at all to pull together at the rate I worked—a week and a half, two at most—so I relaxed as I went through color schemes and photos, templates and fonts.

My emotions jumped from one to the other—excitement, fear, guilt, disgust. Over the past couple of days, my head told me I either had to back out of the contract or tell Victoria who I was. The other side of me, the one I struggled more and more to control, snarled at the thought and told my head to shut the hell up. It whispered I should develop the website, riddle it with bugs and broken links, fixing them whenever Victoria found them, only to create others.

"Don't be stupid," I said, my voice breaking the silence. Victoria and Hugh were well connected throughout Portland, and beyond, so was Stan. If I did a shoddy job, the reputation I'd worked hard to build up would be ruined in an instant.

Maybe it would be better to call off the deal. It would be easy enough to conjure up a family emergency needing my attention, or I could pretend a larger project had been dumped in my lap. Maybe I didn't have to give her any explanation other than I'd changed my mind.

Then again, why not go ahead with the contract and do a perfect job? I needed the money. It meant I could get to know her—and messing with Stan's head was a huge bonus—but still, helping with Victoria's professional success felt counterintuitive. What she should be experiencing, no doubt for the first time in her life, was failure.

Feeling like I'd arrived in front of a crossroads without a GPS or even a torn and tatty map to guide me, I shook my head. Since Dad's death, being shoved aside and learning about Victoria's glitzy life, I could feel myself changing, becoming more bitter and resentful. They say some people can't help themselves from turning into their parents. Was that happening to me? Could I end up as twisted and scheming as my mother, when all this time I'd vowed I wouldn't?

I was still contemplating the terrifying thought when my phone rang. It was Kyle, who rarely called on a Sunday, always insisted it was a family day he spent with his husband and kids. I slid my finger across the screen, slowly put the phone to my ear.

"Hey, Kyle. How are you?"

"Not good. You're late again. The deadline was yesterday."

"Deadline? I—"

"I sent you the details on Thursday," he said, his tone like liquid nitrogen to my core.

I grabbed my laptop, my fingers furiously darting over the keyboard, scrolling through my inbox. There was nothing there, so I flipped to the spam folder, but still came up empty. As a last resort, I zipped through my deleted items. There it was, an unread email from Kyle.

How the hell had this happened? I was always diligent and professional, so terrified of giving people a reason to complain I made sure it never happened. I didn't recall seeing the message. I'd been so preoccupied, I must have hit Delete without paying attention. I was losing it.

"I'm sorry," I said, heart sinking. "I've no idea how, but I—"

"How quickly can—"

"Immediately." I scanned through his note, speed-reading his bullet-point requests. Ten changes in all, simple stuff a toddler could handle. "It won't take more than an hour and—"

"Fine."

I could have kissed him. "Thanks. This will never happen again. I promise."

"No, it won't." He paused, and although—or because—his voice softened, a hundred alarm bells went off in my head, a deafening metallic chorus. "Listen, Eleanor…this arrangement isn't working anymore."

"But, I—"

"Don't get me wrong, you've been great, but you're distracted—"

"I know, I won't—"

"I'm sorry," he said, and I could tell no amount of pleading would help. "I don't want to be a dick but I have businesses to run, and this situation has become untenable." He paused for a few seconds, during which I didn't know what to say. He was right, of course he was. I *had* been unreliable, I'd been useless. "I checked the contract," Kyle continued, "and while I believe I have grounds to terminate immediately, I'm not going to."

"Thank you," I whispered, closing my eyes and sinking onto my sofa in case my legs gave out. This was a nightmare. A total and utter nightmare.

"I'll pay your fee up until the end of the month," Kyle said.

"I'll send the contact details of the new development team leader later today. Please give her all the login details and passwords immediately. If you handle this properly and without incident, I'll consider providing a reference in the future."

"Thank you," I said, making sure I kept the bite out of my voice, determined to remain professional until the bitter end. "I'm sorry, Kyle."

"Me, too. Listen, we'll stay in touch. You never know how these things work out, okay?"

I hung up, gently put my phone on the table before pulling the hospital envelope I'd ignored from the depths of my bag. Heart pounding, I slipped a finger underneath the lip, tore it open and pulled out the paper. My mouth went dry when I saw the numbers, settling on the one at the bottom next to the words *balance due.*

Over five thousand dollars. Five grand I couldn't afford with the amount left in my bank account. I closed my eyes, knowing there was no more room for debate. If I wanted to eat and somehow hope to keep this mediocre roof over my head, I needed to take Victoria's contract, and I had to do a perfect job.

I spent the next few hours on Victoria's designs, laying out pages and searching for stock photographs as placeholders before we had our own. *We. Our* own. I was already thinking about us as a *team.* If Hugh was hesitant about giving me the project, I'd have to convince him with my mock-ups or persuade Victoria it was her decision, not his. She was the one I'd be working for, after all.

A thought crept into my mind, burrowing down deep. What if working together made Victoria want us to become *proper* friends? Besties. BFFs. The kind of women who called each other multiple times a week, had lunch and coffee, and went on mini vacations together.

I batted the ridiculous idea away. She was the exact opposite of me—which said something about the nurture-versus-nature argument. It was highly doubtful she'd want to stay in touch once I finished her project, even though she'd showed me more kindness and attention in a matter of hours than Amy—the sister who knew I existed but preferred to pretend I didn't—had done in years. Still, the idea kept creeping back into my gut and settling there, a cute, cuddly puppy I didn't have the heart to shoo away.

My phone rang as I was getting myself a glass of water. Victoria.

"Hello," I said.

"Eleanor, it's Victoria," she said quickly. "Is this a good time? Can we talk?"

"Uh, sure." My fragile confidence ebbed away. I knew that tone. It meant she'd changed her mind, the project was a nonstarter. I wasn't just up shit creek without a paddle, I'd fallen out of the boat. "Is everything okay?"

"Yes… Well, no, actually. Not really."

"It's okay," I mumbled. "I haven't started the development yet."

"Sorry, what?"

"I meant I haven't spent much time on it. If you've decided you don't want me to—"

"Wait, no, that's not it at all."

"Isn't it?" I said, my chest inflating as if I'd been thrown a life jacket.

"Are you kidding? I definitely want you to do the site—"

"But you've delayed the project? You have a different timeline or budget?"

Victoria laughed—warm, friendly—and I pictured her in her apartment, her hair loose, casually flowing over her shoulders. I could see her sitting on her turquoise sofa, one of the mustard pillows pushed up against her tummy, something I'd noticed we both did.

"Are you trying to talk me out of working with you?" she said. "Because you can't. That's a done deal, I'm afraid. So yes, I called to confirm we're going ahead with the project, but also because I'm hoping you can help Hugh."

"Hugh?"

"Yes. He works for Bell Hops Brewery. Have you heard of it?"

"Yeah, of course. Their stuff's good."

"Isn't it?" she said. "Hugh's one of the partners. He manages the purchasing and he's in charge of the IT department, too, although to be honest, I'm not quite sure why, considering he can be a bit of a Luddite at times, but please don't tell him I said so."

"Okay..."

Victoria's voice sped up as she veered into babble territory. "Anyway, this isn't official yet, so please keep this between us, but their web person has resigned. He got poached by another company and quit on the spot, no notice, nothing."

"Wow, how unprofessional."

"Right? Hugh's freaking out because they're in the middle of a project, and this guy—who he thought was a friend, by the way—has really screwed them over. I've never seen Hugh so stressed. But well, I immediately thought of you."

"You did?"

"I thought maybe you can help or know someone who can," Victoria said, her voice hopeful. "I don't understand any of the technical jargon or anything, but perhaps you two could have a conversation?" She hesitated before quietly adding, "Would you? *Please.*"

"All right," I said, my mind reeling with possibilities and implications. "When?"

"He's at the office right now doing damage control. I'll give you his details." She sighed deeply after rattling off the numbers, her voice slowing. "I know it's short notice again, and you can't make any promises. I can only imagine how busy you are with all your other clients—"

"Yeah, well—"

"—but hopefully you can help him out. I know he'd be incredibly grateful. We both would be. Thanks, Eleanor. I'll send him a text telling him to expect your call."

We hung up, and I sat there, my mind whirling. Could I go through with this? Speak to Hugh about a job, never mind accept it if offered? While neither he nor Victoria had any reason to suspect who I was, the risk of Stan telling them at any time was still very real. I'd lose both opportunities—which would be devastating from a financial perspective—and I'd lose my connection to Victoria. But if I could pull this off, design her site and help out Hugh, my résumé would get a badly needed boost and I'd get closer to her. Screw Stan, I decided and, with rabid butterflies flapping around inside me, dialed. Hugh picked up right away.

"Eleanor? Victoria said you'd call. Thanks for being so quick."

"Of course. She mentioned it was urgent. You're in a bit of a situation?"

"Christ, you could say that. My web guy text-quit this morning, didn't even have the decency to wait until Monday or do it face-to-face, the absolute… Well, I'd best keep those thoughts to myself." He forced a laugh.

"I'm sorry he's put you in such a difficult position. That's rough."

"Yeah, it is. Bell Hops is lean with its IT," Hugh said. "We outsource some, but not the website or systems maintenance. My other person, Genie, can handle the systems. She's great, but we're in the middle of redeveloping the site so it's a critical time of the project. She's not up to speed with that stuff, you know?"

"I understand," I said.

"Well, to put it mildly, I'm scrambling. We're launching a new beer soon, we've got a huge amount of promotion going on and the site's redevelopment is supposed to coincide." He paused, then exhaled with a groan. "It's a disaster. I have to find

a contractor right away and Victoria suggested we speak, so…
here I am. Basically, I'm begging for help."

"I'm flattered she mentioned me," I said, meaning every word.

"Are you kidding? She was so excited by your designs. She
hasn't stopped talking about them." Although his tone had hardly
changed, I thought I detected a hint of jealousy. "I'm glad you're
open to having this conversation, and I was hoping we could
meet. Today, if possible?"

"No problem. I could come to your office now?"

"Could you? Man, oh, man, I'd be incredibly grateful."

"Give me an hour," I said, trying to stop my voice from
trembling.

After Hugh gave me the company address I already knew and
directions I didn't need, I showered quickly, put on some of my
new foundation, blush, a sweep of eyeliner and mascara, before
observing myself in the mirror—without cringing.

Once in my bedroom, I pulled out one of two pairs of black
dress pants and crossed my fingers, hoping I'd be able to get
them past my thighs. I braced myself for the inevitable top-
button fight, but it didn't happen. Not only could I close the
pants with ease, but the waistband sat low, almost on my hips.
I went back to the bathroom, stood on my tiptoes and turned
sideways while taking another look in the mirror. I knew I'd lost
a little weight, and instead of rotund, I looked curvy, almost…
I shook my head. No, not sexy, definitely not, but…womanly.

My breasts fit my bra better, too, I noticed, and had stopped
spilling out the sides. Encouraged, I retrieved a cream-colored
blouse I'd stopped wearing because it had become too tight, and
slipped it on. When the fabric slid over my skin, settling com-
fortably around my chest, I grinned. I reached for my phone to
snap a picture to send to Dad with a funny caption before remembering he'd never see it. I scrunched my eyes shut, bracing
myself for the wave of grief to swallow me whole, the inevitable

flick of the switch to binge mode, making me run to the kitchen and shove a tablespoon into the peanut butter jar.

"*No,*" I whispered. "Stay in control. Stay in control."

Once my cravings had ebbed, I grabbed my bag with the sketchbook and Nikon as well as my long black woolen coat, the single item in my wardrobe I'd splurged on years ago. Boots on, I locked the door and went outside.

The bleak skies above did nothing to dampen my mood, and as I'd managed to blow-dry my hair into a reasonable style and didn't want the coastal winds or incessant humidity to get to it, I opted for a ride-share rather than walking. The driver—a man called Roberto with a face much too young to drive— arrived within minutes. I settled into the back of his Toyota and gave him the address.

"Business meeting?" he said cheerfully.

"How did you know?"

"Uh, because you look like you mean business."

I laughed. "Thanks, I think. I'll take that as a compliment."

As we drove to Bell Hops, I wondered if there was truth in the saying "clothes make a man" or, case in point, a woman. I felt better, more confident, despite where I was heading and what I was doing. It wasn't just because of how I was dressed, my new makeup or my hair. No. Shifts were happening inside me, too, a few seedlings of self-assurance digging their roots in deep, and I welcomed them.

"Good luck," Roberto said when we arrived. "Although, I don't think you'll need it."

I bounced out of the car and walked to the brewery's front door, where I sent Hugh a text announcing my arrival. As I waited for him to come get me, I vowed I *would* work at Bell Hops Brewery. I'd make myself indispensable, convince him my experience and knowledge were exactly what they needed, and I was the only person for the job.

Yes, before he'd unlocked the brewery's front door, casually dressed in a navy blue Diesel T-shirt and matching jeans, his hand outstretched and a charming smile on his face, I'd decided I'd make Hugh F. Watters offer me the role well before I left the building.

CHAPTER TWENTY-FIVE

HUGH DIDN'T EVEN ATTEMPT to put up a fight, and within fifteen minutes of arriving at Bell Hops, I knew the job was mine. "Can I be perfectly candid?" he said, and when he leaned in the V-neck of his shirt fell open, exposing a wisp of dark hair.

I forced myself to look at his face. "Of course."

"My ass is very much, if not completely, on the line here," he said. "I took on the management of the IT department because I was the most qualified, believe it or not, then convinced my partners to bring the web development in-house. You'd be doing me a huge favor if I can show them I contained this crisis in under twelve hours. Plus it'll stop Genie from freaking out. That last thing I want is to lose her, too."

"I'm really not sure I can, though," I said, not wanting to

show how badly I needed the contract. "You know, with my other clients and projects—"

"I'll add ten percent to your rate. Providing you start Tuesday."

My mouth dropped open. Up until then, I'd never had a daily rate. A monthly retainer from Kyle, sure, but one paling in comparison to what Hugh was offering. Despite his assertion, the job wouldn't be simple. The website was only a quarter done, their deadlines ambitious to say the least, and picking through somebody else's code could be as difficult as trying to understand long-forgotten hieroglyphics. Sometimes it was easier, not to mention quicker, to scrap it all and start from scratch.

"You can work remotely, too," Hugh said. "If it helps."

I imagined myself in my apartment, isolated and alone, with nobody to talk to or interact with. It no longer held the same appeal as it did a month ago. "Actually, I'm more than happy to come here. I can meet Genie and immerse myself in the company culture."

He beamed. "Are you saying I'll see you Tuesday morning?"

I hesitated again, giving myself pause to think about what I was doing, infiltrating Hugh's and Victoria's lives. It didn't take long for the thrill to sweep all the nagging whispers away. "Yes. I'll be here."

"Fantastic. Excellent. Thank you, Eleanor." Hugh sat back in his chair, looking as if he might collapse in a heap from relief. "Oh, before I forget—" he took a folded envelope out of the back pocket of his jeans "—here's the deposit check from Victoria."

A shadow crossed his face but disappeared all too quickly. Maybe a trick of the light? I did my best to hold his intense gaze, thinking if there was ever a triple-threat combination of good looks, sophistication and brains, my brother-in-law had lucked out.

Handsome, isn't he? the voice inside my head whispered, and I squashed it flat. Thinking about Hugh that way was a thousand miles too far, no matter how much I thought I'd unleashed my darker side. "Thank you," I said, "So, you were okay with the amount?"

A smile. "Uh-huh. We can't wait for your designs. It's great to see Victoria excited."

I could've sworn I heard him add, "For a change," under his breath but he got up, switching the subject to the weather as we walked to the front entrance, saying how he dreaded the winter and much preferred the cooler temperatures of spring and fall to the oppressive summer humidity.

"Genie will get all of your access and login details sorted out for Tuesday morning," he said when we got to the front door. "Again, thanks so much, Eleanor. You're a lifesaver. Actually, Victoria said you contacting her was serendipitous."

"She said that?"

"Yup, and I agree."

I left on a high, grabbed another ride-share, Victoria's check tucked safely away in my bag. As tempted as I was to ask the driver to take me to a hairstylist, I decided I'd first find out from Hugh or Victoria who hers was. When I did, I'd make an appointment and maybe I'd have my hair colored, streaked and highlighted like hers.

My next thought was whether Lewis would approve and I almost kicked myself. First of all, what did I care? And second, when had I ever pandered to a guy's preferences? Wasn't it exactly why at least two boyfriends had left me? Saying I was too cold, too distant—that I didn't care enough about them or what they thought? In their defense, they'd been right, I *hadn't* cared enough, but nor had I disintegrated into a blubbering mess when they'd said it was over.

When I got home, I discarded the thoughts of what Lewis's opinion of my hair might be, and changed into an old college sweatshirt and a pair of jeans I'd long abandoned hope of getting back into. As I sliced an apple, my phone buzzed with a new message from Lewis, and I wondered if I'd somehow set his ears on fire by thinking about him so much.

Sorry I haven't been around. Pipe burst @ studio. Major mess. Want to cash rain check? Free for dinner tonight?

From nowhere, images of me straddling him and running my fingertips over his chest charged into my mind like a stampede of wildebeests.

Your place or mine? I replied and, before I could stop myself, hit Send. Immediately all of my gutsiness performed a vanishing act worthy of its own headline show in Las Vegas. What the hell was I doing? I typed another message, fingers darting over the keys. Jk. What about Pump House on Wharf?

It didn't take long for his reply. Meet @ 7?

I sent a thumbs-up along with a smiley face and put my phone down, my mind racing off into la-la fantasyland about Lewis taking me out for dinner. If I didn't stop my daydreams, I'd let him become a distraction again, and there was no time.

I wanted to finalize the details for Victoria's site. Maybe take the designs and show them to Hugh on Tuesday, get his input before steering the conversation to Victoria, their history and secrets, although parts of me couldn't help reprimanding me for my snap judgments about them. Perhaps Victoria wasn't like Stan at all. Didn't I owe it to her to at least give her a chance? She was family, after all. She was my sister.

By five thirty I'd usually have stuffed my face with a bowl of predinner chips, but I hadn't bought any and settled for three glasses of water instead, reminding my gut I was in charge, and again it complied. It was nothing to cry victory about. I'd been here many times before, and it ended up with me overeating again and putting back on any weight I'd lost, something my mother habitually remarked upon. For now, I decided, I'd enjoy the longer win.

Showered, hair and makeup done, I swapped my college shirt for a purple V-neck sweater, added silver hoop earrings and a necklace with a camera-shaped pendant. Jacket, scarf and boots on, I checked my reflection in the mirror, surprised when I didn't roll my eyes and look away. Perhaps my face was finally growing on me a little, I thought, smiling at the pun.

My heart raced when I neared the restaurant, as it always did when faced with the prospect of speaking to people one-on-one outside of a work context where I couldn't make technical chit-chat. Unlike some, I fared better in crowds. They allowed for more space to hide.

The Pump House, a two-level, low-key eatery with a dessert menu that could induce diabetes from a single glance, was already three-quarters full. The smell of roasted garlic and fresh basil hit me full-on when I walked in, and the floorboards creaked beneath my feet as the host accompanied me to a table near the far left corner. He handed me a menu and offered a glass of water. I readily accepted, gulping half of it down before he turned his back.

I was ten minutes early, a habit I'd developed because it provided the opportunity to choose the seat facing outward, offering the chance to observe the room. The Pump House's tables stood close together, the one next to ours occupied by two women my age, whose clothes suggested dinner was a pregame before a night of fun at a club. As I took off my jacket, I listened to their conversation about which Chris was hotter, Evans or Pratt.

"It's Captain America," the one next to me said, wrapping a long strand of raven hair around her finger. "He can come save me from myself any day."

"Nuh-uh, it's definitely dinosaur dude," the other one answered, wagging a finger.

"What about Chris Hemsworth?" I said. "Don't forget him."

They turned and gave me a slow, deliberate once-over. "Excuse me, this is a *private* conversation," the woman next to me said, rolling her eyes at her friend.

"Oh, sure. Sorry. The tables are so close. I didn't mean…"

They'd already continued their conversation and I sank a little lower in my seat, grateful to see Lewis walking in through the front door. He lowered the hood of his coat, revealing a head of long, damp hair. He bent over to exchange a few words with the host and looked around.

"Forget them both," the girl next to me whispered to her friend. "Check out the guy who just walked in. Holy cow. Get me his number. *Stat.*"

Lewis spotted me, waved and walked over. He slipped off his coat, his sweater clinging to his shoulders, biceps and the vastness of his chest and I wanted to sigh from the pure pleasure of looking at him. "Hey," he said as he lowered himself into the chair across from me, resembling a beautiful golden giant. "You haven't been waiting long, have you?"

"Not at all," I said, only too conscious of the stares from the women sitting next to us, who had their mouths and eyes wide-open. "It's good to see you."

"You, too. Really good." He reached across the table and touched my arm.

The girl next to me choked on her drink, coughing and spluttering into her napkin. "Are you okay?" I asked, and when I spotted her mascara traveling down her cheeks in little black streams, I dug in my bag for a pack of tissues. "Here, have one of these."

"I'm good," she croaked, turning and arching an eyebrow at her friend.

I made myself refocus on Lewis, silently telling myself their presence didn't matter. Him sitting opposite me after asking me out to dinner did. "You've been busy then?"

"Oh, man, it's been nuts," he said, rubbing his chin. "But good nuts, mainly. My six-thirty slot at the gym was completely full so I opened another an hour earlier. Who knew so many people wanted to be bossed around at that time of the morning?"

"And the burst pipe? Was it bad?"

"Now, *that* was a complete nightmare. I managed to fix it. Got a friend who's a plumber to help. Had to repair the drywall and repaint, though, once it dried. It's all been keeping me out of trouble, plus I hired two new staff. Anyway, how about you? Did you get things sorted out with your client?"

"What? Oh…yes. Everything's great."

Our server came over, rattling off the specials. The shepherd's pie and peas sounded delicious, but it was one of Dad's favorites, and I didn't think I could bear it. Besides, I was on a budget, and as my appetite had all but disappeared, I settled for a side salad with Cajun chicken.

"That's it?" Lewis said after ordering a steak. "You sure? You'll waste away."

The woman next to me coughed again, and whether it had been directed at me or not, it still managed to liquefy my insides, stealing my confidence. I clung to it with both hands, scrambled to pull it back. I wouldn't let it go, I would *not*. This was the kind of passive-aggressive crap I'd dealt with from preschool right through to university. The kind of shit my sister and mother dumped on me. Years and years of utter *shit*. Snide remarks, backhanded compliments, accusing me of being overly sensitive the few times I'd called them out.

I shifted in my seat. All the water I'd drank had collected in my bladder, and I needed the bathroom, but as I was about to get up, the women next to us beat me to it. My initial plan was to wait until they came back, but I didn't think I could. I counted to ten and excused myself to Lewis, planning to sneak into a stall without the women knowing I was there. I quietly opened the bathroom door and immediately heard their chitchat.

"…the way she butted into our conversation. Like, seriously?" It was the voice of the one who'd been seated next to me. "And please say she's his sister or something, or I'm eating carbs and sugar again."

"Tell me about it." The other one laughed. "And what *is* she wearing?"

"Was there a sale at Walmart?"

"Like, maybe ten years ago?"

The cackling grew louder and I retreated out the door, cheeks burning. I'd never be seen as an equal by those types of women. They'd always, always hold the power to make me feel inadequate. My mother's voice floated into my head, *Oh, Nellie. If only you made an effort. Ate less. Moved more. It's not complicated.*

I slunk back to my seat, nodded when Lewis asked if I was okay, wondered why I'd agreed to meet him and what he saw in me. When I looked down, I noticed a roasted cherry tomato on the seat next to me. It must have rolled off a plate and landed there, neatly blending with the fabric's colors and disappearing in the dim light. I was about to reach out and remove it when the women returned and I pulled my hand away. *Fuck you*, I thought. *Fuck you both.*

They sat down and made a show of looking over the dessert menu before declaring they were "way too full" after a tiny salad and "couldn't possibly eat another thing" because they were going to boot camp the next morning. Their pointed looks garnered no attention from Lewis, who didn't glance their way. Mission abandoned, they paid their bill and stood up.

"Oh, my *God*," the one across from me declared as her friend took a step in front of her. "What's on your skirt?" Cue pandemonium, high-pitched voices and abundant hand flapping.

I tilted my head. "Oh, no. What a shame," I said loudly, and tomato girl's eyes met mine. "But you know what? I think I saw that exact skirt on sale at Walmart."

A look of confusion followed by the apparent realization of what I'd overheard spread across her face as if she'd contracted an instantaneous, vile and ugly rash. It suited her. She opened and closed her pouty lips a few times before grabbing the other woman's hand and marching out, her coat still under her arm, the stain on her skirt on prominent display.

"Jesus, talk about high-maintenance. Some people never leave high school, do they?" Lewis muttered and I wanted to leap over the table and hug him. Instead I said something about there being a long line before and bolted to the washroom, making it just in time.

"Come on then, tell me what's been going on with you," he said after I got back and the server brought our food. After taking a bite of steak and making appreciative noises, Lewis continued, "You sure you're okay? Your head's all better?"

"Yes, I'm fine," I said, picking at my chicken. "Thanks again for chasing the guy off."

"You don't need to thank me every time I see you." Lewis grinned but then his face turned somber. He put down his knife and reached for my hand. "What about, you know, with your dad and...*other* dad? Are you all right?"

I shrugged, trying not to move my hand for fear he'd let go. "It's hard. I try not to think about it, if I'm being honest. Work's keeping me busy. I've landed myself two contracts."

"Fantastic, congratulations. Who with, or is it top secret?"

I hesitated, remembered how understanding and encouraging he'd been the other night when I'd opened up about my family woes. "It's... Uh, it's for Victoria."

Lewis's eyebrows shot to the top of his head as he sat back. *"Gallinger?"*

I shifted in my seat, tugged at the neck of my sweater as sweat pooled under my arms, and I wished I'd worn something lighter. When had it become so hot in here? "Yes."

"That's amazing, Eleanor." Lewis reached over and touched my hand again. "I'm so pleased for you. Wow. Did you meet? Was it weird?"

"Yeah, it was, but she's—" I shrugged "—actually she's kind of nice."

"How badly did she freak out when you told her you're sisters?"

"Uh…"

Lewis's brow furrowed. "She knows, right?"

"There really wasn't a good time to bring it up," I said quickly, deciding to stretch the truth a little. "We met at a coffee shop and got talking about her website for a new business…"

"Yeah, I can see how that would sidetrack you. So, when do you think you'll tell her?"

"I don't know, I mean, probably when I'm finished with the contract…"

Lewis nodded, although I didn't think the gesture was necessarily an indication of his approval. "You said you've got two contracts?"

"Yeah, the other is with Bell Hops."

"The brewery? Their stuff's great. A couple of my clients work for them. Who did you deal with? Maybe I know them."

"Hugh Watters. He…he's Victoria's husband." I'm not sure why I told him. I think it was because I didn't want to lie to him again, but when I saw the look on his face, I wished I had.

"Hold on," Lewis said with a shake of his head. "You've taken a contract with your half sister and you're working for your… Well, I guess he's your brother-in-law, but they don't know you're related?"

Feeling as if I was being chastised like a naughty schoolkid at the principal's office, I sat a little straighter in my chair. "Yeah, well, when you put it that way it sounds a bit bizarre, but it's my business, isn't it? In every sense of the term."

"Well, yes, of course. But…I'm not sure you should—"

"Like I said, it's *my* business." I crossed my arms. I didn't want him judging me, telling me what I could or couldn't do. He barely knew me. What did he think? We'd shared some details from our past and now he had the right to criticize my choices, things which had nothing to do with him at all?

"I'm just concerned for you, that's all."

"You don't need to save me, I'm not your mom," I snapped.

"Whoa, that's not what this is about," Lewis said quietly.

"This has been great." I fumbled in my bag for my wallet and pulled out a few bills, my cheeks burning. "I have to go. I've got work to do, despite your disapproval."

"Eleanor, wait. I didn't mean it like that. I'll get dinner, and at least finish your—"

"I'll see you around, okay? Have a good night."

As I walked out of The Pump House, and despite knowing I'd been rude, I wondered if he'd come after me, ask me not to leave or at least offer to walk me home. When we got back to the apartment, he'd take my hand before asking—and he *would* ask, because he was a gentleman—if he could kiss me.

I kicked myself for the thought. I'd become a prickly human porcupine for a reason. I didn't need him. Didn't need *anyone*. For years I'd found people to be unkind, unreliable or downright indifferent, and it was far better being alone in the long run. Except this time, and as much as I tried to convince myself otherwise, one thing stood in the way of my believing it. Victoria.

CHAPTER TWENTY-SIX

WHEN I GOT HOME after deserting Lewis at The Pump House, I paced my apartment. Fifteen minutes later I heard him moving around upstairs, and fought the urge to go and apologize. In the cold light of my living room, I acknowledged I'd gone too far…although he had no right to judge my actions to begin with. He wasn't in my position, didn't know or appreciate all of my family history. But I'd given him details about my life. Therefore I'd invited his opinion, which is all he'd shared.

Ultimately I wondered if it mattered. The way I'd spoken to him, I'd be surprised if he'd even wave if we bumped into each other again.

I groaned and flopped on the sofa, wishing I could go back and not say anything about working for Victoria and Hugh, except it would've meant lying by omission, which was just as bad.

To stop arguing back and forth with myself, I focused on Victoria's designs. By the time I was happy enough to send them to her, it was well after midnight, so I shuffled off to bed, where I fell into a dreamless sleep, woken only once by an ambulance rushing past shortly after three. When my phone rang at nine thirty, I'd only been up a few minutes, had barely had time to switch the kettle on.

"Eleanor? It's Victoria." Her voice sounded eager, as if she were a six-year-old kid who'd woken up on Christmas morning to find Santa's entire bag of loot under the tree. "I'm so excited to talk to you about the designs you sent. You did them so quickly. I couldn't stop looking at them over breakfast. They're fantastic—"

"Thank you—"

"No, thank *you*. My favorite is the third one, the green-and-white layout with the pale gray? It's gorgeous. Seriously, Eleanor, you're so talented. I'd never have come up with anything close to this in a million years, and—" She stopped, sighed and said, "I'm babbling, aren't I? I always babble when I'm excited."

I laughed, her enthusiasm for my work infectious and welcome. "I'm glad you like it so much. Is there anything you'd want me to change? The font, or maybe the—"

"Oh, no. It's perfect. Wait until I show Hugh and my parents."

"Your parents?"

"Uh-huh, they'll be so impressed, especially my dad. You know…I bet I could convince him to let you do some of the designs to market their new properties, because—"

"Oh, no, I don't think he'd—"

"What? Go for a small company because his is huge? Wait until he sees what you do. He'll change his tune."

I wanted to beg her to not mention my name to him at all for fear he'd make her cut ties, but doing so would invite far too many questions. "I'm a bit swamped right now," I said, "and I wouldn't want to blow that opportunity. Thanks, though. Can I let you know when I'm ready?"

"Sure, whenever you want. And you're welcome. That's what friends are for."

The word *friends* bounced around my skull, filling it with joy, turning *me* into the kid at Christmas. "I owe you another thank-you," she continued, unaware of the loop-de-loops my emotions were flying inside me. "I can't tell you how glad I am things worked out with Hugh. He's so happy." The relief in her voice felt thick, rich and luscious enough to cut with a knife and serve on a plate.

"Like you said, that's what friends are for," I said, a slight wobble in my voice.

"Exactly right. So, tell me, what are you doing today? It'd better be something good considering it's your last day of freedom before Hugh buries you in work for all eternity."

"Oh, not much. I haven't really thought about it. How about you?"

"I have the day off. I was supposed to go to the spa with my cousin Charlotte. We had this whole thing planned, but she can't make it."

"That's too bad," I said, remembering the conversation I'd overheard in the bathroom at Le Médaillon and wondering if Charlotte's husband's affair had anything to do with her backing out. Maybe Madeleine or Victoria had decided to tell her about his indiscretions, after all.

"Honestly, I feel terrible, seeing as it's all my fault…"

"Your fault?" I said, my attention snapping back to her.

"Yeah." She sighed. "I convinced her to go roller-skating yesterday. We used to go all the time when we were kids, but it seems our muscle memory wasn't as good as we'd hoped, well, not mine at least. Long story short, I lost my balance, and when I stupidly grabbed hold of her to steady myself, she went down, too."

"Oh, no. Is she hurt?"

"She chipped a bone on her ankle and has to wear this boot thing for a few weeks. She says she's not in much pain, but it could be the drugs talking. I feel awful. I'm trying to think of a thousand ways to make it up to her. I've sent flowers and chocolates and a dozen bottles of her favorite wine, but it doesn't seem enough, you know?"

"Accidents happen, though, it wasn't your fault," I said, and as automatic as the words might have been leaving my mouth, I meant them. "I bet she feels the same."

"You're incredibly sweet," she said brightly. "Well, thanks again for the designs. I'd better leave you to your day. Unless…" She laughed. "No, that's silly."

"What is?"

"Well…what if we went to the spa together? Unless you think it's weird?"

"Uh, well, I—"

"We could chat more about the business. I'd love to have your input and ideas on marketing and promotion, you know, things you've done, and—"

"But what about your cousin? I mean, won't she mind?" I said, my heart thumping, bounding around my chest as if my rib cage were a xylophone.

"Not at all," Victoria said. "She's already made me promise to take her as soon as she feels up to it again. Actually, I'll organize a pampering weekend in Vermont as a surprise. Anyway, I thought about canceling today's reservation as it's for two people, but we could… No, I'm sorry. Of course you don't want to. See? I'm full of stupid ideas. I'll—"

"Yes, I mean, no, I mean—" I made myself slow down. "I'd love to go with you."

"You would? Are you sure? I don't want to make you uncomfortable or anything. But we could have a facial and a mani-pedi. What do you think?"

No clue how much all of this would cost, but as long as I

didn't have to get naked in front of anyone, especially Victoria, I didn't care. The prospect of spending more time with her, and so soon, was too exciting. "Perfect. Tell me where to meet you."

CHAPTER TWENTY-SEVEN

FOUR HOURS LATER I'D been primped, pruned and plucked within an inch of my life. Victoria and I sat at the spa's on-site café, eating quinoa energy bowls and drinking an odd-looking green juice my brain knew was stuffed with spinach and kale, but my taste buds insisted was strawberries. I'd never had a juice so satisfying or, at twelve bucks a glass, so expensive.

"Thanks for coming with me, Eleanor, I really needed a day to unwind," Victoria said, wrapping herself more tightly in her plush pink bathrobe. They were so thick, I'd almost melted into mine as if it were a marshmallow, reveling in its warmth and luxury, a contrast to my threadbare one at home, which sandpapered my skin if I rubbed too hard.

"I'm still not happy about you paying for it all," I said with a shake of my head.

Victoria shook hers more emphatically. "Not at all. I invited you."

It had felt strange, at first, walking into the spa. All of the beauticians wore spotless white uniforms, which I couldn't fathom how they kept clean, and talked quietly, barely making a sound as they drifted across the white tile floor. Instrumental panpipe music played so softly it made me want to put my head down on the reception desk and go to sleep with the gentle aroma of eucalyptus wafting up my nose.

"I've never been to a spa before," I'd whispered to Victoria as the receptionist finalized our reservation and went to fetch our robes.

"You mean this one?" Victoria said.

"No," I answered, my cheeks flushing. "I mean any spa. I've only been to the nail salon down the street, and I think that was about three years ago."

"Seriously?" She looked at me, and I could tell from her expression she wasn't sure if I meant it or was making some kind of pointless joke. "You've never…" When I shook my head again, she turned to the receptionist, who'd walked back in, grinned widely and said, "Could we upgrade to the half-day package, please? For the both of us, and lunch, too?"

Panicking, I put my hand on Victoria's arm. "Oh, no. I can't afford—"

"And everything's on my bill," she continued, smoothly sliding her card across the desk.

I'd protested, but Victoria fobbed me off, insisting it was her idea, therefore it should be her treat. Looking at her now, I couldn't believe her generosity. A few days ago I'd have grumbled about her flashing her wealth around, but that wasn't her angle. It was kindness.

She let out a languid sigh and took another sip of green juice before pulling a face. "Sorry again for walking in on you in the changing room. I thought you were ready."

More heat shot to my cheeks as I remembered standing in front of her, a hand over my naked breasts, her mouth in an O of surprise. "Uh, it's okay. Don't worry about it."

She winked at me. "Cute underwear, though. Where did you get it?"

I couldn't stop myself from giggling, my embarrassment melting away. "Gosh, I can't remember. Most of my underwear is the same. I've got a thing for polka dots."

"Really?"

"Yeah, I've got—" I counted on my fingers "—gloves, pajamas, a scarf, an umbrella, mugs and plates. It's ridiculous."

"Okay, spill. What's with the spotty obsession?"

"Apparently it started when I got the chicken pox as a kid, would you believe? I watched *101 Dalmatians* on a loop with… with my dad, and we counted my spots over and over. After they faded, I was so sad we drew them on with a pen. I've had a thing for polka dots ever since."

"How sweet. And your dad sounds fun." She must have seen my face fall. "What's wrong? Eleanor, are you okay?"

"He passed away," I said quietly. "Cancer. Nearly three weeks ago."

"I'm so sorry," she whispered. "You poor thing."

"It's been awful. And I didn't even get a chance to say goodbye. I got mugged on the way home that night and ended up in the hospital."

"*What?*"

"This guy came up from behind me, punched me like this—" I demonstrated with my hands "—and he hit my head on the ground. I didn't even have any cash on me. I'd forgotten my bag at my dad's hospice."

"I can't believe it. Thank goodness he didn't do more damage, and I'm so sorry about your dad. Do you still have your mom? Does she live in the area?"

"We don't get along or speak anymore."

"Oh, Eleanor." Victoria leaned across the table and put her hand on mine. "That must be so hard. I can't imagine losing my dad and not talking to my mom. She's always been my rock. Do you have any siblings? A brother or sister you can confide in?"

Two virtual paths leading in different directions appeared in front of me, one labeled Truth, the other Lies. I wanted to pick the former, I really did, but if I told her who I was, I risked losing my contract with her, and the job with Hugh, and I needed the money. Except it was by far the prospect of losing Victoria now that terrified me the most. She'd learn I'd betrayed her trust, and our budding friendship wasn't solid enough to withstand my disloyalty. Up until that point, I hadn't realized how much I, well, *cared*.

I expelled the air from my lungs in an emphatic whoosh before answering, "A sister in LA. She's an actor."

"Is she? How exciting."

"She's keeps saying her big break's around the corner. Maybe it'll happen."

Victoria looked at me, took a sip of her drink. "You don't approve of her career choice?"

I shook my head. "It's not about her job. We've never been close, either. We have nothing in common and barely speak."

"Well, you know what they say," Victoria tutted. "You can't choose your family."

I looked at her, almost opened my mouth to tell her she was wrong, I could choose, in this very moment. Instead, I was going to ask how it was growing up as an only child, remembering just in time I wasn't supposed to know anything about her, not officially, anyway.

"Do you have siblings?" I said.

"No," she said before looking down in her lap. "I always wished for a sister, someone to share secrets with or lament about my parents to. Although there wasn't anything to lament about, to be honest. My childhood was great and I've led an überspoiled life. I know how firmly I'm sitting in the white privilege, rich brat camp."

"Well, I wouldn't—"

She waved a hand. "It's okay. I'm well aware of the bucket of luck I was handed at birth. The point is to do something good with it all, right? To make it meaningful and help those less fortunate without coming across as an insensitive, snotty bitch."

"You definitely don't," I said, hoping the reason she'd invited me to the spa wasn't because she saw me as a pro bono project. I didn't ask in case she said yes.

"Thank you, I really appreciate you saying that." She glanced at her phone. I noticed she did so a lot, not in an I-must-check-social-media-all-day way, but with a worrying look crossing her face every time.

"Hugh's going to let me know if he's working late tonight," she said when she caught me staring at her. "I'm usually home when he gets back. He hates walking into an empty house and... Oh, would you listen to me? I'm not a fifties housewife." She put her head back and laughed but it was a smidgen too hard, too loud, more than enough to make me wonder once more whether something was off between them.

When I looked at her again, her eyes had gone shiny, so I leaned forward and lowered my voice. "Hey, is everything okay?"

She looked at me and blinked, and at first I thought she was going to tell me everything was fine but instead she bit her lower lip, her eyes now brimming with tears. "We're, uh, having a bit of a tough time. We...we've been trying for a baby. It's not going well."

"Oh, I'm sorry." I shifted in my seat, not quite sure how to handle such an intimate confession. "Uh, have you been trying long?"

"Long enough. Since we got married. Call me naive, but I thought it would happen right away, because it did for my friends. God, if I hear 'we weren't even trying' one more time, I think I'll scream."

"These things can take time, though, right?"

"Yes, they can," she said. "But it's been a while and both of us had tests done, which indicated some issues, and I...I miscarried in February."

"I'm so sorry,"

Victoria nodded. "Thanks. I was only a few weeks along, the doctor said, but it didn't make it any easier." She tried a smile but it turned into a lopsided grimace. "I found out the day before, but for those twenty-four hours, I was so happy. Finally, *finally* I'd have a baby, the one thing I knew would...I don't know, make things *better*." She closed her eyes and exhaled, her breath coming out in a shaky stream.

"What did Hugh say when—"

Her eyes flew open. "I never told him."

"Why?"

"Because...because I felt so useless and I couldn't stand him thinking I'm not the perfect wife." Her eyes went wide as she pressed a hand to her chest. "Oh, my God. I'm sorry, I'm way out of line. He's your boss now, and—"

"You're my friend," I said quickly, surprising myself with the statement. "Right now I'd say that's more important."

"You're so lovely, Eleanor," she said, looking less flustered. "Honestly, I'm at the point where I'm wondering if the whole baby thing will happen for me at all. It's also why I'm starting my own business, it'll give my mind something else to focus on. Hugh thinks I'm crazy. He says I'll launch the company, get pregnant and then be more stressed than I am now."

"It's not up to him, though, is it?" It came out with more indignation than I'd intended. "I mean, you said it yourself, it's not the fifties. It's your career. You can do what you want."

"He worries about me, is all. He loves me."

I wasn't convinced. The way she looked down when she said

his name, how she wanted to be at home when he got back from work, how he'd called when we were at Jake's Cakes, claiming to have a headache. I knew how a control freak could be, I'd been raised by one. I looked at her, thinking it was odd, being this close—hearing her speak, picking up on her body language—kind of like examining an antique porcelain vase. From afar it looked perfect, but as you got closer, the hairline cracks became visible, the paint a little more faded. Except it didn't take away any of Victoria's beauty; in fact, it added to it, it made her human.

"He's so busy at work, too," she said. "You'll probably see him more than me. No wonder I'm not getting pregnant." She let out a laugh and covered her mouth with a hand. "Oh, crap. *Please* don't tell him I was that crass, or that we talked about any of this at all—"

"Of course not."

"Here I am, complaining about my life when he's had it so much harder..." She sighed, must have decided she owed me more of an explanation. "I'm not his first wife, you see. He was married before, but...she passed away."

I felt my eyes go wide, and this time I didn't need to pretend. I hadn't seen anything about Hugh's first wife online; then again I'd focused almost a hundred percent of my spying mission on Victoria's life, not his. "Oh, my God, that's awful."

"It was terrible."

"Can I ask what happened? Was she sick? She must've been so young."

Victoria shook her head, whispered, "Natalie died in a fire at their home."

"Jesus, that's horrific."

"Truly, truly awful. A group of us were out that night—"

"You knew her, too?"

"Oh, yes, she was my cousin Charlotte's best friend and..." She stopped talking and pulled a face. "I'm sorry. I really shouldn't have brought it up. It's not my story to share and I don't think Hugh would want me to."

"It's okay, I understand." There it was again. The evasiveness, the subtle anxiety.

She smiled. "Thank you. Let's lighten the mood, shall we? Why don't you tell me about your love life instead? What's going on in the dating world these days? I'm out of touch."

I let out a half snort. "There's a conversation that'll take five seconds."

"Oh, come on. There must be someone special in your life."

I thought about Lewis and shook my head. "Never going to happen, I'm afraid."

"Is he hot?" she said, waggling her eyebrows.

"Sun temperature." I looked at her and we burst out laughing in our apparent shared relief to have moved on to brighter topics. "Honestly, he's so perfect, we're a million light-years apart." I laughed again until I noticed she'd cocked her head to one side and tapped her lip with a finger.

"Why are you looking at me all strange?" I said, sinking into my seat.

"First of all, don't sell yourself short about the kind of men interested in you," Victoria said. "And second, I hope you don't mind my asking, but that's not your natural hair color is it?"

"Uh, no." I ran a hand through my mop, smoothed it back. "Home dye-kit disaster. I'll have it redone properly at some point."

"I know a great stylist." A sly smile spread across her face. "Rocco owes me a few favors since I introduced him to a local celebrity who shall remain unnamed. His Instagram following went bananas and he had to expand the salon. I'll call him, if you're game."

"What, now?"

"No time like the present," she said with another mischievous grin.

I got the odd sense she was more excited than me as she pulled out her phone and dialed. She spoke in what had to be almost immaculate Italian, and I managed to pick up the *sì, va bene* and *grazie* I'd heard in movies.

"You know Italian?" I said when she hung up.

She gave me a slow wink. "Two summers of misspent youth with a *very* keen Venetian boyfriend. But never mind him." She grabbed my hand and jumped up. "We'd better get going. Rocco can fit you in now."

CHAPTER TWENTY-EIGHT

ROCCO'S SALON FELT PALATIAL, the kind of place I'd hurried past, too terrified to look in the windows. Elaborate lighting, a gleaming oversize espresso machine churning out one delicious-smelling frothy drink after the other, and busy stylists who might have belonged on Rodeo Drive or in Milan. I sat in the chair, my thighs and torso covered by the silky black-and-silver gown, drab hair flopping around my shoulders. Rocco stood to my left, Victoria to my right, both of them examining me as if I were a specimen under a microscope.

"*Sì, sì.*" Rocco tutted as he ran his fingers through my hair, bunching it up a little at my nape. "Yes, we definitely have to go back to blond, and I will cut the layers, too. It will give more volume, *d'accordo*?"

"Sure...?" I said.

"I can tell you have wonderful curls," Rocco said. "Why do you hide them?"

"They frizz. Whenever the humidity gets to them, I look like a sheep."

"A sheep?"

"*Pecora,*" Victoria said and Rocco laughed.

"Not anymore, *mia cara*," he said with a knowing smile. "I will show you what to do."

Victoria put a hand on my shoulder. "Rocco's an absolute genius."

For the next few hours I let him and his bubbly assistant buzz around me, talking shades and cuts, bangs or no bangs, texture and length. Color was stripped away and added back. My hair washed and conditioned, scrunched with a paper towel before I was plopped under a heat lamp. I sat, mesmerized, watching my locks change into delicate ringlets. Victoria hovered in the background, chatting with Rocco and the stylists, sipping cappuccinos and reassuring me how much of a difference the color already made, how it had lifted my face.

"Perfect," Rocco said when he removed the lamp. "Time for the cut."

"You're going to cut my hair *dry?*" I said, eyebrows raised.

"Ah, tell me, you do not walk around with wet hair, do you?" Rocco laughed, picking up his scissors to continue his quest. "We cut it dry to see how each curl falls, then wet it and style."

Another hour later and he'd demonstrated how to add volume by lifting the wet roots with clips and showed me the proper use of a diffuser. He took a step back to inspect his work, made a few adjusting snips before holding up a mirror behind me.

My mouth fell open. Not only were the gloomy mud-colored strands gone, replaced by a rich strawberry blond, but my hair bounced in gentle curls, grazing the back of my neck. It looked far shorter now than when it was straight, but the person in the mirror appeared younger. Happier.

"Are you sure that's me?" I whispered. "Am I dreaming?"

"You look *incredible*," Victoria said, as she walked up behind us. "What a difference. God, I'd murder for those curls, let me tell you. They're stunning, absolutely stunning."

"*Bellissima,*" Rocco declared, beaming. "Beautiful."

I bit my lip, tried not to cry as I looked at myself. "Thank you. Thank you so much."

"You are most welcome," Rocco said. "And call me or come in if you have any styling questions, okay? Victoria's friend is my friend."

I paid the bill, trying hard not to visibly recoil at the amount despite the twenty-five-percent discount Rocco generously applied. A week ago I'd have scoffed at the self-indulgence, reminded myself looks weren't everything, or *anything*. But the way I felt walking out of Rocco's salon—confidence buoying each step—was as alien as it was undeniable. Could a new haircut make such a difference? Or was it simply the effect of being around Victoria?

"Thanks for a lovely day." She sighed, turning to me. "I'm so glad you said yes."

"Me, too. I mean…my *hair*. I can't believe it. Rocco really is a genius."

"He is. You look amazing." She smiled, her emerald eyes sparkling. "But, well, what I meant was I really enjoyed your company, too."

"Oh." I looked at her, a warm feeling prickling my belly. "I enjoyed yours. Very much."

"Isn't it strange how we've only know each other for a few days but it feels as if it's been forever? This might sound weird but I don't think I've felt this kind of connection with a friend so fast, and—" she tucked a lock of hair behind her ear "—oh, no. Oh, *shit!*"

"What's wrong?"

"I've lost my earring." She felt around her collar, shook out her jacket and looked at the ground. "Maybe I dropped it inside. Back in a sec." She dashed into the salon, but returned empty-handed, her head bent. "It's not there."

"Maybe at the spa?" I said.

"Of *course*. You're so smart. I'll go now. Hugh gave them to me for my birthday and if I don't find it, he'll be so—" her eyes darted around "—*disappointed*."

"But it's just an earring."

"It's not *just* the earring, though," she said, giving an almost imperceptible shudder. "I lost my engagement ring a couple of weeks ago, too."

"Oh, gosh," I said, forcing myself not to break her gaze. "That's…horrible."

"I'm such an idiot, always losing things and breaking stuff. A real Calamity Jane." She gave a tight smile. "Hugh was furious when I came back without the ring, and now this, too? I have to go. I'll call you soon, okay? Thanks again for today."

She fled before I could answer, practically jogged down the sidewalk in the direction of the spa. A part of me wanted to run after her, blurt out I knew where her ring was—snugly wrapped up in a tissue and stuffed away in my bedside table—but I couldn't bring myself to do it. Not because I was a wicked half sister who still wanted to rub my hands with glee and make Victoria's life a little less perfect. That desire had been replaced by more compassion and empathy today, and there was no longer a hint of envy or disdain.

I tried reminding myself I was supposed to be jealous of her, angry she had everything I'd ever wanted, but it wouldn't stick. I *liked* Victoria, and she was right about the connection, I felt it, too; it was as if we'd known each other for years. What the hell was I going to do about the ring, though? And when?

Back at my building, I tiptoed past Mrs. Winchester's door although I needn't have bothered because she had *American Ninja Warrior* on full blast, and closed my apartment door behind me.

Once I'd prepared a small green salad and some grilled chicken with lemon, I settled down at the kitchen table, planned on researching Hugh's first wife, Natalie. As soon as I opened up the browser on my laptop, there was a soft knock on the door.

"Eleanor?" Lewis's voice floated toward me. "Are you home?"

I hesitated, heard another knock, decided my apology was still outstanding. When I opened the door and saw Lewis standing there in jeans and a black shirt, with a jacket slung over his shoulder, I tried not to stare. God, he was a beautiful, beautiful man. So handsome, it almost hurt to look at him.

"Wow." He raised his eyebrows as his gaze swept over my curls. "You're gorgeous."

I don't know what did it. My need to distract myself from the ring and the shift in my allegiances to Victoria, the new haircut bolstering my confidence or that Lewis was the first man to call me gorgeous and sound like he meant it. Maybe it was a mixture of it all. Whatever the reason, I grabbed his hand, pulled him inside my apartment and pushed the front door closed.

Without saying a word, my hands went over his arms, gliding across the bulk of his muscles, the breadth of his shoulders, finally coming to rest around his neck. His gaze didn't waver, his eyes stayed on mine as I stood on my tiptoes, my lips nearing his. When they touched, I felt his warm breath, tasted the mix of mint and coffee on his tongue. Within a moment I was lost in an embrace so intense, I felt my legs give out from underneath me. So much time had passed since I'd let a man touch me—since I'd felt the need to be touched—but I wanted to feel Lewis with every square inch of me. My body ached, yearned for his weight to be on top of me, for him to be inside me, for us to become one.

"Are you sure about this?" he whispered as I pulled his shirt over his head, taking in the smooth skin and acute definition of his abs.

I silently took his hand again and led him to my room, where we sank onto the bed. He undressed me slowly, one piece of clothing at a time, running his hands over my thighs, my stomach—the parts of me I'd always detested, but didn't want him to stop touching. He kissed and stroked, gently murmured as his lips slid over my skin, his fingers teasing, caressing, playing.

I didn't want to wait any longer. Pulling him to me, I moaned softly when he finally slid inside, and wrapped my legs around his, urging him deeper still.

Maybe this was a mistake, something I'd regret come morning, but I didn't care. Right then, the beautiful Lewis Farrier was who I wanted, what I needed, more than anything. For whatever short time it would turn out to be, Lewis was mine.

CHAPTER TWENTY-NINE

THE BEDROOM WAS STILL dark when I opened my eyes. As the remnants of sleep slowly dissolved around me and my senses returned one by one, I froze. I could hear slow breaths that weren't mine. Someone was in my room. Lying next to me. My heart sped up and I almost jumped out of bed until my brain kicked in, recalling the events of the night before. I let out a small sigh of ecstasy-filled relief as I remembered Lewis's hands on my body, my nails digging into his back as I pulled him closer, searched for his lips with mine.

We'd made love again, less urgently than the first time, and he'd kissed my neck, lingered on my breasts, taken his time as his mouth traveled over my middle. I'd gasped when his head settled between my legs, arched my back as he ever so gently, ever so deliciously, pushed me over the edge without letting go of my hand. Our bodies moved with such familiarity, it was as if they'd been destined to be together, made for each other. Afterward we lay with our legs entwined, my head on his shoulder, chests heaving.

"That was a surprise," he said, stroking my hair. "I only stopped by for a cup of sugar."

"No, you didn't." I whipped my head up, searched his face. "Did you?"

He held an innocent expression for as long as he could before laughing—a deep, rumbling sound that made my heart do a few spins. I ordered it to hold still, reminded myself not to get attached. I fully expected what had happened between us to be a half-night stand. Lewis would be gone by morning, slip out the door while I slept. But not now, not yet.

"No sugar, I promise," he said, running his fingers across my shoulder, turning my skin into goose bumps underneath his touch. "I came to apologize."

"Really?"

"Yeah. To say I'm sorry for trying to tell you what to do about your sister."

"It's okay. I was rude and—"

"No, you were right. It's none of my business and I was talking out of my ass. I'm sorry."

"You made up for it." I kissed him again before settling my head on his chest. "Twice."

He pulled me closer, enveloping me in the discreet scent of soap and aftershave. "I aim to please. I've been having increasingly naughty thoughts about you since I first saw you at the mailboxes, and then in the basement, clutching your polka-dot underwear—"

I snorted. "No, you haven't."

"I swear," he whispered. "Scout's honor. It's been driving me crazy, knowing you're down here, poring over your keyboard being all smart and techie. It's hot. *You're* hot."

Glowing heat spread across my cheeks. I was acutely aware I

was naked now, lying next to a hulk of a man who was about ninety percent lean muscle mass while my soft stomach pressed into his side. Panic ensued. At some point I'd have to get up and use the bathroom, but my clothes were strewn somewhere on the floor, out of reach. I couldn't take the entire duvet and wrap it around me like a cocoon, making a chaste escape one hop at a time. That left sneaking around in the dark as soon as he fell asleep, providing I didn't stumble and wake him.

What on earth had come over me? I was no sex goddess— although judging by the groans Lewis had made earlier, he'd enjoyed himself at least as much as me—and I certainly wasn't the kind of woman who proudly paraded around naked.

"Are you okay?" Lewis said, his voice drowsy, indicating sleep already had a good hold on him. "You seem a bit tense."

"No, not at all. I'm fine." I yawned, hoping it would mask how freaked out I was.

"No regrets then? About what happened tonight, I mean."

"Not one," I said, thinking, *Not yet, anyway.* "Do...do you?"

"How could I?" He let out a relaxed sigh. "Can I stay for a while?"

"Of course. As long as you want."

He had, and here he was, still in my bed, at almost five o'clock in the morning, lying on his back, peacefully asleep. I rolled onto my side, careful not to disturb him as I studied his face in the dim light from the window.

His lips, full and soft, were slightly parted, and I pulled back my hands to stop myself from reaching out and touching them with my fingertips. His hair had fallen to one side, making him appear to be a Roman god, or a merman, perhaps. It made no sense to me why he was here, not when I knew he could have his pick of a hundred prettier, smarter women.

As I looked at him, and the more perfect he appeared, my heart hardened, a thicker shell forming around it. No feelings for him would make their way inside. I'd made that mistake in my past and it wouldn't happen again. I didn't need to wonder too hard why he was in my bed. I'd thrown myself at him and he'd gone with it. Why not? I'd been an easy lay. He'd even chucked in a few compliments at the end for good measure, stealthily leaving the door open for future encounters. Neighbors with benefits.

I rolled onto my back, decided to focus on the day ahead rather than the night before. My alarm was set for six, but I'd get up now, shower and prepare for my first day working at Bell Hops. Hugh had warned we'd spend the morning going through HR paperwork and training, and geting me set up on the systems, said I should enjoy my first day because it would be the most relaxing one I'd have in a while. Good, because I'd need the distraction to stop myself thinking about Lewis.

I slipped out of bed and sneaked to the bathroom, where I brushed my teeth and showered, letting the water run over my body, blushing as I washed my breasts and between my legs, all the places Lewis had touched. My senses responded and I blushed some more, felt incapable of washing without aiming the showerhead in strategic places. What had he done to me?

I didn't have time to find the answer because Lewis pulled back the shower curtain. Naked Lewis. Perfect, naked Lewis, who, judging by his body's reaction, wanted me again.

"Good morning," he whispered. His gaze swept from the top of my head to my feet, making me instinctively want to either disappear down the drain or reach for a towel, except his smile stopped me. Fascinated by how he seemed to truly see me, I stood still, letting him stare.

"You're beautiful, Eleanor," he whispered.

I tried to believe it, made a desperate attempt to convince myself for this single moment I shouldn't—wouldn't—care about my paunch, my thighs or the size of my butt. And so, instead of grabbing a towel to cover myself with, I reached for Lewis's hand, led him under the water, pressed my naked body against his, feeling the walls I'd built around my heart crumble.

CHAPTER THIRTY

"WILL I SEE YOU AGAIN?" Lewis said after we'd dried off. I watched him retrieve his boxers and jeans from the bedroom floor and pull them on, his muscles rippling. The definition of his arms was something else, and I planted my feet onto the floor to stop myself from dragging him back to bed like a famished cavewoman.

"Of course you will," I said, forcing a laugh. "You live upstairs."

"I'd hope we're a bit more than neighbors now," he said, a hint of another smile playing on his soft lips. When I nodded, he added, "Will you let me take you out again? On a proper date where I don't piss you off and you leave? How about dinner or a movie one night?"

"Yes, please." The pitter-pattering in my heart quickened,

straining against the protective layer I'd tried to wrap it in. "Sure."

After Lewis left, I stood there for a while, studying the closed door, listening to him moving around upstairs, but then I looked at the time and it snapped me out of my reverie.

"Shit!" I said, rushing around my apartment, pulling on clothes and putting on makeup as fast as I could. I managed to spend enough time on my hair, using the coconut-scented samples Rocco had pressed into my hands, and followed his exact instructions on how to scrunch, scrunch, *scrunch* and clip, clip, *clip* in order to properly lift and define my curls.

It had worked so well, I'd almost done a double take in the elevator mirror when I arrived at work—with two minutes to spare—barely recognizing myself. My old suit and lilac top didn't make me look huge or bunch in any of the wrong places. I wasn't slim by anyone's stretch of the imagination, hadn't lost that much weight, either, but increasingly felt I was a woman with curves where they belonged. Or perhaps having mind-blowing sex with the hot upstairs neighbor three times in the last twelve hours had messed with my vision, along with everything else.

"You look different," Hugh said as we settled in his office, a manila envelope between us, the contents of which had been spread over the conference table.

"It's the hair." I pointed. "Victoria took me to her salon yesterday."

"Of course. She mentioned it. It suits you."

"All credit goes to the mighty Rocco, but thank you," I said, blushing again. At this rate I'd burst all the blood vessels in my face before the end of the morning.

"Okay, can you sign here and here?" Hugh pointed to the spots marked with pencil.

I speed-read the paragraphs, which all seemed standard, picked up my pen and scribbled my name before sliding the forms back across the table.

"Great," he said. "That's the confidentiality and consultant agreements done. Here's your badge to get in and out of the building. All right, we're all set." He paused, furrowed his brow. "Before I show you to your office I, uh, wanted to say thank you—"

"My pleasure. I'm thrilled to work here, and—"

"No, I mean… Uh, of course, thanks for taking the role, but also for spending the day with Victoria." He hesitated, shifted in his seat and fiddled with his watch. "She said she mentioned she's been low, you know, about the baby stuff."

"Ah, yes." Now I was the one squirming. She'd asked me not to mention anything to Hugh, which I wouldn't have regardless. Why had she felt the urge to tell him? Had he demanded to know what we'd talked about? What else had she told him?

"Well, anyway," he said. "Thanks for being there for her."

"No trouble. It was a lovely day."

He pushed his chair back. "Okay, let's finish getting you set up, shall we?"

The rest of the morning sped by. Hugh walked me through the building, an old food processing factory located on Marginal Way, which they'd transformed into a state-of-the art brewery. He introduced me to his partners and team members, told them I was a "website wizard," and each time he said it, the words made my head grow a size. We spent an hour touring the plant while Hugh told me about milling and mash conversion, fermentation and maturation. I could tell how proud he was of the brewery, and the fact he'd founded it with his best friend, two months after he and Victoria had got married.

"We went on a boys' weekend to Vegas. But instead of gambling or partying, we spent the entire time in our room, developing the Bell Hops business plan. Victoria was none too pleased I quit my corporate job," he said with a grimace as we walked up the set of steel stairs. "But she came around. Anyway, this'll be your office."

He pulled open one of two glass doors, immediately silencing the industrial noises once it closed behind us. The roughly two-hundred-and-fifty-square-foot open-plan area was a mixture of brick walls painted gray, huge arched windows that let in copious amounts of light and steel-vaulted ceilings.

I noticed a girl at the desk in the corner. She sat in a yoga pose, her legs crossed, feet resting on her thighs. When she unfolded herself and got up, her long giraffe-like limbs made her tower over me, bringing her eye-to-eye with Hugh. She looked a couple of years younger than us, had long blond hair, huge blue eyes, full lips and a heart-shaped beauty spot to the right of her nose. Heads had to turn on swivels whenever she walked by, especially with that smile.

"This is Genie," Hugh said with a broad grin. "Our systems guru."

"Hi." She stretched out a hand and I spotted a Celtic cross tattooed on the inside of her right wrist. "Am I ever glad to see you. I've been going through the website code, trying to decipher it." She shook her head, exhaled loudly. "I'm definitely in the crapper."

"I'm happy to help," I said, smiling back. "Whatever you need."

"Genie will get you set up with everything else," Hugh said. "She's the best."

"Stop it, boss." Genie gave him a tap on the arm and Hugh smiled at her again.

"I'll leave you to it," he said. "Go easy on her, Genie. Don't scare her off." Before he made it to the door, he turned around. "Eleanor, it's customary to take each new team member to lunch on the first day. There's a small bistro across the road. They have great grilled cheese and tomato soup. Nothing fancy, but delicious all the same. Genie, want to join us?"

She grinned at him. "I really should do my online course… but what the hell. Okay, then."

"Genie's doing a degree in fine art," Hugh said. "Major history buff, the kind of person you want working with you because she's so smart, and on your trivial pursuit team whenever possible, too."

"Ugh." Genie rolled her eyes. "Enough. Don't make me go all red."

"The three of us can grab a quick bite," Hugh said. "You can tell us more about your plans for Victoria's website. I'd be happy to pitch in."

I looked at him, took in his smile. First the compliments about my hair, now offering to take me to lunch. Was he...*flirting*? I smacked the ridiculous thought away; the night before really had messed with my head. "Uh, I was hoping to work on Victoria's site over lunch, actually. There's still a lot to do. Is that okay?"

"Sure, no problem," Hugh said. "I'm in the office next door, if you need me. See you later then, Genie, yeah?"

"Yes, boss, great," she called back, and when I glanced at her, I saw a look of unabashed delight lighting up her face, and little attempt to hide it.

CHAPTER THIRTY-ONE

TIME WENT BY SO FAST, it felt as if I'd blinked and two weeks disappeared. I spent my lunch breaks working on Victoria's site, the rest of the days on the Bell Hops project, and the nights… Well, many of those were spent with Lewis. Gorgeous, kindhearted, generous Lewis. He'd let me sketch him one evening, agreed to me taking his picture with my old Nikon despite being camera shy and he took the time to dial my number instead of firing off a quick text, so he could hear my voice.

"I can't wait to see you tonight," he'd whispered this morning as he kissed me deeply, making delicious shivers run down my spine because I couldn't wait, either.

I hadn't told Victoria about him yet, had preferred to keep our relationship—or whatever it was—a closely guarded secret in case mentioning it to anybody made it pop like a soap bubble. I'd avoided discussing Victoria with Lewis, too, for fear he'd think less of me because she still didn't know who I was.

I spoke to her most days, either by phone or text, and we had lunch at the bistro across the road from Bell Hops a couple of times. Whenever I heard from Victoria, my heart did a little flip, and when I sent her development updates and the logo for final approval, she called me instantly, insisting how marvelous everything was, and I thought I'd burst.

No doubt the connection between us had deepened. I'd deftly avoided speaking about her parents, who were on vacation, but she'd asked me more about Dad. She'd held my hand when I'd become teary-eyed, whispering she was there for me, that everything would be all right and I'd cried harder still because I wished I had the guts to confess we were related.

Hugh, on the other hand, seemed increasingly stressed, staying at Bell Hops far later than anyone else at night. He'd been right about the brewery's project being in a critical mess and it keeping me busy, but on one of the days Genie had gone for lunch with him again, I'd finally found the time to look into his first wife, Natalie. I'd read articles and watched a news report about her death. As Victoria had said, Natalie had perished in a house fire—"a tragic accident," the fire marshal had called it—in which she'd been the only victim. Despite searching for more information, I'd found little and decided to let it be, making sure I wiped my browser history.

On Thursday morning while I was finishing up more code, my cell rang, and when I picked it up, the first thing Victoria announced was that she had "huge news."

"What?" I said, her excitement flowing down the phone and into my ear. "Tell me."

She let out a muffled squeal. "I quit my job."

"You didn't!"

"I did! I signed the lease on the office last night and now that our website's almost done, I gave myself a kick in the butt. I'm officially on two weeks' notice."

"Wow, Victoria. What amazing news. Congratulations."

"Thank you. You've been such an inspiration to me. I couldn't have done this without you. I hope you know how grateful I am."

"I didn't do anything—"

"Sure you did," she said with a laugh. "And I want to repay you."

"Repay me?"

"Relax, it's not my weight in gold or anything."

"Diamonds, then?"

"Ha, better. Are you free tomorrow night? Want to come to dinner at our place?"

"Really?"

Victoria laughed again. "Yes, really. We're friends, aren't we? Don't sound so surprised. Hugh and I have this tradition where I make an Italian feast the week before Thanksgiving. I have a to-die-for meatloaf recipe from Rocco. Best thing I've ever made."

"I love meatloaf," I said.

"Then this one will blow your mind. Will you come? My cousin Charlotte will be there. It's high time you met. I think you'll really get along, and we need someone to help dilute her husband because he's an idiot." She laughed again. "But word of warning, don't tell Charlotte any secrets, okay? I love her to bits but by morning all of Portland will know, too. What do you think? Want to bring someone? Sun Temperature Guy, maybe?"

"Oh, no," I said. "I mean, I'd love to come, but I'll be alone."

As we said our goodbyes, I smiled, my expression becoming broader still when I thought about her enthusiasm while extending me the dinner invitation and referring to us as "friends." I was still grinning when my phone rang again, smiled harder when I saw it was Lewis.

"Hey, gorgeous," he said, then sighed. "One of my clients

asked if I could reschedule her workout for 9:00 p.m. and I'm booked solid before, so I can't see you earlier. Are you free tomorrow night?"

"Sure, I... No, wait. I'm going to dinner at...uh...at a friend's house."

"Okay. I've got stuff going on at the gym all weekend, so how about Monday?"

I didn't want to wait that long to see him. No matter how ridiculous it sounded or how much I didn't want it to be true, I needed it to be earlier. "You could come with me tomorrow," I said far too quickly, and without giving the consequences any thought. It was a stupid idea, I knew it as soon as the words left my mouth, except both he and Victoria were important to me, and I didn't want to keep those parts of my life separate anymore.

"I'd love to meet your friends," Lewis answered. "You sure it's okay?"

"Uh, yeah." I reminded myself how he'd clearly stated that my decision not to tell Victoria or Hugh we were related was none of his business. "I'm sure it'll be fine," I added, way more for my benefit than his, hoping I'd have his support.

As we made plans to meet at my apartment at six thirty the next day, I couldn't bring myself to tell him my "friends" were Victoria and Hugh. He hadn't pushed me for any more details of my relationship with them, but in this situation he'd have valid questions, and I needed time to anticipate them and figure out the answers. Part of me hoped Victoria would say it was too late to add a guest, but when I messaged her, she replied with a thumbs-up.

After work on Friday, I went through my entire closet, dug out a pair of black jeans and a wine-red scoop-neck sweater. I added my camera pendant necklace and silver earrings Dad gave me for my eighteenth birthday, touched up my makeup and studied myself in the mirror.

My hair, no longer a frizzy bush since I'd religiously followed

Rocco's routine, fell in soft spiral curls. I'd examined photos of Victoria's makeup on Instagram, too, had watched a dozen instructional videos on YouTube, and the results were astonishing. Smoky eyes and glossy lips, my puffy, pasty face gone. Since I'd dropped a few more pounds and had taken to drinking four glasses of water for every cup of green tea, my skin glowed, especially with the highlighter I'd bought for an eye-watering twenty-six dollars from Penelope at the drugstore. The result was worth it.

I looked at Dad's photo on the sideboard. "I think you'd be proud of me," I told him, my heart pinching. "I've met a guy. I've made new friends. I'm spending time with *people*, Dad. Can you believe it? And they're really, really nice. I think… I think I'm almost *happy*." I didn't say anything about not telling Victoria the truth. Wherever Dad was, he already knew, and I wasn't ready to have that conversation with him, if only in my head.

At exactly six thirty, Lewis knocked on my door, and I couldn't hide my smile. His jeans hugged him in all the right places, and his fitted dark blue shirt showed off his frame. He held a bottle of red wine in his hand and leaned in to kiss me softly on the lips. "Hi, stranger," he murmured. "You look amazing. Do we have ten minutes to spare?"

"Ten minutes? For what I have in mind, we'd need ten times as long."

He raised an eyebrow. "I'll consider myself warned. And intrigued…"

Once I'd locked up and we made our way down Cumberland Avenue, Lewis took my hand, my fingers disappearing inside his meaty, gloved palm. It felt familiar yet strange, scary yet safe, a jumble of conflicting emotions I struggled to figure out what to do with. *Go with the flow,* I decided, anyone looking at us would think we were a couple. Did that mean we were? Maybe it was too soon to discuss it…but there was one thing I needed to bring up, and it couldn't wait.

"About where we're going tonight," I said. "My friends, they're, uh, Victoria and Hugh."

"Good one," Lewis said, but when he spotted my expression, he stopped and let go of my hand. "You're not kidding, are you? And...am I right in thinking they still don't know who you are?" I shook my head and he whistled. "Well, this might get a little awkward."

"You don't have to come," I said quickly. "I'm quite self-sufficient, and—"

"I know, I know." Lewis sighed. "But I wish you'd told me. Actually...I wish you'd told *them* because now I'm part of the lie."

"I will, eventually," I said, wincing at his choice of words, although he was right, it was a lie, but hearing it out loud made it all the more real. "I really like Victoria," I added quietly. "I don't know how to tell her in case she cuts ties."

"Why do you think she'd do that?"

"You said so yourself, because I lied."

"You might be right," Lewis said. "But it's been weeks and surely the more you delay—"

"I'm not ready yet, okay?" I snapped. "Remember, you said you had no right to tell me what to do. And, again, you don't have to come."

He looked at me. "You're right. And I want to come, I do. It threw me, is all."

At first I felt the atmosphere between us shift, but within a block he'd taken my hand again, holding it as tight as before. I remembered his comment about arguing with Janique on their second date being a bad sign, reminded myself of our disagreement at The Pump House on our first, and he'd still asked me out again. Plus, that was a couple of weeks ago and he'd known about Stan, Victoria and Hugh before then. All that had to count for something, but he felt uncomfortable about who we were going to see tonight and I didn't blame him.

"You're absolutely sure you're okay going to their place like this?" Lewis said as we stood outside Victoria and Hugh's building. "There's still time to back out."

"I want to spend time with her, Lewis," I said. "I really like her, and I know you will, too." I held up my finger and pushed the buzzer, trying to quiet the nerves.

My belly took a while to settle after we arrived, despite Victoria fussing over us, thanking Lewis for the bottle, pressing a glass of white wine into my hand and fetching him a beer, while Hugh introduced us to Charlotte—who sat in a chair with a pair of crutches by her side, her medical-boot-clad foot propped up on a pouf—and her husband, Malcolm.

"I heard about the accident," I said. "How are you? Not in any pain, I hope?"

"Oh, I'm okay." Charlotte waved a hand. "I'll survive."

"She's a trouper," Victoria called over from the kitchen. "Never complained once."

"Speak for yourself," Malcolm said, and his tone added to the instant dislike I'd felt when he'd shaken my hand. I'd had to stop myself from wiping my fingers on my pants when he'd let go. While the rest of us were dressed casually, as per Victoria's instructions, Malcolm looked as if he'd time-traveled from Wall Street circa 1985. Pin-striped suit, slicked-back hair—revealing a widow's peak Dracula would've run through sunlight for—and a chunky monogrammed ring.

He looked at Lewis, pulled a face and put his hands up like a boxer, weaving his upper body around. "Whoa. Nobody told me a fridge was joining the party." His hollow laugh echoed around the room. When the rest of us only half joined in, he coughed. "What do you do, then, Lewis? Careerwise, I mean. We've got the girlfriend department covered."

I caught Victoria and Charlotte looking at each other, rolling their eyes.

"I own a gym," Lewis said.

"Figures. I'm in risk management." Malcolm popped an olive in his mouth, continuing to talk as he ground it with his teeth. "Never enjoyed the gym, all the dudes grunting and sweating put me off. Now, golf, there's a civilized sport. Give me a Friday afternoon with eighteen holes, and I'm all yours. Do you play? The best course I've seen—"

"Sorry to interrupt, Malcolm." Victoria slid her arms around Lewis's and my shoulders, leaning in between us. "I need to talk to these two about dinner." She steered us to the back of the kitchen, saying, "I forgot to ask about allergies, so let's go over what I've made and…" She threw a glance toward Malcolm, who redirected his monologue at Hugh and Charlotte, their eyes no doubt already glazing over.

"Sorry about him," she said. "He can be a bit much at times. His attitude is hit-or-miss depending on his insecurity levels. But never mind that. I'm so glad you two are here. It's such a pleasure to meet you, Lewis."

"Thanks for extending the invitation at such short notice," he said.

Victoria laughed again, tilted her head back as she patted his arm. "Oh, you're welcome. You're already in my good books for impressing Malcolm. Anyway—" she turned to me, her smile growing "—give me the details. Where did you meet? How long ago? Tell me everything."

"Uh, well, we're neighbors," I said, and Victoria raised an eyebrow.

"Sounds…*convenient*," she said.

"We first met at the mailboxes," Lewis added. "I kept hanging around the hallways, hoping to catch a glimpse of her. It took me a while to work up the courage to ask her out."

"Really?" Victoria and I said in unison and I thought I caught the slightest hint of something judgmental in her tone, but decided I was projecting.

Lewis chuckled. "Yes. Trust me, Malcolm's got me all wrong. I'm a big cuddly bear. Eleanor's the intimidating one."

"*Me?*" I said.

"Oh, he's right," Victoria said. "When we first met, I felt like an idiot."

"No, you didn't," I said. "Did you?"

"Yes, because you're so knowledgeable," she said. "You were designing logos and talking about WordPress and Java, which, incidentally, I thought meant coffee, and all I could do was nod so you wouldn't figure out I didn't have a clue."

"What? But that's exactly how I felt. You're so glamorous and beautiful, and I look like something the cat dragged in after a ten-mile trek backward through the woods."

Victoria clicked her tongue and patted my arm. "No, you don't, but isn't it funny how we can get so caught up in wishing for what another person has?" She smiled at me again before turning to Lewis. "Did I hear you say you own a gym?"

"Yes," he said. "It's called Audaz."

"Spanish for *bold*. How fantastic. Actually I've been thinking about switching. My place doesn't do it for me anymore, you know? I've hit a major rut. Same routine, different day."

"You should check us out," Lewis said. "It's not your average place, though, we do lots of high-intensity circuit training, with tire flipping and such. It's not your standard cardio mill."

"Ooooh." Victoria's eyebrows shot up. "Sounds way more fun than what I'm doing."

"Have a few sessions on the house if you'd like to give us a try," Lewis said.

It made sense for him to offer. He already knew how well connected Victoria and Hugh were. If she enjoyed the gym, it could mean access to a large—and wealthy—client base, but still... I tensed as I imagined her working out with him, her lithe limbs bending and stretching under his watchful eye.

"I'll come with you," I said quickly. "I'd love to give working out a try."

"Will you?" Lewis beamed, turning to me. "That's not what you said in bed."

"In bed?" Victoria said. "You *are* a dark horse, Eleanor."

"Yeah, well—" I turned to Lewis, doing my best to ignore my glowing ears and Victoria's stare boring into the side of my head "—I should make more of an effort. Walking to the coffee shop twice a week isn't cutting it."

Lewis rubbed his hands together. "This'll be fun. In the meantime, may I use your bathroom, Victoria?"

"Of course. Third door on the left," she said, grabbing my hand as soon as he disappeared down the hallway. "Please tell me he's Sun Temperature Guy. I can't take it if there's someone more attractive walking around Portland. My head will explode."

I grinned, blushing again. "Yes, it's him."

"And he's your neighbor? God, lucky you. And when did you—" she waggled her eyebrows "—*get* together?"

"The day we went to the spa and I got my hair done."

"What? That was two weeks ago. Why didn't you tell me?"

"I don't know," I said, covering my mouth to stifle a giggle. "And I don't know what came over me, either, but when he stopped by that night—"

"He fell under the spell of your gorgeous curls?" Victoria grinned.

"Something like that."

"I want way more details—"

Relief flooded me as the doorbell rang. I'd never been one to share stories about my sex life. It was too exhibitionist, and I couldn't stand the thought of anyone imagining what we'd been up to. Victoria squeezed my arm and excused herself as Lewis returned.

"This is a bit bizarre," he whispered as she went to answer

the door. "And I still wish you'd told me, and them. But you're right, Victoria's great. She seems lovely."

"What about him?" I said quietly. We looked over to where Hugh sat next to Charlotte. Malcolm towered over them, talking about cost accounting and EBITDA, his hands waving around for emphasis, his voice slightly raised as if he wished he had more of an audience.

"You mean his ability to bore the pants off everyone?" Lewis said.

"Hugh, not Malcolm," I said with a laugh.

Lewis shrugged. "He seems all right. Haven't had much time to form an opinion."

I was about to reply when we heard people in the hallway. Footsteps coming our way, voices, one of them—a man's—sending ice down my spine. I knew that voice. Recognized it in an instant.

Stan Gallinger. My *father*.

CHAPTER THIRTY-TWO

I GLANCED AROUND THE KITCHEN, wondered if I could disappear into the bathroom or the pantry until he'd left. A thought hit me—what if they'd come for dinner? Victoria hadn't mentioned it, but why would she, and what if they stayed the entire evening? So many times I'd played out this scenario in my mind—where Stan found out I'd secretly befriended his daughter—but now the prospect of it happening made me want to throw up. If Stan told Victoria who I was, here, now, I'd lose her friendship. I'd probably never see her again.

I wanted to make my excuses and run, but doing so meant walking past him, and I didn't think my feet would carry me that far without stumbling. And so I stood, unable to move, waiting for Stan to see me, bracing myself for his reaction, hoping he'd long forgotten who I was, that I even existed. Maybe he wouldn't recognize me with the different hair and wearing makeup. My heart pounded, my palms damp.

"Your mom said Malcolm and Charlotte were here and suggested we stop by," Stan said as he walked in behind Madeleine, both of them smartly dressed and wearing long black coats. "I hope we're not interrupting anything."

"Of course not," Victoria said, and I could barely breathe. "I'm so glad to see you both. How was your trip? Did you have a good time?"

"Incredible." Madeleine sighed, her face perfection, and still, I didn't move. "We're quite tired, so we won't stay long. We'll say a quick hello to Charlotte and Malcolm, then… Oh—" her smile broadened when she saw Lewis "—I didn't know you had more guests. Hello." Madeleine peered around him to get a better glimpse of me, hiding. She held out her hand, shook Lewis's, then mine, and I hoped she wouldn't feel the tremble of my sweaty fingers. "I'm Madeleine, Victoria's mom. This is my husband, Stan."

"Mom, Dad," Victoria said, "this is Eleanor and her boyfriend, Lewis. Lewis owns a gym and—" she reached over and patted my arm "—Eleanor's designing my new website."

"And she saved my bacon at the brewery, too," Hugh said as he walked over, giving his in-laws a hug each. "Don't forget that part. She's a frigging whiz kid."

I managed to look at Stan—his blue-eyed stare digging straight into my skin—but was unable to form a single word in my mouth, not even a quiet "Hello." I wanted to shrivel up and float to the ground like an insignificant speck of dust. If he continued looking at me so intensely, maybe I'd spontaneously combust and get my wish.

"You hired someone?" Stan's gaze didn't waver, his tone cool. If he recognized me, he deserved every single Best Actor award in the history of the Oscars. "Well, this is a surprise."

"I'd told Dad I'd speak to some of his connections while he

was away," Victoria said. "But I didn't need to. You contacted me before I got the chance. It was fate."

Stan's Adam's apple bobbed and I wondered what he was thinking, how he felt, seeing his illegitimate daughter, knowing I could open my mouth and drop him into an industrial-size vat of stinking, rancid family shit. The thought made my spine grow an inch, and my resolve harden. In comparison, I'd done nothing wrong. Nothing. I wasn't the one who should be scared.

"Definitely fate," I said, matching his stare, unblinking, until he looked away.

"Did you know each other from before?" Madeleine said to Victoria. "School, maybe?"

"Yeah, now that you mention it, you do look kind of familiar, Eleanor," Charlotte called over from her perch on the sofa.

"N-no," I said, my heart thumping as I tried not to look at Lewis. "We'd never met."

"Well, in any case I'm glad to hear you're helping my daughter," Madeleine said, giving me another smile before walking over to Charlotte. "How are the girls and how's the ankle?"

"The girls are cheeky monkeys," Charlotte replied. "In a week or two I can get rid of this stupid boot and get back to chasing them properly. I can't wait to feel normal and not have to ask Malcolm to—"

"Yeah, so am I," he said, talking over her. "All the women in my house think I'm their man-slave or something."

Madeleine and Victoria exchanged a look. Had they told Charlotte he was cheating? If so, she was an incredible actor, too. And if not, what were they waiting for? Maybe the right time—when she got rid of the boot and could smack him over the head with it.

"Got a minute to talk about the lease?" Stan said to Victoria.

"Sure." Victoria wiped her hands on a kitchen cloth and set it on the counter. "The food won't be ready for another ten. Let's go to the office. Help yourself to drinks and snacks, guys," she called over. "Back in a minute."

As I exhaled slowly to get my heart back under control, Lewis leaned in. "I'm guessing he's your dad? Do you want to go home? I could say I'm not well and we could slip out."

Shaking my head, I said, "No, but I need the bathroom."

The long hallway had three large doors on either side, and one at the back, which I assumed was the master bedroom. I hadn't been in this part of Victoria and Hugh's apartment, hadn't had an opportunity to dig around or snoop through her things, but now I no longer wanted to invade my sister's privacy that way. Instead I crept past the sleek white chest of drawers with a vase of sweet-smelling purple lilies on top, ignored the framed prints and other art hanging on the walls and edged my way closer to the only door from which soft light and voices spilled.

"...yes, I understand I was away," Stan was saying. "But my question is why *her*?"

"Look at the designs," Victoria said. "And her prices were reasonable—"

"You know very well the other companies would've matched her fees, and what's more, they came recommended."

"Sure, they may have charged the same," she said, "but Eleanor... She *gets* me, Dad. She knew exactly the kind of look I wanted without me being able to express it clearly. It's as if she's a psychic, or we're twins, or something."

I stifled a grin as I imagined the look on his face, one he'd no doubt tried to hide. Did I feel sorry for him? Not really. After all, he'd brought this upon himself. He hadn't wanted me three decades ago, had rejected me again when offered another chance. His shitty deeds were catching up to him. Apparently his past was biting him in his rich ass.

"Okay, but why invite her to dinner?" Stan said. "You know my rule about contractors."

"Yeah, yeah. Keep them at arm's length or they'll start taking advantage, I know." Her voice sounded jaded, bordering on petulant, making me smirk. I wasn't sure how our parents regressed us to teenagers at times. My mother could have the same effect on me, too.

Stan sighed. "Correct, so why did you—"

"Because I love hanging out with her, Dad. She's a great person."

"You mean you've *hung out* with her before? What for?"

"What do you mean, what for? You don't even know her."

"I know enough to tell you haven't had the same upbringing—"

"*Upbringing?* God, you're such a snob, Dad," Victoria said, and I almost punched the air. "First of all, no, she may not be from a super wealthy family, but so what? Neither were you."

"I'm not—"

"*Second*, she's smart. She runs her own business, as you do, and as I'm going to." She drew a breath, during which time I thought I might hear Stan fall to the floor from heart failure. "And third," Victoria continued, "although I don't have to justify who I'm friends with or give you any reason other than I *like* her, Hugh thinks she's great, too."

"And she's working there, as well?" Stan voice sounded as if he'd got a giant fluff ball stuck in his throat.

"Yup. His website guy quit without notice. Thankfully Eleanor stepped in."

"That's not a good idea—"

"What is it with you today, Dad? You haven't tried to meddle in who I'm friends with since middle school, and it didn't work back then, either, remember? I love you, but please stop. Eleanor contacting me has been fantastic, and—"

"How did she contact you, exactly?"

"Sent me a LinkedIn message, offering her services." Victoria's voice sounded triumphant. "Her timing was perfect."

"I bet it was."

"You should trust me," she snapped. "Look, I've got to get the food out of the oven."

I darted down the hallway and back to the living room, where I joined Charlotte, Lewis and Hugh, who were in the middle of a conversation about Lewis's time in the army. Hugh filled my glass and Lewis put his arm around me, and I leaned against him as I observed the room.

Madeleine and Malcolm stood at the far end of the kitchen. She was whispering in his ear, his face paler than the white stone countertop. He nodded, his jaw tight, and she arched an eyebrow, giving him a steely glare. No need to guess what they were talking about.

When Victoria and Stan walked in, a fake-happy expression slid over Stan's face but not before he'd directed a look of absolute fury my way. I'd long stopped wondering if he'd recognized me, but although my nerves had subsided, I still speculated what he'd do about it.

"We should go, Madeleine," he said curtly.

"*Déjà?*" she said. "We've barely arrived. Hugh offered to make me a martini—"

"I have to unpack and go over a few things," Stan said. "Let's leave these guys to it."

"Oh, well, all right, then," Madeleine said. "It was a pleasure meeting you, Eleanor, and you, Lewis. Hope to see you again. Take care, Charlotte, won't you? Kiss those beautiful girls for me. And, Malcolm?"

"Yes," he said, swallowing hard, his eyes shifting left and right like a trapped animal's.

She gave him a cool look. "Don't forget what I said about looking after your wife."

Malcolm looked as if he might empty his bowels right there in the living room, and when I looked at Victoria, I almost blanched, too. The venom-filled hatred she directed his way made me promise myself two things: I'd never get on her bad side, and I'd somehow sort out the lies I'd created between us, before it was too late.

CHAPTER THIRTY-THREE

"**H**OW DO YOU FEEL** about coming upstairs?" Lewis asked when we got back to our building. He raised my hand to his lips and kissed my fingertips. "Would that be okay?"

"Yes, very much okay," I said. "Give me a few minutes, and I'll be right there."

"It's a date." He gently pulled me toward him, pressed his lips to mine. When we broke apart and I stepped inside my apartment, I closed the front door and rested the back of my head against it, listening to his footsteps disappearing upstairs and thinking about the last few hours.

Despite the shock of seeing Stan and Madeleine, I'd had a fantastic evening, the rest of my nerves dissipating soon after they'd left, helped, no doubt, by two more glasses of wine. Victoria might have called her food simple, but it was delicious—juicy meatloaf served with perfectly cooked, buttered, al dente pasta and a crunchy green salad she'd dressed with a lemon and caper vinaigrette. Hugh had stopped at Jake's Cakes on his way home and picked up melt-in-your-mouth cannoli, all of us groaning with joyful indulgence when we took our first bites, despite our initial protests of not being able to eat more food. The best part was that for the first time in years, I ate without guilt, the snide little berating voice holding its tongue all night.

In contrast to Malcolm, Charlotte turned out to be equal parts funny and charming, regaling us with stories of her family's flower shop, including how there had been an unfortunate mix-up with the deliveries for a funeral and a wedding.

"Thankfully, I managed to make it right with a minute to spare," she said, shaking her head. "At least the funeral home didn't have to wonder for too long why someone had sent a mammoth bouquet with a banner saying Congratulations, and thank God the bride-to-be never saw the condolence wreath. Phew."

Like Victoria, Hugh had been an attentive host, refilling glasses, helping her with dinner and, alongside Lewis, insisted on cleaning up. Still, I couldn't help noticing how flustered Victoria became when she'd tipped over a glass of water, how she'd apologized to Hugh far more than Malcolm, to whom the drink had belonged. The trend of her seeming nervous and on edge around Hugh had continued, and she'd gone out of her way to please and appease him.

I pushed the jumble of thoughts about Victoria and Hugh's marriage to one side and headed for my bathroom, turning back when my phone rang. It was almost eleven thirty, late for anyone to be calling, and although I didn't recognize the number, I still answered.

"Hello?"

"Stay away from my daughter," Stan said. "Do you hear me? Stay away."

"You don't get to tell me—"

"*Yes.* Yes, I do. I said from the beginning I don't want anything to do with you."

"I'm not having anything to do with *you.*"

"I don't know what you think you're playing—"

"I'm not playing—"

"What, you mean you *coincidentally* ended up working for Victoria? And Hugh?"

"It wasn't—"

"What do you want? What's your endgame?" Stan said quietly, and when I heard a dog barking, and a police siren in the distance, I knew he'd slipped outside to call.

"I don't want anything from you. Not anymore."

"Oh, come now," Stan said through clenched teeth. "If there's one thing I've learned in life, it's that everybody wants something. You've been a good strategist, and I underestimated you. My bad, as they say. What's it going to take for this to end?"

"Why are you so desperate to make me go away?"

"What do you *want*?" he repeated. "Tell me now."

"I want a relationship with my sister. That's all."

"Half sister," he snapped. "And under false pretenses, no less. I wonder what she'd say if she knew who you really are."

"I wonder, too," I said without missing a beat, "and what she'd make of you buying off my mother and making this big a decision for her."

His voice rose, his tone exasperated. I'd hit a nerve. "If you tell her—"

"Careful, *Dad,*" I said. "It almost sounds as if you can't handle not getting your own way. How does it feel? A little uncomfortable, I'd imagine." As the line went dead, a smile stretched across my face. I'd got to him. Again.

Ten minutes later when I knocked on Lewis's door with newfound energy, I felt victorious, a little dangerous, even, as if I could do anything I put my mind to.

"I thought you'd changed your mind," he said, nuzzling my neck and leading me inside.

It wasn't the first time I'd been in his apartment but I paid minimal attention to the decor—bright white walls, a brown sofa with cream cushions—before I took him to his bedroom and pushed him onto the bed. As I straddled him, unbuttoning his shirt and loosening his belt, letting my hands wander, he groaned.

"You're killing me," he said, his hands moving over my hips. I lowered myself to kiss his chest, slid my lips downward as I worked on the buttons of his jeans, shivering at the thought of my hang-ups disappearing, no longer worried about the lights being on. Lewis could see me. I *wanted* him to. It meant I could see him, including his expression—one full of lust and desire, and which I'd put there.

I awoke the next morning to the aroma of fresh coffee. When I pulled on Lewis's shirt, which I'd ripped off him the night before, and walked to the kitchen, I found a blue-and-white polka-dot coffee mug on the counter with a neatly penned note underneath.

Hey, Sleepyhead,
New client = early start. Stay as long as you want. See you tonight?
Lewis x
P.S. Hope you approve of the mug. It made me think of you.

I filled the cup with black coffee and wandered around Lewis's apartment. His place was far nicer than mine, its walls freshly painted, its kitchen refitted, the taps still shiny. There was no water-stained ceiling or patchy carpet, either. He'd told me he'd done some of the work, and I wondered if he'd chosen the accent pieces or if it had been a former girlfriend. The blue of the heavy linen curtains complemented the other soft furnishings dotted around the living room—the cream cushions and a fuzzy beige blanket folded over the back of the sofa. Black-and-white framed pictures of misty mountains and the ocean hung on the wall, giving the place depth rather than sullenness. The photographs were of professional quality, and they made me want to grab my Nikon and go out for a walk so I could get some long-overdue practice.

Smaller framed pictures stood on a teak sideboard. One was of Lewis with a group of guys, all dressed in army uniform. Another of an elderly lady sitting in a restaurant in front of a giant plate of calamari—his Spanish grandmother. I picked up the third photo, one of an older couple hiking in the mountains, people he'd told me were his mother and stepfather. Would I meet them, I wondered? If Lewis and I stayed together, would we fly out to Colorado at some point? The thought made my palms clammy and I put the photo down, wishing I was able to introduce him to Dad, too, and the sudden stabbing pain made me well up.

Although grateful I could imagine Lewis in his own environment when I heard him moving around upstairs, after sitting on the sofa for a few minutes I began to feel self-conscious. I needed to get to work if I was going to meet Hugh's project expectations, and I'd be up late most nights if I wanted to polish Victoria's site, too, getting ready for her company's launch.

Last night after Malcolm and Charlotte had left, and Hugh and Lewis were discussing their favorite Netflix shows, Victoria had confessed she couldn't stop freaking out after quitting her job.

"Do you really think I did the right thing?" she said, and chewed on her lip.

"Yes. Why? Don't you?"

"Yes, well, mostly. I'm not sure at times. I'm not that confident—"

"Are you kidding me? You're one of the most confident people I know."

She glanced at Hugh, shook her head and whispered, "I'm not. It's all an act. Most of the time I'm scared shitless everyone will figure out I don't know what I'm doing. I feel like a downright fraud most days. Does that ever happen to you?"

"All the time," I whispered back, albeit, I suspected, not exactly for the same reasons.

"Apparently it's called impostor syndrome." She looked at me and I made myself hold her gaze. "And it's exactly what I am. An impostor."

"No, you're not. And you're going to be great."

"Come with me." She reached for my hand and jumped up, pulling me into the hallway. "I have a surprise for you."

"A surprise?" I said as I followed her.

"I was going to wait until you finished the website, but…"

Laughing, she ushered me into their bedroom, which was almost as big as my entire apartment. A king-size bed with a padded sapphire velvet headboard stood on the far wall. The white bedding looked crisp, with the word *Hugh* embroidered in blue on the left pillow, and *Victoria* on the one on the right. Books filled his bedside table whereas hers was bare, except for a heavy-looking paperweight made from turquoise glass. A cream-colored chaise longue sat in the corner, and I imagined her draped over it, sipping a green tea or a foamy cappuccino, reading a book on a lazy Sunday morning.

One of the pictures hanging on the left wall drew my eye—a black-and-white photograph of a naked woman's arched back, her hands loosely tied behind her with a string of pearls. Although the curve of her hip, buttocks and left breast were barely visible, it made the photo more intimate, more erotic somehow. Eleanor caught my stare.

"Oh, God," she said. "How embarrassing."

"It's you, isn't it?"

"Yeah," she said, wrinkling her nose. "Hugh went through this phase of taking naked pictures of me. I didn't enjoy it much, to be honest, but it made him happy."

I forced my gaze away and looked around. "This is a lovely room. It's huge."

"Thanks. The pillows are a bit over-the-top, aren't they? I mean, it's not as if we'll forget which side of the bed we sleep on, but they were a present from Charlotte. Anyway…" She gestured for me to join her at the dresser, where she slid open the top drawer, making the duo of silver rabbit ornaments standing on top of it wobble.

Curious, I peered inside the drawer, my eyes going wide. "You have a *gun?*"

Victoria laughed. "Yeah, but don't worry, that's not your surprise."

"But…why do you have a weapon?"

She shrugged. "Dad bought it for me years ago, insisted I learn how to shoot. It's a SIG P226." She picked it up and held it out. "Want to hold it? Don't worry, it's not loaded."

"Uh, no, thanks. Guns really aren't my thing."

"Yeah, mine neither, but Dad said it was for—" she made quotation marks "—'self-defense.' Anyway, never mind that stupid thing. This is what I wanted to give you." She set the gun down and picked up a small parcel wrapped in gold paper, complete with an elaborate ruby-red bow. "It's a small thank-you for taking on my project at stupidly short notice, and, well…for becoming such a good friend."

"Victoria, I can't—"

"Yes, you can." She pushed the parcel into my hands. "It's not much. Open it."

I tore into the paper, uncovered a black velvet box the length of a deck of cards. Fingers trembling, I opened the lid, blinked hard. Inside was a silver necklace with a diamond-encrusted infinity-symbol-shaped pendant and matching earrings.

"I can't accept this," I said, looking up.

"Why not?" Her smile faded, replaced by abjection.

I wanted to tell her I couldn't take her beautiful gift because I'd stolen her ring. Why hadn't I brought it with me tonight? I could've hidden it somewhere in the apartment, hoping she'd find it, but I hadn't had the courage in case she caught me with it somehow.

"Don't you like them?" she said, her voice faltering.

"I love them." My fingers grazed the precious stones. "But it's...it's too much."

Victoria closed my fingers over the box, pressing it further into my palm. "No, it isn't, I promise. If it helps, they're zirconia, not real diamonds. Oh, and before I forget..." She walked to her closet and pulled out a white plastic bag. "I went through my clothes the other day and, well, I hope this doesn't sound weird or anything, but I found these tops. I bought them on a whim but they don't suit me, the color isn't right, you know? I think they'll look great on you."

She opened the bag and pulled out two sleeveless V-neck shirts, both of them a different shade of red. The first one had little black embroidered roses, the other spirals of tiny sequins sewed into the satin fabric. I saw the label, recognized the brand and shook my head.

"Victoria, I can't take these. You should return them and get your money back."

"I can't," she said. "I don't have the receipt. Besides, they're worn."

"Still...they'll be too small—"

"Take them," she insisted, pushing the bag into my hands. "They're a bit big for me. I bet they'll fit your lovely curves perfectly. You'll look amazing, trust me."

Still, I hesitated. "You're sure?"

"Positive. But do me a favor?"

"Of course, anything."

"Can you not mention the gifts to Hugh?" She fiddled with her wedding ring, spun it around her finger with her thumb. "He, uh, said I spend too much, especially with me quitting my job… He's not too happy about my lost jewelry, either, because I was careless."

"I won't say a word to anyone, I promise."

In a heartbeat Victoria threw her arms around my neck and hugged me hard, the scent of her floral perfume enveloping me.

"Thank you," she whispered, giving me a peck on the cheek before pulling away, as if embarrassed by her sudden display of affection. "I knew you'd understand."

"Can I ask you something?" I said.

"Of course you can. Anything."

"It's… Well…uh, is…is everything okay between you two?"

"What do you mean?" She blinked, her voice light, but a trace of a frown on her face.

"Sometimes I can't help wondering—"

"Oh, we're fine," she said, her eyes darting around the room. "We're great. Gosh, I'd better get back and make more coffee. Put the shirts and jewelry in your bag, okay? And please don't tell Lewis, either, in case he mentions it to Hugh. Those two seem to have hit it off." As she turned, her elbow knocked one of the rabbit ornaments over, and it fell onto the carpet with a thud. I bent over and picked it up.

"Thanks," she said. "Jeez, these stupid things keep falling. Just put it in here." She opened the drawer and after I'd placed the rabbit inside, she led the way back to the living room.

I wasn't sure if she'd avoided being alone with me afterward, or if it was through circumstance, but I continued watching her with Hugh, and I knew she'd noticed. The way she put her hands on his shoulders, how he draped an arm around her waist, both of them the perfect, attentive couple. Was there actually any negativity between them? I'd asked Lewis his opinion.

"They seem like a great couple," he'd said as we'd walked home. "Happy. Solid."

And yet, here I was, sitting on Lewis's sofa the next morning, and the thoughts remained, burrowing deeper. I finished my drink, washed the mug and scribbled a quick note.

Thanks for the coffee.
Message me later? xoxox
P.S. Love the mug

I hesitated before adding a drawing of a woman with curly hair blowing a kiss, and writing another set of *x*'s and *o*'s beneath.

Once downstairs, I retrieved the velvet box from my bag, admired the necklace and earrings before carefully putting them on and looking at myself in the mirror. It had been an unexpected and thoughtful gift—making my heart melt, and my gut contract with guilt.

I walked to the bedroom and retrieved the folded tissue, taking my time to unwrap the contents, staring at Victoria's ring as it lay twinkling in the palm of my hand. I wished I'd never taken it, that I'd handed it in without being so impulsive, so stupid. What had Hugh really said and done when he'd found out she'd lost it?

On the surface he appeared doting and kind, both toward Victoria and everyone else, but something was wrong between them, I could feel it. Whether it was abuse—mental, physical or both—I wasn't sure. I hadn't noticed any bruises when we'd been at the spa or since. Then again I hadn't seen her in her underwear as she had me, but I knew from experience there didn't need to be physical evidence for someone to be suffering.

The longer I stood there, my fingers touching the delicate chain around my neck, my other hand grasping Victoria's ring, the more determined I became to figure it out. I felt a compelling need to ensure she was safe. Including from her husband.

CHAPTER THIRTY-FOUR

LEWIS AND I SPENT Saturday night together, but much as we wanted to stay under the covers all Sunday, duty called. "I'll see you soon," he said as I left his apartment, kissing me deeply, his lips tasting of the breakfast he'd surprised me with in bed. When I'd woken up to the sound of him moving around in the kitchen, the sweet scent of cinnamon sugar in the air, he'd walked into the bedroom holding a tray filled with plates of French toast, tangy raspberries and grilled bananas. Once we'd finished eating, I'd thanked him for his perfect hospitality by pulling him back under the covers and removing his boxers.

I practically skipped down to my apartment and collapsed on the sofa. Over the past weeks I'd not only opened my heart to the gentle giant upstairs, but I'd also let my guard down—had *chosen* to let it down—giving him more details about the relationship with Amy and my mother, including the lurid story of their failed blackmail plans.

"Have you spoken to them since?" he'd said as we lay in bed.

"No, and I don't intend to," I said, rolling onto my side. "Anyway, enough about them. Tell me more about your mom and your stepdad."

"Jackson's a rancher, through and through. Mom's a psychiatrist."

"God, how was that, growing up? Did she psychoanalyze you?"

Lewis chuckled. "All the time, but she was clever. I never caught on until I was much older, by which time it was too late. She's a master at reverse psychology. She actually wrote a book about it."

"And you never wanted to move to Colorado?"

"I'd miss the ocean too much," he said with a shake of his head. "I get to see them a few times a year. They're usually in Portland at least once, and sometimes I make it there for Christmas or over the summer. Anyway, I got used to being away."

"You're not visiting them for Thanksgiving?" I left the implication hanging between us. The holiday was this coming week, and we'd yet to discuss plans. I hadn't found the nerve.

"No, not this year. Are you doing anything?"

I tried not to think about how Dad and I would've spent the day together, roasted a chicken before treating ourselves to his homemade pumpkin pie. Would Lewis have come with me? Would Dad have whispered, *Good choice, Freckles, good choice*, after meeting him, because there was no doubt they'd have got along.

My heart ached, and I shook my head before quietly saying, "Nothing special."

"Would spending the weekend with me be special enough...?"

The pain in my chest eased as I took in his green eyes, the curve of his mouth. Yes, I wanted to spend the weekend with him, and the one after, and each one after, that, too. The thought of letting him into my heart this quickly terrified me, but I couldn't help it. "As long as we don't eat turkey, and I can hide from all the Black Friday madness."

Lewis pulled me closer, the warmth of his body spreading across mine. "Deal."

I'd let him hold me, my head nestled on his chest, relishing the thought of his hands and tongue on my body, the sound of his voice calling out my name. It was more than sex. I felt comfortable with Lewis, I felt safe. While it was something I'd long convinced myself I didn't need, it was also something I'd never thought I'd want, and part of me tried to resist and fight the sensation. I never had any intention of relinquishing my independence for anyone. And yet, with Lewis, I felt it was okay to not always be wary, because I trusted him.

Resurfacing from last night's memories, I fired up my laptop, preparing to finish the corrections on Victoria's website. Once she'd signed off on the final photographs and given me the edits for the text we'd drafted together, we'd almost be finished. Would it be the right opportunity to tell her who I was? I'd still be working for Hugh—we'd estimated until around Christmas—although he'd hinted there could be a longer contract in the works.

I couldn't decide what to do. If I followed my gut, stopped lying and told her I'd known all along we were related, her trust would disappear. Once she spoke to Stan and he filled her in on my prior visits and conversations, she would refuse to see me again, and I couldn't imagine not having Victoria in my life anymore.

One alternative stretched out before me. Maybe I could convince Stan to call a truce. Perhaps we could agree I'd never say anything to anybody about who I was, so Victoria would keep both of us in her life, although it was doubtful he'd agree. Funny how I'd started off on this journey wanting to get back at Stan, and subsequently Victoria. Now I wanted to stay close to her and had to figure out how to do so without causing any damage to everyone around me, even if it meant sparing my coldhearted biological father.

I found myself wishing for Dad, to be able to call him, hear him say, "Jeez, Freckles, you're in a bit of a pickle," and help me figure it out.

I let myself sit with the grief, felt it clamp around my heart for a while until I shook my head and forced myself to get back to work. Once done, I made myself a tea and sat at the table with the hospital invoice I'd steadily ignored in front of me. I'd had a message from Accounts Payable already, and I knew I'd have to settle the amount before the matter went further. I fished out my checkbook, preparing to make a partial payment, but as I was about to scribble the date, I paused.

Heart pounding, I grabbed my phone, brought up the calendar and flipped through it. Back and forth. Back and forth. Counting and recounting the days, my mind a jumble.

"No," I whispered. "No, no, *no*."

I checked again and, once more, found the same result each time I swiped. With everything else going on, I hadn't noticed—or paid enough attention—to the Due entry at the beginning of last week. Surely I couldn't be…

But of course I could. The first time Lewis and I had slept together, we'd been so caught up in everything, we'd been more than a little lax about protection. We'd used condoms ever since, but still… I tried to reassure myself my almost always reliable period was a few days late because I was overworked, overstressed, with way too much going on in my head. Yes, that was it. It *had* to be. The alternative was too petrifying.

I got up, stumbled to the bathroom and fumbled around the cabinet. When Tony and I split up, my period had been a day late and I'd bought a double pack of tests in a panic. The first one had been negative. I'd never needed the other. With shaking hands, I yanked it from the wrapper and went to the toilet, my fingers trembling so hard I couldn't aim straight, let alone put the cap back on securely. Somehow I managed to do both and sat on the edge of the tub, clutching the small plastic object, which held infinite, life-changing power, in my hand.

Tick, tock, tick, tock…

I urged the next three minutes to move at quadruple the speed but time seemed to pass more slowly. It didn't matter. Within sixty seconds there was no longer a single blue line, but a second one, too, growing stronger and stronger, filling the plastic window, mocking me, taunting me.

I was pregnant. *Pregnant!* There was a baby, a tiny human being, growing inside me.

Lewis's child.

No idea how long I sat there with my heart racing, the pregnancy test clenched between my fingers, cold sweat collecting under my arms. I couldn't get up. Couldn't move.

This wasn't part of my plan. I was broke, could barely keep a roof over my own head, let alone be responsible for a child. And as for Lewis… The bed upstairs was still warm from where we'd lain, and whenever we were apart, I ached for his touch, longed to hear his voice. But we'd dated for weeks, not months or years, we weren't ready for any kind of commitment. This would be our first Thanksgiving together, and the other morning I'd wondered if we should exchange Christmas gifts or whether it would be too much, too soon. Now I was poised to present him with the biggest surprise of all.

Because, despite all the reasons why not to, I already knew having this child was my only option. My mother hadn't wanted me. Stan had pushed me away. There was no way I could get rid of this baby and look myself in the mirror the rest of my life or make it through unscathed.

CHAPTER THIRTY-FIVE

I'**D BARELY MOVED FROM** my perch on the tub—barely moved at all—when the doorbell rang an hour later, and while my first instinct was to ignore it, whoever it was rang again and then a third time. I didn't think it was Lewis and assumed it was Mrs. Winchester, so I threw the test in the garbage can and quickly washed my hands. But when I opened the door, it was Victoria. She wore head-to-toe workout gear, her impossibly long, toned legs disappearing underneath her jacket, her cheeks flush from the cold.

"Hey. Lewis gave me your address. I thought I'd stop by so we can look at the website," she said, and when I gulped, she frowned. "Are you okay? You don't look well."

"Headache," I whispered. "You saw Lewis?"

"Yeah, we worked out this morning." She smiled brightly.

"I woke up super early and decided to stop by Audaz. What a place. I signed up on the spot. It's fantastic, isn't it?"

"I don't know. I haven't been yet."

She looked at me, eyes wide. "Oh, you...you don't mind, do you? Have I upset you?"

"No, it's not—"

"I know you said you might go, but with the work Hugh and I have piled on you—"

"That's not it," I snapped.

Victoria looked at me. Without another word, she stepped inside the apartment and closed the door, led me over to the sofa and, very gently, pushed me down onto it. "What's going on?"

"Nothing."

"I'm not leaving until you tell me. Is it Lewis? Is something wrong?"

I looked at her, wanted to explain but couldn't, not yet. "No, sorry. It's just my head."

She narrowed her eyes but nodded in an apparent sign of acquiescence. "I'm not sure I believe you, but when you're ready to talk, I'm here, okay? You can tell me anything."

"Okay," I whispered. "But I'll be fine, honest."

Victoria smiled and looked around. "So this is where you do your website magic. It's—"

"Sparse?" I said with a forced laugh, imagining seeing my apartment through her eyes.

"I was going to say *efficient*," she answered with another smile. "It's bijou."

"Now I'm not sure I believe *you*," I said, my shoulders dropping, vowing to pretend everything was normal. "Want some coffee?"

"No, thanks, working out gave me enough of a buzz." She retrieved a lip balm from her bag and as she was putting it back, glanced at the papers on my coffee table. She pointed at one of them. "Jesus, is that the hospital bill? Five grand? That's insane. You have insurance, right?"

I waved a hand. "I have kidneys. Maybe they'll take one of those."

She looked at me, furrowed her brow. "I don't want to intrude or be rude or anything," she said slowly, "and feel free to tell me to get lost, but do you... Would it help if I paid the other half of your invoice now?"

"No, it's fine." The prospect of scrimping until she paid me, and I got the first check from Bell Hops, not to mention—I shivered—what was happening inside me all felt exhausting, but I still couldn't push away my pride. "I'm okay, thanks for the offer, though."

"Do you have a pen?" she said, fishing around in her bag until I got one from the drawer. She pulled out her checkbook, filled one in and handed it to me.

"What's this for?" I said.

"I haven't dated it, so you cash it when you want to, okay?"

"I can't—"

"It's not a gift, Eleanor. Consider it a buffer and now you don't have to ask. If you don't need it, tear it up and throw it away." She smiled as I stared, incapable of speaking. "Anyway, how about we look at the website? And can I use the bathroom first?"

I remained speechless as I started up my laptop and went to the kitchen for glasses of water. As I was filling up the second, Victoria walked in, holding something in her hand.

"You're pregnant?" she said.

The test. When I'd put it in the garbage, I hadn't covered it up. I wanted to lie, tell her a friend had come over or fabricate some other story, but I couldn't bring myself to.

"Is it Lewis's?"

I nodded, my bottom lip quivering. "Yes."

"Does he know?" she said, and I shook my head. "How far along are you?"

"I'm not sure. I'm about a week late."

"You're five weeks then."

"What? But I can't be, we only had sex a couple of weeks—"

"You start counting the first day of your last period," she said with half a smile, but I could tell it was forced. I hadn't forgotten her comment at the spa about her friends getting pregnant easily, how desperate she was, and more guilt coiled around my gut, squeezing hard.

"I'm sorry... I don't know what to do, I—" I let out a sob as the tears came, and Victoria rushed to put her arms around me. She held me forever, whispering everything would be okay, she was there for me, before leading me to the sofa and fetching one of the glasses of water, encouraging me to take small sips until I calmed down.

"When will you tell him?" she said, taking my glass and setting it on the table.

"God, I don't know. I haven't got that far yet. I'm terrified."

"He thinks you're awesome. He kept talking about you, how smart you are—"

"Not smart enough to use contraception properly."

"It takes two to make a baby," she said sternly. "Don't you go blaming yourself, you hear me? And Lewis is a gem, incredibly buff and handsome, obviously, but he's so kind and...I don't know...*honorable*. I can't imagine it's the kind of situation he'd run from, whatever you choose to do."

"I already know," I said. "I'm keeping the baby, with or without Lewis around."

Victoria grabbed my hand. "Are you sure?"

"Yes," I said, surprised at the determination in my voice. "Yes, I am."

"I'll help you. Whatever you need. Time, support, money, stuff. I'm here."

There it was again, the connection between us, getting stronger each time we were together. I considered coming out with the truth, spilling my guts right there on the sofa, but I couldn't. The bond between us was still fragile and easily broken. I wouldn't risk her walking away, not now. I needed her. More than ever.

"I'm sorry," I said. "I know you and Hugh are having trouble, and I'm such a—"

"Please, don't."

"But it's not fair, and it'll happen for you soon, I know it—"

"It's okay—"

"—and you'll make an awesome mom, Victoria—"

"I don't think—"

"—far better than me, and—"

"*Stop it!*" she yelled, making me flinch and stop talking at the same time. She took a few shallow breaths before closing her eyes and whispering, "I know why I can't get pregnant…"

"What do you mean? Did you have more tests?"

She looked at me for a long time before shaking her head and saying, "No…it's…it's because of what happened to my sister."

CHAPTER THIRTY-SIX

A **THOUSAND THOUGHTS TORE THROUGH** me at once, one of them aiming for the center of my brain. She had to be talking about me. There'd been no mention of any other sibling, anywhere.

"You have a sister?" I said, trying to think three moves ahead, plan how I'd respond, and what to tell her, but coming up with nothing but panic.

"She…she died," Victoria whispered, and her words and the distress in her eyes almost made my heart stop beating. "My sweet little Angeline died."

"Oh, my God, that's awful," I said. "I didn't know. I had no idea."

"We never discuss it," Victoria said. "My parents are extremely private about her." She hesitated, as if trying to decide how much to tell me and whether breaking the family silence would be worth it. "She was almost seven years younger than me," she continued. "My mother had trouble conceiving. I guess it runs in the family. Anyway, they called her their little miracle, and she was the cutest thing you'd ever seen. Blond curls and big blue eyes… She looked like a doll." She studied my face. "In a way she reminds me of you."

My heart pumped so hard, I thought it might break. "You don't have to—"

"It happened the day before my eighth birthday…" Her voice was so low, I leaned in to make out what she'd say next, but instead of speaking again, a sob escaped her lips. She shut her eyes, shook her head.

"It's okay, it's okay," I said, reaching over. "If it's too difficult, you don't have to—"

"It's all such a blur…" Victoria didn't bother to wipe the tears streaming down her cheeks. "She'd started walking, toddling around on her wobbly legs. One afternoon we were in our bedrooms. Angeline was napping while I drew a picture or something, but I got bored, so I sneaked down to the kitchen to look for my birthday cake, and…and…she fell down the stairs."

"Jesus—"

"Mom kept telling me how dangerous they were. It's why they'd put up the stairgates. Everyone assumed Angeline climbed over the one at the top of the stairs because she'd started getting out of her crib."

I looked at her, unsure whether to ask my next question, deciding I should because I could feel she needed me to. "You don't think that's what happened?"

"I *know* it isn't," she whispered, the words tumbling out thick and fast, barely leaving enough time for me to process them. "I forgot to close the stairgate. It was all my fault. My baby sister… my darling Angeline died because of *me*. I *killed* her."

"But it was an accident. Or maybe you don't remember it properly? Perhaps—"

"You don't understand," she said, shaking her head. "I heard her fall, and when I found her at the bottom of the stairs and saw the stairgate open at the top... I—I ran up and...I closed it."

"Are you sure?"

"*Yes!* And I've never told anyone. I feel so guilty—"

"But you didn't mean—"

"I never *told*," she said, almost yelling now. "I let them think Angeline climbed over it when it was *my* fault. I left it open. What kind of a person does that, Eleanor? What kind of a person keeps secrets from their family?"

"I don't think—"

"I'll tell you. An awful, despicable, horrible one." She gulped in a lungful of air. "People get punished when they tell lies. What if I'm not meant to have children because of what I did? What if having a miscarriage was only the beginning?"

"That's not how it works," I said gently. "It wasn't your fault. You didn't mean to hurt her. What if you talked to your parents? They—"

"My parents? No, *no*. I couldn't—"

"But maybe they'd—"

"*No*. You won't say anything to them, or Hugh, will you? Do you promise?"

"I won't say a thing, I swear."

"I shouldn't have told you. You've got enough to worry about." She exhaled deeply and covered her throat with her hand. "Could I have a glass of water, too, please? Really cold, with ice, if you have it? My throat feels so raw."

I patted her arm and went to the kitchen, let the tap run until the water was frigid. My head wrestled with Victoria's revelation. I wanted to take her guilt and make it disappear, could well imagine the waves of it slamming into her over and over, relentless and pounding, eating away at her core for years.

She blamed herself for Angeline's death the way I blamed myself for Dad's, and while there was nothing we could do or say to each other to bring either of them back, would telling her we were sisters somehow help heal our broken hearts? Or would it appear a crass, opportunistic move on my part? Either way, I couldn't imagine how she'd held on to her secret, hating herself for what she'd done. As I took her the glass of water, I vowed I'd do whatever I could to help her, as she'd done for me. She didn't have to cope with this alone. Not anymore. Not now that we had each other.

When I went back into the living room, Victoria wasn't there, and I found her in my bedroom. I watched as she walked over to my shelf and reached up to retrieve Dad's snow globe, and as she did, her shirt slid up her back, enough for me to catch a glimpse of the angry palm-size bruise above her left hip. A shade of deep purple. Fresh.

"What happened to you?" I said and Victoria spun around.

"Oh, you scared me. Sorry. I was having a look—"

"I meant your hip. How did you get that bruise?"

"What? Oh, uh, I tripped and fell into the sideboard. I'm such a klutz."

"You tripped *backward*?"

"Yeah," she said. "It's nothing I—"

"I'm going to ask you something." I set down the glass of water while telling the rage building inside me to keep still, to stay calm. "And I want you to tell me the truth. Has Hugh ever laid a hand on you?"

"What?" Her voice went up a few notches. "No, of course not."

"Because I swear to God, I'll kill him if he has."

"He *hasn't*," Victoria said. "I tripped. I *did*. Honestly."

I waited for her to change her story, to tell me what really happened, but she remained silent. "There's more, I can tell." I moved toward her, put a hand on her shoulder.

"There's nothing going on."

"Victoria—"

"Eleanor, please." She shook me off and put the snow globe back. "I'm fine."

I followed her to the living room, anger simmering inside me. I was sure now Hugh had hurt Victoria, and I needed her to tell me, but if I pushed too hard, I'd risk scaring her away or, worse, strengthen her warped loyalties toward him. I knew it was hard for anyone to admit they were in an abusive relationship, and things weren't as perfect as everybody thought they were from the outside. I'd have to bide my time, tread lightly until she was ready, but how long would it take, and what if he hurt her again? How could I protect her if she didn't open up to me?

"I'd better go," she said, gathering her things, but I put my hand on hers.

"You're my best friend. I'm here for you, always and no matter what. I'll do anything for you, do you understand?"

"Anything?" she said. "Really?"

"Anything. All you need to do is ask."

CHAPTER THIRTY-SEVEN

LEWIS AND I SPENT most of Thanksgiving together, but by
Sunday night I felt so exhausted from pretending everything
was normal, I couldn't think or keep my eyes open. We sat on
my sofa, watching a movie I'd wanted to see for ages, but which
hadn't held an iota of my interest, my thoughts about the baby
and Hugh and Victoria all running circles through my head.

I'd called her a few times over the past week but our conversations had been quick, and she'd fobbed me off on account of
being too busy with the new company setup. While I'd almost
told Lewis about my suspicions regarding the state of Hugh and
Victoria's relationship a few times, I didn't want to betray her,
needed her to confide in me.

"I like your necklace and earrings," Lewis said, bringing my
scattered focus back to him. "They suit you." When I didn't
reply, he added, "Are you okay? You seem really preoccupied."

"Oh, you know. Website stuff," I said, working hard to make it sound believable.

"Why don't you let me take you to bed early?" He brushed his fingers down the side of my face. "I can think of a few ways I might be able to get you to relax."

I tried not to flinch or pull away as I shook my head. I'd feigned a classic headache twice and had to come up with something else. "Not tonight. I'm really tired and can't switch off. I need a long bath and a good night's sleep. Would you…uh, mind if I spent the night alone?"

"Whatever you need," he said, leaning over, kissing me gently. "Tell you what, you get some rest and I'll call you after the conference."

"Conference?"

"The fitness pros one tomorrow. I did tell you about it, didn't I? I know I mentioned it to Victoria at the gym the other day but I'm sure I told you, too."

"Maybe… I can't remember."

"See? Preoccupied. It's at the Marriott on Fore. I'll be there until late, these things tend to go on forever, and there are a few people I want to catch up with. I'll see you Tuesday?"

After kissing me again, he left me alone in my apartment, and I wished I hadn't asked him to go, that I'd had the courage to tell him about the baby. I was too scared to let him inside my heart more than I already had, was terrified of his reaction. He'd think I did this on purpose, I was trying to trap him, force him into being with me. He'd walk away, exactly how Stan had from my mother.

On Monday afternoon Lewis sent a few messages asking how I was, telling me he missed me, but when he phoned I let the call go to voice mail. Later, I listened to his husky whispers of how he couldn't wait to see me, how he was so glad we'd met, and I forced myself to not call him back and blurt out I was pregnant with his child. Victoria had suggested I wait awhile to tell him, that I should do so once I was sure how I felt about everything, and I knew she was right.

Still, when there was a knock on my door shortly after nine, I wondered if Lewis had abandoned his conference buddies in favor of coming home early, but instead it was Victoria. She looked around, peering past me, frowning.

"Are you alone? Lewis isn't here, right?"

"I'm alone. What's going on?" I said as I shut the door behind her. "Are you okay?"

"No. No, I'm not. I'm *angry*. I'm fucking *furious*." Her eyes narrowed some more, and her lips pursed as she shook her head and started muttering to herself.

"Victoria, calm down. Tell me what happened."

"Men," she said, her hands on her hips. "That's what's happened. Fucking *men*."

"Okay...but I think you have to give me a bit more context."

"When you asked about Hugh...about him hurting me, I... I lied."

The air felt as if it had been sucked out of the room. While I'd had my suspicions, I hadn't expected her to be so direct about her situation, so brazen and forthcoming. I felt taken aback, didn't know how to respond. The way she stood there, so bold and strong, I could tell something had changed. Something had snapped. This was a woman who'd had enough. A woman on the edge.

"How...how long has it been going on?" I said.

"On and off. It's never been anything bad—"

"Anything is bad," I said, her fury igniting mine. "He gave you that bruise on your hip, didn't he? He physically hurts you?"

"It's the first time he's ever touched me, I swear," she said. "It was never like this before. Up until now it was all emotional, you know? The things he said, the way he said them, what he allowed me to do or not do. I kept trying to reason it was because he was under pressure at work or worrying about money or whatever. Well, *bullshit*."

"Tell me what happened," I said. "Tell me what he did."

"I didn't lie about falling into the sideboard, but I didn't trip. We had an argument and he pushed me after I accused him of having an affair, and—"

"Wait. What? He pushed you and you think he's seeing someone else?"

"I'm positive. It started weeks ago. Around when you and I met, actually. He'd switch off his phone when he said he was still at the office. Then he started coming home way later than usual, and I could tell he'd had a shower."

"Still, it could be—"

"I buy his body wash, Eleanor, and it doesn't smell like *that*." She paused, but I kept quiet because I could tell more words were preparing to rush out. "I'm such an idiot. Do you know what I told myself up until now? That he may be controlling and a bit nasty at times, but at least he was loyal." She laughed and threw her hands in the air. "Can you believe it? I appeased myself with the thought that it could be *worse*. How pathetic. I'm such a goddamn loser."

"No, you're not," I said. "You're *not*."

"I *am*. I haven't told my parents about him. Dad thinks the sun shines out of his ass and Mom would think I'm weak and a failure for him not treating me the way Dad does her."

"She wouldn't—"

"She *would*, because I've never been allowed to fail at anything." She shook her head. "We Gallingers live in such a bubble. Everything's always got to be just *so*. God help us if we have a hair out of place or don't RSVP to a party the proper way or, dear Lord, get *divorced*. And so here I am, making excuse after excuse for the way Hugh treats me—"

"Victoria, you're human and, believe me, you're not alone.

Lots of us make excuses when the ones who are supposed to love us hurt us the most."

"Maybe you're right," she said, "but I can't live this way anymore. I won't. And let me tell you something, I've had enough of men taking advantage of us, of thinking they're better than us, smarter, faster, stronger and—"

"They don't all think that way," I said.

"Yes, they do. My dad, God love him, is exactly that way. He's ruthless."

I tried not to shiver. "Maybe, but not *my* dad. And not Lewis."

Victoria's face fell and she reached for my hand. "Oh, sweetheart..."

"What?" As she squeezed my fingers, a giant lump grew in the pit of my belly.

"Nothing. It's nothing," Victoria said. "I'm sure—"

"Stop. Why did you say, 'Oh, sweetheart,' like that? Do you know something?"

She hesitated, spun her wedding ring around her finger with her thumb. An almost imperceptible move, but I knew her now. It meant she was uncomfortable, hiding something.

"Tell me," I said. "Whatever it is, you have to tell me."

"Are you sure you want to know?" she whispered. "Because I can't take it back."

"Tell me," I repeated. "Does he know about the baby? Did you tell him by accident?"

"No, of course not. I wouldn't betray you. How are you feeling, anyway? Are you—"

"*Stop.* Just tell me what you meant. Please."

Victoria looked at me, shaking her head. "I saw him. I saw the dirty *fucker.*" She spat the word with such vehemence, it made me take a step back.

"What do you mean? You saw Lewis? Where?"

"I didn't want to be home when Hugh got back, couldn't face

looking at him, so I went for a walk to try to figure out what to do, you know? Anyway, I went past the Marriott on—"

"Fore Street," I said, a tremble in my voice.

"Yes. You knew Lewis was there?"

"He said he was at a conference," I whispered.

"Well, maybe that's true, but he was at the bar, I saw him through the window, and, oh, Eleanor, I'm so, so sorry... He was with another woman. They were...kissing."

I was sinking, drowning, right there in my apartment. "No, he wouldn't—"

"And it wasn't innocent. It wasn't innocent at all."

It was as if I'd been punched, as if the mugger had attacked me all over again, hitting and pounding me in the head with his fists. Stumbling, I grabbed the back of the chair to steady myself, felt everything spin, threatening to pull me to the floor. My mother's voice filled my head, telling me I shouldn't be surprised. I was unworthy, unlovable, hopeless, pointless, a waste of space. I tried to push the words away, thought I'd almost stopped believing them, that Lewis wasn't like that, he'd never hurt me because he cared and I meant something to him.

"No," I said, the remaining fragments of hope disappearing one by one. "He *wouldn't.*"

Victoria's face fell. "I'm so sorry. I wasn't sure what to do, whether or not to tell you, but I couldn't live with myself if I lied to you. I can't let him do to you what Hugh's doing to me, not when you're...when you're pregnant."

She handed me her phone and my legs threatened to collapse entirely when I saw the photo. Although blurry, Lewis was unmistakable, and a petite brunette dressed in a red shift dress and silver heels had her lips locked to his, her slim arms draped around his neck, her breasts pressed against him. Precisely the kind of woman I'd always pictured him with, the kind I could never be or compete with. I stared at the shot, tears of rage, disappointment, frustration, disbelief all mixing together as I let out a sob.

Victoria swore and threw her phone back in her bag. "Don't you dare cry, do you hear me? They're not worth our tears, not Hugh or Lewis. Here we are, bending over backward to make them happy, and what do we get in return? *Screwed.* Well, there's to be no more, let me tell you, Eleanor. We're done. It's you and me now. The two of us and—"

I sank down on the sofa as she continued to rant but I stopped listening. I didn't need to wonder anymore how Lewis felt about me. Whatever it was, it had never been much. What we'd had was over, he was already moving on, it had only been a matter of time. I'd known from the beginning I'd never be enough for him, but he'd had me so convinced he liked me—maybe loved me a little, even—I'd let my defenses down. I'd let him in.

You stupid bitch, the voice in my head whispered. *You stupid, pathetic little* bitch. *You thought he'd want to stay with you? That you could make him love* you? *You're nobody. You're nothing. You're—*

"*No,*" I shouted, silencing the words, and Victoria's. "I'm not nobody. I'm worth more than this."

"That's right," Victoria said, nostrils flaring. "You're worth ten of him. A hundred."

"I'm not taking this shit," I shouted. "I. Am. Not. Taking. This. *Shit.*"

Victoria's chest was heaving now, her hands on her hips, eyes blazing like a thousand bonfires. "What are we going to do? We can't let them get away with this. We *won't.*"

"I'm going to tell Lewis to go fuck himself. Are you going to do the same to Hugh?"

Her face hardened some more, chin raised. "We have a prenup."

"Brilliant."

"Yes, but if I can prove he's having an affair, he'll walk away with almost nothing."

"Okay, then let's figure out who Hugh's been seeing."

"Good. That's good. I've been through all his clothes and pockets and everywhere else I could think of at home. There's nothing there but he wouldn't be that stupid." She bit her thumbnail, furrowed her brow. "I'll follow him when he goes out next time and says it's with his friends, and... I know it's a lot to ask, but could you get him out of the office tomorrow? For lunch, maybe? Let me know when, so I can snoop around? I'd only need fifteen minutes."

"But other people will be there. They'll see you, and when they tell him you were in, he's bound to become more careful, especially after you accused him of cheating already."

Her shoulders dropped. "You're right...unless—" she snapped her fingers "—unless I wait until he's asleep, take his badge and go to the brewery. He'd never know, would he?"

"What if he wakes up and you're gone? And he looks at the badge logs every so often to measure efficiencies or whatever. I mean, it might not matter, but—"

"No," she said, shaking her head. "I definitely don't want him to know what I'm doing... *Shit!* I can't let him get away with this. I have to get into his office."

"I'll go in early tomorrow," I said. "It'll be far less conspicuous, actually, not conspicuous at all. With the hours I've been putting in, nobody will blink."

"You'd do that for me?" she whispered.

"Of course I would. Do you know the password for his computer?"

She shook her head again. "No, he changed it... I don't know about this, Eleanor. You're not a private detective, and I know how to handle him."

"Your bruise tells me otherwise," I said. "Let me do this. Please?"

She sank down on the sofa, reminding me of a deflated,

week-old balloon, looking like she'd given up. "I…I'm going to divorce him, aren't I? I'm going to be all alone."

"No, you won't. You'll have me. You said so, it's going to be us now."

"And the baby," she said. "It'll be the three of us against the world."

I felt exhausted, spent, and when I tried a smile, it probably resembled a pathetic grimace, but as I looked at Victoria, I felt it transform itself into something stronger.

"The three of us." I touched my new necklace. "You have no idea how good that sounds."

CHAPTER THIRTY-EIGHT

BY SIX THIRTY THE next morning I was at Bell Hops, surrounded by darkness. The cursor on Hugh's screen blinked at me, daring me to try again as I forced my brain to remember the password I'd seen him enter a few days earlier when Genie had come in to run a quick systems check, which I thought could have waited. I closed my eyes, pictured myself sitting next to him, attempted to see his fingers moving across his keyboard in my mind's eye. Three attempts before being locked out, and after using two of them, I accepted Victoria was right. I was no sleuth, no Sherlock Holmes or Lara Croft, but I wasn't defeated. Not yet.

I opened the top drawer of his desk, looked through everything with enough stealth to not displace things and make it obvious someone had searched for something. There was nothing in the top drawer, but in the middle one a folder with Bell Hops's latest financial reports caught my eye, and I flicked through the profit and loss statement. I'd assumed the company was doing well, and while I wasn't an accountant like my mother, I knew enough to tell Bell Hops was in trouble. Big trouble. Over half a million dollars lost this year alone. I turned the page, studied the balance sheet, compared assets and liabilities. The debt load was huge and I estimated if they didn't do something soon, their cash flow wouldn't last the winter.

I shook my head, refocused on my hunt for evidence of Hugh's affair, spotted a plain white cardboard box at the back of the third drawer, hidden behind the hanging folders, about a third of the size of a shoebox.

I lifted it out and opened it up, hands trembling, my throat dry. Tucked underneath a stack of business cards was a set of birth control pills, a week of them already punched out. Why the hell did Hugh have them in his drawer? Was it an old pack belonging to Victoria, perhaps? But why would he have it at the office? Maybe it belonged to his mistress, but that didn't make sense, either.

I put the pills down and kept going, still unsure of what I was looking for, exactly, and hoped I'd know when I found it. But after searching through the rest of the drawers, I'd found nothing screaming *adulterer*. I dug through a pile of old papers on the floor next to me, flipped through binders and notepads, coming up empty again and again, my frustrations rising.

Time was disappearing fast, and soon the first of my colleagues would arrive. I crossed to the bookcase and pulled out a few binders, found nothing and moved on to one marked Obsolete. As I did so, a small orange envelope fell to the floor. I snatched it up and emptied the contents on the desk, letting out a loud gasp.

Photographs. Three black-and-white close-ups of a naked woman on a bed, her head deliberately cropped out. In one of the shots her legs were slightly parted as she knelt on the pillow, one hand placed strategically enough it still left something to the imagination, the other covering a breast. I knew where they'd been taken, I'd seen those pillowcases before, and while the embroidered word was almost obscured by the woman's thigh, there was enough for me to know exactly what it said. *Hugh.*

As far as nudes went, they'd been tastefully shot, and were reminiscent of the picture of Victoria hanging in their bedroom. Except it wasn't her, and I knew this because of two things. One; with her back arched, I could see this woman's hair spilling in waves over her shoulders—not dark hair like Victoria's, but a light shade of blond. And two, the hint of a Celtic tattoo I could just about make out on the woman's wrist. Both Hugh and I knew someone with that kind of a tattoo, someone he saw and interacted with every day. Often had lunch with. Someone who fluttered her eyelashes whenever he walked into the office. *Genie.*

"You bastard," I said, stuffing the photographs into my bag before reconsidering. If Hugh knew Victoria was on to him and Genie, he'd dispose of any other evidence, and Victoria would lose the advantage. It would be easy enough for her to hire a proper private detective to follow her husband around and get all the evidence she needed. I smacked the pictures down on his desk and took photos of them with my phone.

As I went to slip them back in the envelope, I spotted something on the floor. A piece of paper—it must've fallen when I'd pulled out the pictures. I unfolded it, my eyes darting across the page. It was a letter dated a few weeks ago, responding to the request to increase Victoria's life insurance, confirming it was "in process."

"Jesus Christ," I whispered. "Five million?"

Had Victoria known about the change? Had it been approved since the letter had arrived? For an amount that large she would've seen the original request, surely? She'd have signed it, and what about a medical? She hadn't mentioned anything, then again we hadn't gone into any detail about our personal finances. Aside from her comment about her lack of interest and leaving it all to Hugh, she'd said nothing. Still, she had to know about such a hefty increase.

Unless Hugh had got her to sign something while fobbing off her questions. But why?

I shuddered as the numbers on Bell Hops's financial statements zoomed into my brain. The company was losing money, and a lot of it. But… I shook my head. No, Hugh *wouldn't*. Adultery was one thing, but… I could barely get myself to think the word *murder*, except once it was in my head, I couldn't make it leave. I grabbed my cell and dialed the number for the insurance company's twenty-four-hour helpline. A representative called Sloane with a soft Texan drawl asked a set of security questions to verify my identity as Victoria Gallinger, all of which I answered with ease.

"Okay, now, let me check." She made tutting noises. "Oh, my stars, our system's really slow right now. It's been buggy for the last hour. No…wait…and we're back. All righty, then. How can I help y'all?"

"Uh…" I'd called on impulse without thinking things through. I struggled to stop my voice from sounding frantic and forced a smile, knowing it would alter my delivery. "Well, my husband and I spoke about increasing my life insurance, but I can't remember the details." I let out a small laugh and squeezed my eyes shut tight, trying to keep my voice steady. "I'm pregnant, and I've got a serious case of baby brain."

"Congratulations," Sloane said as she tapped on her keyboard. "I mean about the pregnancy, not the baby brain. Oh, my, I remember when my first—"

"I'm sorry, but I'm in a bit of a rush," I said, cringing at my bluntness.

"Oh, sure, sure. Let me see… Here it is. The coverage increased from two to five million."

"Increased? You mean it's already been approved?"

"Yes, ma'am. The payment cleared last week."

"And who's the beneficiary?"

Another few keyboard clicks. "Your husband. He's listed as the sole beneficiary."

"Is that new, too?"

"Yes, ma'am. Your previous policy listed your husband as the beneficiary, but if there were any children they were to receive fifty percent of the policy, split equally between them."

My hand dropped down and, without saying another word, I hung up. A shiver traveled down my spine as I tried to put the pieces together in some kind of logical order. Hugh was sleeping with Genie, probably. Bell Hops was going under, that was a certainty, and he stood to lose whatever he'd invested unless he poured more cash into the business. Cash he might not have in the first place, and certainly wouldn't get if Victoria left him and enforced the prenup. But the life insurance increase had been applied for before she'd accused him of having an affair. Did that mean he'd been planning this—whatever *this* was—for a while?

Somehow he'd managed to change her insurance and exclude children from being beneficiaries. I tried telling myself it made sense if they couldn't have kids, but then why change it at all? And then I knew… Victoria *had* become pregnant, and while she said Hugh hadn't known, maybe he'd found out. Had he caused the miscarriage somehow? Was that why he had birth control pills in his desk? Had he been giving them to her to make sure she didn't get pregnant again before the insurance policy changed?

Another shiver went through me at the thought of Hugh's possible intentions. I couldn't grasp he could be so evil. He'd seemed genuine on the surface, and a good boss, too—"The best I've ever had," Genie had told me—but if still waters ran deep, he was the human equivalent of the Mariana Trench.

I wanted to call Victoria and warn her, but couldn't afford for her to shut down on me, and while the photos were evidence of an affair, the insurance information was pure speculation on my part. Except another terrifying thought occurred to me. Hugh's first wife, Natalie, had *died*. Had the fire really been a terrible tragedy, or was there more to it? Before I made any kind of allegations about Hugh, I needed to do more digging into his past, and as I stood there, I realized I knew just the right person to help.

It wasn't quite seven thirty, but I grabbed my phone and called Charlotte, grateful she'd insisted we swap numbers at the end of Victoria and Hugh's pre-Thanksgiving dinner.

"Hi, Charlotte, it's Eleanor."

"Eleanor," she said, sounding more than a little surprised. "Is everything okay?"

"Uh, yeah, I'm good. Sorry to call you so early—"

"Oh, don't worry, the kids always get me up by six." Her voice became muffled. "Girls, *girls*. I'm on the phone. Keep it down. Sorry, Eleanor."

"It's okay."

"Would you believe there's been a power outage at their school since last night? They had to cancel class for this morning at least. I was hoping for a quiet day, instead I'm on my second coffee already. Ugh. Anyway, it was lovely meeting you and Lewis the other week."

"Yes, it was," I said, pushing a new level of bubbliness into my voice. "Victoria was so sweet to invite us."

"She's a darling, she really is. Always has been."

"Actually," I said, my mind speeding ten miles ahead. "I was thinking of throwing a surprise party for her. You know, to celebrate launching her new business. I've got a few ideas, but I'd love your input as the two of you are so close."

"Oooh, sounds lovely," Charlotte said. "Tell me what you have in mind?"

"Uh, well, can we meet? I could come over now."

"Well…is there a big rush? Can we talk about it on the phone?"

"Some of my party ideas are a bit…uh, elaborate, you know? And I can show you some examples if we meet face-to-face. Besides, brainstorming works far better in person." I crossed my fingers. I wanted to sit opposite her and gauge her reaction when I steered the conversation to Hugh and Victoria, and then to Hugh and Natalie.

"Hmm… I promised to take the kids to Crackle today, God help me," Charlotte said with a laugh. "It's a new paint-your-own-pottery place they've been begging to go to for weeks."

"I could come there?"

"Well, okay. If you don't mind being surrounded by kids…"

I glanced at my stomach and closed my eyes. "Not at all."

"I'll send you the address. Meet me at nine?"

"I'll bring you a latte."

"Ha. Can you add a shot of Baileys?"

Before I could answer, the lights went on in the hallway and I heard a deep laugh, followed by a pair of voices, one of them Hugh's. *Fuck.* Victoria was supposed to have texted me when he left their place, but she hadn't, and now I stood in his office, in the dark.

"I'll see you later, Charlotte," I said, hanging up and scrambling to shove the photographs and insurance letter back into the envelope before returning it to its original place on the shelf. I ducked out of his office at the exact same time Hugh's and Genie's heads appeared at the bottom of the stairs, her luscious blond hair bouncing with every step, her three-quarter-length sleeves revealing the Celtic tattoo on her wrist.

"Oh, hi," she said when she saw me. Was a blush creeping up to her ears?

"Morning." Hugh beamed, not looking even slightly phased. "Couldn't sleep, either?"

"Not really, no," I said, plastering ten layers of fake cheerfulness over my face. Two could play at the lying game. What he didn't know was how much practice I'd had in recent weeks. "There's a lot going on."

"Anything I can help with?" he said, and as his eyes dropped to my neck, I saw a small frown cross his face.

My hand instinctively flew up to cover the jewelry from Victoria. Hugh hardly knew me—or my wardrobe—well enough to suspect it was new or that she'd given it to me, but I wasn't taking any chances, not if my suspicions about him were even partially true.

"I really should get to work," I said, brushing past him and Genie, but as soon as they went to his office, laughing and chatting, I grabbed my bag and jacket and left Bell Hops without looking back.

CHAPTER THIRTY-NINE

I SHOWED UP AT CRACKLE a few minutes early and peered in through the windows. The place was already busy, at least half of the dozen tables filled with tired-looking parents. Eager kids dressed in smocks had half-painted pieces of pottery in front of them, brushes clutched in their tiny hands, budding artists ready to create their masterpieces. I didn't spot Charlotte, so I waited outside, stood under the awning to get out from the drizzle. She arrived ten minutes later, red-faced and blotchy, her updo more of a down-do as she hobbled along on her crutches with her mini-me girls in tow.

"Hey," she said. "Good to see you. Daisy, Lily, this is Eleanor. She's a friend of mine and Auntie Victoria's." They looked up at me, muttering a quick hello. "Let's go inside," Charlotte continued. "Now, remember, girls, you can pick two pieces each, okay? Be careful and take your time. Don't break anything."

It took a while for us to settle down, and I wondered how I'd get Charlotte to open up, given the fact we sat at a tiny table, my legs already cramping from being on a chair the size of a toadstool. Lily, tall and dancerlike, chose a frog and a race car, whereas Daisy, the younger one with a face full of freckles, selected a pumpkin and a piggy bank. The owner came over and distributed paint to the girls, and after Charlotte and I helped them put on their smocks and roll up their sleeves, they got to work.

"About this party," Charlotte said, turning to me. "What were you thinking?"

"Uh, well," I said, remembering a corporate event from years ago, "I thought we could start with a treasure hunt. Give her a single clue leading to another and another."

"That sounds fun. We could take her all over Portland."

"Sure, why not," I said quickly.

"And we could end up at her new office, decorated to the hilt. I could ask Hugh—"

"No," I said, and both Daisy and Lily looked up at me, their eyebrows raised in surprise. I lowered my voice. "Let's keep this a secret from both of them. He's been so involved with the business, it would be great to do something nice for him, too, don't you think?"

"Oh, yes. I completely agree," Charlotte said.

"He works so hard, he deserves a break." How could I talk like this without throwing up?

"Yes, he does."

I paused, gave a long, dramatic sigh Amy would've given me a standing ovation for. "Actually, sometimes I think he does far too much. I think... No...no, never mind..."

"What's wrong?" Charlotte said. "Is everything okay?"

"Well...I'm a little worried about him, to be honest," I whispered.

She moved her chair a little closer to me, our knees almost touching. "Why?"

"He's always staying late at the office. I mean, I work long hours, but he's worse."

Charlotte sat back and smiled. "Oh, well, that's nothing new. He's always been—"

"Can I go to the bathroom, Mommy?" Daisy asked.

"Sure, babycakes. Want me to come with you?" When Daisy shook her head, Charlotte added, "Okay. Lily, go with her, would you?"

Lily rolled her eyes but dutifully trudged to the bathroom holding her younger sister's hand, lining up behind a few kids already waiting. The opportunity gave me a bit of time to speed things up, so I made a quick calculation in my head and opted for a new angle.

"Your girls are adorable," I said. "They're so well behaved."

Charlotte shook her head and blew out her cheeks. "Not always, believe me. Twenty minutes ago, I'd have sworn they were the spawn of Satan."

"Still, kids are great. You're lucky… Victoria told me they've been trying, and I was so sorry to hear things aren't working out for them. It's incredibly hard for her."

"I know." Charlotte leaned in. "It's such a shame. So many of her friends have had babies and she feels so left out. She was in tears the other day, and I didn't know what to say. I felt guilty because I have two lovely girls. She dotes on them, of course, but it's not the same as having your own."

"No, I suppose it isn't. But…I feel for Hugh, too," I said, trying not to grit my teeth. "I mean, with what happened to his first wife, Natalie…? I couldn't believe it. How horrible."

"Gosh, yes, heartbreaking." She rolled a paintbrush under her fingers, her eyes welling up. "Nat was such a lovely person. I still miss her every day."

"Oh, Charlotte, I'm sorry." I was going to hell for all the

manipulation and the lies I was telling, but I had to keep going, I didn't have much time. "I didn't know you were so close."

"Best friends," she said.

"And Victoria knew her, too?"

"They weren't as close as Nat and me. But she still cried for weeks."

"You all knew each other then? From before? And Hugh, too?"

"Kind of. I knew Nat from work and had introduced her to Victoria," she said. "A month later we went to the movies. Victoria was late so we kept a spot for her between ours, and Nat ended up next to the only other spare seats in the entire theater. Anyway, when this guy arrived with a friend, he asked if the seats were taken, and he and Nat started talking."

"And that was Hugh?"

"Yeah. They were great together, and a few months later they were engaged." She smiled at the memory. "When they got married, Nat thanked Victoria for her crappy timekeeping because if she hadn't been late, she might have ended up sitting next to Hugh and marrying him instead. God, talk about premonitions."

"Can I ask what happened to Nat? Victoria mentioned a fire, but…"

"Oh, it was awful," Charlotte said. "Nat wasn't well so she decided not to come out with us one night when we went to a club. When she got home, she drew herself a bath and lit some candles, you know, usual stuff…"

"And the fire…?"

"They said she must've forgotten the candle in the bedroom. The draft blew the curtains over the flame, and by the time she realized, she couldn't escape." She shivered.

"Weren't there any smoke detectors?"

"Yes, but not in the bedroom with the en suite, and both doors were closed. The alarm in the living room didn't go off. Hugh blamed himself for that. He tested it about six months earlier but hadn't checked more recently. Nat had noise-canceling head-phones in the bathroom, too. They were a birthday gift from Victoria, so you can imagine how she felt about giving those to her. No wonder they ended up together, she and Hugh, with so much guilt between them."

"Wasn't it strange?" I said carefully, unsure how much I'd get away with. "I mean, them ending up together so soon after Natalie passed?"

"I can see why you might think so from the outside," Char-lotte said slowly, with a warning edge to her voice. "But to all of us, it felt natural and organic how their relationship devel-oped. Hugh was lucky to have Victoria as a friend, we all were, and you can't make judgments like that when you haven't lived through it yourself."

"No, you're absolutely right. I can't imagine. It must've been horrific."

"Oh, it was hell. The police interviewed Hugh—"

"The police?"

"Yeah, isn't it standard procedure when there's insurance money involved?"

"There was life insurance?" I tried hard to keep my innocent look while my head wanted to scream at her that Hugh was a murderer. He was *dangerous*.

"Yeah, she'd had it for years. I'm not sure how much. Enough for them to ask questions."

"But how would money have been a motive?" I said. "He came from a rich family."

"Not really." Charlotte glanced around, lowering her voice even more and I said a silent prayer to the gossip gods for be-stowing her with such a loose tongue. "His father declared bank-ruptcy a month after Nat died. All Hugh's inheritance—" she snapped her fingers "—gone. And when that happened, the cops hauled him in for questioning again. All that suspicion really hurt him, it was so unfair."

"Because he had an alibi, thank goodness."

"Oh, yes, and it was titanium. We were all at the club together. Victoria, Hugh, Malcolm and me, some of our other friends. There were at least ten of us who confirmed he was there all night."

I hesitated, didn't know how far or hard to push. "He's lucky you were there for him."

"Still, it was really hard. Victoria helped him through it all. So did her parents."

"*Her* parents?"

"Yeah, Stan's girlfriend died in a car accident when he was younger, and Madeleine supported him. I guess kindness runs in the family. Anyway, they were a rock to Hugh. He was distraught. Blamed himself. Couldn't eat or sleep for months. In the end I'm sure even the cops could see you can't fake that much grief for that long."

Or could you? I wondered. It wasn't impossible, especially not with cash on the line. He might have found out about his father's bankruptcy well before it was declared, and decided his next move was to kill his wife. Had he increased Nat's insurance, too? If he'd got away with murder once, wouldn't it have bolstered his confidence, made him feel invincible?

"Anyway, Hugh found solace in Victoria," Charlotte said, "and they're such a great couple. He's taking her on a Caribbean cruise after Christmas. She was telling me the details the other night. Hugh arranged it all. Can you imagine? Watching the sunset from the deck? Counting down the New Year? It sounds amazing. I wish Malcolm would take the hint, I've told him a thousand times I need a vacation and—oh, hi, girls. All set?"

As Daisy and Lily sat back down and Charlotte fussed over them, helping them decide how to decorate their pieces, my mind whirred. Victoria hadn't mentioned the vacation, and while a cruise ship might be the perfect place to watch the sun go down, wasn't it also the perfect place for an accident? Maybe Victoria would slip overboard. Go missing one morning as she went for a stroll on the deck, or after dinner, when Hugh could blame it on her having one too many nightcaps he'd plied her with.

The more I thought about it, the more I knew Victoria was in danger. Worse, she had no idea. She thought her only problem was a cheating husband. I had to tell her, had to warn her. I'd left the hospice when Dad needed me, ignored all the signs. I wouldn't make that mistake again. I had to do something.

"I have to go," I said, jumping up, almost knocking the girls' pieces off the table.

"Already? But we haven't talked about the secret party yet."

"Uh, yeah, but I got a message from Hugh." I waggled my phone in the air. "Website emergency. I'll call you later."

Without waiting for her reply, I ran out of Crackle. My fingers stabbed at my cell, attempting to dial Victoria's number as my brain debated what I'd say, how I'd tell her what I'd found out and, most of all, whether she'd believe me.

CHAPTER FORTY

VICTORIA DIDN'T PICK UP the first time I called. Nor the next, nor the third. I dialed and redialed. Hanging up each time I got her voice mail without saying a word. I sent her a text. PICK UP YOUR PHONE; another saying, NEED TO TALK; and still, no answer. I considered contacting the detective who'd called after I'd been mugged but couldn't remember his name. Besides, what would I tell the police without sounding crazy? I had no proof, just a possible chain of stitched-together events, but that didn't mean I was wrong. I tried calling Victoria again and, finally, after another half a dozen attempts, she answered.

"What do you want?" she said, and I frowned at her tone. She sounded angry—no, *livid*—even more than she had at my apartment the night before when she'd told me about Hugh.

"You were right," I said as I ran down the street. I'd decided

I'd give her some details on the phone, but go to her place and share the rest in person. "I found naked photos—"

"Oh, *really*? Print them off the internet, did you? As a diversion?"

My brow furrowed deeper as I tried to understand. "What? No, I need to tell you—"

"What? More lies about who you are and what you've been doing?"

Her words stopped me cold, and my feet refused to budge another inch. Oh, Jesus, *no*. She'd found out who I was. Stan had finally decided to tell her. She *knew*. My head threatened to shatter as I grappled with the knowledge, attempting to work out how to control the impending explosion, convince her my identity was irrelevant right now, how she could hate me later. In the meantime there were bigger things at stake, far more important ones we had to tackle, together.

"Victoria, I can explain. I'm coming over. We'll sit down and—"

"Don't bother. Because I never want to see you again. *Ever*."

"I'm sorry, I didn't want you to find out—"

The cold, hard sound of Victoria's laugh bounced around my skull. "Sorry? You think saying *sorry* will make it all better?"

"What did he tell you?" I whispered.

"Hugh never told me anything."

"Wait. Hugh?"

"Yes, Hugh. My *husband*. You two thought you were so clever, didn't you?"

"I don't know what—"

"Why do you think I didn't warn you he was on his way this morning? Because there was no point, was there? You already *knew*. You've probably been screwing him on your desk and making fun of me for being such a stupid, trusting bitch."

"But we never—"

"*Stop it.* I went through his briefcase when he was in the

shower this morning," she said, each word a poisoned dart flying my way. "I found them, Eleanor. I found them."

"Found what? What are you talking about?"

"Your underwear! Your fucking polka-dot panties. You slutty *bitch*."

"Victoria, wait. Whatever you found, they're not mine."

"You were wearing the exact same pair at the spa. What's that? Coincidence?"

"They're not mine, I promise. I'm not the one having an affair with Hugh."

"I don't believe you." Victoria lowered her voice to a terse whisper. "All this time I've been confiding in you, sharing secrets with you, and you've been sleeping with—"

"*I didn't!* I'd never do anything to hurt you. I found photos at his office and… I'm coming over. Stay—"

Victoria hung up.

I tried calling again, redialed over and over, sent a dozen messages asking her to pick up or call back, I needed to speak to her. When she didn't reply, I sent another and another. I told her I was coming over. I'd stay until she opened her door. She had to speak to me.

All I wanted was for her to believe me, and this time, I'd tell her everything. The entire truth about who I was, and what I'd done, right from the start. The irony of it being me—a liar and a fraud—finding proof of her husband's infidelities didn't escape me. But I was her half sister, her *family*, and the thought made me stronger than I could've ever imagined. There was no more question about where my loyalties lay, something I had to make her see. Whatever she thought she knew about what I'd done to hurt her, she was wrong, and I'd make her understand. And afterward, if she never wanted to see me again, I'd walk away, providing she was safe. It would break my heart, but her well-being and her future were all that mattered. They were paramount.

As I went to hail a cab, Lewis's number flashed up on my screen, and although I wanted to let it go to voice mail, the pent-up frustration inside me threatened to bubble over. There was no telling what I'd do if I didn't let some of it out. I waved the cab past and picked up.

"Why are you calling me?"

"Eleanor? Are you okay?"

"I said, why are you calling me?"

"What's the matter? Has something happened?"

"You know exactly what's happened, you *asshole*," I said. "You were seen."

"Seen? What are you talking about?"

"At the bar, kissing another woman."

There was a pause. Long enough for him to deny it, but he didn't even try. "Don't ever call me again," I said. "Don't stop by my place. Don't contact me. Just…*don't*."

"Eleanor, wait, I didn't know her, I promise. She walked up to me and—"

I let out a laugh. "Is that the best you can do? Honestly, do you think I'm that stupid?"

"I promise I didn't—"

I hung up, willing myself not to cry. Why hadn't I been more careful? Why had I let him into my heart and my bed, the latter of which would have lifelong consequences? I threw my phone back into my bag and continued walking, gulping in lungful after lungful of cold air. When I saw another cab, I flagged it down, jumped in and directed the driver to Victoria's apartment, forcing myself to calm down. Her thinking I was having an affair with Hugh was a misunderstanding. We'd sort everything out, together. It would be the two of us again, just like we'd said last night, and, in time, it would be three.

When I got to her place and stood with my finger pressed on the buzzer, she wouldn't let me in. Finally, after waiting and ringing on and off for three minutes, one of the other residents opened the front door and I pushed past her, bounded up the stairs, two at a time, banging on Victoria's door with the palm of my hand so hard, one of her neighbors popped his head out of his apartment to see what the fuss was about.

"It's me," I shouted. "Let me in, Victoria. You have to let me in."

"Enough," she yelled when she opened up, and I thought she was going to punch me, but she let her hands drop by her sides. "I'm begging you, Eleanor, stop."

"I didn't sleep with him. Please, you have to believe me."

She stood still for a second, looking at me, before finally stepping aside and letting me in, closing the door behind us. "You remember what I told you about the prenup? If it's money you're after, you're screwed."

"Stop. I have to show you something." I pulled out my phone. "These are the photos I found this morning in Hugh's office."

She stared at them, then at me. "But that's not you, it's... Wait, that's—"

"Genie, yes."

"Oh, my God... *Genie*? I thought she had a crush on him, but—"

"Show me the underwear you found. Please?" I said. Victoria hesitated at first, then pulled out a pair of black-and-red panties from her pocket and I gasped. "These aren't mine. They're the same pattern as the ones I have, yes, but I don't own a single thong, Victoria, and they're tiny. Look. They'd never fit me."

Hope spread across her face. "So...you're...you're really not sleeping with him?"

"No. No, I'm not. I promise. I'd never hurt you. Never."

Victoria threw her arms around me, tears running down her face as her body started to shake. "I was so sure it was you," she whispered into my hair. "I'm sorry, I'm so sorry."

"It's okay, it's okay." I hugged her tight, not wanting to let go. It was going to be all right, everything would be all right now. Finally I made myself pull away. "But we need to talk about something else. And we have to do it now. I found a life insurance policy letter."

"For Hugh?" She blinked hard, wiped away her tears.

I shook my head. "For you. Did you know your insurance has increased to five million and he's the sole beneficiary?"

Victoria shook her head. "No. No, that's not right. It's far less, and if we had kids, I think half would go to them. It's what we agreed..." She covered her mouth with a hand before letting it drop by her side. "I signed a document about a month ago. He told me it was to do with my new business. I didn't even question it. But he wouldn't. He couldn't possibly—"

"Bell Hops is going under. It's losing money."

"*What?*"

"This is going to be really hard to hear," I said, taking a step closer. "But I...I think he might be planning on hurting you, and I think he might have done it before, to...to Natalie."

Her head snapped upward, and I saw the glimmer of something in her eyes. "What do you mean? What do you think he did to her?"

"The fire. What if it wasn't an accident?"

Victoria stumbled backward, put a hand against the wall. "What?"

"I spoke to Charlotte—"

"My *cousin?*"

"She told me you were all at a club the night of the fire."

"We were," Victoria said. "All of us were there. Together."

"But were you with Hugh all night?"

"Yes."

"Are you sure? Could he have slipped out somehow?" I said, and when Victoria opened her mouth, she didn't speak, but instead a pained expression slipped over her face. "You've wondered about it, too, haven't you? You're not sure?"

"It's not..." She looked at me, and I watched as the final pieces of her life came crashing down. "When I went to the bathroom on the night…when…when…"

"The night of the fire? When you were at the club? What happened?"

"I…I saw him coming in from the service entrance," she said. "He told me he'd gone out for a cigarette—that was when we still smoked—but…but it wasn't until much later that I remembered…"

"*What?* Tell me."

She shuddered. "He didn't smell of cigarettes, Eleanor. But the fire was an accident. He said so. The *police* said so."

"Did you tell them?" I said. "Did you tell them what you saw?"

She bit her lip. "He asked me not to…and I didn't want him to get into trouble. But he didn't… He wouldn't hurt Natalie. I'm sure of it. He loved her. He *wouldn't*."

"What if he did, Victoria? And what if he wants to hurt you, too?"

"I don't know… I don't know." She gasped and grabbed my arm. "Oh, my God, I called him, right after I hung up on you. I was so mad. I yelled at him, told him about the underwear and that I wanted a divorce. He yelled back at me, called me a bitch and worse."

"Oh, Christ. What if he's on his way home? We need to get out of here."

"But where will I go? If I go to my parents, he'll—"

"You'll stay with me. Grab your things. Hurry. We can't be here when he gets back."

"Can you help me? Please? It'll be quicker."

I dropped my bag on the floor and followed Victoria as she ran to the bedroom, and I stood in the doorway as she pulled a suitcase from the closet and threw it on her bed, stuffing it with pants and T-shirts and sweaters, shoving them in without removing the hangers.

"Pass me some of my underwear?" she said. "Top drawer on the left."

As I slid the left drawer open, my eyes settled on the SIG. "Victoria, your gun..."

She whirled around. "Oh, fuck, we can't leave it here. Put it on the bed—we'll take it with us when we're done." When I hesitated, she said, "Eleanor. *Please.* It won't bite you. Pick it up and put it on the bed."

I did as she asked, then handed her bras and panties while she fished out some shoes, frantically stuffing them into the case. "Eleanor, can you grab—"

"Victoria?" The voice came from the hallway. *"Victoria?"*

We were too late. Hugh was home.

CHAPTER FORTY-ONE

VICTORIA PUT A FINGER to her lips, slipped silently to the door, closed and locked it, her fingers trembling, her eyes wide and full of fear. "Where's your phone?" she whispered.

"Bag. Front door," I mouthed back with a shiver. "Yours?"

"Kitchen counter. What are we going to do? What are we going to *do*?"

"*Victoria?* Where are you?" Hugh's voice was closer now, his footsteps traveling down the hallway, bouncing off the walls. The door handle rattled, making us both gasp. "Are you in there?" he said "Victoria? What's going on?"

She grabbed hold of me, her entire body trembling, and I knew, finally understood how much she feared this man, a person she was supposed to trust with her life. For years she'd pretended to everyone, and herself, that their marriage was perfect, knowing people envied her, envied *them*, but it had all been a lie, and now I was the one who had to protect her.

"Open the door," Hugh called out, banging again. "Victoria? Open up."

"Go away," I said, taking a step closer. "Go away *now*."

"Eleanor?" Hugh said. "What the hell? Open the door."

"No."

"Where's my wife?" He pounded on the door again. "What have you done—"

"She's gone. I'm collecting some of her things."

"What do you mean she's gone? Gone where? I don't believe you. Open the door. *Now*." The pounding resumed, harder and louder. "Victoria? *Victoria?* Talk to me."

"Help me," Victoria whispered. "I don't know what he'll do if he finds me here. He won't let me go. He's said it a thousand times. He'll never let me go."

"I won't let him hurt you," I said, crossing over to the bed and grabbing the gun, closing my shaking fingers over it, the cool steel heavy in my hand.

"It's not loaded," she said. "It's useless."

"Not if I can make him think it is."

"Eleanor," Hugh yelled and Victoria let out a scream. "Open the door, *now* or I'll kick it in, I swear to God."

"I have Victoria's SIG," I said, planting my feet on the floor, hips wide. "Leave, or—"

With an almighty crack, the door flew back on its hinges, coming off one of them and lodging itself, lopsided, into the wall. Hugh stood in the doorway, his right foot raised, his face barely recognizable. He looked like a beast, ugly and twisted, and that was when I knew Victoria's life wasn't the only one in danger.

His eyes darted from me to Victoria, who had slid to the floor and cowered, her hands over her face, shoulders shaking. She let out another scream as he lunged for me, and my immediate self-preservation reflex was to pull the trigger.

Another crack, from the gun this time. Hugh lurched, his head snapping back before our eyes met again. A look of bewilderment appeared on his face as he put one hand to his chest, his fingers touching the patch of deep crimson that had already appeared. His knees buckled and he went down on the carpet with a dull thud, wavering for a full three seconds as if he were about to say a silent prayer. Another one, two beats, and he crashed to the floor without putting out his hands to stop the fall or making another sound.

"Oh, my God," I shouted. "Jesus Christ. No! *No!* It was loaded. The gun was loaded."

As I turned to Victoria, all I saw was a flash of something coming at me, something turquoise and made of glass. It hit me on the side of the face. Pain erupted through my skull in the same way it had when I'd been attacked in the street, except this time, I knew my assailant. Unable to speak or cry out, I went down, too, falling a few feet away from Hugh, whose eyes were open, unblinking, already glazed over.

Victoria grabbed hold of my shirt and rolled me onto my back. She yanked on my hands, curling my limp fingers before scraping them across her face and chest, leaving angry, deep red gouges in her buttery skin. I pulled my hands away, but she tugged down my sleeves, digging her nails into my flesh, so I tried to roll over and push myself up. I let out a cry as she hit me again with what I now knew was the paperweight from her bedside table, and shoved me onto my front, this time pulling my hands behind me, tying them together with what felt like a scarf. I could barely move, barely think, and as I tried to pull my hands away again, she twisted my thumbs back so far, I thought I heard them snap.

"V-Victoria...stop. Please. L-let...m-me...go," I stammered.

She didn't answer, didn't utter a word. Instead, she got to

work on my feet, tying them together, too, immobilizing me completely. Once done, she stood over me, looking down with a satisfied grin on her face.

I didn't understand. Wanted to ask why she was doing this, why she was hurting me, but my eyes rolled into the back of my head. The entire room faded to black, pulling me toward unconsciousness as everything began to soften around the edges. Everything except the grip of her fingers as she knelt down and tugged on my hair, and the sound of her ice-cold voice as she put her mouth to my ear.

"Be still now," she whispered. "There's a good sister dear."

CHAPTER FORTY-TWO

I DON'T KNOW HOW MUCH time passed until I came to, but when I opened my eyes, slowly, painfully, I managed to lift my head and turn it to one side. From my vantage point—flat on my stomach, my hands still bound behind me, my feet tied at the ankles—I made out two police officers. They stood in the doorway of Victoria and Hugh's bedroom, their bulky silhouettes obstructing the last slivers of light fading behind them like wispy ghosts.

My eyes landed on the crumpled body lying six feet away. I didn't want to see it again. Didn't need to. I knew Hugh had drawn his final breaths, his once strong, healthy heart had stilled forever. Although I turned away, I could smell the rusty scent of his blood—a dark, sticky pool seeping deep into the carpet as it inched its way toward the bed.

"It was self-defense," I croaked, making the officers turn. "He attacked—"

"You're *lying*," Victoria shouted, pushing past the policemen and silencing me as a sob escaped her lips. "Stop *lying*. You threatened me. You shot him. You *killed* him."

"No." I looked up at the three of them staring down at me with varying expressions of judgment and disgust. "I didn't mean to—"

"He came home and she *murdered* him," Victoria said before collapsing against one of the officers—the taller man with hair darker than coal, caramel skin and big brown eyes, not the pallid potbellied one with the acne-scarred face, despite the latter standing two feet closer. As the officer's thick, muscular arms went around her tiny waist, she turned to me, her voice hoarse.

"How could you do this?" she said. "You said we were best friends."

I felt my mouth fall open, my words—protests—wrapping themselves around my throat, squeezing tighter and tighter until I thought I'd pass out again. My head throbbed, and I attempted to convince myself I'd somehow landed in the middle of a nightmare. None of it was real. I'd wake up soon. Oh, how I wanted to wake up soon.

"Hugh warned me." Victoria spoke to the officers now and let out another sob she tried to stifle by covering her mouth with a hand. "He warned me this morning. Said she'd stolen from us. He wanted to fire her but I told him not to because I didn't believe him. Then she kept calling and calling, and came over, so I asked Hugh to come home. And now my husband's dead. Oh, my God. He's *dead*. What am I going to do? What am I going to *do*?"

I tried to fathom for how long she'd rehearsed those looks of pretend panic, the sounds of disbelief and despair. Minutes, days or weeks, it didn't matter. It had been long enough to distill them to pure perfection. She pressed herself against the officer's chest and tilted her head so only I could see the small, sly smile gently pulling her lips upward, emphasizing the cold, dark pools her eyes had become.

It was the moment I knew nothing I said would make a difference.

Nothing I did would get them to change their minds.

They already believed her.

CHAPTER FORTY-THREE

CLEAR-CUT, **THOSE WERE THE** words my lawyer, Ms. Allerton, said when we met, after she offered to take on my high-profile case pro bono, explaining it would raise the notoriety of her firm when I asked why. At first I'd argued and fought, insisted and wept, before accepting I'd been unequivocally fucked by my half sister. I watched Ms. Allerton's ruby-red lips as she talked, but didn't hear her words. Instead I let my mind wander off in different directions. I pondered how she got her lipstick to stay on for so long, if it smudged when she ate, ending up on her brilliant white teeth. It's understandable—I was in shock.

"The evidence against you is compelling." Ms. Allerton tap-tapped her notepad with the cap of her fountain pen. "It doesn't look good, but it's by no means over."

She didn't need to lay everything out, but she did, anyway. There was the fact I'd lied to Victoria and Hugh about who I was, right from the beginning. There were my clandestine visits to Stan, which he and his assistant, Steven Marshall, were all too happy to confirm. The photographs they'd found—many, many photographs—on my old Nikon, ones of Stan and Madeleine, and Victoria, all of them taken when they'd had no idea I was there. A few of them were leaked to the press, who labeled me a stalker, especially when somebody told them I'd contacted Victoria via LinkedIn for the website job without sharing my true identity.

And then there were all Victoria's things. Her engagement ring they'd found hidden away in my bedside table, her red shirts and the earring she'd "lost" at the spa, which had turned up in my bathroom. The jewelry I insisted she'd given me, but which, as it turned out, Hugh had custom-made for her as Christmas presents—they even had the receipt and store footage to prove it, in which you could hear Hugh say how excited he was to have found the perfect gift for his perfect wife. Zirconia, my ass. They found a silver rabbit ornament tucked away in the back of my bedroom drawer, too, my fingerprints all over it, and the undated check Victoria had written out with my pen. She'd even changed her handwriting so it looked like a forgery.

As if all that wasn't enough, there were the dozens of frantic phone calls I'd made to Victoria the day Hugh died, the neighbor who confirmed I'd slipped past her to get into the building and the other who'd shared how I'd banged on Victoria's door so hard, he thought it might break. And, of course, the coup de grâce: my prints on her SIG, and the gunshot residue on my hands. Mine, not hers, because she hadn't fired the gun.

"Hugh and Genie were having an affair," I insisted. "He was going to kill Victoria. He increased her life insurance. He killed his first wife, Natalie. Look into it. It's all true."

Ms. Allerton shook her head. The nude photos in Hugh's office weren't of Genie, they were of Victoria. She and Hugh often engaged in role-play, apparently. Victoria still had the blond wig and the photographs on Hugh's camera to prove it. As for the tattoo—upon closer inspection similar but not identical to Genie's—it had been one of a few temporary ones, all part of Victoria's persona, part of the excitement and mystique she liked to build. My eyes had seen what they'd wanted to see—what *she'd* wanted me to see. And the life insurance? They'd both increased their policy amounts, and had the beneficiaries changed.

Victoria was in for a hell of a payday, and I'd been played harder than Go Fish.

But none of those things were as hard to come to terms with as hearing how Lewis had told the police I'd shared the details about Victoria and me being half sisters with him right from the start. My refusal to tell her, he'd said, was because I'd wanted to get to know her, which immediately got spun as "infiltrate her life." I was branded crazy, jealous, the half sister from hell, a madwoman.

I didn't blame Lewis for his testimony. All he'd done was tell the truth, but the prosecution reveled in arguing I'd latched onto Victoria because Dad had died, and I didn't have a relationship with my mother or my sister, Amy. The last one wasn't hard to prove. Neither of them showed up when I was arrested, and I doubted they would ever visit me in prison. A clear albeit mostly false picture of me emerged. Manipulative, deceitful, blinded by envy...almost ironic how at one point that had all been true.

Facedown and tied up on the bedroom floor, next to the man I'd killed, I'd known I was in trouble. What I hadn't bargained for were the lengths Victoria had gone to, the strategic planning and patience it must have taken. Under any other circumstance, I'd have been in awe.

"This is a good deal," Ms. Allerton had said when she'd come back with an offer, laying out the consequences if I accepted the lesser charge of manslaughter.

"Lesser charge?" I whispered. "It's eighteen years. *Eighteen*."

"Yes," she'd said, crossing her slender legs and rearranging the long string of blue beads hanging around her neck. "But if this goes to trial, you have to understand you could be convicted of murder. Life in prison. Are you sure it's a risk you're willing to take?"

I wasn't. And so, a few months after shooting Hugh, I stood in front of a judge, bowed my head and answered, "Guilty," when asked how I wanted to plead.

Victoria's victim impact statement was the final, crushing blow, and a manipulation masterclass. "She's pregnant," she said quietly, looking drawn and skinny, continuing to play the part of the beautiful, grieving widow to perfection. "But I want to show mercy, Your Honor, and I hope you will, too. The only reason I agreed to the manslaughter plea is because she's having a child…and whatever she did, the fact is, she's still my half sister. She's my family by blood. And…I have to keep believing that counts for something."

The judge had dabbed at the corner of his eye, setting off an entire row of people at the front while I sat there, according to the news reports, stone-faced and unrepentant.

The news of the murder went national, Victoria's face splashed across the front pages of the papers, and everywhere online. Even in prison, I couldn't escape her.

"I thought we were friends," she said during one of her many interviews. "She even told me we were best friends. I can't believe how naive I was, how stupid."

"Why do you think she killed your husband?" the reporter said, her voice soft, coaxing.

Victoria sighed and bent her head before looking up from underneath those goddamn eyelashes, the ones she'd used to enchant everyone with, witch powers I now knew for sure she had. "I've asked myself that question a million times," she said, her voice silky smooth, everyone in the room gulping it down like hot chocolate. "How could she hate us so much? What did we do to deserve what she did? Other than her being jealous, I just don't know."

"And do you think you'll ever find any kind of peace?"

"Peace?" She shook her head. "I think peace is still a long way out of reach."

Victoria was a far better actor than Amy, and as I listened to her words, watched her swipe at her tears with a crumpled tissue in her hand and a pained expression on her face, I wondered how I'd got everything so wrong.

So utterly and completely wrong.

CHAPTER FORTY-FOUR

Ten months later

I GAVE BIRTH TO YOU on a Wednesday, Gemma, four days after my sentencing, to all glorious seven pounds, nine ounces of you. I sweated and screamed, panted and writhed—not because I wanted to force you out of me, even though I'd become so big I could barely sit. No, if it had been up to me, I'd have carried you ten times as long, and longer still. Because I knew once you'd left my body, they'd take you from me. For the next eighteen years, I couldn't be your mom, not properly, no matter how much I wanted to.

The nurse let me hold you for an hour, gave me tablets to stop my milk from coming, and then they took you, and I thought I might die from the pain of losing you. Not long after I signed the custody papers for your father, each pen stroke a cut to my shattered heart. Although it's better this way, I know it is, and he promised he'd come once a month, on a Wednesday, so I can see how much you've grown. He's a good man, your father. A wonderful man and I have to stop myself from thinking how different everything might have been if I'd listened to him.

My heart soars as I'm summoned to the visiting room, despite its clinical look and its hard white tables and seats bolted to the linoleum floor. It soars because it's Wednesday, and today you're exactly six months old. I've made you a little card on the pink paper one of the officers gave me. I drew a picture of me holding you, which my cellmate said was "nice," and I know that means it's awesome, because she never compliments anyone on anything.

I walk into the visiting room and look around, my heart beating fast, my smile growing as I try to find your beaming face among the tables. You have teeth now, two of them at least, and I can't wait to see. But you're not there, and neither is your daddy. Instead I see the devil herself, her smooth mahogany hair tied back in a ponytail, her long legs crossed in front of her, disappearing underneath an emerald dress that matches her eyes.

She's chosen the table the farthest away from everyone, including the guards, undoubtedly so no one can hear us. I'm certain she's here for me, so I walk over, lower myself into the chair, unable to take my eyes off her. Why has she come? Where are you, my sweet little Gemma? It's already been a month and I need to see you, smell the top of your head and take in your scent. Without it, I'll surely wither away to nothing.

I haven't seen *her*—I can't bring myself to think her name—in person since the sentencing, and yet here she sits, a ghost of my past still haunting my present, and smiles.

"Hello, sis," she says. I don't reply. "It's good to see you, too. Wow, you're slim."

She means it. I'm thinner than ever before, all muscle and sinew. Working out has had that effect, the group therapy sessions, too.

At least that's what I let people believe. But I know my bingeing became a thing of the past when the void inside me filled with a million mountains of rage. It took locking me up to rid myself of some inner demons, only to see them replaced by other, darker ones. Ironically I miss the comfort of my curves. It's something else she's taken. I won't tell her this, of course.

"I lost my appetite," I say.

"Ah, but you look great. You've almost got the figure you wanted."

I deflect the jab. My outer shell is so strong these days, almost nothing gets through. "I don't have long, so whatever it is you're here for, get on with it. I'm expecting someone."

She looks at me and smiles again, and it makes me want to climb over the table and push my thumbs into her eyeballs, feel them bulging and popping underneath the pressure like grapes. Maybe I would if I thought the guards wouldn't have time to stop me.

"I feel bad," she says, but I know her too well to believe it. "I owe you a few explanations—"

I put my head back and laugh. It's an awful sound. "I think I've got you figured out."

"Do you? Indulge me."

I understand how this is another game to her, and yet I can't stop myself from entering the arena, ready to play. "You did all of this for money. Exactly like Hugh did to Natalie."

She has a dangerous sparkle in her eye, one I've never seen before, but which turns her into a beautiful, dangerous feline creature, and she's ready to pounce. "Did he? Are you sure?"

"It wasn't him, it was you," I say with a distinct lack of surprise—not much shocks me anymore. "You set the fire. You were the one who went for an alleged cigarette. Hugh covered for *you*." When Victoria doesn't answer, I say, "But why? Did you plan it together? You wanted her insurance money, too?"

"Oh, please," she says, and I realize I've actually offended her.

"Hugh wasn't clever enough for that, and it wasn't even a million. No. I wanted *him*, right from the start, except he only had eyes for *her*." She pauses, taps her fingers on the table. "But my mother always told me some people are easier to maneuver out of the way than others."

My brain whirs and clicks, fits more pieces together. "Madeleine killed Stan's girlfriend, the one who died in the car accident that almost killed him, too. She did, didn't she?"

"Perhaps," Victoria says, sounding bored. "I never asked her. What I do know is Mom grew up around cars, and that woman was supposed to drive home alone, not with my father."

"Rotten apples fall close to rotten trees. You didn't have to turn out like your mother, you know. You could've taken a different path—"

"You mean the way you didn't?" She laughs and shakes her head.

"What do you mean? I'm nothing like my mother."

"Aren't you?" she says, amused. "According to my mom, Sylvia Hardwicke is—" she counts on her fingers "—calculating, cold and manipulative. Just not shrewd enough. That sounds familiar, doesn't it?"

While I don't blanch at her saying my mother's name out loud, I'm unable to stop grabbing the scraps she dangles in front of me. "Madeleine knew about Stan's affair?"

She breathes in deep. "She had her suspicions."

"She told you?"

"My mother would never admit to any kind of weakness, not even to me," Victoria says. "I've only ever seen her lose control once, at a Christmas party. I was fourteen. She'd had too much to drink, and when I helped her to bed, she told me I was far prettier than my sister." She shakes her head. "I thought she meant Angeline until she whispered, 'Sylvia Hardwicke and her ugly little Eleanor.' She cursed you both to hell and back that night, but never mentioned anything again. I never forgot. And you were easy enough to find."

"Why didn't you ask her or Stan about me," I say, "if you knew all along?"

"Remember what I told you about Angeline?"

"You didn't leave the stairgate open by accident," I answer. "I worked it out already."

"Well done," she says, staring at me so hard it makes me want to vomit. Her callous admission of responsibility in her baby sister's death shouldn't come as a surprise but it slams into my chest like a dozen sledgehammers all the same. When she smiles, I know I'm sitting opposite the embodiment of malice. A sociopath. And she's my sister. How couldn't I have seen it? How could I have been so blind?

She leans in and whispers, "I didn't want you around, either."

I try my hardest not to react, not to show any kind of emotion. "Except I showed up."

"At exactly the right time, thank you for that." She sits back with a sigh, and it's a long, contented sound, as if she's stretched out, sipping a margarita on a sunny beach somewhere. The thought almost kills me because it will be years and years before I see the ocean again.

"You made me believe Hugh was hurting you, that he was having an affair—"

"You saw what you wanted to see, in part anyway, and you were so desperate to help, so anxious for my approval—"

"I wasn't—"

She laughs. "And you impressed me, you really did, first jumping to conclusions and finding my clues in his office so quickly. And seeing Bell Hops's financial statements, talking to Charlotte, well, that was all you. But you know my favorite part?" She waits, and when I don't answer, she continues, anyway. "You shooting Hugh like that. I thought I'd have to finish him off and blame it on you, but my goodness, did you ever exceed my expectations."

I can't stop myself from wincing. I killed a man. An innocent man. That's something I'll have to deal with for the rest of my life, and part of me knows I deserve to be in here, no matter what she did. "But you hurt your father," I say. "The news about him having another daughter coming out—"

"Actually, you wouldn't believe how my business has taken off," she says. "How many contracts he's thrown my way to make it up to me. He's *so* proud of me. I wonder if you could ever say the same about Bruce."

A gasp escapes my lips as her words cut into me, slashing deep, right to the bone. I can't bring myself to think about Dad in front of her, what he'd make of me now, were he still alive. Would he believe her, too? The thought makes me want to scream. "How long had you been planning this? Since the day we met?"

She smiles. "Don't flatter yourself. Things hadn't been good between Hugh and me for quite some time, way before you showed up. I'm afraid he wasn't what I'd expected, in the end. He'd spent all his money, and went after mine. He thought I wouldn't notice. Like I said, he really wasn't that smart."

I shake my head. "You know, most people get a divorce."

"Ah, yes." She actually winks at me. "But it's not nearly as lucrative. Besides, he would've fought me on everything, dragged the whole process out. And, for the record, it was supposed to be Genie, not you. It would've served her right for flirting with him the way she did. But then you bumped into me outside Dad's office, and when I saw you after the spin class and at Le Médaillon, I knew you were following me, so I set the first trap."

"The ring," I say, and she smirks.

"You stole from me," she says, her eyes colder still. "You had every chance to give it back, to tell me who you were, but you didn't. You tried to make a fool out of me."

"You manipulated all of us. Hugh, me, Lewis. I know you set him up at the bar with that woman who kissed him—"

"Crazy what some people will do for ten bucks."

"Even Charlotte. You made her fall on purpose when you went roller-skating—"

"But we had a lovely spa day because of it, you and me, didn't we? And don't forget to add the web designer at Bell Hops to your list. I thought it was particularly genius, putting him in touch with one of my friends, getting him out of the way in preparation for you to take his place. It took no time at all."

"You're a monster—"

"That's a matter of perception."

"—and you'll get your dues. Someday, I promise, you *will* pay for what you've done."

She touches her lips with a fingertip before saying, "Let me tell you a secret, Eleanor. We're all monsters. Every single one of us is evil on the inside. To varying degrees, maybe, but evil nonetheless. The difference is some of us choose to accept it."

"You're insane."

"Am I? All you need to do is look around. This whole—" she adds quotation marks "—*'good triumphs bad'* shit is nothing but an illusion, a complete fantasy. It's what people tell themselves, and each other, to hide from the truth because admitting the world is a despicable place, full of greed and hatred, is too terrifying for most. They can't cope." She shakes her head, and when she speaks again, she sounds wistful. "But when you accept the fact, when you give in to it…it's *liberating* beyond anything you could ever imagine."

"I don't understand," I say. "Why did you come here? Why tell me all this? I've already worked out you're a fucking psycho. What the hell do you want?"

She doesn't flinch at my words. It's as if she already knows, has a deep understanding of who and what she is and is proud of it. Leaning in, her eyes harden some more. "I want you to know exactly what I'm capable of. Lewis and I never—"

"*Lewis* and you?" Whatever blood is left in my face drains away, leaving me light-headed, making the room spin.

"We never want to hear from you again, Eleanor. No visits, no letters, no phone calls… It's just the three of us now." She shakes her head and pulls out her left hand from under the table, points to the brand-new sparkling solitaire on her ring finger.

"No," I say, realizing she's not just come here to taunt me, but to let me know she owns me, now and for years to come, possibly forever. I can't let her do this. "*No*. You aren't… You didn't—"

"I was grieving," she says with a perfectly innocent look as she puts a hand to her throat and bats her eyelashes. "He felt responsible. Told me if only he'd known how desperate you were, he might have been able to stop you. He's such a sweetheart."

"No—"

"Isn't he manly and protective?" she continues. "The savior complex is a real turn-on, didn't you find? And he's a fabulous father. The ring might not be as big as the one you took from me, but Lewis makes up for that in so many other ways."

I want to lunge over the table, wrestle her to the ground and bash the back of her head against the floor until I hear it crack like an egg and it splits apart in my hands, but I can't. I have to control the fury inside me. Losing it would only lead to spending more time away from you, Gemma, and I can't let that happen. It's not something else I'll let her take from me.

"Why are you doing this to him?" I whisper, tears pricking the backs of my eyes, and I blink them away. I will not cry. I will *not*. Not in front of her. "He's a good man. An honest man."

"Oh, Eleanor," Victoria says. "You love him, don't you? Are you hoping he'll change his mind about you? It's never going to happen, I'll make sure of it. It wouldn't be good for the baby. Little Gemma needs a stable environment."

The sound of her uttering your name makes me sit up straight. "Don't talk about my—"

"She saved you," she says, silencing me. "If you hadn't told me you were pregnant, I would have killed you and Hugh." She leans back in her seat. "And when you think about it, it's perfect. I can't have children. You're in here. Who better to raise darling Gemma than your own flesh and blood?"

"I won't let you take her—"

"Oh, but I already have, sweetheart. I already have."

"Why?" I whisper. "You're incapable of loving anybody but yourself."

Victoria smiles. "I don't let anyone tell me what I can or can't have. Not even my own body. Having a child will be my little experiment. See if I can bring out the worst in her."

I let out a whimper, a small, pathetic sound of defeat. "I won't let you do this."

"Lewis's mother and stepfather adore her," Victoria says, ignoring me as she cocks her head to one side. "You should see Jackson's ranch, it's incredible. The only thing worrying me is that it's a real tinderbox, with all that wood. I can only imagine what might happen if there was a fire and someone was trapped inside…"

I want to say something, but all my words have shriveled up, dry as ashes. It isn't until Victoria gets up to leave that my voice returns. "Why did you agree to the manslaughter charge instead of murder?" How I hate that she holds this power over me, that she still has answers to my questions, and I detest myself for being incapable of letting her walk away with them.

She sighs deeply, sounding *content*. "You never know who'll end up on the jury. What if one of them had convinced the others somehow you really were innocent?" She smiles. "This way we ensured a conviction. Which reminds me. Ms. Allerton sends her regards."

"Ms. Allerton? My attorney?"

"Yes, isn't she great? Alison and our father go way back."

The final pieces slot into place, the heavy lid of a sarcophagus sealing my fate as she buries me alive. "She took my case because you asked her to," I whisper.

"Eighteen years." Victoria gives me a sad look as she shakes her head. "Rumor has it the assistant attorney general offered twelve."

It's the last thing Victoria says before she leaves, her sweet floral perfume trailing after her, hanging in the air like a noose. I watch her go, now understanding what I'm up against, and all I can think is *eighteen years*.

As the door closes behind her, it rips the hinges off another, the one in my heart marked Evil. The one she said was there, which I now know is true. And from where I'm sitting on this cold hard seat in this despicable place, my sentence seems barely long enough to plan my revenge.

Just over seventeen years before I can come for you, Gemma. Before I can save you.

I just hope it won't be too late.

★ ★ ★ ★ ★

ACKNOWLEDGMENTS

The best part of being an author is the people, and writing the acknowledgments in their honor is an absolute treat. It's the fourth time I've had the pleasure of doing so, and I'm incredibly lucky to have a long list of individuals to whom my gratitude extends.

First of all to *you*, the reader. Whether you're a librarian, reviewer, blogger, book club member, work at a bookstore or are "just" an avid reader: thank you for spending time with my characters. It's a privilege that you chose this story and I hope you found it time well spent. Special shout-outs to the incredible social media and #bookstagram communities I've had the pleasure of discovering. Kate, Sonica, Suzy, Tonni—among many—your joy and enthusiasm keep me going when I want to hit Ctrl+A, Delete.

To Carolyn Forde, agent and person extraordinaire—thank

you for all your expertise and advice. I'm thrilled to be safely tucked under your wing and can't wait to see what we do next.

Huge thanks to Michelle Meade for falling in love with the initial concept of this novel, and to Emily Ohanjanians for taking over as my super talented, gracious editor. Your savvy input moved the story to another level, and I've absolutely loved every minute of us working together.

To the wonderful Harlequin, HarperCollins Canada and MIRA teams, including Cory Beatty, Peter Borcsok, Nicole Brebner, Audrey Bresar, Randy Chan, Heather Connor, Carol Dunsmore, Lia Ferrone, Emer Flounders, Heather Foy, Olivia Gissing, Miranda Indrigo, Amy Jones, Sean Kapitain, Linette Kim, Karen Ma, Ashley MacDonald, Leo MacDonald, Lauren Morocco, Melissa Nowakowski, Irina Pintea and colleagues: you're my heroes. Thank you for everything!

Thank you, HarperAudio, BeeAudio and the incredible performers who turn my work into audiobooks and make them accessible to disabled individuals, too. I'm forever grateful. Hope to hear you on the next one, Alex. To Brad and Britney at AudioShelf—thank you for your fun-filled support. Love you two!

I'm continually humbled by the generosity of those who take the time to answer my weird (and downright evil) questions with good humor. Special thanks to Bruce Coffin for making Victoria more despicable than I'd planned, and to Sam Blaney for the medical advice. Kudos to Harlan Gingold, Erik from Jones, Rich & Barnes Funeral Home, and Dina from Maine Medical Center for not hanging up when I said, "I have a few strange questions but I'm an author, honest."

Waving at the brilliant Sarah Lewis and Jo Gatford from WritersHQ.co.uk (Plotstormers rules!) and my local writing group, Donna, Lyanne, Mary and Shauna.

To my GTA clan: Sam Bailey, Karma Brown, Amy Dixon, Molly Fader, Jennifer Hillier, Lydia Laceby, Jennifer Robson,

Marissa Stapley and K.A. Tucker, who continue showing me how it's done with skill, flair and finesse. Farther-away hugs to Wendy Heard—thanks for having my back.

In a very short time I've met so many authors I'm honored to call my friends. It makes for a huge list, and I'm terrified I'll leave someone out, but here goes: Amy, Alex, Elizabeth, Emily, Gilly, Heather G, Heather Gk., J.T., Jill, Julia, Kaira, Karen, Kate, Kerry, Kimberly, Laura, Mary, Mindy, Pam, Penni, Rebecca, Robyn, Roz, Samantha, Shannon, Vicki, Wendy W and all the others I've met since writing this—you are brilliant, fierce authors and inspire me every single day. Thank you for your advice and encouragement, and for always being there. The writing community truly is like no other I've experienced.

To Mum and Dad, Joely & Co.: lots'o'love and thanks for believing in me from the start. To my in-laws, Gilbert and Jeanette and my extended families, much love also. Thank you for reading my books and spreading the word. Thank you to Becki for always telling me, "Yes, you can."

And finally, to Rob, love of my life and man of my (ICQ) dreams, who became my world more than two decades ago, and to our boys, Leo, Matt and Lex. I've no idea where I'd be without you, but wherever it is, there's no way it would be this much fun.

SISTER
DEAR

HANNAH MARY McKINNON

Reader's Guide

mira

1. How much did Eleanor's upbringing influence her personality, behavior and obsessions? If her childhood had been different, what might have happened instead?

2. What do you make of Bruce and Sylvia keeping Stan's identity from Eleanor? In what situation do you think that choice might be justified?

3. How do you think the story would have unfolded if Eleanor hadn't taken Victoria's ring? Did that moment decide her fate, or do you think it was something else? If so, what?

4. What do you think Eleanor was most terrified of? How did Victoria use those fears to her advantage? What, if anything, was Victoria afraid of?

5. Victoria and Eleanor both seemed to turn out like their mothers, whether they wanted to or not. Might this be inevitable? Do you think sociopathy runs in either of the families, and if so, what are you basing that observation on?

6. Did your allegiances switch from Eleanor to Victoria or vice versa—and back again? Why and when? Was there a point where you felt sorry for Eleanor or do you believe she got what she deserved?

7. What scene was the most pivotal in the story for you? How would the novel have changed if it had been different or hadn't taken place? What did you expect to happen?

8. What surprised you the most? What didn't you see coming? What was obvious?

9. At what point did you realize Victoria had manipulated Eleanor into doing her bidding? What could Eleanor have done to escape her half sister's clutches and when?

10. At the end, Victoria says, "This whole 'good triumphs bad' shit is nothing but an illusion, a complete fantasy. It's what people tell themselves, and each other, to hide from the truth because admitting the world is a despicable place, full of greed and hatred, is too terrifying for most." What do you make of that?

11. How do you feel about stories where evil wins, at least temporarily?

12. What do you expect will happen next to Eleanor, Lewis and Victoria? How do you think Gemma will grow up? How much impact will Victoria have on her? What can Eleanor do to protect her daughter?

This is your fourth novel. What was your inspiration for *Sister Dear*?

I heard a radio segment about a woman who'd found a wedding ring at a playground, and she was trying to locate the owner through social media. It got me thinking—what if the woman found out the ring's owner had a dream life, and felt jealous? The more I thought about it, the more twisted my imagined outcomes became. I realized the individuals had to be related somehow, and if I made them half sisters, it would add to the drama and intrigue. It seems some of the most despicable acts are carried out within families. That was something I wanted to explore.

Did any of the characters appear fully formed? Did the story end the way you'd initially thought?

Not fully formed, no, my characters don't arrive in that state, never mind how much I'd like them to. However, I knew one of the sisters would have a distinct lack of confidence, particularly regarding her physical traits. She'd perceive herself far more negatively than anybody else does—primarily because of her relationship with her mother—and suffer from a kind of body dysmorphia. I wanted to show how the attitude of others can impact a person, how we carry these things forward and what they can do to us. It made Eleanor complex and interesting to write, and most of the time I wanted to give her a hug. Having said that, while I hoped the reader felt sympathy for her, I didn't want it to be so during the entire novel. She did make some rather dubious choices, after all.

In contrast, Victoria was always going to be Eleanor's alter ego, but she presented another challenge—she had to fool everyone, including the reader. I had to develop her side of the story almost in secret, and make a list of what she wanted and how she'd get it, before feeding all that in without making it obvious. I hope I succeeded.

As for the ending, I plotted this story far more than my previous novels, and that's likely why the conclusion didn't change much from my original plan, with one exception. In my first draft, Victoria was pregnant, not Eleanor, but the level of malice skyrocketed when I flipped it around. I remember sitting in front of my computer, rubbing my hands together thinking, "Yes, this is way more evil." (Cue maniacal laugh.) I think sometimes my husband worries about me...

What did you have the most fun with, character or plot?

Both! I've had trouble plotting novels in the past because I tend to get overexcited about the story and impatient about writing it, so I jump in too fast. Doing so has led me to typing about thirty thousand words very quickly, before meandering around an awful lot because I've lost my way. Not so this time. I took a course called Plotstormers with WritersHQ.co.uk, during which I outlined this novel, and it streamlined my approach. I slowed down, used lots of sticky notes I put all over my dining table to develop the story, completed far more character interview sheets and wrote a clear sixteen-point plan which I broke down into thirty-two smaller steps. It sounds technical, but I didn't get stuck this time.

As for the characters, I adored developing Eleanor. Taking her from self-conscious to brazen to distraught was quite the ride, and I could feel her backbone growing and collapsing the more I typed. Victoria was a treat to write, too, because I knew how scheming she was from the start. And Lewis...he was my guilty pleasure. I love writing male characters (my last novel, Her Secret Son, was written exclusively from a man's point of view) and he was the person in the story with the strongest moral compass. I needed him to keep me grounded.

You write about some pretty messed-up families. Why do you think that is?

I'm not entirely sure, considering my family is anything but messed up. I was raised in a traditional nuclear family environment. My parents have been together since the early '60s, They're generous, loving and open and have always supported us. I get along very well with my sister, too, and we all enjoy spending time together whenever we can. I'm extremely fortunate. Maybe that's why I write these dramas—having a highly dysfunctional family frightens me; it would rip away a large part of what gives me stability and comfort, and what my husband and I want to provide our kids with. Writing about it lets me explore those fears from the safety of my keyboard and reminds me not to take what I have, and the privileges that come with that, for granted.

Do you ever include anything about your own life, or people you know, in your stories?

It seems the more I write, the less I draw on my personal life and people I know, with one notable exception in this book. Candidly, I share some of Eleanor's body image issues, which I've found hard to deal with, yet somewhat therapeutic to address. It's a work in progress.

There are also a few anecdotes here and there, things my husband or kids will chuckle at because they know the backstory, but I'd never take a real person and drop them as they are in my books. I'm an author; it's my job to make stuff up. Creating these characters and the worlds they live in is always an interesting challenge; it's part of what stretches me as a writer. I spend a lot of time thinking about my cast (and talking to them out loud, which is weird, I know). Readers telling me they felt the characters were so real, they almost expected them to walk in through the door, or that they missed them after finishing my novels, or even that they felt strongly enough to absolutely detest them, truly is the highest compliment.

How has your approach to writing changed since the publication of your first novel?

The biggest change is that, four books in, I feel more in control. That being said, it doesn't necessarily get easier. Self-doubt always, always creeps in, particularly when I'm writing my first "skeleton draft," which is a first, very loose version nobody will ever see. It's rough, dirty and...terrible—my skeleton drafts always have been.

However, I've learned to trust my writing process. If I can get the bones of the story on paper, I'll subsequently add layers and complexity as I go over the novel again and again in preparation for my editor's eyes. I've learned the finer details will come. Just like most people who draw, paint or write music or books, the first draft will never be my best work and I'm glad I've accepted that—it stops me from being overly self-critical when I start a project. I'm also more disciplined than in the past because I have deadlines from my editor. And I've always loved deadlines—especially beating them.

What can you tell us about your next novel?

It's another psychological thriller about a man who wakes up on a beach, not knowing who he is or how he got there. When he makes it back to his hometown in Maine, he discovers he'd abandoned everyone and everything two years prior. Not only *do some of the locals suspect him of murder, but he's also faced with the daunting challenge of figuring out the truth about what he did, and to whom. I'm very excited to introduce you to another cast of messed-up characters!*